T0159094

BLIND
KNOWLEDGE

elizabeth b. splaine

authorHOUSE®

AuthorHouse™
1663 Liberty Drive
Bloomington, IN 47403
www.authorhouse.com
Phone: 1 (800) 839-8640

Published by AuthorHouse 01/18/2019

ISBN: 978-1-5462-7594-7 (sc)
ISBN: 978-1-5462-7593-0 (e)

Library of Congress Control Number: 2019900521

Print information available on the last page.

Any people depicted in stock imagery provided by Getty Images are models, and such images are being used for illustrative purposes only. Certain stock imagery © Getty Images.

This book is printed on acid-free paper.

To the plucky, real-life Molly Elizabeth and her
old-soul brother, Henry Alexander.

Ohana means family. Family means no one gets left behind. But if you want to leave, you can. I'll remember you though ... I remember everyone that leaves.

—Lilo from the movie *Lilo & Stitch*

Button jar cover photo courtesy of Farrellandholmes.com.

CHAPTER 1

The convertible shot like an arrow through the midsummer afternoon, only slowing slightly while rounding the curves on Route 2, just northwest of Boston. The air, which was thick with August humidity from a recent thunderstorm, blew April Stanton's auburn hair back. She glided her right hand in waves as the car accelerated once more on a straightaway.

A carefree giggle escaped her rouged lips as she glanced at the car's driver. Luke Marshall, who was the quarterback of Lexington High's football team and the most popular boy in the entire school, had chosen her to be his most recent fling, and she had no idea why. Sure, she was a cheerleader, but she didn't consider herself particularly pretty or engaging. Her grades were strong, and she had every intention of going to college. As much as she liked this boy, she wasn't going to do anything, today or any other day, to jeopardize her future. But that didn't mean she couldn't have a little fun.

Tracing his profile with her eyes, she tried to commit it to memory. April knew this *relationship* wouldn't last long once Luke discovered she wasn't going to put out—at least not much. So she decided to simply enjoy the moment and ride the wave of contentment as her right hand rode the air currents.

"Whatcha thinking?" Luke turned to her with that incredible toothy grin he saved for the pretty girls. April had seen him smile that way a hundred times, never dreaming she'd be the lucky recipient.

April was thinking that Luke should be wearing his seat belt, but instead, she lifted an eyebrow in reply and slid her left hand up his right thigh. Luke glanced down at her hand and then sideways at her.

"Me too." Luke turned up the volume on the radio as the car's engine responded to his heavy foot on its accelerator. American Authors' "Best

Day of My Life" blared from the vintage Corvette's jacked-up speakers. April laughed, feeling carefree and a little reckless.

"How long 'til we get to the lake?" April yelled over the music.

"Just past the hospital and down on the left. Hey, April, I have to tell you, you're gorgeous." Luke grinned.

She glanced at him and rolled her eyes. "Uh-huh."

He turned down the radio and was suddenly serious. "I mean it. I've been watching you for a while now, trying to figure out a way to ask you out. I mean, why would a girl like you want to go out with a blockhead like me?"

April turned to face him with knitted eyebrows and tried to determine his sincerity. "Are you serious?"

"Dead serious."

Gazing into his hazel eyes, she felt herself softening, drawn in by that mysterious force some people have. As she leaned in to kiss him, something caught her eye. For a split second in her peripheral vision, she thought she saw a—

"Oh, my God, Luke, *stop!*"

Without thinking, Luke's foot reacted to her command as his attention returned to the road. Slamming down the brake pedal, he immediately saw what had forced such a dramatic scream from April. The car, which was traveling at seventy-five miles an hour, was careening toward what looked like a child standing in the middle of the road. The child remained stationary as the Corvette spun in ever-tightening circles toward her. April's hands clawed frantically at empty air as they desperately tried to find something—anything—to hold onto while the car's vicious movements tossed her head back and forth like a bobblehead doll. Losing sight of the girl as her world spun out of control, April screamed and reached for Luke, wildly grasping at his tank top as his body flew impossibly fast out of the car as if clutched by some large invisible hand.

The Corvette slammed into a massive maple tree which had stood in Concord, Massachusetts for over one hundred years. The little girl hadn't moved or even blinked as she witnessed the crash. Her face had been an inscrutable mask as she had clutched a jar of buttons close to her chest.

CHAPTER 2

Having just recuperated from a gunshot wound to his left shoulder, Julian was looking forward to a brief getaway in western Massachusetts with his girlfriend, Alex. The recent rain and accompanying barometric pressure changes had the injury throbbing, and Julian unconsciously rubbed it.

Out of the corner of her eye, Alex took note of the movement and flinched. "I know I've said this a million times, but I'm really sorry I shot you."

Julian turned to her. "And for the millionth time, you thought that crazy doctor was going to inject me with poison. You reacted as any good cop would. You aggressively went after the bad guy—or girl in this case—to save the incredibly handsome victim. Wait a minute. You weren't actually aiming for me, were you?"

Although the dramatic roll of Alex's eyes went unnoticed by the blind man seated next to her, the tone of her voice did not. "Not that time, but you better watch it because next time I might be aiming for you, and clearly I'm a good shot, so ..."

Julian laughed. "Clearly." He extended his hand palm up.

Like a well-worn glove, Alex slid her hand into his and said, "At least we have some time off together."

Julian smiled lasciviously. "Hey, if being shot is what it takes to spend some time alone with you, I'd gladly do it again."

"Watch it, mister. You're still hurt, remember? Didn't the doctor specifically say that you should avoid all strenuous activity for at least another month?"

Julian's smile widened. "Yes, he said that *I* should avoid strenuous activity, but he didn't say that I couldn't be the *recipient* of strenuous activity."

"God, you're incorrigible." Alex laughed.

"That's a big word, cop lady."

"Yeah, I know. Look it up. It means you're a pain in my ass."

Julian's phone buzzed, and he commanded Siri to answer it on speaker. "Dr. Julian Stryker."

"Hey, Julian, it's Jesse. I'm at your house with the cutest puppy dog in the whole world. Yes I am." Although Jesse was speaking into the phone, his words were obviously directed at the dog. He was using the baby voice he reserved for cute animals and men he was currently dating. Julian could hear Oscar, his English mastiff/Lab mix, panting in the background.

"We just got back from a long walk. Yes we did, didn't we, buddy? And we were wondering where you left the dog treats."

"I'll answer you, Jess, but you've got to drop that sickening voice before I vomit."

"Jeez, Julian, so serious. This is why your dog loves me more than you. Isn't that right, Oscar boy?"

Julian turned to Alex, who was laughing and shaking her head. "Don't drag me into this, Julian."

"Oh, hey, Alex," Jesse said.

"Hi, Jesse," Alex responded.

"Alex, do me a favor and don't let Julian drive. His insurance rates are already through the roof."

"That joke was old the first time you told it, Jess," Julian said as he chuckled.

"And yet you laugh every time. Maybe that's why I haven't found a better job. You need me."

It was true. Julian had taken a chance on hiring Jesse many years ago when the young man had been in search of a job, a fresh start, and some true friends. Julian had never regretted his decision. Jesse had become invaluable to him after an attack by one of his adolescent psychology patients had left Julian blind. If it hadn't been for Jesse, Julian's psychology practice would have disintegrated. Instead, the practice was thriving, and Julian and Jesse had forged a relationship stronger than steel.

"The dog cookies are in a canister on the pantry's top left shelf," Julian said.

"Okay, thanks. Hey, you guys have a great time. I know you'll miss me but try to carry on. Don't worry about old Oscar and me. We're gonna have a great time too, watching the tube and eating TV dinners. Two men keepin' it real."

"You really need to get a boyfriend, Jess, and a life. Hey, what happened to the guy you brought to my hospital room after I was shot? Oliver, right?"

"Oh, he's definitely still in the picture, but I'm not ready to settle down. Not yet. Oliver *is* quite a catch though," Jesse trailed off dreamily.

"Glad to hear you guys are still seeing each other. He seems like a really stand-up person. The best part is he's emotionally available, unlike so many men," Julian finished.

"Blah, blah, blah. Stop psychoanalyzing my boyfriend, will you? Anyway, gotta go. Oscar and I have a date with some dog treats and a bath. This dog stinks, Julian."

Julian laughed, thanked Jesse, and rang off.

"You really love Jesse like a brother, don't you?" Alex asked.

Julian smiled. "Honestly, I think I'm the luckiest man in the world. Between you and him, my life is close to perfect."

Alex shook her head. "You're the only blind man with a gunshot wound from his girlfriend that I know who would say his life is close to perfect. Seriously, your glass is always half full."

"Happiness is a choice, Alex. Every morning we're fortunate enough to wake up, we have a choice to be happy, bitter, angry, or sad. It's simple for me. I always choose happy."

"And that's one of the many reasons why I choose you," Alex stated matter-of-factly.

CHAPTER 3

James McClelland was a fastidious man. Standing five feet six inches tall, his petite stature might lead one to believe that he suffered from a Napoleon complex. On the contrary, since childhood, he had known exactly what his strengths had been and had nurtured them. James, or Jimmy as he had come to be called, had built a solid network of friends and confidants whose loyalty to him was unquestionable.

In seventh grade, one of the middle school's bullies had made the mistake of giving Jimmy a swirly in the girls' bathroom. Jimmy had endured the humiliation even as several of the popular girls had looked on in amusement. Biding his time, Jimmy had gathered personal information on the perpetrator and his friends and had collected money surreptitiously from those who'd been victims throughout the years. Then, using the pseudonym Kee Smyas, he had bribed a company to run a billboard add that featured pictures of the bullies with a caption underneath that read, "I'm a bully because I have a small *ick."

When the billboard had been taken down (for obvious reasons), Jimmy had placed flyers throughout the school and town that had listed the names, addresses, phone numbers, and social security numbers of the bullies, along with a list of their transgressions. These, too, had been removed within two days of their placement, but not before the bullies had received their fair share of calls and personal visits from people expressing discontent at their behavior. Six months later, two of the three bullies had found that their identities had been stolen using their social security numbers, which had rendered any future possibilities of obtaining good credit next to impossible.

When the principal had called Jimmy into his office to discuss what had happened to the bullies, Jimmy had pleaded the fifth and had refused to answer any questions. The principal had threatened Jimmy with suspension. When that hadn't worked, he had threatened expulsion if Jimmy wouldn't address the allegations, but Jimmy had remained mute. He had been confident in the belief that his actions had been justified, based on the ill-treatment he had received. Without any solid evidence or admission of guilt, the principal had had no choice but to release Jimmy with a warning. That had been the beginning of a long and illustrious career as *a fixer*.

In college, Jimmy had realized that he could make a lot of money dealing drugs. By the end of his freshman year, he had amassed a small fortune to accompany his 4.0 GPA. When other dealers had threatened him physically for broaching their territory, Jimmy had always looked them in the eye and had calmly said, "You will most likely regret harming me," in such a way that they had backed down.

The power and money had never gone to his head though. Jimmy had chosen to major in accounting (a practical choice for his field of work), and in his spare time had devoured books that dealt with money sheltering, laundering, and investment. By the time he had graduated summa cum laude, he had been worth well over $1 million. Most of it had been housed in offshore accounts. Not bad for a twenty-one-year-old.

After college, Jimmy had taken to loan sharking and had continued to rake in money, using the proceeds to purchase several dry-cleaning stores, which had served as legitimate moneymakers as well as a way for him to launder illegal tender. Very few people had defaulted on their loans because Jimmy had ensured that each client had heard the story of Terrence Schultz, a degenerate gambler who had borrowed money from Jimmy and had lost it all, causing his wife and children to leave him. Sadly, Terrence had been found in his study with a single bullet wound to his temple—an apparent suicide.

Although Jimmy had kept a low profile, his savant-like abilities to make and hide money had come to the attention of local Italian mob bosses, who had offered him a lucrative position with opportunities for advancement. Coming in on the ground floor, Jimmy had run money for the mob before working his way up to become primary accountant and personal financial advisor to Paolo Torchia, the current reigning head of the Italian mafia in Boston.

As Jimmy had gained stature in the family, the don had suggested that he marry and have children so as not to stand out in any way. Being an efficient, goal-oriented person, within three years Jimmy had found a wife and had produced two children—a boy named Joseph followed by a girl named Molly.

The McClelland family lived comfortably in Winchester, Massachusetts, an upscale suburb of Boston where Jimmy was active in local politics. A quiet but popular councilman known for representing his constituents well, the community was shocked to learn of his premature death because he was on the ballot to run for a second term.

CHAPTER 4

Five-year-old Molly McClelland followed the car with her large brown eyes as it came to an unceremonious, violent stop at the trunk of a huge maple tree. Following the straight line of the tree trunk as it soared toward the sky, she wondered if she could climb it or if the tree might be too tall.

A clarion demanded her attention, and she returned her gaze to the crash scene. The car's horn blared and seemed to be getting louder. Tucking her jar of buttons in the crook of her right elbow, she covered her ears with her hands in an effort to find relief. When none came, Molly decided that she'd have to fix the problem herself.

Approaching the car cautiously, she noted that the driver was missing but that the driver's seat had been forced forward and was leaning against the horn. Placing her button jar carefully on the cool, dark green grass, she tugged at the seat until it disengaged from the horn and returned to its normal position. That was better.

Molly retrieved her precious jar of buttons and examined it, evaluating it carefully to ensure that no harm had come to it while being away from her for a time. Satisfied, she turned her attention once more to the car. A girl was slumped in the passenger seat with her head on her chest. Her hair was matted with blood that covered her entire face.

Molly had seen a dead body before, but this one was different. It bothered her that she couldn't see the dead girl's face. Carefully, she walked around the car and gently grabbed the girl's auburn hair in her small fist. Pulling slowly, she forced the dead girl's head back against the headrest. In the girl's open mouth, Molly could see that some teeth were missing. Molly ran her tongue around her own mouth. She, too, was missing a tooth. That realization brought a smile to Molly's lips as she remembered that the tooth fairy had come and exchanged money for her tooth. She wondered whether this girl would get money for her missing teeth when she went to heaven.

A sudden exhalation of air caught Molly by surprise. She stumbled back as the dead girl's head lolled back and forth. Staring in abject horror, Molly paled as the dead body moaned and cried. The dead girl touched her nose and then groaned as she opened her eyes and took in her surroundings. "What happened? Who are you?"

Molly continued to stare at the ghost as her eyes bored holes into her. "Am I dead?" the ghost asked. Molly nodded dumbly, surmising that she, too, must be dead because the ghost was speaking to her.

The ghost touched her forehead, glared at her hand, and then at Molly. "Oh my God! What happened? Where's Luke? Oh my God, Luke!"

The ghost unlocked her seat belt, opened the car door, and fell out onto the beautiful grass. Attempting to rise, she fell twice as she made her way to a body that Molly hadn't noticed before.

Molly haltingly followed as the ghost knelt next to the body of a boy. The ghost screamed his name over and over. After exhausting herself, the ghost turned quickly to Molly and pointed a finger at her. "This is all your fault! What were you doing in the middle of the road? He's dead! You know that? Luke is *dead*!"

Molly was confused. If the ghost was saying that the boy was dead, then perhaps the ghost was in fact, alive, which meant that Molly, herself, was still alive. A wash of relief swept over her, and she hugged the jar to her chest, smiling.

"What are you smiling about, you freak? You killed him! It's your fault!" The auburn-haired girl stood up, called for help, and ran around in circles until she ended up back on the road.

Molly turned her attention once more to the boy, who was truly dead. She approached him, knelt, opened the jar, and carefully reviewed her collection of buttons. She settled on one that was royal blue with sparkles around the edges. Laying the button gently on the boy's chest, she placed her hand over it and silently recited the same prayer she'd said when she had found her daddy hanging from a rope in his bedroom.

CHAPTER 5

"What's the name of the hotel we're staying in?" Julian asked as Alex accelerated onto route 2 from the highway. Julian gripped the door with one hand and placed his other hand on the dashboard.

Alex smiled as she glanced at Julian. "It's an inn, not a hotel. And it's called 1862 Seasons on Main Bed and Breakfast."

"It's not one of those places where we have to sit with other people and have breakfast, community dinners, sharing plates, and stuff like that, is it?"

Alex pulled a face. "What are you talking about? You love those kinds of places."

"Usually, yes. But this getaway is different. I want you all to myself, that's all."

"Well, I can't really argue with that. Tell you what, we'll do our best to stay in our room as much as possible. Sound good?"

Julian waggled his eyebrows in Alex's direction. "Sounds perfect. I have plans for you, my dear."

"Oh my God."

"Yeah, you should be saying, 'Oh my God.' I'd be happy to tell you about my plans."

"No, no, not that. There's an accident up ahead. It looks like a car is wrapped around a tree. Oh jeez, Julian, it's bad. There's a girl standing on the side of the road covered in blood. We need to stop and help."

Julian tucked his sense of humor in his back pocket and asked Alex to describe the scene as they pulled off the road. "Older Corvette, skid marks on the road leading to where the car veered off. Maybe the driver was trying to avoid hitting something? There are lots of deer around here. Could've been that."

"Where's the girl that's covered in blood?"

"She's about twenty feet in front of us. She's clearly in shock because she's staring at us but doesn't seem to register that we're actually here. C'mon, let's go talk to her."

Julian grabbed Alex's arm. "Be careful, Alex. Everybody reacts differently when in shock. Some people literally lash out while others are docile. Either way, try not to scare her when we approach."

"Got it. I'll come to your side of the car." Alex got out and continued to observe the teenage girl as she crossed to Julian's door, opened it, and took his arm. "She's not even blinking, Julian."

"I'll speak first, okay?"

They approached the girl while making as much noise as they could, hoping that she'd acknowledge them, but she didn't.

Stopping ten feet from her, Julian cleared his throat. "Hi there. My name is Julian, and I'm wondering if you might need some help."

The girl turned toward them and stared. "No, I'm fine, but thank you."

Julian took a step forward as Alex remained watchful. "What's your name?"

The girl looked confused for a moment as she brushed her blood-soaked hair from her forehead. She stared at her bloody hand and attempted a smile. "My name is April."

"Hi, April. You've been in a car accident, and I want to make sure you're not hurt. Can I come and sit with you on the grass for a while and talk?"

April's eyebrows came together as she contemplated Julian's offer. "I guess that'd be okay."

"Great. April, I can't see so I'm going to need you to help me, okay? I'm going to ask you to let me take your arm, and then you can guide me to the grass where we'll sit and talk. Can you do that, April? Can you help me?"

Giving her a job seemed to help April focus. "Oh sure."

As Alex walked Julian over to where April was standing, Alex whispered, "FYI. Broken nose and some missing teeth. Could be other issues including internal injuries." Julian nodded his head almost imperceptibly as he took April's arm. As they walked to the side of the road, Julian casually asked her if she was hurt. "Just my head, I think."

"Okay. My friend Alex will call 911, and they'll be here soon. Can you tell me what happened here?"

April stared through Julian as if she did not see him. "We were driving."

"Who was in the car, April?"

"What? Oh, Luke and me. Just the two of us. We were headed to Brindell Lake to—" April cut off abruptly and started to cry.

Julian touched her arm. "Take your time, April. It's just you and me sitting here. Just the two of us talking. You talk only when you're ready. Excuse me for one moment."

Julian turned around and spoke evenly, "Alex, a boy named Luke was driving and needs to be accounted for."

"I'm on it," Alex responded.

Julian returned his attention to April. "Sorry for the interruption. Please continue when you're ready."

April sniffled, hugging her legs up against her body. "It's okay. I can go on. We were going to the lake to get away. I really don't know Luke that well, but—oh, I guess I should say that I *didn't* know Luke that well. He's dead, right?" April craned her neck looking for Luke but couldn't see past the wrecked car.

"April, can you focus on me? My friend Alex is checking on Luke and will take good care of him. She's actually a police officer, so you don't need to worry."

April ran her sleeve under her nose and then wiped her eyes with the other arm. "I must look awful."

Julian smiled. "You look okay to me."

April paused and then barked out a laugh, which quickly morphed into a crying jag.

"April, Alex told me that there are tire marks on the road, which makes me think that Luke hit the brakes pretty hard before you went off the road. Why did Luke brake so hard?"

"Um, I'm not sure. I don't remember. It's, um, all kinda fuzzy but …" Julian waited as April worked through her memory. When April finally spoke, it came out as a whisper. "The girl … It was the girl."

"What girl, April?"

"The girl in the middle of the road. Luke slammed on his brakes trying to avoid hitting the little girl in the middle of the road. She wouldn't move.

She was like some kind of zombie from the movies. Even after the accident she acted really weird. She was smiling at me like some kind of fucking freak show!"

Julian held out his hands palms up toward April. When he was sighted, he would ask patients to look into his eyes in an effort to calm them. But since that was no longer an option for him, he'd learned to use touch instead. Except for patients who were contact avoidant, Julian had found that touch worked wonderfully. "April, do you see my hands reaching out to you? Can you please place your palms on mine?"

April, her rising anger momentarily subdued, wrinkled her brow but complied. Sirens were beginning to sound in the distance.

"Where is this little girl now?"

"I don't know. I went for help, and she walked in the other direction. I know she's only little, but I'm telling you, there's something really odd about that girl."

CHAPTER 6

Alex had dialed 911 as Julian had walked off with April. Julian's ability to talk people down was truly remarkable. He had worked his magic with her several times since they'd been dating. The first was related to a child abuse/murder case they had worked together.

The other two had had to do with her mother's overinvolvement in Alex's life. With Julian's guidance, Alex's relationship with her mother had improved dramatically. With a kind word here and a gentle suggestion there, Julian had aided Alex in understanding that her mother truly wanted what was best for her, even if her mother's methods of communicating were not always crystal clear.

Alex had observed Julian as he had touched April's arm. After initially hesitating, April's shoulders had relaxed, and then Julian had suddenly turned toward Alex and asked her to find the boy who'd been driving the car.

Alex turned her attention to the twisted metal that used to be a car. Jogging over, she scanned the surrounding area. One of the side mirrors had detached and lay face up, the sun reflecting off its mirrored surface. The front bumper had partially shattered, and plastic and fiberglass were strewn haphazardly in various directions. The car was too old to have airbags, and although the passenger's door was ajar, the driver's door was closed tightly, leading Alex to surmise that the driver might have been thrown from the vehicle.

Alex mentally replayed the crash in her mind, using the tire marks to guide her to where the driver might have been ejected. She walked quickly forward and to the left, scanning the long grass as she went.

Alex rounded a tree to witness a little girl pulling something out of a jar and placing it carefully on the chest of a body that lay unmoving. As

Alex approached, the little girl closed her eyes and placed her hand over the object. The girl's lips moved silently, and Alex felt she was intruding on a private and almost holy event.

"Hi, honey." The girl's eyes flew open and danced around trying to find the speaker. Alex emerged from behind the tree. "I'm sorry. I didn't mean to startle you. My name is Alex. Who's your friend?"

Alex approached the body, holding the little girl's brown-eyed gaze. "How's he doing?" Alex knelt and felt the neck for a pulse. Finding none, Alex glanced again at the little girl, who slowly shook her head while keeping her tiny hand on the boy's chest. Alex leaned back on her heels as sirens sounded in the distance.

"What's under your hand?" In response, the little girl glanced at her jar, and Alex's eyes followed. "What's in the jar? Are those buttons?"

Slowly removing her hand, the child allowed Alex to see the beautiful blue button that lay on the dead boy's chest. Alex returned her gaze to the girl, whose eyes seemed to be searching Alex's for something.

"Is that your button? Why did you place it there? Do you know this boy?" Alex asked. The girl's stare was unwavering, and Alex was beginning to feel uncomfortable. It was as if she was being scrutinized and wasn't living up to the girl's expectations. The sirens drew closer.

"Were you in the car when it crashed?" The girl gazed past Alex and then nodded her head. "So you know this boy and the girl that was in the car as well? Is he your brother? Where did you come from? What's your name?"

The little girl glanced past Alex once more and then dropped her eyes, sadness enveloping her features. When she looked up once more, a single tear traced a clear path down the left cheek of her dusty, dirty face.

CHAPTER 7

Ashton Beaufort had been a cop on the Concord, Massachusetts, force for exactly three weeks when a call came across the radio requesting officers to report to a motor vehicle accident on route 2 near Brindell Lake. The only action that Officer Beaufort had seen so far had been a speeding vehicle with a driver whose wife had been in labor, and a raccoon that had broken into a local garage to find a good meal. Grabbing his radio, Officer Beaufort tried to keep the excitement out of his voice as he responded. "Car five responding to MVA. I'm in the area, so I'll get right over there."

Dispatch immediately replied. "Thanks, five. Do me a favor and try not to sound so excited about this, will ya?"

"Roger that … sorry." Despite the slight reprimand, Officer Beaufort turned on his siren and smiled as he sped down the road.

Arriving at the scene, Officer Beaufort pulled onto the shoulder of the road, entered his current coordinates on the car's computer so dispatch would be aware of his exact location, donned his Concord Police Department cap, and exited the vehicle. Placing his left hand on his night stick and his right hand on his gun holster, Officer Beaufort walked cautiously toward the minivan, which lay on its right side as oil dripped steadily from its underbelly. The back door of the vehicle was wedged against a tree that was completely blocking rear access.

"Hello? I'm Officer Ashton Beaufort of the Concord Police Department, and I'm here to help. Everyone okay?" Hearing no reply, Officer Beaufort continued his trek around the car to peer through the shattered windshield. He could discern two people who were both still wearing seat belts and were either dead or passed out.

"OhmiGod, ohmiGod. Okay, don't panic, Ashton," he whispered to himself. Officer Beaufort ran back to his car and snatched the radio from its cradle. "Dispatch, it's me. Um, this accident's really bad. You need to send help fast. Um, there are two people, and I think they're dead!"

"Officer Beaufort!" a voice boomed through the speaker. "Get yourself together and tell us exactly what the situation is out there."

Officer Beaufort stood a little straighter. "Um, sorry, sir. I mean captain, sir. Uh, there are two bodies that I can see through the windshield. The black minivan is on its right side. Its windshield is smashed, and there is no access to the rear of the vehicle because it's against a tree. I can't see inside the back of the car at all at this point. Airbags must have deployed, making it even more difficult to determine the conditions of the two victims that I can see. Um, requesting backup, fire, and paramedics immediately."

"Well done, officer. What is your job until additional help arrives?"

Officer Beaufort struggled through his panic to remember what he had learned in the academy.

An exasperated sigh blew through the speaker. "Attend to the victims, officer. Get to them and apply any necessary lifesaving techniques until the paramedics arrive."

"Yes, sir!" Ashton replied, but the captain had already clicked off.

After grabbing a collapsible step stool, heavy gloves, and a glass-breaking hammer out of his trunk, Officer Beaufort returned to the rolled minivan and climbed onto the side of the car. He ensured that there was no one in the back seat, and then aimed the hammer at the back edge of the rear window on the driver's side. He turned his head away and tapped firmly three times on the corner of the window before the glass splintered and then spider webbed, which allowed him to use his boot to push the window slowly into the vehicle.

"Can anyone hear me? Please respond." Officer Beaufort strained to listen and was rewarded with a hawk screeching as it flew directly overhead.

Avoiding stray glass, he lowered himself into the back seat of the car. Because the vehicle was lying on its right side, he ended up standing on the other back seat passenger's window. He took note of the way the limp bodies in the front seat were situated.

The driver's head was lolling to the extreme left—an angle that even in his rookie opinion, a live body couldn't achieve. Despite this involuntary mental observation, Officer Beaufort removed his gloves and reached forward to feel for a pulse. The woman's neck felt cool, and the officer wondered how long she'd been dead.

Turning his attention to the passenger, Officer Beaufort was saddened to see that he was a boy of no more than six or seven years old. By law and logic, he had been too young to be in the front seat where the unstoppable force of the airbag erupting at an incredible speed had shattered his nose and most of the bones in his face. His left eye dangled out of its socket, secured only by the optic nerve. Officer Beaufort retched and then covered his mouth as he scrambled out the way he had come in.

Paramedics arrived as Officer Beaufort finished wiping his mouth on a towel he kept in the trunk of his car. The captain's car trailed behind the ambulance, whose siren had announced their arrival.

As the paramedics exited the ambulance, they glanced at Officer Beaufort. He shook his head and said, "Take your time." Ignoring his comment, both professionals rushed over to the minivan and scrambled up the step stool.

"How are you doing, Ashton?" The police captain leaned down and placed a hand on the young man's shoulder.

"I'm okay, Dad. Thanks for asking."

"You did well, son. I'm proud of you."

Ashton shook his head as if to clear the memory of the boy's dangling eye. The captain removed his hand from Ashton's shoulder and stood up straight once more. "Get to work now, Officer Beaufort. Start taking photos, measuring any skid marks, and writing up your report. I expect to have it on my desk by the end of the work day."

"Yes, sir." Ashton leaned into the trunk of his cruiser once more to find his Nikon 360 camera and a measuring tape.

"Hey!" yelled one of the paramedics.

Ashton raised his hand to block out the sun as he answered, "What?"

"Where's the kid?"

Annoyance crawled up Ashton's back and settled into his jawline. The paramedics were messing with him, knowing he'd vomited at the sight of the boy's eye. "He's in the front seat, moron."

As Ashton returned his attention to removing the camera from its leather case, his radio crackled. "Officer Beaufort, you're in an incorrect location. Repeat, you're in an incorrect location. The site of the MVA that was called in to me is approximately two miles east of where you are. Over."

"No, not the dead kid, the other one," the paramedic said as he leaned out of the black minivan and tried to get Ashton's attention.

"What? Stop messing with me, asshole. There is no other kid!" Ashton spat.

His radio crackled once more. "Officer Beaufort, please respond."

Ashton grabbed the radio in frustration. "Ruby, I don't know what you're talking about. I'm at the scene of the accident, and there are two dead bodies."

"Well, apparently there's another MVA down the road two miles, Ashton. You better get your ass over there. A Boston cop called it into 911. Three victims. One adult male dead, one adult female injured, and one little girl seemingly unharmed. Over." The radio crackled and then went silent.

The paramedic approached Ashton abruptly as if trying to pick a fight and said, "Listen, buddy, there's a pink car seat in the back of the minivan that has ice water in a sippy cup. The ice hasn't fully melted, and there are snacks in a plastic container in the seat's other cup holder. Both containers were jammed into the cup holders pretty good, so they remained in place during the accident. I'm thinking there was a young girl in the seat when the car crashed. So … back to my original question. Where's the kid?"

CHAPTER 8

One paramedic evaluated April. She had two broken teeth, a broken nose, and a lacerated forehead with a slight concussion. The other paramedic verified what Alex and Julian knew to be true: Luke Marshall was dead. Alex drew Julian aside and told him about how the little girl had placed a button on Luke's chest and prayed.

"A button?" Julian asked.

"Yeah, I know. It's weird but yes, a button. It was bright blue with little rhinestones around the edges. I got the sense it was important to her."

"Where did she get it?"

"Out of her jar of buttons."

"Her *jar* of buttons? Are you kidding me?"

"Do I sound like I'm kidding, Julian? She has a jar about seven inches tall, and it's filled with buttons of varying sizes, colors, and designs."

"I wonder where she came from? Tell me about the surrounding area, Alex."

"What do you mean, where she came from? She was in the car when it crashed. It's amazing she wasn't hurt. Not a scratch on her actually."

Julian shook his head. "I think you're mistaken, Alex. She wasn't in the car. April told me that it was just her and Luke in the car. The girl was standing in the middle of the road, and Luke swerved to avoid hitting her. That's why they crashed."

Alex turned to look at the little girl who sat stoically as a paramedic performed a physical examination. "Huh. The girl told me that she was in the car when it crashed."

"She said that?"

"Well, not exactly."

Julian smiled. "Alex, I know you're not a big fan of children in general, but kids, especially young ones—how old is she?"

"I'm not sure. Five, six maybe?"

"Okay. Well, young children are usually pretty black-and-white literal thinkers. So, what *exactly* did she say about being in the accident?"

"Well, let's see. I asked her if she was in the car when it crashed, and she nodded."

"Has she actually spoken at all?"

"No."

"Is she able to speak?"

"I don't know, but she understood everything I said to her."

"Did she do anything before she answered your question about being in the crash?"

Alex twisted her mouth as she reviewed her brief conversation with the girl. "Yes, actually. She looked past me before she nodded yes. Then I asked her where she came from, and she stared past me again and started crying. I wonder why she lied about being in the car when it crashed?"

Julian shook his head. "I don't think she lied, Alex. I think she misunderstood your question. Where is she? I want to talk to her."

Alex led Julian over to the grass where the girl sat alone with the button jar in her lap.

"Alex, while I sit with my new friend, would you please get my briefcase from our car and bring it to me?"

"Of course. I'll be right back."

Julian removed his sunglasses, revealing his blindness. The little girl evaluated Julian openly with an unabashed look of curiosity in her delicate features. Julian sat directly in front of her, close enough that their knees almost touched. He waited while tipping his face toward the sun. After a full minute, he spoke. "It's warm today, isn't it?"

Receiving no response, Julian tried a different approach. "Do you understand what I'm saying to you?"

The little girl tilted her head and was confused as to why he would ask such a question. She placed her hand on his knee to indicate yes.

"Have you ever heard of someone named Helen Keller?" Without waiting for an answer he knew she wouldn't give, Julian pressed on. "She was a lady who couldn't see or hear, so she communicated using her hands like this." Julian held out his left palm and made a fist with his right hand. He took his fist and rubbed the knuckles against his left palm in an up-and-down motion. "She used this motion on people's hands to answer 'yes' to a question."

He then took his right hand and straightened the fingers and thumb, bringing them together like a duck's bill. He opened and closed them against his palm. "And she used this motion to indicate 'no' when communicating with people. Can you and I try that?" Julian held out his palm toward the girl.

The girl smiled, liking this game. She balled up her right hand and rubbed her knuckles against Julian's palm. Julian grinned. "Excellent! My name is Julian. Is your name Harriet?" The girl made the "no" sign on Julian's hand.

"How about Millicent?" He received another "no."

"Mildred?" This drew a giggle from the child as she indicated "no" once more.

"Huh," Julian reasoned. "Well, since I can't guess your name, why don't you just tell me?"

The little girl clutched the jar of buttons against her chest and withdrew both physically and mentally from Julian. Julian heard the buttons rattle against the glass and felt the girl pull away. He knew he had made a mistake by moving too fast.

Grinning broadly, he announced, "I know your name. It's Buttons McGee!" The little girl laughed out loud at this and grabbed Julian's hand, rubbing her knuckles hard against his palm.

"What's so funny?" asked Alex as she approached and joined in the laughter.

"Alex, I'm pleased to present to you Miss Buttons McGee, sign language interpreter extraordinaire. Buttons, this is Alex, the best police officer you'll ever meet."

Alex bowed her head and said, "It's a pleasure to meet you, Miss McGee."

"You can call her Buttons. All of her friends do."

"Am I your friend?" Alex asked the tear-streaked, earnest face that was turned upward toward her own. The girl smiled shyly and then nodded.

"That makes me happy, Buttons. Please call me Alex." Buttons smiled and nodded, gently taking Alex's hand and pulling her down to sit with them in the cool grass. She glanced at the briefcase and then at Alex.

"Julian, I think Buttons wants to know what's in the briefcase."

"Ah, the briefcase." Julian rubbed his hands together and then wiggled his fingers. "You should know that although this is not a magic briefcase, what's inside of it can tell me a lot about you, Buttons. Do you want to see inside?" Buttons briskly rubbed her knuckles against Julian's hand.

"Alex, can you please open the special briefcase and remove the pad of white paper and the crayons?" Alex did as Julian had asked.

"Buttons, everyone has a family. It doesn't matter whether they're related to you or not. Your family is anyone that is special to you and wants to help or take care of you. It could be your mom, your dad, an aunt, or even a friend—anyone who is really important in your life. Can you draw a picture of your family?"

Buttons gently took the box of crayons and pad of paper from Julian. He heard her open the box and then heard scratching sounds as she began drawing. After several minutes, Buttons handed the picture to Julian. Leaning over his shoulder, Alex described it for his benefit. "Wow, Buttons, so many beautiful colors. Is that you in the center with the pink dress on?" Buttons nodded and was clearly proud of her work.

"And I'm guessing that's your mom and dad on either side of you and maybe your brother on the other side of your mother? The yellow sun looks very bright in the sky, and there's a Christmas tree on the right side of the picture. Am I correct?" Buttons nodded again. This time, she took the picture from Julian and stared at it for a long time. Placing it gingerly on the grass, her expression dropped as she picked up the pad of paper and began drawing once more.

Julian had been an adolescent psychologist long enough to know when to keep his mouth shut, and this was definitely one of those times. It took Buttons several minutes to draw her next masterpiece, and when she was finished Alex's breath caught in her throat. Julian felt the tension in Alex's hand on his shoulder. Buttons extended the drawing to Julian but kept one hand on it as Alex described the scene.

"Buttons, in your first picture, you used so many beautiful colors, but in this one, you used only a black crayon. I see your mom, dad, and brother, but they're not wearing any clothes. The sun is gone, and the tree is on its side. Did it fall down?" Buttons' eyes were glued to the previous colorful drawing, which lay on the grass. She nodded.

"I don't see you in this picture." Buttons slowly lifted her gaze from the colorful drawing to meet Alex's. Her brown eyes became glassy, and her eyebrows came together as if in confusion.

Keeping her hand on Julian's shoulder, Alex knelt. "Did you go away? Is that why you're not in this picture?" The little girl finally broke Alex's stare and slowly took Julian's hand in her own. Making a duck bill with her right fingers and thumb, she signed "no" to Alex's question.

Julian paused, knowing he had to ask the next questions but not wanting to. "You didn't go away, but they did? Did your parents and brother go away?" Buttons took Julian's hands and placed them on either side of her face. She wanted him to feel her nod.

CHAPTER 9

Officer Beaufort silently berated himself for not having noticed the girl's car seat in the back of the minivan. He'd been so distracted by the boy's dangling eye that he hadn't noticed other important items at the scene. *Lesson learned*, he thought as he pulled up to the second accident scene.

As he exited his cruiser, a tall, fit blond walked over with her right hand outstretched. "Alex Hayes, Boston Homicide. And you are?"

"Ashton Beaufort, Concord PD. What the hell is Boston Homicide doing here?"

Alex lifted her eyebrows while shaking her head. "Getting into a big mess that I would've loved to avoid if possible, but as you can see ..." Alex trailed off as she swept her hand across the entire accident scene.

"Jesus," Ashton whispered. "Two in one day. When it rains, it pours."

"What do you mean 'two in one day'?"

"I just left another MVA. It involved a minivan about two miles west of here. Two are dead. It looks like a mother and a son."

"Any ID?"

Blood rushed to Ashton's cheeks. "Uh, I didn't have time to check. I was busy ensuring the victims were okay."

Alex squinted. "But I thought you said they were dead."

"Well, they were. I mean, they are, but anyway, I didn't find any ID."

"Because you didn't look?" Alex said and then smiled. "Officer Beaufort, was that your first dead kid?" Ashton examined the dirt on his shoes.

"It's okay. It'll get easier. I promise. You never get used to it, but it gets easier. What about the license plate?"

Officer Beaufort gained courage from being on solid ground again. "The car came to rest with its rear bumper against a tree, so I couldn't

26

see it. The tow truck was on its way, so I should know about the license plate shortly." It suddenly occurred to Ashton that he was answering questions that were posed by a person who was completely unrelated to the investigation.

"I'm sorry, how did you come to be here, detective?"

Alex turned around and pointed to Julian, who was sitting quietly on the grass holding Buttons' hand. "My boyfriend and I were heading off for a weekend in the Berkshires when we happened upon this accident. The driver, a teenage male, is dead, and his one passenger is being treated in the ambulance."

Ashton smiled sadly as he observed Julian with the little girl. "Your daughter must be pretty shaken up seeing all of this blood and stuff."

Alex paused, unsure what the officer meant, but then quickly understood. "Oh, she's not my daughter. According to the witness, she's what caused the driver to swerve and crash. She was standing in the middle of the road, and he yanked the wheel hard to the right to avoid hitting her."

"Where's she from? Where are her parents?"

"We're not sure. My boyfriend is a child psychologist, and he's trying to get her to open up, but so far she hasn't spoken. She was able to tell us through drawings that her family went away—whatever that means."

A pit yawned in Ashton's stomach. "Oh God," he moaned.

"What is it?"

"A little girl was missing from the MVA that I was investigating down the road. I wonder if that's her. But that's two miles away from here. Did she really walk all that way?"

"Let's go find out."

Alex and Ashton approached Julian and Buttons, and Alex made introductions.

"Her name is Buttons?" Ashton asked Alex.

"It is until we find out her real name," Alex said, reaching down and touching the child's shoulder. "She carries a jar of buttons that are very important to her."

"Okay. Well, Buttons," Ashton started, crouching down to be at eye level with the little girl, "My name is Officer Beaufort. Were you in a car that crashed into a tree today?" Buttons looked at Alex and then leaned into Julian, seeking permission and comfort at the same time.

"It's okay, Buttons. He's a friend," Julian said. Buttons nodded slowly while signing into Julian's hand so that he could be included in the conversation.

"Did you walk from your black car to here?" Again she nodded and signed.

"Why?" Alex's heart seized as the child's eyes wandered around. She was clearly lost and desperately sought an anchor in her horrible personal storm. Finally, after what seemed like an eternity, she simply shrugged and slouched against Julian.

Officer Beaufort continued. "It's okay. Were your mother and brother in the car with you?"

"Were?" Julian asked.

Officer Beaufort paused, realizing his gaffe, but it was too late. Buttons was a sensitive, intelligent child, and the past tense of the verb had not been lost on her. She closed her eyes and quietly began to weep, a private affair where she retreated inside of herself for solace.

Julian knelt down, placed his arm around her, and pulled her close. "You walked along the road because you were trying to get help, weren't you, Buttons?" Through her tears she nodded against his chest. Julian thought back to the girl's second drawing—the one in black crayon. "Buttons, was your father in the car?"

She took Julian's hand and signed "no."

"But you said he had gone away."

She remained perfectly still.

"Buttons, I think you're able to talk, but that some scary things have happened recently, and you're choosing not to talk. Is that true?"

She nodded with her face wedged tightly against Julian's chest in an effort to shut out the world. Julian took her shoulders, gingerly pulled her slightly away from him, and said, "One scary thing was the crash, right? But I think there was something else. Something happened before the car accident. Was the other scary thing related to your father?" Buttons paused, staring with unseeing eyes at some distant vision.

"Is that when you stopped talking?" Tears traced lines down her face as she nodded once more.

"When you said that he 'went away,' did you mean that he died?" The little girl wiped her face on Julian's shirt and then stared hard at Julian's sunglasses. The glare of the sun bounced off the lenses and hurt her eyes.

"Buttons?" Grabbing Julian's hand, she ground her knuckles into Julian's palm.

"Are you sure your father died?" Without hesitation the girl signed "yes" again, as if her emotional floodgates had opened and she wanted to rid herself of the burden.

"How are you so sure, honey?" Alex asked quietly.

The little girl suddenly straightened and set her mouth in a thin, tight line, making her seem older than her five short years. Her beautiful, expressive eyes darkened as she remembered walking through the house and calling for her father. With eyes unblinking, she recalled rounding the corner of the door jamb to find her father's feet dangling at eye level. Being confused, she had looked up to see his swollen, purple face and huge tongue sticking out of his mouth. Despite her terror and confusion, she had managed to silently pray for her father, quickly gather her button jar, and run out of the house to where her mother and brother Joey sat in their idling car waiting for her.

"Buttons, did you hear Alex? How are you so sure your father died?" Julian gently prodded.

The little girl turned to Julian and gently removed the sunglasses from his destroyed eyes. Regarding him thoughtfully for a moment, she sighed and whispered, "Julian, I'm sorry your eyes are broken. My daddy's head was broken too. That's how I know he's not alive anymore."

CHAPTER 10

FBI Special Agent in Charge Northeast Division Vinny Marcozzi was having a very good day. He had spent the night in the company of Annabelle Andrews, an intriguing, intelligent woman, who happened to be a Boston assistant district attorney.

Being a confirmed bachelor at forty-two, Vinny had abandoned the notion of meeting Ms. Right and had thrown himself into his career when he had spotted Annabelle at a fundraising dinner for Boston's mayor. Observing her from a distance, he had watched as she had taken in the room, clearly evaluating and determining the people with whom she would spend her time and energy. Once she had settled on her lucky recipients, she had approached them directly and captured their attention simply by becoming an intent listener. Vinny noted that she rarely spoke, and when she did, people leaned in to listen.

From his vantage point, Vinny couldn't be sure what motivated her calculated actions. She seemed to be one of those people to whom others were irresistibly drawn and he'd known he had to meet her. When he'd finally approached her, she'd cocked her head and commented, "Took you long enough, didn't it?" Vinny had been smitten at once, and they had spent many nights together since then.

The antics of the previous evening drew a smile to Vinny's lips, and he picked up his phone to text Annabelle. In the middle of composing the text, his assistant Marcie approached his desk quickly, threw down a thin folder, and quipped, "Oh my God, Vin. Enough with the sexting. Here's the *Spooks Report.*"

The *Spooks Report* was a weekly review of Vinny's agents' interactions with CIs (confidential informants). The cover was marked "Classified-Highly Confidential," and Vinny reluctantly put down his phone.

"I wasn't sexting!" Vinny called after Marcie, who had already disappeared. Vinny flipped open the report's cover to find a piece of paper that had five columns on it: "Agent Name," "Date/Time of Meeting," "Place of Meeting," "CI Code Name," and "Y/N," which indicated whether the scheduled meeting had taken place.

At a glance, he could see how many meetings had occurred over the last week and which of his agents had been involved. If the last column contained a *Y*, the agent was required to follow up within two business days with a written report outlining exactly what had happened during the meeting. Running his finger down the "Y/N" column, he found twenty-seven *Y*s and two *N*s. Focusing on the two *N*s, Vinny noted the agents' names and then called each one.

"Andy, it's Vinny. No meeting with your CI this week? How come?"

"It's legit, Vin. He's sick—in the hospital, actually, with pneumonia."

"Are you sure he's not playing you?"

"Yeah, I'm sure. I'll get on him when he gets out."

"Okay. Keep me posted then."

"You got it."

Vinny glanced at the second agent's name on the report: "Sid Nickerson." Sid was a career man who had been with the bureau since being recruited from Yale in his senior year. He was smart, had great people instincts, and held the current record for managing the most CIs at one time. Vinny glanced at the name of Sid's CI and shook his head. Sid had given him the codename of Walter Mitty, the agent's idea of a bad joke. Vinny dialed Sid's number, and the call immediately went to voicemail.

"Hey Sid, it's Vin. Call me back. There was no meeting this week with Mr. Mitty, and I'm wondering why. Thanks."

***

The man Sid had nicknamed the Ogre smiled as he saw Vinny's call go to voicemail. "It looks like your boss left you a message, Sid. Shall we listen to it?" He pressed the voicemail icon and smiled as the message played through the phone's speaker.

"Well, that clears up at least one of my questions, doesn't it, Sid? See, that wasn't so hard. If you'd told me the code name several hours ago, I wouldn't be so tired from working on you, would I?"

The Ogre lifted Sid's chin and pursed his lips as he examined Sid's face. "You don't look too good, Sid. Let's end this, okay? Cause I got dinner reservations and don't wanna be late. You know how wives are, am I right? So, I'm going to ask you once more. What else do you got on my boss?"

With gargantuan effort, Sid lifted his head and stared hard with his one functioning eye at the thug who'd been questioning him. He smiled as bloody mucus dripped from his split lips. Laughing hurt his broken ribs, but he managed a chuckle before spitting and whispering, "Fuck you, asshole. Go to hell."

CHAPTER 11

"Are you sure that little girl will be okay with your friend Julian?" Ashton asked as he drove and glanced at Alex in the passenger seat of his cruiser.

"There are other cops there now if you're worried, but trust me, that kid is in the best hands imaginable, especially given her recent trauma."

"What happened to Julian's eyes?"

"One of his patients took a knife to his face several years ago."

"Jesus."

"Yeah, it was bad. Kid was tried as an adult though, and isn't going to get out for a long time."

"Good to hear, but God, what a nightmare. We're here." Ashton pulled off the road as the black minivan was being loaded onto a tow truck.

"Virginia," Alex said.

"What?" Ashton turned to her.

"The license plate on the van. It's a Virginia plate. Can you run it?"

Using the laptop computer mounted in his cruiser, Ashton accessed the state of Virginia's license plate database and entered the numbers on the van's plate. "No matches," Ashton said. "Must be stolen or fake."

Alex wrinkled her brow. "A mother and her two kids are driving a minivan with a fake license plate that looks real enough to have fooled you and me? That's not normal."

"Not to mention that the dead woman's husband is also deceased and that her remaining child is wandering the roads of Massachusetts carrying a jar of buttons," Ashton finished while shaking his head.

"Let's ask about ID," Alex mumbled, as she exited the car and walked purposely toward the officer in charge. Ashton hurried after her, and they made their introductions.

"Nope. No ID found. Absolutely nothing," the officer stated matter-of-factly as he directed traffic.

"What about the registration?" Alex asked.

"Nothing."

"How about the VIN?"

"It's been completely scratched out."

"Are you sure? Because—"

"Let me be perfectly clear," he said while turning to her. "There was absolutely no form of any identification in the car. No registration, no purse, no driver's license, no phone. Nothing. We're going to have to ID the vics using dental records. At least that's what the coroner said. He's over there if you want to talk to him."

Alex was miffed. Her very much-needed vacation had been at best, postponed and at worst, ruined. After hearing that the black minivan and its deceased occupants had no identification, she marched over to the coroner as Officer Ashton hustled behind her.

"Hi. Alex Hayes, Boston homicide. I understand you're the coroner."

A tall, stately, gray-haired man turned slowly and evaluated Alex over red half-glasses. After looking her up and down, he nodded and said, "Dr. Hamilton Lippincott, medical examiner for the town of Concord. How may I help you?"

"I understand that no identification has been found on the victims."

"That is correct."

"Do you plan on using dental records to ID them?"

"Again, correct."

"When do you think you'll have that information?"

Dr. Lippincott removed his glasses, extracted a silk handkerchief from the breast pocket of his navy blue cashmere jacket, and began cleaning the lenses. "You cannot rush science, my dear. I understand that you are in a hurry to solve this case, but I must do my job correctly and thoroughly or not at all. If I rush, I might miss evidence that could be germane in the investigation and the eventual conclusion of this complex case."

Alex pursed her lips and squinted at the man. Having encountered people like Dr. Lippincott throughout her career, Alex had honed her method of working with them. She usually stroked their incredibly large egos while gleaning valuable information from them, but not today. Today, her vacation had been ruined. Today, she had witnessed a little girl whose life was in a shambles and who was clinging to a jar of buttons. Today was not a normal day, even in Alex's world.

***

Buttons lay asleep with her head in Julian's lap and her face turned away from the sun. Rubbing her back slowly, Julian used the same circular motions his mother had used to soothe him when he was a child. Although her breath came evenly, every so often her body would jerk as her subconscious began the unpredictable process of working through the horrors she had recently endured.

Julian's mind wandered back to another child he had never known but whose trauma had formed the foundation for an adult serial killer later in life. Touching his left shoulder, he wondered if he could have done anything further to help Dr. Linda Sterling, the person Alex had been targeting when she had accidentally shot Julian. Linda had been about Buttons' age when her trauma had begun.

"Julian?" Buttons' tiny voice interrupted his thoughts. "Why did you stop rubbing? It felt so good." The girl yawned and sat up, causing the buttons to rattle against the glass jar with her movements.

"Oh, sorry, Buttons. I was just thinking about a woman I knew."

"Was she a friend of yours?"

Julian smiled. "I wouldn't say that, but she went through a lot of tough stuff when she was a child—kind of like you."

"Oh. Where is she now?"

In his mental musings, Julian had let his professional wall weaken and, like most children, Buttons had managed to find the crack and wedge her hand through it. Because he was now trapped, Julian knew that the worst move would be to lie to this child who had already seen and experienced more than most adults.

"She's in heaven, Buttons."

"Oh," Buttons answered, as if expecting his response. "It seems like everybody's going to heaven these days."

"May I ask you a question?"

"Uh-huh," she answered, yawning and rubbing her eyes.

"Why do you carry that jar of buttons?"

"Because my daddy gave it to me."

"Is there something special about the buttons?"

"Yes, very special."

Julian leaned in conspiratorially. "What?"

Buttons squinted at Julian as she considered his request. She remembered the words her father had used each time he had given her a button to add to her collection. He had said, "This button is very special, Molly, just like you. There's only one like it in the entire world, just like you. Promise me you won't lose it, and won't tell anyone—not *anyone*—about these buttons, okay? It's our secret."

She had agreed, of course, as her father's love and approval had meant the world to her. After all, if he had given these most precious buttons to her and trusted her to keep such an important secret, she must not ever let him down.

As much as she liked Julian, she couldn't break her father's trust. Buttons made her decision and leaned her forehead against Julian's. "I'm sorry, Julian, but I can't tell you," she whispered.

CHAPTER 12

"Okay," Julian smiled. "I respect that you can't tell me why the buttons are so important to you. But can you at least tell me your name?"

Buttons giggled and leaned into him. "Julian, you're funny. It's Buttons, remember? You just gave me that name. Did you already forget?"

Julian tapped his head and said, "Oh, right. Silly me. But I think you have another name, Buttons. It's one that your parents gave you when you were a baby. Can you tell me that name?"

Buttons' mouth twisted in thought. On the one hand, her parents had told her never to share personal information with people she didn't know. On the other hand, neither of her parents was alive anymore and Julian seemed awfully nice. He wasn't *really* a stranger.

Sensing her hesitation, Julian said, "You know, it occurs to me that we haven't been properly introduced. The name that my parents gave me is Julian Robert Stryker. It's a pleasure to meet you, Miss ..." Julian held out his right hand, hoping that Buttons would take it.

As Buttons raised her left eyebrow and tilted her head, a slow smile graced her lovely countenance. She rose, took his hand, and bowed theatrically. "Hello Julian Robert Stryker. My name is Molly Elizabeth McClelland, but my friends call me Buttons. You may call me Buttons, by the way, because you're my friend, right?"

Julian lifted his head and maintained his firm grip on her right hand. "I am your friend, Molly Elizabeth, and you can always count on me no matter what."

Julian could feel the tension ease out of Buttons' hand as he spoke. The trauma the little girl had suffered over the past hours had been more than most adults see in a lifetime. Julian knew that she most likely was still in a mild state of shock. The extent of the damage to her life wouldn't fully be comprehended for years. She would need significant counseling and emotional support from family, friends, and professionals.

"Buttons, do your grandparents live near you?"

"Nope. They all died."

"What about cousins, aunts, and uncles?"

Buttons shrugged. "I don't think I have any of those either," she stated matter-of-factly. "Julian, can I go home now? I'm tired."

Julian's heart broke as he gathered Buttons in his arms and hugged her tightly. What she didn't realize—couldn't realize at this point—was that her home, as she once knew it, no longer existed and never would again. He didn't want to lie but couldn't face telling her the truth, so he said, "Soon, Buttons, soon."

***

As Alex was about to unload on the pretentious coroner, her cell phone buzzed. Glancing at the screen, she smiled. "Excuse me. *Doctor* Lippincott. Be right back."

Alex sauntered away and pressed the green button to answer the call. "You just saved my ass one more time, Stryker," she quipped. "I was about to let an arrogant medical examiner have it. What's up?"

"Always glad to be of service, my love. Listen—Buttons has shared her name with me. It's Molly Elizabeth McClelland, and she's from Winchester. I suggest someone get over to the McClelland house and see if her dad's there. If you recall, she said that her dad's head was broken, but maybe she misunderstood. He could be in the house, hurt but alive."

Alex sighed. "It's just as well because there's nothing else to be done here in Concord at either accident scene. God dammit!"

"What's wrong?"

"We're not going on vacation, are we?"

After a beat, Julian said, "Yes, we are. Let's just go. This isn't our case. I can contact Stacey Goldberg to take care of Buttons—I mean Molly—and we can go."

Alex's spirits lifted. "Okay, great! I'll be back there in five minutes. Call Stacey and we'll be on our way."

"You got it."

Alex disconnected the call and returned to the accident scene. "Excuse me, Dr. Lippincott," Alex started sweetly.

The medical examiner, appreciating her softer, more respectful tone, inclined his head and replied, "Yes, dear?"

"I just wanted to let you know that I'll be leaving now so that you can carry on your important work. Oh, and one more thing, I did half your job and discovered that the surname of the two deceased people you're examining is McClelland and that they live in Winchester. Have a nice day … *sir*."

She then turned to Ashton, who had witnessed the exchange between the two professionals as if observing a skilled tennis match. "Ashton, please take over here. I need to return to the other scene." Alex walked back to her car with her head held high, watched by an awed Ashton Beaufort.

CHAPTER 13

Kellie Moser had owned her housecleaning company, Dirty Secrets, for five years and had managed to build quite a clientele in the greater Boston suburbs. Because it was known to be thorough, fast, and fair-priced, the business had grown via word of mouth to include local celebrities. Most important, however, was Kellie's discretion. What she witnessed and heard in each client's home was never repeated, locked in the mental vault that she reserved for important information.

When tabloids broke the story about a local news anchor philandering with his nanny, Kellie simply smiled as her coworkers prodded her for information. Of course she had seen evidence in the home and had cleaned up after their trysts, for goodness sake. But she would never share any of their family secrets. It just wasn't right. She'd been raised better than that. Plus, it wasn't good business.

The McClelland family had been one of Kellie's clients since they had purchased their Winchester home seven years ago. In Kellie's opinion, they were a typical family, in that the father, Jimmy, owned several dry-cleaning stores, and the mother, Isabella, stayed home with their two children. They were good people who gave to charities, made sure Kellie received a bonus during the holidays, and always remembered to ask about her family.

Isabella always had a cup of hot, fresh chai tea waiting for Kellie on the kitchen table next to her payment. Kellie found that she looked forward to the ten-minute chat she and Isabella would enjoy each week. It was never anything too complicated. It was just two ladies sipping tea and sharing family anecdotes.

This particular morning, however, as she pulled into the McClelland's driveway, Kellie immediately felt that something was amiss. There was an emptiness about the property that set her nerves on edge. She gathered her cleaning supplies while evaluating the house and trying to determine what seemed out of place. As she approached the garage, she noted that Isabella's minivan was missing, yet Jimmy's car was there. That was odd for sure. By now, Jimmy should have been at work for several hours, and Isabella would be waiting for Kellie inside.

Her cell phone buzzed, causing her to jump. Chastising herself for being so skittish, Kellie answered the call and was quickly enveloped in a one-sided conversation with her autistic son. Apparently, his father was trying to get him dressed for school, but his pants were too itchy. As Kellie used key phrases the psychologist had taught her to calm her son, she reached for the front door handle, only to find the door slightly ajar.

"Connor, Connor, put Daddy back on the phone. Mommy needs to go to work. I know, Connor, I know. I'll talk to Daddy and tell him to let you wear the red pants—the soft ones—okay? Now please put Daddy on the phone. Thank you."

After a moment, her husband Frank came on the line. "Frank, let him wear the red pants 'cause I can't deal with this right now. Something's not right at the McClelland house. I'm not sure, but I need to go. I'll call you back when I can. Love you too."

Kellie pushed the door open just wide enough to squeeze her head through. Normally she'd simply walk in, but the back of her neck felt prickly, and her gut told her to walk away or to even call the police. But then the reasonable side of her brain took over. *What would I tell the police?* she thought. *The door's ajar? C'mon, Kellie, you're being ridiculous.*

"Isabella? You home?" There was no response. "Jimmy? Is anyone home?" Kellie dragged her cleaning supplies through the front door and stood in the foyer while she determined her next steps. She entered the kitchen and found a clean, empty teacup on the table, which was obviously meant for her. Her check was next to it. *Clearly Isabella remembered I was coming today*, she thought.

After walking through the downstairs and finding nothing amiss, she decided she was being silly, called her husband to update him, and was relieved to learn that Connor had finished dressing without incident. Feeling content, she started her weekly cleaning and completed the downstairs within an hour. She then vacuumed the front stairs and the upstairs hallway. She was continuing into the master bedroom when she backed into something. Instinctively, she mumbled, "Excuse me," as she turned to see what she'd hit.

Kellie Moser had seen and heard many things in her career, but she was completely unprepared for the vision before her. James McClelland's body was swinging back and forth, striking her again and again. His neck had elongated as gravity had worked its magic on the weight of his body, and he had soiled his pants.

Kellie heard herself screaming and dropped the handle of the vacuum cleaner on her foot as she scrambled to press 911 on her phone. She stumbled backward to disentangle herself from the body that seemed intent on accosting her, but miscalculated her footing and tumbled backward. Kellie's neck broke in two places as she rolled down the stairs and smashed her head against the mahogany banister. Her body came to rest on the bottom landing, a heap of twisted and broken body parts. Her phone lay next to her while a confused 911 operator repeatedly asked, "911, what's your emergency?"

CHAPTER 14

Although some silent 911 calls were hoaxes—teenagers completing some ridiculous dare—this one struck the seasoned emergency operator as significant. He had pinpointed the caller's location using satellite GPS technology and had forwarded the information to the Winchester precinct, which was the closest one to the neighborhood. Winchester police officer Thelma Grace was dispatched to investigate.

Officer Grace pulled into the driveway, exited her vehicle, and approached cautiously, glancing in the windows on either side of the front door as she knocked firmly. "Winchester police! Please open the door."

Tilting her head to listen, she thought she heard someone moan. She knocked even harder while slowly drawing her gun. "Winchester police. Open the door now!"

She heard another soft moan. Speaking into the walkie-talkie on her shoulder, she informed headquarters of her location and requested immediate backup. With her gun aimed at the ground, she twisted the doorknob and entered the house, quickly raising her firearm in front of her. Completing a fast visual sweep of the foyer and the living room, which was to her left, she heard a sound behind the door.

Coming around the door quickly, she found a woman's twisted body lying at an impossible angle on the stair's landing. The woman was moaning softly as her eyes rolled back in her head. Officer Grace spoke into her walkie-talkie once more and requested that an ambulance be sent immediately to the scene.

She knelt next to the woman. "Ma'am! Ma'am! My name is Officer Grace. An ambulance is on the way. Don't move please. Is there anyone else in the house?"

Kellie Moser managed to focus her eyes on the face swimming

above her. Her brows came together in confusion and then raised as she remembered the horror she had seen in the master bedroom.

"Ups-upst-," she couldn't make her mouth say what her brain was thinking.

"Upstairs?" the officer said, pointing up the stairs.

"Yeh."

"Okay, like I said, help is on the way. I need you *not to move*. Is that clear? Moving could actually hurt you more. Do you understand?" The woman blinked. "I'll be right back."

Turning her attention to the top landing, Officer Grace hugged the wall and crept silently up the stairs. As she climbed, she noted three rooms that were off the main hallway and to the left and another to her immediate right. Raising her weapon in front of her, she turned quickly into the doorway on the right and found herself pointing the gun at Jimmy McClelland's knees. Officer Grace glanced at his face, swallowed the bile that had risen in her throat, and quickly checked the other rooms before radioing in the updated situation. She then returned to the base of the stairs where Kellie Moser was more coherent.

"You saw him?" Kellie whispered while her eyes filled with tears.

"Yes, I saw him. Do you know his name?"

Tears rolled freely down Kellie's cheeks and dropped heavily to the oak wood landing where she lay. "Jimmy McClelland. I don't know where his wife, Isabella, and their kids are though. They might be in danger."

The wail of the sirens crescendoed as the ambulance and police cars approached the house.

"What's your name, and how did you end up at the bottom of the stairs?" Officer Grace asked Kellie as she opened the door for the paramedics.

"It's Kellie Moser, and I tripped and fell backward while calling 911."

"I know you're in pain, but you'll be at the hospital soon," Officer Grace said kindly.

"Actually, it's kind of weird, but I can't feel anything from my neck down, so I'm okay, really." Officer Grace stared hard at the woman who clearly didn't comprehend the fact that she might be paralyzed.

CHAPTER 15

"No need for vulgarity, Sid," the Ogre said, smiling. "We're all friends here. Now, you told me to go fuck myself. I believe that's what you said, wasn't it? And then I believe that you told me to go to hell." The man stood up and slowly shook his head as he crossed behind Sid and flexed his hands open and closed. "Sid, I don't think you are in full understanding of your situation here."

Sid attempted to turn his head and was rewarded with a stabbing pain that shot down his back, forcing him to abandon his efforts.

"Despite hours of conversation with you, it was your boss who graciously gave me the code name you used for your CI. Walter Mitty." The Ogre smiled and shook his head. "Great name, by the way. Very fitting for a man who seemed so inconsequential but was actually so powerful. What I need to know now though is what Mr. Mitty told you before he met with his untimely demise."

Despite his training and many years in the bureau, Sid was surprised and showed it. "Jimmy's dead?"

The man stopped pacing behind Sid and stood in front of him. "Oh, did I neglect to mention that? Yes, Jimmy died, this morning actually. Poor man hung himself in his bedroom. The note he left said something about no longer being able to live with the fact that he had been cheating on his wife. Couldn't live with himself, poor bastard, so he ended it. Sad really, if you think about it."

Sid's mind was reeling. No wonder the Ogre had gotten to Sid so quickly. Jimmy had probably babbled everything he knew in an effort to save his own life or perhaps the lives of his family members. Jimmy must have omitted some pertinent information, however, or Sid wouldn't be in this predicament. Sid quickly reasoned that his only leverage would lay in the information Jimmy had given him over the years as a confidential informant. If he spilled what he knew, he'd be killed.

"Let's talk about your wife, Sid."

Sid's head snapped up quickly. "What about her?"

"And those two beautiful kids you have. Teenagers now, right? Annie, sixteen, and Joshua, fifteen, am I right?"

Sid's upper lip lifted as a growl escaped him. "I swear to God, if you hurt them—"

"You'll what? Kill me? Please, Sid, like I said, we're friends, you and me. Don't be so damn melodramatic. I'm not gonna kill them. I'm not stupid, for fuck's sake."

"Did you kill Jimmy?"

The man looked at him with eyes that registered a mixture of surprise and hurt. "Of course I didn't kill him. I could never do that."

Despite the pain, Sid started laughing and ended up vomiting. He spit and then said, "You can do this to me, but you can't kill someone? That makes no sense."

The man knelt down in front of Sid and placed his hand on Sid's knee. "Seriously, Sid, I have integrity—standards. I might rough you up, but I'd never kill you or your family. You gotta believe me." The man stood and gestured behind him. "But he might."

A large bald man walked into the room and stood stoically with his hands crossed almost demurely across his abdomen. Although Jimmy McClelland had mentioned him in verbal reports, Sid had never imagined he would lay eyes on the person Jimmy had referred to simply as the Muscle—the person to whom Don Paolo entrusted all life-ending physical enforcement.

"Did *you* kill Jimmy McClelland?" Sid asked the Muscle.

The Muscle looked at Sid as if registering his presence for the first time. "Yes."

For the first time in Sid's lauded career with the bureau, he was genuinely frightened. It wasn't the fact that the Muscle had so readily admitted to murder, but rather the manner in which he had done it. It was as if taking someone's life, snuffing it out *forever,* was a mundane occurrence. Sid dropped his eyes and sighed heavily.

"There we are. Welcome to the party, Sidney," said the Ogre smiling.

"Now I know that you understand. You see, Sid, I'm not going to kill you, and neither is the Muscle. We won't need to. Because if you don't start cooperating with us, the Muscle will first pay a visit to your gorgeous, ripe Annie and then to your wife. After that, he'll—"

"Okay!" Sid bellowed. "I get it! Enough!"

"Fantastic. Now, here's what's going to happen. You're going to tell me everything that Jimmy told you, and then you're going to go back to work as if nothing has happened. Oh, except that you're going to wreck your car in order to explain your injuries. In the future, you will report to me any information the FBI has on my boss, Don Paolo. Any ongoing investigations, updates, and things like that. Hey, you're kind of like my confidential informant—like Jimmy was to you. Why do you look so sad, Sid? It'll be fun."

CHAPTER 16

Julian phoned Stacey Goldberg, a social worker friend he had known since graduate school. Stacey had aided Julian on several occasions, and he knew that if anyone could figure out the next steps for Buttons, it would be Stacey.

"Hey Stacey, it's Julian Stryker."

"Julian! I heard you'd been shot, by Alex no less. Seriously, what did you do to piss her off that much?"

Julian chuckled. "It wasn't quite that simple, Stace. I wish it had been."

"I know, I know. I heard the whole story from Jesse. I know he has a flair for the dramatic, but it sounds like the lady you were dealing with— what was her name? Linda Sterling—was a psychopath. In all seriousness, I'm glad you're okay."

Julian rotated his damaged shoulder and sighed. "Yeah, I honestly wasn't sure I was going to come out of it alive. Linda was ... really broken. I wish I could have helped her."

Stacey blew out air on the other end of the line. "You're very gracious, Julian. Even after she tried to kill you, you're still wishing you could have helped her? You're either really empathetic or just flat-out stupid."

"A little of both, I think," Julian answered and then tried to change the subject. "Anyhow, Stace, I need your help." Julian explained the entire situation and finished by saying, "So I'm not sure there's any family left. I don't want her thrown into the child-welfare system. Can you take personal ownership of Buttons' case?"

"Julian, I'm not a child caseworker."

"I know, I know, but you know people that can ensure her safety and security. She's special, Stacey, really special."

"Mm ..."

"Please, Stacey? I'll owe you."

"Oh, my goodness, Julian! You already owe me for so many other things. Why do I do these things for you?"

"Because I'm really empathetic and flat-out stupid."

Stacey burst out laughing. "But really clever. Don't forget that."

"Can you tell Alex that I'm clever? Because I'm not sure she knows that."

"Oh, she knows, believe me. Yes, I'll come get … what was her name again?"

"Buttons. Well it's really Molly, but her friends call her Buttons."

"Something tells me she won't want me calling her Buttons when she finds out why I'm there," Stacey mumbled. "I'm on my way."

"Thanks, Stacey. You're the best." Julian told her where they were and rang off. Pleased with himself, Julian turned his face toward the sun.

"You're leaving me?" Buttons' voice seemed smaller than it had been only moments before. "But … but … you said that I could count on you no matter what. That's what you said."

Julian knelt down. "You *can* count on me, Buttons. I'm your friend. But Alex is also my friend, and I made a promise to take her on a little vacation. Just because I'm going to keep my promise to Alex doesn't mean I'm abandoning you. I have another friend named Stacey Goldberg who's a social worker. She's going to come here, meet you, and help you find somewhere to stay until—"

"Somewhere to stay?" Buttons screeched. "What does that mean? I want to go home! Julian, you lied to me. You lied! You said I could go home soon. You said that!"

The terror in Buttons' voice struck Julian as if he'd been hit with a hammer. He *had* said that she would be going home soon. Caught up in the moment and trying to make her feel better, he had lied and told her that she would be going home soon, even though he knew it wasn't true. He silently berated himself for allowing his professional guard to drop for that split second. Children were honest, and they expected honesty in return. The truth might have been difficult, but they deserved nothing less. That was one of Julian's professional tenets. It took only one lie to unravel the fragile bond of trust that had been carefully woven between them, and it had happened.

Buttons collapsed on the grass, the button jar rattling against her heaving chest. Her sobs rang out against the silent, humid summer day, and Julian could feel her loneliness—the empty void that would never be filled no matter how many people cared for her. The severed bond lay naked between them, and Julian felt impotent to reach out across the chasm.

Alex had arrived and had heard the last words of their exchange. Staring at the weeping child, her heart clenched. Alex wiped her eyes, slipped her hand into Julian's, and said very quietly, "We're not going on vacation, are we?"

Julian faced her. His face was a mask of sadness, and he didn't trust himself to speak. Alex squeezed his hand, leaned in, and whispered, "Julian, you're the most honest, wonderfully kind person I know. I know you don't want to disappoint me, so I'm going to make this decision for us. We're not going on vacation. We're going to stay with Buttons."

Julian squeezed her hand in return and whispered back, "Thank you, Alex."

CHAPTER 17

Julian and Buttons rode in the back of Stacey's car while Alex followed closely behind in her Mustang. Stacey was on speakerphone with her assistant trying to reschedule several patients that had been misplaced due to Julian's recent request. Smiling, he reminded himself how fortunate he was to have friends who would drop what they were doing to help.

In fact, Julian remembered when he had met Stacey many years ago on Massachusetts Avenue in front of the Starbucks that was close to Boston University, where they both attended. Stacey had been sitting in the middle of the sidewalk next to a wounded pigeon. When Julian had asked her what she was doing, she had replied that the pigeon had been struck by a car, and although she had made numerous calls to animal shelters and even animal control, because it was only a pigeon and was so severely injured, no one would help.

Julian had commented that her actions were kind but had wondered aloud what she could do for the poor animal. She had looked defiantly at him and had said, "I'm not sure, but at least he won't die alone." Julian had sat down next to her, and for the next two hours, they had exchanged stories about family and friends as the bird had lain there panting. Inevitably, the bird had passed, and Julian had placed his hand on Stacey's shoulder as she had shed a tear. Stacey Goldberg possessed honor, integrity, and a drive to help others, which made her great at her job, not to mention a fantastic colleague and friend.

Buttons had fallen asleep within minutes. She was curled in the fetal position with her arms wrapped tightly around her jar and her head in Julian's lap. Stacey had been correct about Buttons' reaction to her arrival. When the little girl had realized that Stacey was there to take her away,

Buttons had told her that she may call her Molly, and had refused to look her in the eye.

Julian had apologized to Buttons for lying to her and had suggested that perhaps he and Alex might accompany her. It had taken some work, but eventually, Buttons had forgiven Julian, had acquiesced to go with Stacey (as long as Julian rode with her), and even allowed Stacey to call her by her nickname.

Julian leaned his head back and reflected on how beautifully the day had started and how quickly it had turned ugly. His phone buzzed, and he commanded Siri to answer it.

"Hey, it's me. How is she doing?" Alex asked.

Julian spoke quietly. "She's asleep—poor little thing."

"We did the right thing by staying with her."

"I believe we did. Thanks for that, Alex."

"Well, she's a kid, and a tough one at that. The least we can do is give her a fighting chance. Do you really think she has no family left?"

"I don't know. Stacey said she's going to do some digging to figure that out. In the meantime, I guess Buttons will stay with whomever the court deems appropriate. A foster family maybe?"

"Mm."

"What?"

"I've seen some foster families that made my skin crawl."

"Me too, Alex, but what other choice do we have?"

Alex paused for a long time before answering. "Us."

Julian pulled the phone away from his ear and then replaced it. He was sure he had misheard her. "Did you say, 'us'? What do you mean?"

"You and me. Us. We could take care of her just until Stacey finds somewhere else for her to go, that is."

Julian was stunned speechless. Alex was literally the last person who would consider fostering a child, not because she wasn't a great human being but because she had never expressed an interest in children at all, much less having one in her own home.

Alex said, "You know what? You're right. It was a terrible idea. Forget that I mentioned it. Really, forget it. Listen—I gotta go. Someone else is calling me. I'll see you at your office." Julian didn't have time to react before she disconnected.

Alex pressed the swap icon on her phone, disconnecting her call from Julian and connecting the new one. "Alex Hayes."

"Hello, Detective Hayes. This is Chief Daniel Schmidt of the Winchester Police Department. There's a message on my desk that says that you needed to talk to me?"

"Yes, hi, Chief Schmidt. My partner and I found a little girl this morning in Concord. She had been in a car accident in which her mother and brother had been killed. We found her wandering down the road in shock. After speaking with her for some time, she told my partner her name. It's Molly Elizabeth McClelland, and she's from—" His quick intake of air stopped Alex short. "You know her?"

"I don't know the girl, but I know her parents—specifically her father. Or should I say, I *knew* her father. He was very active in local politics."

The hairs on Alex's arms stood on end as she remembered Buttons' comment about her father's head being broken. "Mr. McClelland is dead?"

"Oh, he's dead, all right. Hung himself in his bedroom from one of the rafters. The McClelland's house was a barn before they bought and restored it. I haven't been over there yet, but my investigators think that Jimmy must've slung a rope over one of the rafters, climbed a ladder, put the rope around his neck, and then kicked the ladder out from under himself."

"Geez. Did he leave a note?"

"Yup. Apparently he was having an affair. Couldn't deal with the guilt anymore. Wait a minute, did you say that the girl's mother and brother were killed in the accident this morning?"

"Yes I did."

The chief paused and then said quietly, "So she's an orphan. Poor kid."

Alex nodded as if he could see her. "Yes, chief, she's an orphan."

CHAPTER 18

Julian's mind was still trying to wrap itself around Alex's offer to foster Buttons when Stacey, Buttons, and he arrived at his office. Grasping his cane in his right hand and holding Buttons' hand in his left, he made his way through the front office door and immediately heard Jesse talking on the phone.

"No, you listen to me. Dr. Stryker doesn't have time for these games. Either pay this claim, or I'm going to file a suit against the insurance company. You and I both know that this claim is legit, and I have a business to run, so don't waste my time … uh-huh … okay … well then, thank you, and I look forward to receiving that check. You have a good day too. Say hi to Marge. Bye."

Julian stood in the doorway, smiling proudly.

"Jesse, what would I do without you? It's like having an attack dog in the finance department."

"Yeah, well, if *you* want to continue seeing patients, *I* need to make sure the business end functions, right? Anyway, speaking of attack dogs, I—"

Before Jesse could finish his sentence, Oscar came bounding out of Julian's office. Hearing his paws hit the floor, Julian immediately surmised that the dog had been lounging on his very expensive leather couch. Julian braced himself for the onslaught he knew was coming. Oscar rounded the corner panting, and rammed his head into Julian's crotch before rubbing against him and nearly knocking him over. Buttons squealed while jumping up and down yelling, "What a big puppy! What a big puppy!"

After leaving an appropriate amount of drool on Julian's pants, Oscar turned his attention to Buttons, whose face was at his eye level. He sniffed her and completed his examination by gracing her with a facial tongue bath, which left her in giggles on the floor. Julian was grateful to Oscar for doing the one thing none of the humans could—making Buttons laugh.

Julian ruffled Oscar's head and said, "Okay, buddy, that's enough. Lay down." Oscar obeyed, his tail thumping against the ground as it wagged wildly.

"Hi, Stacey, great to see you. Slumming with Julian, I see," Jesse said.

Stacey smiled. "Something like that," she mumbled.

Jesse focused his gaze on the little girl. "And who is this beautiful princess I see before me?" Jesse stood and came around the desk to kneel in front of Buttons.

Buttons withdrew from Jesse and hid behind Julian's leg. "How did you know she's a princess?" Julian asked, feigning astonishment.

Jesse rolled his eyes at Julian. "Julian, *clearly* she's a princess! Look at the way she walks and holds her head. She's simply royal, that's all."

Buttons twisted her mouth, trying not to smile, but lost the battle. She grinned and peeked at Jesse from behind Julian's leg.

"Oh, you know what?" Jesse continued as he stood up quickly and crossed to his desk. Julian heard him rummaging through drawers until he said, "Ah-ha! Here it is. Royal Princess, I do believe that this is yours." He knelt and bowed his head as he presented Buttons with his find.

"A tiara!" Buttons exclaimed, grabbing it and placing it on her head. "Can I keep it?"

Jesse smiled and nodded. "Of course. It's yours. My name is Jesse. What's yours?"

Buttons stepped forward and placed her hand on Jesse's shoulder. "My name is Moll—I mean, Buttons. My name is Buttons."

"Is it because you have that jar of buttons?"

Buttons looked down at her jar, and the recent events came flooding back. Her face dropped, and she became silent. Sensing the dramatic change, Jesse switched topics. "What are you doing here anyway, Julian? Last I heard, you and Alex were on the road to paradise."

Julian cleared his throat. "We came across Buttons and decided to spend some time with her instead. Right, Buttons?" The little girl had returned to Julian and had taken his hand, retreating into herself. Her eyes remained downcast.

Jesse had worked with Julian long enough to understand that Julian didn't want to speak openly in front of the little girl. "Where's Alex?"

"I'm right here," Alex said, entering the room.

Stacey cleared her throat and said, "Shall we go into your office, Julian, and discuss next steps?"

Buttons rushed over to Alex and clasped her hand, pulling her until she stood next to Julian. Grasping Julian's hand, she joined Alex's and Julian's hands and then placed her small hand over theirs. "Look," she said quietly, glancing from Alex to Julian and back again. "We're a family."

CHAPTER 19

Sid walked into Vinny's office and lowered himself gingerly into one of the chairs across the desk from him. Vinny's face registered shock and confusion as he finished a phone call. "Sid, what the hell? You look like shit."

"Yeah, sorry, Vin. I know you left me a message, but I was in a car accident and ended up in Beth Israel Hospital. They wouldn't let me use my cell phone. It had something to do with it interfering with X-rays or some other bullshit like that. Anyway, that's why I just got your message. So to answer your question about meeting with my CI, I didn't meet with Mr. Mitty because it turns out he's dead. Hung himself in his house. He was cheating on his wife and couldn't take the guilt anymore."

Vinny's eyebrows narrowed as he examined Sid. "Sid, let's break this down. One thing at a time. First of all, how did you end up wrecking your car?"

Sid grimaced, pain shooting through his midsection as his two broken ribs shifted. "It was stupid, really. I was on my way to meet Mr. Mitty when my wife texted me. All I did was glance at the screen, and when I looked up, there was a car stopped in front of me at a red light. I smashed right into it. Thank God, the guy wasn't hurt. It could've been so much worse. I feel lucky to be alive."

Vinny had known Sid for many years but had never known him to be so reckless. In fact, two weeks earlier, Vinny had taken a phone call while driving, and Sid had chastised Vinny on the dangers of distracted driving.

"What make and model?"

"I'm sorry?"

"What make and model was the car you hit?"

"Oh, uh, I think it was a Toyota Camry. It was blue if I remember correctly."

"And the other driver sustained no injuries, you say?"

"Yeah, lucky for both of us, I guess."

Vinny bit his lower lip in thought. "And this Mitty guy is dead?"

"Yeah, hung himself because—"

"Yes, you said that, Sid. The guilt of cheating. So now that he's dead, what was his name?"

Sid paused. It was common practice in the FBI to allow as few people as possible access to sensitive information that could compromise them, the agency, or the case in question. Under normal circumstances, Sid would have answered Vinny's question immediately. With his confidential informant dead, there was no reason Vinny shouldn't know the CI's name. But the circumstances in which Sid found himself were nothing close to normal, so he paused.

"Sid! What's going on, man? You okay? What's the CI's name?"

"Yeah, sorry, Vin. James McClelland—Jimmy."

Vinny's eyebrows shot up. "Your CI was Jimmy the Shark McClelland? Jesus, Sid. I had no idea."

"Yeah. Now that he's dead, the case I was building against Paolo Torchia and the mob is also dead."

Vinny threw his hands outward. "What are you talking about? Jimmy's given you a lot over the months. When did you roll him?"

"About six months ago."

"Okay. So let's you and me go over everything Jimmy told you. You got any other CIs in the mob?"

"Nope. Jimmy was it, and I only had him because two of his dry-cleaning stores incurred safety violations a year ago, which got the local police nosing around. I have a friend on the Winchester police force. She contacted me and had me look into Jimmy's businesses. They're legit, but after digging a little deeper, I found that the numbers in the books didn't seem to equal the amount of business coming into his stores. I approached him quietly and directly, and he agreed to snitch in exchange for full immunity."

Vinny was shocked. He had never known Christopher Smith to grant full immunity to anyone since coming into the office of district attorney several years ago. "The DA agreed to *full* immunity?"

"No, it was an ADA named Andrews."

"Annabelle Andrews?"

"Yeah, you know her?"

"Yes, very well, actually. I remember the case, but I didn't know it was Jimmy that had flipped." Vinny thought a moment. "Is it possible that his suicide wasn't a suicide at all? Could it have been a hit?"

Blood rushed to Sid's cheeks. He was at a moral and ethical crossroads. Until this point, he had not lied about anything that might affect the FBI's case against the Torchia crime family, but now he had to make a choice. He could mislead Vinny in an effort to derail the case and in so doing, save his own family, or tell the truth and go into witness protection to avoid persecution from the mob. Over the years at the bureau, Sid had known nine people who had gone into witness protection, and only four of them were still alive. The others had been discovered and murdered by the people they had been hiding from. He made his choice.

"No chance it was a hit. First of all, he hung himself and kicked the ladder out from under his feet. Secondly, he did have a mistress. He was open with me about it because he wanted to make sure she was taken care of if anything ever happened to him. It was part of his deal with me."

"What's her name?"

"Who?"

"The mistress."

"Oh, uh, I don't remember. I'm sure it's in my notes."

"Check on that and get back to me. We may want to talk to her."

"Sure, sure."

"Okay. So let's you and I get together again in a couple days when you're up to it. Seriously, you look awful. You're sweating like a pig. You sure you're okay?"

Sid wiped his forehead on his sleeve, making an effort to smile. "If it's all right with you, I'd like to go home and lie down."

"Of course. Feel better and keep in touch, okay?"

"Thanks, Vin." With great effort Sid stood, his right hand gripped the arm of the chair while his left hand cradled his broken ribs.

Vinny winced as he watched his friend struggle. "That must have been some accident, Sid."

Sid examined Vinny's eyes, trying to gauge whether or not Vinny was suspicious. He found nothing but honesty and concern. His guilt level rose as he said, "Some people say that there are no accidents in this world, Vin, and that everything happens for a reason. But sometimes bad stuff happens to good people, doesn't it?"

A cloud crossed Vinny's countenance as he considered Sid's words. "Yeah, Sid. I guess."

CHAPTER 20

Sid left Vinny's office, limped quickly to the bathroom, and dry heaved. The effort left his ribs screaming in pain as he sank to the floor exhausted. His mind was reeling from his conversation with Vinny and he desperately tried to determine what Vinny already knew and how much information he'd have to divulge at their next meeting. His phone buzzed as the screen lit up with a message.

> Hope you're having a good day, Sid. I thoroughly enjoyed our conversation yesterday and am looking forward to another one if things don't work out. Meet me at Rosa's at noon.

Sid closed his eyes and breathed deeply. He thought about an agent he had known who had been compromised by the same people who were blackmailing him. Agent Anthony Mora was a twenty-two-year-old recruit who had a baby face and an uncanny ability to morph himself into whatever his target required him to be.

Paolo Jr., the don's eighteen-year-old son, was an egotistical and secretly homosexual person, and took immediate notice of the raven-haired, green-eyed boy who gazed at him during math and science classes. After propositioning Anthony in the bathroom, Paolo Jr. and he became inseparable under the guise of being best friends. The don never questioned his son's choices, grateful that the boy kept his *tendencies* private.

Thus began the most successful two-year infiltration of any mob family in the history of the Boston bureau. It led to the arrest of several lower-level deputies and included Paolo Jr. The DA had been unable to mount a case against Don Paolo, so he had remained free, which explained why things hadn't ended well for Anthony Mora, whose body parts were delivered parcel post to his family, piece by piece, over the next several months.

In agreeing to work with the Ogre, Sid knew he had made a pact with the devil, but what choice did he have? They were threatening his children, for God's sake. In theory he had always thought he could withstand any threat that was thrown at him. He had listened with disdain to stories of agents who had become rats for the mob. He had judged them and had thought they were weak. Now the tables had turned, as his family members' lives were hanging in the balance. The decision he had made had actually been no choice at all. His primary goal had been ensuring his family's safety.

Sid wasn't stupid though. He didn't plan on being a snitch for the mob forever. After his meeting with the Ogre, he had stopped at home and had told his wife of nineteen years that he was working a local project for a little while and then retiring. After he had assured her that his car accident had left him bruised but functional, they had sat at the kitchen table with their heads huddled together over coffee and had planned when and where they would go in retirement.

Sid had told her that the kids weren't to know about their plans because he wanted it to be a surprise. She, too, must remain silent, as the project he was working was top secret and he didn't want the bureau to know about his retirement plans just yet.

Kathleen had looked at him questioningly. He had taken her hand and had asked her, this one time, to not ask too many questions and to just *go with it*. In all of their years together and Sid's years at the bureau, Kathleen had never felt that she or the children had been at risk. Although Sid's recent actions and behavior had worried her somewhat, she had decided that she didn't want to make things worse for her husband, so she had agreed to maintain her silence.

***

Vinny watched his subordinate and friend make his way toward the bathroom. Sid had been acting strangely. *It's most likely from the accident,* Vinny thought. Before he could draw any more conclusions, a ding from Vinny's phone indicated that he had a new text.

Hey, handsome. How about dinner tonight?

Vinny smiled and texted back.

If by "dinner" you mean sex and then dinner … yes!

The texted response was,

What if it is really just dinner?

Vinny laughed, composing his response as another text appeared.

Just kidding! Of course it's sex and dinner. Meet me at 6:30 p.m. at my place.

Vinny was still smiling when he picked up the phone to call Beth Israel Hospital. "Hi, this is FBI Special Agent in Charge Vinny Marcozzi of the northeast division."

"Wow! That's a mouthful," the operator quipped.

Vinny smiled. "You got that right. May I please speak with the person in charge of your emergency room?"

"Sure. Hold on please and have a good day."

Vinny was picturing Annabelle in his bed when a voice interrupted his reverie.

"Sarah Sterns, may I help you?"

"Hello Ms. Sterns, my name is Vinny Marcozzi, and I'm the FBI special agent in charge of the northeast division."

"Okay," she replied cautiously.

"I'm just following up on a victim you had in the ER last night. It was a man by the name of Sidney Nickerson. He was in a car accident."

"I'm sorry Mr. Marzcoli—"

"Marcozzi," Vinny corrected her.

"Right, sorry, Mr. Marcozzi, but I'm sure that as special agent in charge, you know that I am unable to release any information about a patient without a subpoena."

Vinny grimaced. "Of course, of course, Ms. Sterns. You see, Sid is actually one of my subordinates, and I'm trying to understand the extent of his injuries so that I can determine when he should return to full duty."

"Well, Mr. Marcozzi, I would assume that an organization like the FBI would have a form that Mr. Nickerson and his physician could complete together in order to make that determination."

Vinny swore under his breath. He'd been hoping he could speak to an inexperienced person who might let some information slip. It was just his luck to have ended up with an intelligent Nurse Ratchet on the phone, who apparently wasn't done stating her opinion.

"I would also think that an organization like the FBI would allow its workers to get enough sleep so that they wouldn't do things like drive into the edge of a bridge due to fatigue."

Vinny's eyes flared as the pieces began to fall into place. "Like Mr. Nickerson did?"

"Exactly. Thank God no one else was injured."

"You mean like the person in the blue Toyota Mr. Nickerson hit?"

"Are you not listening, Mr. Marcozzi? The man drove into a bridge, for goodness sake. There was no blue Toyota. Now, unless you have a subpoena you'd like to drive down here and present to me, I'm a very busy person. Will there be anything else?"

Vinny's eyebrows raised as he smiled. "No, Ms. Sterns, you've been incredibly helpful." Pressing the red icon to end the call, Vinny's smile died as he watched Sid exit the men's room.

CHAPTER 21

Buttons' comment about the three of them being a family caught Jesse by surprise, and his hand flew to his mouth. Having grown up as an only child, Jesse hadn't known a lot about children when he had accepted Julian's offer of employment. He had been a quick study, however, and had learned a lot on the job.

Years later, Julian's patients now loved Jesse. Perhaps they innately understood that he had once been a lost soul who had found a home in Julian's life, and they were hoping to do the same thing as Julian's patients.

The small girl who stood before Jesse sporting a tiara had commanded his attention from the moment she had crossed the threshold. Unable to define exactly what it was that held his focus, Jesse noted that even in her grief, Buttons carried herself with an air of authority combined with empathy. Jesse decided that the tiara was well placed on her fragile head.

"Jesse, how is it that you came to possess the tiara that was residing in your desk?" Julian asked disbelievingly.

"Ah, trade secrets can never be revealed, my friend. Besides, like I said, clearly this tiara belongs to her royal majesty, Princess Buttons." Jesse bowed theatrically before continuing. "Now, Princess, may I escort you to your throne while Julian, Stacey, Alex, and I chat?"

"You may," Buttons responded, giggling.

Grabbing a bottle of water, Jesse took Buttons' hand. He led her into Julian's office, gave her the water, and hoisted her onto Julian's couch, which was still warm where Oscar had been lying on it.

"Do you need anything else right now?" Jesse asked.

Buttons made a show of thinking. "That will be all for now, thank you. Oh, can Oscar sit with me for a while?"

Jesse smiled. "I think that can be arranged. Oscar!"

The mutt bounded eagerly through the door as drool swung from his jowls. "He's kind of messy right now. Is that okay?" Jesse made a face.

Buttons smiled and looked down at her clothes. "I'm kind of messy too, I think. Oscar and I will be fine. Thanks, Jesse." Buttons patted the couch next to her, and Oscar wasted no time bounding up, wedging himself against her, and collapsing with a groan of contentment.

"I'll be back soon, okay?"

Buttons yawned, nodded, and lay her head against Oscar. For the second time in ten minutes, Jesse's heart broke a little.

Returning to the group, Jesse noted that Alex's body language seemed odd and closed. Her eyes were downcast, her arms were folded across her chest, and her feet were planted as if she were about to shoot her weapon. Jesse then turned his attention to Julian, who hadn't moved from his original spot. Stacey was glancing back and forth between the two of them and was obviously uncomfortable. Her eyes found Jesse's as she raised her eyebrows in a questioning gesture.

"What's with the awkward silence?" Jesse asked. "Something going on I need to know about?"

"Absolutely not," Alex answered a little too quickly.

Julian twisted his mouth and shook his head. In all of their years working together, Jesse had never seen his boss at a loss for words. Julian had always seemed to know how to handle every situation they had encountered—even ones that no one in his right mind could fathom. Until now, Julian had always known what to say and what to do to de-escalate a situation. But this was different. Jesse's stomach rolled a bit at the realization that everyone, even Julian, had his limitations.

"Okay then. Shall we talk about the beautiful little girl in your office and why she's here today?" Jesse asked the group while staring directly at Stacey for reinforcement.

"Yes, let's do that. Julian, I'm kind of in a time crunch, so …" Stacey trailed off.

"Of course, yes. I'm sorry, Stacey. Thanks so much for altering your entire schedule at my request. What's the plan regarding Buttons? Where will she go?"

Jesse looked confused. "What do you mean, Julian? What happened this morning?"

Julian updated Jesse on the two accidents that had ended up being related to Buttons and how she had lost her entire family in one morning.

"That explains her comment about you, Alex, and her being a family," Jesse said quietly.

Alex abruptly cleared her throat. "So back to the original question. Where will Buttons go?"

"Assuming she has no extended family members who can take her in, legally she needs to go into the child-welfare system. It'll take me at least a day to do a thorough search for her family."

"And in the meantime?" asked Jesse.

"She'll stay in a group home just until I can figure out which foster family will take her in."

Jesse threw his hands into the air. "Stacey, you cannot expect a kid like Buttons to go to an orphanage. She just lost her entire family, for God's sake! And you want her to go to some group home where there'll be bullies and other scary shit?"

"Jesse, Buttons might hear you," Julian said quietly. Jesse reined in his emotions while crossing his arms over his chest. His face was a mask of pent-up anger.

"All I'm saying," he stage-whispered, "is that Buttons is special. She's sensitive and kind. She'll get eaten alive in a place like that."

Stacey blew out a mouthful of air. "Jesse, as I mentioned to Julian, child welfare is not my area of expertise. I agreed to do Julian a favor by looking into Buttons' situation. I'm doing the best I can."

Jesse shook his head and pulled Stacey into a hug. "I'm sorry, Stacey. You've been wonderful to Julian, me, and this practice. I shouldn't have gotten so emotional."

Stacey hugged him back. "It's okay. I understand. But this is exactly why child welfare is not my thing. Tensions and emotions always run high where kids are concerned. I couldn't do this every day."

"I'll take her," Alex said.

"Alex?" Julian asked.

Alex turned toward Julian. "I said I'll take her. As a member of the Boston police force, I am allowed, under law, to retain a minor whose life might otherwise be threatened. If what Jesse said about the orphanage is true, I am obligated to exercise my duty as a police officer and to detain the child until appropriate accommodations can be made."

Julian turned to Stacey. "Is Alex correct?"

Stacey shrugged. "Yeah, she is."

"Then it's settled. Buttons is coming home with me tonight."

CHAPTER 22

Buttons ran her hand through Oscar's fur. She had always wanted a dog, but her parents hadn't allowed it due to her brother's allergies. As she leaned over and put her head on him, Buttons relished the warmth of the large dog's body and the way his soft fur brushed against her cheek. Oscar groaned and lifted his big head to lick her face. Buttons giggled as she listened to the grown-ups talking in the other room.

Although she couldn't hear their exact words, she heard Jesse raise his voice and then lower it again. *He sounds angry*, she thought. *I hope he's not angry at me.* She liked Jesse and felt comfortable with him like she did with Julian. *Maybe they can all come to live with me in my house*, she mused, feeling proud of herself for thinking of such a clever plan.

Buttons yawned again and shifted her tiara so that it wasn't pressing into her head as she snuggled even closer to Oscar. The dog was snoring, and Buttons focused on his breathing and the way his torso lifted and fell with each breath. Although she fought it, sleep lured her.

"Molly!" *her father called.* "Molly, come find me!"

"Where are you, Daddy?"

"Well, honey, if I told you, the game wouldn't be called hide-and-seek. It would be called I'll-hide-and-then-tell-you-where-to-find-me, wouldn't it?" *Her father always had a way of making games even more fun by saying silly things like that.*

"Okay! Here I come!" *Molly looked in all of her father's usual hiding spots—behind the door to the basement, the downstairs' closet, the kitchen pantry—but he was nowhere to be found.*

"Molly, why haven't you found me yet?"

"Where are you, Daddy? I can't find you!"

"I'm here, honey. You need to look harder, that's all. Don't quit. You can do it. You can find me."

Molly stood at the base of the stairs staring up into the darkness. "Are you upstairs, Daddy? It's very dark. I don't want to go up there."

"You have to find me, Molly. You're the only one who can do it. You must. I know you're scared, but you can do it. You can do anything!"

Swallowing her fear, she slowly ascended one step at a time. The creaking boards made her wince as she neared the top.

"You're getting warmer," her father said playfully.

"Daddy, you're scaring me. Please stop hiding. Please just come out."

"I can't do that, honey. I can't come to you. You must find me."

Molly rounded the doorjamb of her parents' bedroom and looked up. Mobiles were hanging from the rafters. They were the kind that her parents had put above her crib when she had been a baby. Buttons were attached to the wooden dowels of the mobiles, and they were moving. No, they were dancing! Thousands of them by the look of it. Molly had never seen anything so beautiful.

A rainbow of light streamed through the window, making the buttons glisten like colorful morning dew on the grass. Rhinestones on some of the buttons threatened to blind her as they spun to a tune only they could hear and in harmony with the silent music and each other.

"What do you think?" Suddenly, her father's voice was next to her, and she whirled to throw herself into his arms.

"It's so beauti—where are you, Daddy?"

"I'm here, sweetheart, right next to you. I'm everywhere and nowhere all at once. I'm in the buttons and in the music you can't hear that's making them dance."

Molly sank to the floor, and the buttons ceased their movement. "But, Daddy, I need you. Please don't go away. Please ..." she trailed off, sobbing.

Suddenly, her father appeared, sitting cross-legged in front of her. Her heart leapt. She knew he would come back if she wanted it badly enough.

"Molly, listen to me. You're a very, very smart girl, so I know that you understand that I'm not coming back, and I know that makes you sad. But you have an important job to do." He glanced down at the button jar in her hands. "Do you know why I gave you those buttons?"

"Because they're pretty?"

"Yes, that's true. But there's another reason. They're incredibly important, Molly. You must guard them at all costs. They are your freedom."

"I don't know what that means, Daddy."

"I need to leave now, Molly. Look for the key."

"What key? I don't understand. Daddy, please don't go!"

"Molly, I will be here for you as long as you need me, okay?"

"That'll be forever, Daddy."

Jimmy McClelland smiled and shook his head. "No, love, it won't. Someday soon, you won't need me anymore. But for now, if you need me, just think of me, and I'll come. I promise."

As her father disappeared, the mobiles recommenced their jig, but this time, Molly could hear the music. She recognized the song. It was from her father's favorite opera, Carmen. The mobiles moved to the rhythm as the music's volume increased exponentially. Molly closed her eyes and covered her ears in an effort to find relief, but none came.

After an eternity, the music ceased. She opened her eyes, and the mobiles had disappeared. Glancing directly above her, she saw her father's feet. Unable to stop herself, she stood up and stared at his grotesque tongue, which wiggled obscenely like an obese worm. Terrified, Molly gathered her button jar and scrambled out of the room with a silent scream frozen in her throat.

CHAPTER 23

Sid arrived at Rosa's Ristorante in the North End of Boston at 12:03 p.m. It didn't take him long to find the Ogre, who sat in a corner booth rolling spaghetti on a spoon, a napkin tucked into the collar of his shirt.

"God, you're a caricature of every Italian mobster in the world," Sid commented as he took the seat opposite the Ogre.

"First of all, Sid, that's incredibly rude and beneath your status as a snitch. Secondly, have you tried Rosa's spaghetti? It's just incredible. Wine?" The Ogre held up his hand, and a waiter appeared. "A glass of red for my friend from the FBI."

The waiter disappeared as Sid glared at the Ogre, who glanced at him and shook his head. "Sid, I really don't think you get the fact that I own you. You're mine from now until one of us is gone from this earth." The Ogre swallowed and wiped his mouth with his napkin. "And of the two of us, Mr. Nickerson, who do you think will die first?" The Ogre raised one eyebrow and chuckled.

"You can't just *summon* me," Sid whispered, glancing around to see if anyone was watching them.

Confusion overtook the Ogre's face as he paused with his spoon and fork in midair. "Yes, I can, and I did. Tell me what Jimmy told you. I want everything."

Sid sighed as he found himself at another crossroads. The weight of knowing what he *must* do versus what he *wanted* to do was crushing his soul. Sid dropped his head in his hands and raked his fingers through his hair.

The Ogre said, "Annie, Kathleen—"

"Stop it!" Sid hissed. "Stop it, you fucking psychopath!"

The waiter appeared, placed Sid's red wine on the table, and evaporated.

"Sid, I'm not a psychopath. I'm a businessman who has a job to do. It's nothing personal. It's just business. I like you, actually. I think you and I are a lot alike and that maybe we could be friends."

Sid stared blankly at the man sitting across from him. "Explain to me how you can talk about killing my family and then in the next breath, think that you and I could ever be friends."

"Because it's business and not personal, like I said."

"But see, here's the thing," Sid started, his brow knitting, "your business runs on the blood of personal vendettas. Do you really not understand that?"

The Ogre thought for a moment. Sid could see that he was truly considering Sid's words. "Yeah, I see your point. But you and I are a lot alike, no?" The Ogre grasped his wine glass and gulped the remnants, raising it to indicate to the waiter that he needed a refill.

Sid leaned forward with his elbows on the table. Peering into the Ogre's eyes, he saw contentment there. The man was truly enjoying his conversation with Sid, as if they hadn't a care in the world. They were just two friends out for a nice lunch in the Italian neighborhood of Boston.

Finally, Sid shook his head. "You and I are nothing alike and never will be. I changed my mind. You're not a psychopath. You're a sociopath."

The Ogre tilted his head as the waiter returned with his glass of wine. "What's the difference?"

"A psychopath has a conscience but commits crimes anyway, whereas a sociopath has no conscience."

A genuine smile lit up the Ogre's face. "Huh, I learned something today. Interesting." He took a large bite of spaghetti and spoke with a full mouth. "Well, if I'm a sociopath, you must be a psychopath."

Sid guffawed as he leaned back in his chair and drained his wine glass in two gulps. "How do you figure?"

The Ogre's eyes danced with amusement. "You're about to divulge everything the FBI knows about Jimmy and Don Paolo despite the fact that it will destroy years of governmental work that used resources equaling hundreds of thousands of dollars. You know that what you're doing is wrong, but you're doing it anyway. Isn't that the definition of a psychopath?"

Sid shook his head. "This is different. You've made it clear that my family's safety depends on my telling you what I know."

The Ogre shrugged. "Is that the best you've got, Sid? Will that hold up in court if you ever make it that far? I'm no attorney, but I think not. Didn't you take some type of oath when you joined the FBI? You know that you're about to commit a federal crime, but you're going to do it anyway, knowing that it will cause irreparable harm to the agency you serve. You can't escape my logic, Sid."

The Ogre leaned back, tore the napkin from his collar, wiped his mouth, and folded it neatly on the table. He was clearly pleased with himself. "Yup, you and I are a lot alike, and you, my friend, are a psychopath."

CHAPTER 24

"Am I a good man, Kathleen?" Sid put his phone on speaker and spoke to his wife while maneuvering his rental car through a narrow intersection on his way to the McClelland house.

"What? Sure, Sid. You're a good man. Where is this coming from?"

"I don't know. I just need to know that I've done well in my life."

Kathleen sighed. "Obviously you're determined to keep me in the dark with regard to what's really going on in that complicated head of yours, so let me tell you this. There is a difference between doing well and doing good. By working hard and performing well, you have worked your way up the ranks in the FBI and have done much good for this country. Do you understand, Sid? You've done both. You've done incredibly well by doing the greatest good. Does that help?"

A sad smile crossed Sid's face. "Hey, remember when we were first starting out and had no money? We agreed not to get a Christmas tree that year."

Kathleen smiled. "Of course I remember. I went out that very day and got a tree to surprise you. No one should be without a tree at Christmastime, for goodness sake."

"And that's exactly what you said when I protested. You said, 'Some things are just nonnegotiable.'"

Kathleen laughed. "I did say that, yes."

Sid turned serious. "It turns out that everything's negotiable, Kath, everything."

"Okay, Sid, now you're scaring me. What are you talking about? What's negotiable?"

"I gotta go, but please remember that I love you and the kids more than anything in this world. Do you know that?"

"Of course I know that, Sid. But what's—"

Sid clicked off as he pulled into the McClelland driveway and parked behind a van that had "Massachusetts Forensic Pathology" etched on its side.

Sid sat in the car and stared absentmindedly at the van as he silently reviewed everything he'd told the Ogre. Six months of hard-won information meticulously detailed by a precise man whose reward for betrayal had been being slung up in his own house for his family to find. Six months of information and twenty years of honor and integrity spilled in a matter of minutes to a man who wouldn't think twice about killing Sid's family to further the Torchia family's goal: becoming the most powerful crime family not only in Boston but on the entire eastern seaboard.

Sid swallowed hard and focused not on his treachery—no, he should be exact in his wording—his *treason*, but instead he chose to dwell on the *reason* he was betraying the oath he had taken when joining the FBI: saving his family.

After popping two TUMS into his mouth, Sid exited the car and straightened his tie before flashing his badge to the officer who was stationed at the front door of the McClelland house.

"You look like shit," the young officer quipped.

Sid turned abruptly as his eyes flashed with anger. "Excuse me, officer?"

"Sorry, sir," the young man responded with downcast eyes.

Sid leaned toward the cop and spoke quietly. "Here's a piece of advice for you, my friend. Just because you think it, doesn't mean you should say it. Remember that."

"Yes, sir."

Sid entered the foyer and found the place buzzing with activity. Reaching down past the white paper runner, he grabbed two blue booties and placed them over his shoes. The house smelled of the sweat borne of too many bodies in one area, making Sid wonder if the air-conditioning was broken or had been turned off. Straight ahead of him in the kitchen, techs in white coats were dusting for fingerprints. To his left, a forensic photographer was busy in the living room snapping pictures of what was once a happy home.

"Careful, careful!" a loud voice commanded at the top of the stairs.

Mindful to avoid the bloodstains on the bottom landing, Sid climbed the stairs to find a man with a pained look directing two uniformed officers on ladders. The two cops were cutting the rope that held Jimmy McClelland's body while two other police officers gripped the dead man's legs to avoid his body from crashing to the ground once the rope was severed. The anguish in the director's face was unmistakable, and Sid knew in an instant that the man was the forensic pathologist assigned to the case. Who else would take so much care while removing a dead body?

"Ah! Careful there, young man. Watch his head."

The young uniform glanced at Sid and rolled his eyes, not relishing his role in the macabre play that was unfolding.

"Please pay attention to the task at hand, gentlemen. Your care and precision is the last gift this dead man will receive. We need this body in pristine condition in order to determine the manner of death."

The uniform chuckled. "I'm no expert, doc, but I'm thinking this man died of hanging."

"Not necessarily. Assume nothing until you know something. That's my MO."

"Your what?" the young officer asked as he and his partner lowered Jimmy's body to the clean white paper sheet that had been laid out for it.

"My MO, young man. My modus operandi. That's Latin for—"

"The way he does things. That's what it's Latin for," Sid interrupted, extending his hand toward the physician. "Sid Nickerson, FBI. And you are?"

CHAPTER 25

The forensic pathologist regarded Sid's hand as if it were covered in E. coli. "My name is Dr. Hamilton Lippincott. I'm the medical examiner for Concord. May I ask why the FBI is here?"

Sid withdrew his hand and stuffed it in his pocket. "You may ask, but I won't answer. Here's a question for you though. Why is the ME for Concord working in Winchester?"

Dr. Lippincott raised his eyebrows as he slowly removed the latex gloves he had been wearing, balled them up, and placed them in an evidence bag. "I'm the only forensic pathologist for three counties right now. Dr. Perkins is on maternity leave, and Dr. Sharon passed away two months ago. I'm told that state budget cuts are not allowing for the hire of someone to replace him. So for now at least, I'm it."

Sid nodded. "So what do you think about Jimmy?"

Dr. Lippincott inclined his head. "Do you always refer to the deceased by their first names? Did you know him?"

Sid glanced sideways at what remained of the man he had flipped, coached, and come to begrudgingly respect over the last few months. It was difficult to look at a dead body, much less someone you knew.

"Yeah, I knew him." Sid didn't elaborate, and Dr. Lippincott didn't push him.

"Well, Mr. Nickerson, I can't really tell you how the deceased met his fate until I get him on the table in my lab."

"It certainly looks like he committed suicide, doesn't it?" Sid suggested, glancing at the stool that lay on its side about ten feet away from the body.

Dr. Lippincott followed Sid's gaze to the stool. "Yes, it looks that way, but if there's one thing I've learned in this business over the past decades, it's assume nothing until—"

"Yeah, yeah, I know. Until you know something. When *will* you know something?"

"What's the hurry on this one? I have three other bodies in my lab from two separate car wrecks this morning that will take precedence. They're the priority, followed by your friend here."

Sid reached into his wallet and withdrew a business card. "When you've autopsied Jimmy, please call me directly with the results. No one else. Just me, okay?"

Dr. Lippincott's eyes narrowed, but he accepted the card and slid it into his jacket pocket. "Sure, Agent Nickerson. I'll be sure to do that."

Sid's eyes shifted to Jimmy's pants, which were stained with urine and feces that had been released when his bladder and sphincter had relaxed after death. *Or maybe he pissed and shat himself as he was being strung up*, he thought. He shuddered involuntarily and pictured Jimmy begging for his life as the Muscle hauled on the rope.

Maybe Jimmy hadn't begged. Maybe he'd seen the end of his life as the inevitable outcome of his decisions and had gone quietly. Either way, he was dead, and Sid was determined to do whatever he must to ensure that his own family would not meet the same fate.

Sid walked downstairs and entered a room that seemed to be the office. The space was small but beautifully arranged. Because of its custom drapes and ornate wallpaper, it felt different than the rest of the house, which spoke to simplicity and functional living. Sid quickly surmised that this must have been Jimmy's private office—a retreat where Jimmy completed business he didn't want his family to know about. A petite leather couch with embroidery-adorned, overstuffed silk pillows graced the west side of the room, and a plush oriental rug covered the hardwood floor. Across from the couch sat a cherry-wood desk with a leather chair tucked into its softly curved top.

Sid donned latex gloves, removed the rolling chair from its resting place, and knelt down. Using a pen flashlight, he visually examined the underside of the desk before feeling every inch of it with his hands. Nothing struck him as being out of the ordinary, and he turned his attention to the drawers.

The desk contained seven drawers: a thin one across the top and three on each side that became progressively bigger as they descended. The center drawer contained pens, paper clips, Post-it notes, staples, and other supplies. All three of the left side's drawers were empty. The top drawer on the right contained family stationery with the four family members' first names listed under their surname. The second drawer held printer paper, and the bottom drawer held files.

Sid rifled through the files hoping to find some information he could bring back to the Ogre so he could prove that he was working on his side and trying to protect the Torchia family from potential prosecution. But the files held only family related information: bills, bank statements, and tax returns.

One file tucked into the back of the drawer caught Sid's eye because it was red instead of the perfunctory army green color. Sid removed the file and found himself staring at the birth certificates of Jimmy's children. *The children. Where are they? And where is Jimmy's wife, Isabella?* Sid thought. He'd been so busy unraveling his own nightmare that he hadn't given Jimmy's family much thought. Had the Muscle killed them too?

Sid jumped out of the chair and returned to the stairs where two officers carrying Jimmy's body bag blocked his way. "Has anyone found the rest of the family?" Sid asked the lead officer.

"I have no idea. Ask the doc up there."

Sid took the stairs two at a time and rounded the doorway to find the doctor kneeling by the overturned stool. "Hey, doc, is Jimmy's family accounted for?"

"Hmm?" The doctor turned with his brow furrowed in thought. "His family? I know nothing of any family nor have I heard any mention of them from anyone else. Does this strike you as odd?"

"Does *what* strike me as odd?"

"It seems to me that this stool was kicked an extreme distance from the deceased's body, doesn't it? Why so far?"

Sid felt sweat beads forming across his upper lip. "Maybe Jimmy didn't want to give himself the chance to change his mind, so he kicked the stool far away."

"Perhaps. Yes, that's a thought, I suppose. But he was not a large man nor was he very powerful, and yet he managed to kick a heavy stool this far while hanging by his neck from a rope. It just seems odd and almost unbelievable the more I think about it."

"What was it you said about assuming nothing until you know something?" Sid asked, attempting to sound friendly and nonchalant.

The doctor stood abruptly and waggled a long bony finger at Sid. "Ah, you're a quick study, aren't you, Agent Nickerson? But of course, you're correct. Enough with the assumptions. To the lab!" Like some twisted, death-related superhero, Dr. Hamilton Lippincott walked quickly and with purpose toward the bedroom door. He stopped suddenly and poked his digit in the air once more.

"Ah! Oh, my goodness. I forgot." He turned and stared hard at Sid and then rapidly approached him. "I owe you a sincere apology, Mr. Nickerson. Please forgive an overburdened and understaffed older man."

Sid shook his head. "Forgive you for what?"

Dr. Lippincott tapped the side of his head. "This brain is tired and overworked, Mr. Nickerson. Two people in one of the car wrecks this morning had the last name of McClelland. At least that's what a bossy, blond officer told me at the time."

Sid's neck tingled, and prickles of perspiration erupted at his hairline. "If I recall, doctor, you told me that a mother and son were in that car. Was there a little girl in the car as well?"

Dr. Lippincott shook his head firmly. "No little girl, but there was a pink car seat that I heard the police talking about. They were wondering if she'd been in the car and had walked away or was never in the car at all. Either way, she's still alive."

CHAPTER 26

Jesse came bursting through the door to find Buttons crying with her face buried in Oscar's fur. Alex, Stacey, and Julian followed closely behind him.

"Buttons, what is it? What's wrong?" Jesse knelt next to the child and gathered her into his arms, her tiny frame trembling. His frantic eyes met Alex's, desperately seeking help.

"Julian, you should take this one," Alex whispered.

Julian felt his way to the couch and sat on the other side of Oscar, placing his hand on Buttons' back. He, too, could feel her tremble, but over the next few seconds, the movements slowed as she dug her face into Jesse's chest.

"Buttons, can you tell me what happened?" Julian said as he rubbed her back in slow, even circles.

"He was there," she mumbled.

Julian leaned toward her. "I can't hear you very well, Buttons. Did you say, 'He was there'?"

"Yes," she stated with a stronger voice. "My Daddy. He was there."

"In your dream?"

"Yes."

"Did you see him?"

"Uh-huh."

"Did you talk to him?"

"Yes." She started humming a tune that sounded familiar to Julian, but he couldn't quite place it.

Jesse smiled. "Buttons, that's the "Habanera," isn't it? It's a song from an opera called *Carmen*,

Buttons exclaimed, "You know it, Jesse? It's Daddy's favorite!"

"Know it? I love it!"

Buttons hugged Jesse tightly. "Me too, Jesse. It was playing in my dream, and there were mobiles dancing to the music. It was beautiful and then …" Buttons stopped talking as her eyes grew big and tears spilled down her face.

"You can tell us what happened when you're ready, Buttons. Take your time," Julian said quietly.

Wiping her nose on her sleeve, Buttons straightened up and said, "And then the music stopped, and the mobiles weren't dancing anymore. My daddy was above me with a big ugly fat worm wiggling in his mouth." Because Buttons was unsure, she paused. Then she made a decision. "He's dead … forever. He's not coming back. But he told me that he'd come in my dreams if I need him."

Jesse wasn't sure which was more heart-wrenching: Buttons crying like the little girl that she was or Buttons trying to be brave.

Buttons glanced at her jar, which she clutched tightly against her chest. "He told me something else too."

Julian noted that she had straightened her back and that the shaking had ceased. He removed his hand from her back, and as he did so, Buttons took the opportunity to right her tiara, which had slipped sideways on her head.

"What else did he tell you, Buttons?" Julian asked, genuinely interested in where this plucky little girl's subconscious had taken her.

"He told me that the buttons in this jar are my freedom and that I must guard them."

Everyone glanced at each other around the room, except for Julian, who was trying to hear any unspoken message Buttons might be trying to convey. "What did your father mean when he said that the jar of buttons was your freedom?" Julian asked.

Unconcerned, Buttons shrugged and shook her head. "I don't know, but I'll figure it out when I find the key."

"What key, honey?" Stacey asked.

Buttons looked from one adult to another until her eyes settled on Julian. "I don't know that either, but I know I have to find it. Daddy said so."

CHAPTER 27

Vinny pulled up in front of Annabelle's condo and switched off the car's ignition. The 2001 Acura sputtered, coughed, and lurched before coming to a violent halt in the small parking space. Vinny patted the dashboard and said, "Good girl, Maisie," before exiting the vehicle and making his way into the lobby of the building. He waited patiently for the elevator while an elderly woman with several bags of groceries glowered at him. Taking the hint, Vinny kindly offered to carry some of her bags, but she declined and continued to stare at him.

They entered the elevator, and Vinny pressed the button for the third floor. He glanced at the woman and raised his eyebrows, silently asking her which button he should press on her behalf. She simply nodded, indicating that the third floor was fine.

The elevator crept slowly to the third floor, whereupon the doors opened, and Vinny indicated with a sweep of his hand that the woman should exit before him. Without acknowledging his chivalry, she exited the elevator and walked in front of him to her front door, which happened to be right next to Annabelle's. Vinny mumbled, "Excuse me," as he squeezed by her in the hallway, and she gave him one last nasty look before disappearing into her condo.

Vinny knocked on Annabelle's door as he wondered how some people could be so angry. *What's her problem?* Vinny thought as Annabelle opened the door wearing a coat.

"What's with your neighbor?" Vinny asked.

"Do you mean Mrs. Cranky Pants next door?"

Vinny smiled. "I think we're most likely talking about the same woman."

"She hates me. I think it's because I'm an independent, sexually aggressive woman, and she's not. I'm a threat to her kind."

"Her *kind*?" Vinny asked. "What's that mean?"

"You know, Vin. The type of old-fashioned woman who thinks men should run everything—relationships, money, sex."

"May I infer from your last statement that you believe that men shouldn't be in charge of those things?"

"You tell me." Annabelle unbuttoned her coat to reveal her naked body underneath. In spite of himself, Vinny's breath caught in his throat. Time froze as his eyes started at her red, heeled shoes and worked their way up her lovely body. Eventually, they settled on her face, which wore raised eyebrows over heavy-lidded eyes and a half-smile.

"You coming in ... or what?" she practically purred.

***

Sid sat on Jimmy's son's bed, staring at the royal blue letters hanging on the wall that spelled out the boy's name: J-O-E-Y. Running his fingers through his hair, he recalled what the medical examiner had said about Jimmy's daughter: "Either way, she's still alive."

Sid had met Jimmy's children only once in passing when he had attended an impromptu meeting at a local park. Joey hadn't approached him, but Molly had. She was a beautiful child with red ringlets and large, honest brown eyes that searched Sid's as he knelt down to say hello.

"Are you my daddy's friend?" she asked him.

Sid smiled and said, "I like to think so," before glancing up at Jimmy to evaluate his response.

Jimmy had scooped up Molly in his arms and said, "This is someone Daddy works with, Molly."

"At one of the dry-cleaning stores?"

"No, honey. Somewhere else. Why don't you run and play?"

The girl had smiled shyly and then kissed her father's cheek before departing.

Sid's mind wandered back in time to when his own children had been that age. He couldn't imagine what Molly must be feeling now that she had lost her entire family. Did she even know? And where in the world was she?

Sid quickly searched Joey's room for anything that Jimmy might have stashed there regarding his relationship to the mob. Finding nothing, he chastised himself for even looking. Odds were that Jimmy wouldn't have put his family in jeopardy by involving them in his business dealings. Jimmy was an honorable man in his own way, and like Sid, family came first with Jimmy.

Sid went downstairs and returned to the front porch where the officer who had mouthed off earlier stood reading a text on his phone. "Are you frickin' kidding me?" Sid asked, grabbing the phone out of the young man's hand.

The cop stood at attention and said, "Sorry, sir ... again."

Sid shook his head and leaned in to see the name on the man's badge. "You're a piece of work, Officer Sinnex."

"May I have my phone back, sir?"

"Who from the Winchester Police Department is in charge here?"

"Officer Grace found the bodies, sir."

"Bodies? Plural? I only saw one body inside."

"Yeah. Apparently there was a woman who fell down the stairs when she found the deceased. She was taken to the hospital and is alive but might be paralyzed. I haven't heard anything else about her condition. Officer Grace is over there if you want to speak with her."

Sid started to walk away when Officer Sinnex said, "Sir?" Sid turned around slowly as Officer Sinnex said, "May I have my phone, sir? Please?"

Sid looked the man up and down. He remembered when he had been that age and how dedicated he had been to the bureau. Nothing had come before the badge.

He approached the young police officer and placed a hand on his shoulder. "Son, do you have any idea what a privilege it is to wear that uniform and serve your squad, your town, and your country?"

The cop paused and was unsure of where Sid was going. "Y-yes, sir," he stammered.

"Do you have a family, Sinnex?"

"I have a mom and dad but no family of my own yet."

Sid smiled. "That'll come, Officer Sinnex. Enjoy the freedom you have now, but remember, people died so that you could have the opportunity to represent the fine people of this town and country. Every decision you make and every action you take reflects on the uniform you wear. So, think, Sinnex." Sid tapped his head. "Think before you act, okay? Don't waste the incredible chance you've been given. Never do anything to jeopardize your honor and integrity." Sid returned his phone.

The young man nodded. "Yes, sir."

CHAPTER 28

Vinny lay exhausted on the lavender sheets of Annabelle's bed and listened to her sing the latest Sam Smith song as she showered. He smiled as she crooned her way through the bridge, realizing with a start that he was falling in love. Sitting up quickly, he thought for a moment, approached the bathroom, and then leaned against the doorjamb with his arms crossed over his chest. "You're pretty good, you know. Your singing, I mean."

Annabelle turned slowly and smiled. "You think so?"

"I do."

"I was thinking about going on *The Voice* but then decided against it, what with my whole law career and all."

Vinny wasn't sure if she was being serious and said so. "Of course I'm not serious, Vinny!" she said while stepping out of the shower. Vinny handed her a towel. "But thanks for the compliment."

"Where shall we go for dinner?" Vinny asked.

"Actually, I have steaks marinating in the fridge and a Caesar salad already prepared."

"How clever and somewhat presumptuous of you," Vinny said, gathering her in his arms.

"Yes, well, I just had a feeling we'd be pretty hungry right about now, so I decided to take dinner matters into my own hands."

"What an independent, sexually aggressive woman you are." He kissed her deeply.

"White or red?" Annabelle mumbled into Vinny's lips.

"What?"

Annabelle pulled away from him as she reached for her robe on the back of the bathroom door. "Wine. Do you want red or white wine?"

Vinny shook his head, amazed at how adept Annabelle was at

controlling her emotions and how she could compartmentalize so quickly. He said, "Red please."

Annabelle wrapped her hair in a towel and walked quickly toward the kitchen to remove the marinating steaks from the fridge. She placed some store-bought mashed potatoes in a bowl and then nuked them on high in the microwave while simultaneously heating the pan to sear the meat. After popping the cork on a bottle of cabernet, she handed Vinny the bottle and two glasses and asked him to pour. She then took the precut lettuce from the fridge and tossed it with homemade Caesar salad dressing.

Vinny poured two generous glasses of wine and held one out to Annabelle, who accepted it as she placed the steaks in the pan. Vinny held up his glass and toasted. "To the most beautiful woman I know, who can bring home the bacon, fry it up in a pan, and never, ever let me forget I'm a man."

Annabelle burst out laughing. "Seriously? An Enjoli commercial from the eighties?"

Vinny shrugged. "Hey, if it ain't broke, don't fix it. It actually describes you perfectly."

Annabelle shook her head as she stirred the mashed potatoes before returning them to the microwave for another minute.

"Tell me about Jimmy McClelland," Vinny said.

Annabelle turned so quickly that some of the potatoes that were on her spoon fell to the floor. "What?"

"Jimmy McClelland. You granted him immunity in exchange for becoming an FBI informant. Didn't you?"

Annabelle paused before turning her attention to the steaks. "Yes, I did."

"Without informing your boss?"

"No, not without informing him. Rather, I informed him upon completion of the arrangement."

Vinny smiled while tilting his head. "That was rather lawyerly stated, Ms. Andrews. The fact is that you didn't have the authority to grant Jimmy full immunity, yet you agreed to the deal his attorney put forth."

Annabelle turned to face Vinny. "That's true. It was in the best interest of the case we were trying to build against the Torchia family, Vin. I told the DA about it when it was done, and he said I'd made a good decision and a good deal. What's this about?"

Vinny stared at Annabelle. "Jimmy's dead."

Annabelle screwed up her face in shock. "What?"

"Yup. Found dead in his house. According to Sid, he hung himself."

"Sid Nickerson?"

"Yeah. Sid was running him."

"Huh. That's a shame." Annabelle returned her attention to the meat.

Vinny pulled back. "That's a shame? That's all you have to say, Annabelle? What about the state's case against the Torchias?"

Annabelle shrugged as she placed the steaks on two plates and loaded them with mashed potatoes and salad. "Don't get me wrong, Vin. It's a blow, but I'll figure out a way to get the job done. I always do. Shall we eat?"

They sat in silence while wolfing down their dinners. Afterward as they snuggled on the couch with refilled wine glasses, Annabelle lay her head on Vinny's chest. "What about the family?"

"What family?"

"Jimmy's. He had a wife and two kids. Are they dead too?"

Vinny pulled away from Annabelle and looked at her. "Why would they be dead? I told you that Jimmy killed himself."

"Why did he do it?"

"He was cheating on his wife and felt guilty."

"Cheating, huh? I guess it makes sense."

"Why?"

Annabelle shrugged. "You know how those Italian guys are. All the mobsters seem to have something on the side. You know, some uncontrollable love affair."

"There are two problems with that statement. One, Jimmy was Irish, and two, I'm Italian and don't have anyone else on the side. Stop generalizing."

"Hey, stereotypes come from somewhere, right?"

"Why did you ask me about Jimmy's family? Do you know something I don't know?"

Annabelle kissed Vinny's lips. "Sh, Vinny, sh. Speaking of uncontrollable love affairs, didn't I mention something about always getting the job done?"

Every other thought was lost as Annabelle sank to the floor and knelt in front of Vinny.

CHAPTER 29

The setting sun splattered orange, pink, and red hues across the sky as Alex drove. "I wish you could see the sky, Stryker. It's absolutely gorgeous."

Julian leaned his head against the headrest. "Describe it, please. Try to outdo your last attempt at descriptive description."

Alex smirked. When they had first started dating and Julian had asked her to describe something, she had used broad words to paint a general picture of an object. She had learned through trial and error that Julian craved specific words to create a detailed mental picture. Over time, she had become more adept at the practice and indeed, had learned to observe everything with a more critical, detailed eye.

"Okay, it's 7:33 p.m. It's July in Massachusetts, so the sun will set at about 9:15 p.m., right?"

Julian smiled. "Good so far."

"The maple trees we're passing are in full, fat, leafy bloom. They have the kind of leaves that feel thick and cool to the touch on a warm, sunny afternoon. The green of the leaves is akin to the dark—"

"Akin to?" Julian laughed.

"Shut up. I'm just getting started." Alex cleared her throat. "Where was I? Oh, yes. The green of the leaves is akin to the dark, rich color of a spruce's pine needles. The bark on the trees feels bumpy and firm to the touch."

"Wow! I'm impressed. Keep going."

Alex was into it now. "About half of the sun is peeking above the horizon and seems desperate to keep its hold on the day. But alas, it will lose the battle and succumb to the darkness, which hunts it like prey on the savannas of Africa. How am I doing?"

Julian nodded his head approvingly. "You need to stop this whole cop thing and become a writer."

Alex laughed and continued. "The sun, in its futile effort to maintain dominance over darkness, is splashing a myriad of colors onto the canvas that is the sky. The pink of a dozen roses rises to the challenge, only to be met with an orange found only in the best citrus fruit Florida has to offer. Both of those colors run lazily into a red that is found only on iron as it is forged in a blacksmith's fire."

Julian burst out laughing and said, "Enough! I can see it in my mind's eye. Please, no more!"

"Ha! I did it. I bested your imagination, didn't I?"

Julian nodded. "Absolutely. Now how about I best your imagination regarding—"

"Stryker! Have you forgotten we have company this evening?" Alex glanced in the back seat and found Buttons staring out the window. Her jar was on the seat next to her fastened with a seat belt. "Buttons, how would you describe the sky to Julian?"

Buttons was slow to come out of her reverie. Surveying the sky, she said, "It's pretty like in Daddy's stores."

"Your father has paintings of the sky in his dry-cleaning stores?"

"No, not of the sky. His stores have different colors in them."

"I'm sure his stores have a lot of colors in them."

Buttons shook her head slowly. "You don't understand."

Julian turned his head in her direction. "Can you explain it to me, Buttons?"

A long sigh escaped her lips. "No, Julian, I can't."

Alex placed her hand on Julian's knee and squeezed it while speaking to the child. "It's okay, Buttons. It's going to be okay."

They parked in front of Julian's house, and Buttons examined the structure as if she were a discerning home buyer. When Alex had offered to take Buttons for the night, Stacey had been adamant about two things: Julian should remain with the girl because Buttons seemed to have latched onto him, and Buttons should not return to her home to obtain clothing or belongings. Not only was it a crime scene but Stacey was concerned about Buttons reliving the moment when she had found her father hanging from a rafter. Julian had agreed wholeheartedly from an adolescent psychology standpoint, and the decision to have Buttons go to Julian's home with both Julian and Alex had been made.

Alex unlocked the front door while Julian helped Buttons out of the car. After straightening her tiara and tucking her jar into the crook of one arm, Buttons used her free hand to take Julian's. The two of them walked up the six steps to Julian's front door where they heard Oscar barking excitedly on the other side.

"How did Oscar get here?" Buttons asked, clearly thrilled that the mutt was greeting them.

Julian leaned down and whispered in Buttons' ear. "*Somebody* doesn't like the smell of dog in her car, so Jesse was kind enough to drive Oscar home ahead of our arrival."

Alex twisted her mouth. "I can hear you, you know."

Buttons turned her alabaster face toward Alex. "You don't love Oscar?"

Julian relished the moment and decided to join in. "Yeah, Alex. You don't love Oscar?"

"It's not that I don't love Oscar. It's just that he's ..." Alex looked into Buttons' eyes and saw so many emotions competing for release. Sadness, fear, and love but most of all, hope. Alex saw her hope and knew in that moment that she could not disappoint the little girl.

"He's what?" Buttons asked innocently.

"He's just ... the most wonderful dog in the whole world!" Alex finished, hip bumping Julian in the process.

Julian opened the door, and as Oscar bounded forth to greet his new favorite friend, Julian placed his forehead against Alex's and said, "You, my love, are remarkable."

CHAPTER 30

Winchester police officer Thelma Grace was exhausted. Almost ten hours ago and at the end of her regular eight-hour shift, she had discovered Kellie Moser at the bottom of the stairs and the grotesque body of James McClelland. She glanced up at Sid from where she was seated in the kitchen and said, "Forgive me if I don't get up, but I've been here for …" Thelma looked at her watch and calculated. "I've been here forever."

Sid held up a hand. "I get it. Been there, done that. Sid Nickerson, FBI. You're Officer Grace?"

"That's me." Thelma removed her glasses, cleaned the lenses on her shirt, held them up to the light, and then returned them to her face. "How can I help you, Agent Nickerson?"

"I have some questions about your findings today. Can you describe what the scene was like when you arrived this morning?"

Thelma sighed. "Sure. I responded to a general call. Dispatch said that a nonresponsive 911 call had come in. When I arrived, I heard moaning coming from inside the house. When no one responded to my repeated attempts at communication, I opened the unlocked door and found Kellie Moser all broken up at the bottom of the stairs. I called for paramedics, and while we were waiting, she told me that she had discovered Mr. McClelland's body hanging upstairs. Apparently, in her haste to call for help, she slipped and fell down the stairs."

"Did she say where the rest of the family was?"

"She didn't know, and it worried her somewhat. She seems to know the McClellands very well."

"Did she say anything else about her relationship with the family members?"

Thelma looked confused. "Um, not a lot. Nothing really."

Sid smiled and spoke patiently. "Well, which was it? Nothing or not a lot?"

Thelma's eyebrows came together. "Listen—I know you're FBI, and I'm just some stupid beat cop, but forgive me for not remembering *exactly* what Ms. Moser said ten hours ago after I'd already completed an eight-hour shift!"

Sid looked at the ground. "My apologies, Officer Grace. I meant no disrespect. I'm told that Mrs. McClelland and her son, Joey, were killed in a car crash this morning. I'm simply trying to ascertain what Ms. Moser knew about the family in an effort to find the one remaining member of the family who is *alive*. A little girl named Molly."

Fatigue overwhelmed Officer Grace, and she placed her head in her hands. "Oh, God. That poor kid."

"Which hospital was Ms. Moser taken to?"

"Winchester."

"Thanks. You've been a great help. Now, why don't you go home and get some sleep."

Thelma stood up and rubbed her lower back. "I might go home, but I can tell you this. After what I've seen today, I don't think I'll be sleeping any time soon."

***

Kellie Moser awoke with a throbbing headache. Confused about where she was, she tried to remove the blanket covering her legs. To her amazement, her hands wouldn't move. She could move her arms a little, but the harder she tried to move her hands toward the top of the blanket, the more they seemed to remain still. With gargantuan effort, she attempted to swing her legs over the side of the bed, but to no avail. As excruciating pain and panic threatened to overwhelm her, she decided she was experiencing a nightmare and tried to wake herself up.

"Well, hello, Kellie. Glad to see you're awake. My name is Maria, and I'm an ICU nurse here at Winchester. Are you comfortable?"

Kellie stared at the woman dressed in multicolored scrubs who spoke as if Kellie was a customer at a spa. "Where am I?" she asked.

"You're in Winchester Hospital. You suffered a fall this morning. Dr. Stanisford will be in shortly to discuss your condition."

"My condition? What does that mean?"

"Are you in pain, Kellie?"

"Um, my head hurts—a lot."

"Why don't I get you some medication for your pain?"

"What did you mean when you said 'your condition'?"

"Dr. Stanisford will be here in a few minutes. I'll be right back with your medication, okay?"

Maria whisked out of the room leaving Kellie alone with her thoughts. *ICU stands for Intensive Care Unit.* Kellie had seen enough hospital shows to know that in the ICU doctors used words like *stat* and *severity.* Her eyes wandered down the blanket following the line of her body, which lay unmoving underneath. Although she had no recollection of the fall that had landed her in the hospital, Kellie had a bad feeling about her—what was the word the doctors always used on TV? Prognosis. She had a bad feeling about her prognosis.

A man appeared and placed his hand on her shoulder. "Hello, Kellie. I'm Dr. Stanisford. How are you feeling?"

"My head hurts."

"Yes, Maria told me that she's getting you something to make your head feel better. Does any other part of your body hurt, Kellie?"

Kellie thought for a moment. "No, nothing hurts. But I can't seem to move. Did you give me medication to keep me still? The nurse said that I fell this morning. What happened?"

Dr. Stanisford crossed his arms and pursed his lips. "There's no easy way to tell you this, Kellie, so I'm just going to be honest."

A commotion kicked up outside of Kellie's room, and the door swung open to reveal six young people in white coats. Dr. Stanisford waved them in and introduced them as first-year medical students. "These students have not yet had the opportunity to see someone in your condition, so I've asked them to observe as we chat. Is that okay with you, Kellie?"

The vise that was crushing Kellie's skull tightened, but she agreed.

"Good. Now, as I was saying, Kellie, the fall you experienced resulted in fractures to two cervical vertebrae, which caused great pressure on your spinal nerve. We performed surgery to alleviate the pressure on your nerve and fused the cervical bones that were fractured, but I'm afraid we won't know for several weeks or even months the full extent of your paralysis.

"The brace you're currently wearing around your head is designed to keep your neck and head completely still as you heal because any movement could jeopardize the possibility of your being able to regain the use of your hands and legs again." With her mouth agape, Kellie stared at the doctor and then at the six young faces who gawked at her as if she were an animal at the zoo.

CHAPTER 31

"Do you have Nutella, Julian? My mommy says that Nutella is better for you than peanut butter. It has more nutrums."

"Do you mean nutrients, Buttons?"

"Yeah, those. Mommy says Nutella has more nutrients."

"I don't have Nutella, but how about I make you some homemade pancakes instead? Those have a lot of nutrients that will fill you up, make you strong, and put hair on your chest."

Buttons giggled. "You're so silly, Julian. I don't want hair on my chest! That's for daddies only. Pancakes sound yummy. Can I go watch TV?"

"Sure. I'll call you when dinner's ready."

Buttons slid off the chair and ruffled Oscar's ears to entice him to follow her into the living room, which he did with gusto. Alex entered the kitchen as Buttons was leaving and found Julian smiling sadly. "What's wrong?"

Julian shook his head. "I keep thinking about the dream Buttons had of the dancing mobiles made of buttons. Did she have that kind of dream because she's been carrying that jar all the time? And what's with those buttons anyway? She says that her dad gave them to her, that they're her freedom, and that she's supposed to find a key." Julian shook his head. "None of it makes sense."

Alex hugged Julian. "It makes sense to her on some level. She just hasn't figured it out yet. If we only knew someone she could talk to— someone who's really good with kids."

Julian smiled. "Ha ha. I tried talking to her about the jar, and she clammed up, Alex."

"Give her some time, Julian. Some women need time to warm up to the idea of releasing information about themselves and their thoughts, desires, and dreams."

"Are we still talking about Buttons?"

"Yes, but me too, as you know. Buttons and I are a lot alike. Maybe that's why I like her so much. I think I understand how her mind works."

"Then maybe you should go in there and see if you can pry some information out of her. Come tomorrow, she may end up leaving for a relative's house—that is if Stacey can find one."

Alex kissed Julian and went into the living room where she found Buttons lying on the floor. Her head was on a pillow that she had pulled from the couch, and her feet were gently rubbing Oscar's belly as he snored. She looked as if she belonged in the house and was an integral element that had been missing but found its way home. The television volume was low, and the screen showed brightly colored humanlike creatures singing a song about inclusion.

"Buttons, how are you doing?"

Buttons placed her finger to her lips and whispered, "Sh, Oscar's sleeping. Please talk quietly."

Alex lowered herself and sat cross-legged next to the girl. Leaning into her, Alex whispered. "You okay?"

Buttons nodded. Her eyes were glued to the screen. Alex picked up the jar of buttons and held it up to the light. Rhinestones caught the light and shimmered through the glass.

"That's mine."

"I know it's yours. Can you show me some of the buttons in here?"

"You mean take them out?"

"Yes. Can we do it together?"

Buttons considered Alex's request for a moment and then nodded. Alex gingerly unscrewed the top of the jar and placed it on the floor. Removing a button, Alex examined it. "This is pretty."

Buttons nodded. "That one is from Daddy's red store. Daddy said it's red like my cheeks get when I've been running around."

Alex placed the button on the rug and withdrew a green one. "And this one?"

"Daddy said that reminded him of green grass on a warm summer's day. It's from his green store."

Alex smiled as Buttons sat up and drew closer with excitement in her eyes. "How about you pick some out and tell me about them?" Alex suggested.

"Okay." Oscar expressed his displeasure at losing his cuddle partner by getting up and walking toward the kitchen where the smell of pancakes permeated the air.

"This one is purple. It's from Daddy's purple store. It's very important."

"Why?"

"I don't know. Daddy never told me, but he said this was one of the most important ones." Alex examined the button and saw nothing unique or unusual about it. She placed it on the carpet next to the red one.

Alex pulled out a flat, army green button. "What about this one?"

Buttons stuck out her lips. "I don't know about that one. I don't remember seeing it before. Sometimes Daddy would put new buttons in my jar and not tell me."

Suddenly Oscar came rocketing in from the kitchen, a 120-pound missile that was heading straight for them. Alex grabbed Buttons and jumped up as Oscar reached the area where they'd been sitting a second before. In the dog's excitement, he knocked over the jar and buttons spilled out over the carpet and rolled in all directions.

A scream escaped Buttons' lips as she writhed to break free. Falling to the floor, she frantically scrambled to gather the treasures in her tiny hands. Alex watched as the child managed to collect most of the fallen buttons into a pile. Buttons' hands shook, and her lips quivered.

Oscar sat nearby with his head hanging low. He did not understand his role in the fiasco but felt the little girl's stress. Turning to the dog, Buttons stroked his large head and kissed his muzzle. "It's okay, Oscar. We all make mistakes. I know you didn't mean it."

Alex struggled to maintain her composure as she watched Buttons comfort Oscar. This little girl who had lost so much was offering comfort to a dog. As Alex leaned down to speak to Buttons, she noticed a shiny object that must have been flung into a corner of the room when the jar had spilled. Assuming it was a button, Alex walked over, bent down, and grabbed it. She returned it to Buttons. "Buttons, in your dream, didn't your father ask you to find a key?"

"Yes."

Alex held up the silver, shiny object she had retrieved from the corner. "I think I just found it."

CHAPTER 32

Marcie entered her boss's office and found him gazing out the window. She dropped the folder she had been carrying onto Vinny's desk and waited for him to respond, but he didn't. "Everything okay?" she asked. Receiving no answer, she tried again. "Vin, you okay?"

Vinny turned his desk chair around and stared hard past Marcie into the office beyond. "You ever get the feeling that someone's not telling you something, and it's not for your own good?"

Marcie followed his gaze and found it settled on Sid's empty desk. "Yeah, sometimes, I guess. You don't tell me a lot of what's going on around here, but I've always assumed it's for my own good. Either that or it's none of my business."

Vinny looked at Marcie. "But what if it was your business and it would help you to know it, but I wasn't telling you about it. Would you come after me to find out the information, or would you continue to assume it was for your own good?"

Marcie sat in the chair opposite Vinny's desk. "Vin, it comes down to whether or not you trust the person in question. In the case you just outlined, I trust you implicitly and would assume that you were acting in my best interest by not telling me. Having said that, if you did something to make me question the faith I have in you, I would come down on you like a ton of bricks and demand answers."

Marcie stood, closed the door, and returned to her chair. "Listen, Vin, I know I'm just your assistant, but you and I have worked together for a long time. I can tell something's eating at you, and I'm guessing it has to do with Sid. You know better than I do that the life of an agent running CIs is a vortex of secrets, lies, and manipulation. You've known Sid a long time too, and he's always been loyal to you and the bureau."

"He lied to me, Marcie. Flat-out lied."

"About what?"

"The car accident he was in. Jesus, I'm not even sure it *was* a car accident. And Annabelle didn't help last night when—"

"Annabelle? What's she have to do with this?"

Vinny slumped in his chair. "I don't know. Probably nothing, but it's just …"

"What, Vin?"

"I don't know. Something doesn't feel right."

"Okay, well, it seems to me you have two choices. Do something, or do nothing and wait and see what happens. And honestly, you've never struck me as a wait-and-see kinda guy." Marcie stood and smiled at Vinny. "Hope that helped."

Vinny glanced at her and nodded. "It did. Thanks, Marcie. And for the record, you're way more than just my assistant. You know that, right?"

Marcie tilted her head and nodded. "If that's your way of saying that you couldn't make it without me and that I'm completely indispensable in your work life, then, yeah, I know."

Marcie walked toward the door. "Open or closed?"

"Closed, please. Thanks again, Marcie."

Vinny tilted his chair back as he thought through Marcie's advice. He could confront Sid with his suspicions or wait to see what—if anything—developed. A thought struck Vinny, and he picked up his cell phone, found the number for the Winchester Police Department, and dialed.

"Winchester Police Department. How may I direct your call?"

"I'd like to speak to the chief please."

"And who is calling?"

"Vinny Marcozzi, FBI, calling in relation to the McClelland case."

"Hold on, sir."

Vinny hummed his way through an entire Muzak version of "Boogie Nights" before hearing Chief Schmidt come on the line.

"This is Chief Daniel Schmidt. Sorry it took me so long, but I wanted the file in front of me when I took the call. How may I help you, Agent Marcozzi?"

"That's okay, chief. I was thoroughly enjoying the 'Boogie Nights' Muzak."

The chief chuckled. "Yeah, sorry about that. The town decided to go with a local company for our on-hold music and has regretted its decision ever since. Now, I understand you have some questions about the McClelland case?"

"Yes. For the last six months, Jimmy was a confidential informant for us and—"

"What? Why?"

"He ran money for the mob, chief."

"Are you fucking kidding me? In *Winchester*?"

"Yes, in Winchester."

The chief exhaled heavily. "Wow. He's been on the city council for—"

"I know the story, chief. He was an upstanding citizen. They planned it that way so no one questioned his motives. Anyway, I just wanted your take on the death."

Vinny heard rustling as the chief opened the file and scanned its contents. "It looks like a legitimate suicide according to the officers' notes from the initial scene. There's a copy of the suicide note here. Apparently, Jimmy was having an affair, which shocks me, to be honest."

"Why?"

"Jimmy was … meticulous, almost neurotic in his exactitude, if exactitude is even a word. Anyhow, you get my point. He was, for lack of a better word, nerdy. Or at least I thought he was. It's not that he didn't get things done, but rather, that he got everything done. He dotted his I's and crossed his T's. I just can't see him cheating on Isabella."

"Any reason to believe that this was anything but a suicide?"

"Why do you ask?"

"We're dealing with the mob, chief."

"Based on the file, the suicide looks legit. But the ME in charge is Hamilton Lippincott if you want to talk to him."

Vinny jotted down the ME's name. "Okay, I will. Are you aware that Jimmy's wife and son were killed in a car wreck yesterday?"

"Yeah. It was the weirdest thing. Yesterday a cop from Boston happened by another car wreck that involved Jimmy's daughter. She's okay, but the cop called me so she could learn more about the girl's family. It was hard for me to have to tell her that Jimmy was dead."

Vinny was taking notes. "What's that cop's name? I want to talk with her about the girl."

"Uh, let me see. I didn't write it down, but if I remember correctly, it was Alice Hays or Rays—something like that."

Vinny's pen stopped moving. "Did you say that it was a Boston cop and that her name was Alice Rays?"

"Uh-huh."

"Could it have been Alex Hayes?"

"Oh yeah! That's it. Alex Hayes. Do you know her?"

"You could say that. I took a bullet for her in Mexico a couple years ago."

CHAPTER 33

"You look nervous, Sid," the Ogre said as he approached the man sitting on a park bench gnawing a thumbnail.

"No, just bored of waiting for you."

The Ogre slapped Sid on the back. "Ah, my friend. You're a bad liar. You look tired too. Didn't you sleep well last night? I slept like a baby."

Sid turned to the large man and fixed him with a harsh stare. "Let's get this over with. I am not your friend. Why are we meeting?"

The Ogre raised his eyebrows and shook his head. "You really don't seem to learn, Sidney." He leaned in and draped his arm around Sid's shoulders. "You are not only my friend but my informant, my rat, and my patsy if things go south. So, I suggest that things don't go south. Now, what did you find in Jimmy's house?"

Sid raked his fingers through his unkempt hair. "Nothing! I have nothing for you!" he growled. "But not because I didn't try. When I got to Jimmy's house yesterday, it was still an active crime scene. There were cops and techs everywhere. I looked but found absolutely nothing related to his ... business dealings with you."

"No, no, not me, Sid. The family. Let us not forget that I am simply a tool that's used on occasion, much like my friend who you met the other day at the end of our...discussion."

"The Muscle."

The Ogre leaned back. "That's what you call him? Huh. Great name for him actually. I'll have to remember that. What's your nickname for me?"

Sid looked at him directly. "The Ogre."

The man laughed out loud. "You're too much, Sid, too much. I love it. It suits me. Bottom line is you can call me whatever you want as long as you get the job done, okay? Now, go back to the house. There's gotta be something there. Something you missed. My guys have been to all of Jimmy's dry-cleaning stores, and there's nothing in any of them, so it's gotta be at home."

Sid shook his head. "Maybe Jimmy didn't keep any records of his conversations with me. Maybe he doesn't have information on the family."

"Good try, Sid. Really, very nice. But you and I both know that Jimmy McClelland would have a backup plan. The only reason he snitched is because the FBI called him out on some bad behavior."

"You mean money laundering?"

"Yeah, whatever. Bad behavior. But he wasn't stupid enough to think that he would've been protected if the family had discovered that he was talking with you on a regular basis. No. He would've prepared an escape plan for himself and his family, in case, as I mentioned before, things went down the shitter, which, for the record, they clearly did. Now, the same fate does not need to befall you, my friend. You find the information, and you're free. It's that simple."

Sid observed two children playing tag. "Nothing's ever that simple."

"I disagree, Sid. It really is that simple. The fact is that the FBI would've taken down the Torchias by now if the information Jimmy gave you had been enough. But he died before delivering the coup de grace. I know Jimmy though, and that information is out there somewhere waiting to be found. We need to get it before the FBI does. And that's where you come in. You do this for Mr. Torchia, and you're done. No strings attached. You have my word."

Sid guffawed. "Your *word*? Are you friggin' kidding me? That's worth shit, and you know it."

The Ogre appeared genuinely wounded. He straightened his back, lifted his chin, and crossed his arms over his chest. "I pride myself on keeping my word, Sid. You're right when you said that we're not friends. But like it or not, we are business associates. I didn't get this far in business by not keeping my word. So, understand that I mean it when I say that finding this information and either delivering it to me or neutralizing the threat to the family will release you. You have my word."

As Sid examined the man's eyes, he saw determination and truth with no hint of guile. Much like his feelings toward Jimmy, Sid found that he was beginning to feel a grudging respect for the man. He certainly didn't like him, but he could respect his position and duties to the people he served. Ironically, he felt that the Ogre respected him as well—as a man, a father, and an FBI agent. Sid realized that to the Ogre, there was truly nothing personal in their transactions.

To his complete astonishment, Sid found himself apologizing to the man who had brutalized him only hours before. "Okay, okay. I'm sorry. I shouldn't have said that your word is shit. I believe you. I don't like you, but I believe you."

The Ogre slapped Sid's back. "Okay then. We're back on the same page. Get to Jimmy's house and get your job done so that you can move on with your life, Sid."

Sid nodded. "Okay."

"I'll check in with you tomorrow to see where we stand, okay?"

Sid's phone buzzed. As he glanced at the screen, the Ogre leaned in. "Oh, that's sweet. Your wife is texting you that she loves you and is proud of you. That's some family you got, Sid."

Sid's eyes teared up. "Yes, it is."

The Ogre put his arm around Sid's shoulders and pulled him in close. "I'd hate to see anything happen to them, Sid."

Sid wiped his eyes and glared at the Ogre. "Nothing's going to happen to them."

The Ogre stood up and straightened his jacket as he watched children playing on the swings. "Well then, that's up to you now, isn't it?"

CHAPTER 34

Alex, Julian, and Buttons sat at the kitchen table before a smorgasbord of pancakes. Buttons poked at her food, moving it around the plate but rarely putting any into her mouth.

"Buttons, you need to eat something. You haven't eaten all day."

"Okay," she mumbled, "but I'm not hungry."

Alex gave Julian's knee a nervous squeeze. Ever since she had found the key and had presented it to Buttons, the little girl had remained distant and quiet.

Julian held out his hand to Buttons, who paused but then grabbed it as if it were a lifeline. "Buttons, it's okay to be sad. It's okay to be confused, scared, and maybe even angry. Do you feel those things?"

Buttons gazed into the distance. "Have you ever been lost, Julian?"

"What do you mean? Like out on a walk?"

"I was lost once in a store, but I didn't know it. I wanted to play hide-and-seek with my mom, but she said no, so I ran away from her. I didn't mean to run so far, but I did. I heard her calling for me, but I couldn't get back to her. I couldn't find her because the clothes were so high."

"You mean the clothes racks were too high for you to see over?"

"I guess so. I guess that's what I mean."

"So what did you do?"

"I went to a lady and told her that my mother was lost and asked her if she would please find her."

Alex smiled and covered her mouth. "You thought your mother was lost and not you?"

Buttons nodded and spoke matter-of-factly. "I knew where I was, but I didn't know where she was. So, she was lost, not me."

"Then what happened?" Julian prompted.

"That nice lady spoke into a phone, and I could hear her voice all around the store. She said, 'Will the lost mother of Molly McClelland please come to the desk?' Mommy came right away and cried when she saw me. I asked her if she was crying because she was scared that she was lost, and she laughed and said, 'yes.'"

Buttons came and sat in Julian's lap. "That's how I feel right now, Julian. That I'm lost. But this time there's no phone for the nice lady to speak into, and I know my mommy isn't going to come even if the nice lady could call her. No one's coming."

Alex felt a lump in her throat and excused herself from the table as Julian wrapped his arms around the little girl. "Alex and I are here, Buttons, and so are Stacey and Jesse. We're all here for you. No matter what happens, we'll always be here for you. I promise. Do you remember when you and I were sitting on the curb, and I asked you to draw a picture of your family?"

Buttons took Julian's hand and made the "yes" sign against his palm, eliciting a smile out of him.

"Do you remember how I told you that family doesn't have to be just your mom, your dad, and your brother but that family can be people you choose to love like they're actually related to you?" She placed Julian's hand against her cheek so he could feel her nod.

"Well, all of us—me, Alex, Jesse, Stacey—we can be part of your family now. That doesn't mean that you're going to live with us forever, but we'll always come for you if you need us. Does that make sense?"

"You'll come even if I'm lost?"

"I would travel to the ends of the earth to find you, Molly McClelland."

"Promise?" Buttons asked, putting her head on Julian's chest.

Julian pulled her away from him and took her tiny face in his hands. He could almost close his hands around her head. A stray thought occurred that she might have been a premature baby.

"Cross my heart, hope to—" Julian paused, mid-sentence, realizing that Buttons didn't need to hear any more about death. Instead, he fabricated a rhyme on the spot. "Cross my heart, hope to fly, on a rainbow in the sky."

Buttons giggled. "That's not how it goes."

"You didn't learn it that way?"

"No, but I like it better than the real way. Hey, what about Oscar?"

"What do you mean?"

"You said that you, Alex, Stacey, and Jesse were my family now. But what about Oscar? He's very important you know."

Hearing his name, the mutt approached and pushed his large muzzle under Julian's arm, attempting to extort a head scratch. Julian acquiesced and smiled. "Oh, believe me, I know how important Oscar is. He helped me a lot after I became blind."

"How did you lose your eyes, Julian?" Buttons asked quietly, gingerly reaching out and stroking Julian's face.

"Well, a boy that I was trying to help cut me with a knife."

"Did it hurt?"

"Yes, it hurt a lot, and it was very scary, but with a lot of help from the same people who are helping you now, I got through it."

Buttons closed her eyes for a moment. "It's very dark for you, isn't it, Julian?"

"Yes, it is, Buttons. But I remember what it was like to see the sun, and I remember all of the colors."

"Do you miss them? The colors?"

Julian smiled. "I do. I miss them a lot. But now I see things differently."

"I don't understand."

"I see through my other senses, Buttons. I feel the warmth of the sun and remember how bright it was in the sky. I feel the wind and know a storm is coming. I hear the leaves rustle on the trees and know that they are drying out and will soon fall because summer is coming to an end. When we go to the beach, I can tell how rough the waves are by the way they sound."

"But you can't see people when you meet them."

"You're right, but blind people have a different way of figuring out what people look like."

"How?"

"May I show you?"

"Okay."

"I'm going to place my hands on either side of your head so that I can use my fingers to feel your face. Is that all right?"

Buttons smiled. "Okay."

Julian cupped her head and ran his thumbs against her hairline. She had a cowlick in the center of her forehead.

"What color is your hair, Buttons?"

"Orange. Mommy calls it ginger, but it's orange."

Julian's hands traced either side of the girl's head, feeling the soft curls that surrounded her face. Smiling, he returned his thumbs to her forehead and ran them down her perky, upturned nose. His fingers felt her plump little lips, and she giggled, saying, "Julian, that tickles!" He finished by feeling the cleft in her strong chin.

"Wow, I've met some pretty people in my time, but you are one of the prettiest!"

Buttons twisted her mouth and was embarrassed as she mumbled, "Thank you."

"And one of the smartest, toughest, and politest to boot," Julian finished, grinning.

"I know," she stated confidently.

"And most humble too," Julian chided.

"What does that mean?"

Julian hugged the child hard and said, "It means you're absolutely perfect just the way you are."

CHAPTER 35

After dinner, Alex suggested a warm bath and then straight to bed for the exhausted child. Led by Oscar, they retreated upstairs and Alex ran the bathwater while Buttons investigated her new surroundings with Julian.

"Am I sleeping by myself?"

"Yes. In the guest room, okay?"

"Can Oscar sleep with me?"

"I don't know. Let's ask him. Oscar, would you like to sleep with Buttons?" In response, Oscar jumped onto the bed, circled three times, pawed the covers to create a nest, and plopped down with a groan. "I think that's a yes," Julian said.

Buttons smiled and rubbed Oscar's head. "Thanks, buddy. Good boy."

After a bath that involved a game of find-the-soap and a lot of splashing, Julian dressed Buttons in one of his T-shirts, which fell below her ankles. They tucked her in and diligently checked for monsters in the closet and under the bed. Julian told her a story while Alex stroked her hair. Oscar's head lay on Buttons' belly, and before Julian had finished the story, Buttons was asleep. Alex gently disentangled the tiara from her hair and placed it carefully on the nightstand. Leaving the door slightly ajar, they tiptoed to Julian's room, tumbled into bed, and slept.

The next morning, Alex awoke to find Julian's side of the bed empty. She checked on Buttons, who was still asleep and curled around Oscar. She walked quietly downstairs, where Julian sat in the kitchen sipping a steaming cup of coffee. "I had a good sleep," Alex sighed, rubbing her eyes and yawning.

Julian sighed. "Yeah, me too. You okay?" Julian reached out across the table, and Alex took his hand.

"I'm okay. You?"

Julian smiled. "I'm good. You're here, so I'm good. I love you, Alex Hayes."

"I love you too, Stryker."

A heavy silence sat between them, interrupted only by the symphony of crickets singing to find their mates. It always impressed Julian how nature found a way to thrive, even in the middle of a city like Boston.

"Do you really want Buttons to live with us, Alex?"

Alex shrugged. "I don't know. Kind of."

Julian squeezed her hand. "But you and I don't even live together. How would we make that work?"

"Well, maybe we should."

Julian raised his eyebrows. "You want to live together?"

Alex hadn't been sure about her feelings until she heard Julian speak the words aloud. "Yes, I do. I think it's time." Then she paused and was suddenly insecure. "What do you think?"

Julian's brow creased as he pulled his hands away from hers. "Gee, I'm not sure. Let's make a list of pros and cons and see where we land. On the pro side, you're a smokin' hot mama. On the con side, you're very, very messy. On the pro side, we'd save all the money you're currently paying on rent, utilities, etc. On the con side, you're very, very messy. On the pro side—"

Alex slapped his hand. "I am not very, very messy!"

"You are, but I'm willing to overlook that because clearly the pros outweigh the cons. I say we go for it."

Alex shook her head. "You are truly a huge pain in my ass, you know that, Stryker?"

Julian reached across the table, grabbed both of her hands, and quickly pulled her toward him, speaking quietly and vehemently. "Alex, I would have asked you to move in with me the day we met, but you would have said no. I've loved you forever and couldn't ask for a better girlfriend. Of course we should live together." He kissed her deeply, and she sighed as he withdrew. "Now that we've settled that," Julian said, "do you really want Buttons to live with us?"

Alex leaned back in her chair and covered her face with her hands. "God, I don't know, Stryker. She's just ... I don't know what it is about her. You know kids. Why does she strike me as different?"

"She *is* different, Alex. First of all, she's been through more death in one day than most people experience in their lifetimes. But I agree with you. It's the way she's dealing with it that makes her stand out. She is very stoic."

"Maybe that's it."

"Be aware, though, that eventually her sadness and anger will surface, probably in an unexpected manner or circumstance. It can't stay locked up forever inside that little head. I'll continue to work with her on processing her experiences."

"Okay. And let's wait and see what Stacey uncovers regarding her extended family. She must have someone that can take her in."

"Hopefully." They sat in silence for a moment. "Can you tell me about the key that spilled out of the jar?"

Alex picked up the key from the table and placed it in Julian's hand. "It's small. Reminds me of a locker key."

Julian felt the length and the width of the key. It was lightweight and had a scrolled top. "No. Too fancy for a locker key."

Alex smiled as she took the key from Julian's hand. "It reminds me of a diary key that I had when I was a kid."

"Maybe it is a diary key."

"Don't you think Buttons is too young to keep a diary, Stryker? I don't think she can read and write yet."

"Yes, she is, but her parents weren't. Maybe it's her brother's. Why would her father put the key in her very important jar of buttons?"

"You're assuming this jar of buttons that she's so attached to is truly important?"

"Her father said so, Alex."

"In a dream, Stryker. It wasn't real."

"I disagree. Dreams are the subconscious pathways to reality, Alex. I think this jar of buttons is as important as she says it is. Maybe not for the reason she thinks, but it's important. And the key was inside of it, placed there by her father."

"According to her."

"Yes, according to her, it was placed there by her father. I think if we find the item to which that key belongs, we will be a lot further along in helping Buttons to heal."

"Okay, so where do we start?"

Julian thought for a moment. "At her house."

"I thought you said she shouldn't return to her home."

"Not her. Us. We'll go to her house."

A terrified scream pierced the early morning. Alex bolted out of her seat and rushed to the stairs, taking them three at a time. Arriving in the guest room with Julian in tow, Alex found Buttons clinging desperately to Oscar, who looked as frightened as the girl did.

"Buttons, it's okay." Julian soothed, kneeling next to the bed.

Buttons shook uncontrollably and was unable to stop crying. "The key, the key, the key!"

"What about it, sweetheart?"

"We have to find it!"

"You did find it, Buttons, remember? In your button jar."

Buttons shook her head back and forth chanting, "No, no, no, no, no!"

"Okay, okay, Buttons. I need you to take my hands." Julian held out his hands to her, palms up.

"No, no, no, *no!*" she screamed and lashed out with her fists, catching Julian on the jaw and sending him reeling backward onto the floor. The little girl started hyperventilating and thrashed around as she looked wildly back and forth between Alex and Julian. Petrified, Oscar jumped off the bed and ran to Julian, who commanded him to sit and stay.

"Julian, what do I do?"

"What do her eyes look like?" Julian asked, rising from the floor.

"What?" Alex asked in confusion.

"I think she might be having a night terror, Alex. Is she looking *at* us or *through* us?"

Alex looked hard at Buttons, whose breathing continued to be labored. Alex shook her head. "I don't know. Her eyes are wild, Julian. There's no other way to say it. What should I do?"

"Do not touch her under any circumstance."

"Yeah, I figured that out when she punched you."

Julian approached the bed, making sure he was far enough away to avoid any physical contact. "Buttons, it's Julian. You're having a bad dream, and I need you to wake up. Molly!" He clapped his hands three times.

The little girl abruptly stopped hyperventilating and stared at Julian. "What happened?" she asked. Then she fainted and fell off the bed into Alex's arms.

CHAPTER 36

Alex was on her thirty-sixth lap around the emergency department's waiting room.

"Alex, please come sit down. You're making me nervous. The heels of your boots clicking against the tile floor is excruciating."

Alex returned to her seat next to Julian and picked at a fingernail.

"She's going to be okay, Alex. The MRI is simply a precaution to ensure nothing is physically wrong with Buttons."

"How can you be so fucking calm, Stryker?"

"Because I know that her night terror and accompanying fainting spell are directly related to the extreme stress she endured yesterday. Her emotional defenses are depleted, and fainting was her body's way of reacting."

"How can you be so sure?"

Julian turned to face her. "Because the exact same thing happened to me. After my attack when I returned home from my initial hospitalization, I was truly alone for the first time with complete blackness and I just freaked out. Of course my psyche didn't let it happen during the day when I was awake because that would show weakness to the world. My subconscious took over during my sleep and created terrible night terrors—horrible dreams that seemed so real.

"The final dream that made me seek help was when I awoke in the kitchen wielding a knife, ready to lash out at my imaginary attackers. I passed out on the kitchen floor and woke up several hours later. I'm sure if someone had found me and taken me to the hospital, the doctors would have wanted to do an MRI on my brain as well." Julian took her hand. "I am positive that's what's happening with Buttons."

"God, Julian, every time I think you've told me everything about your attack and the aftermath, you divulge new information. I can't believe you suffered so much alone."

"I wasn't alone, Alex. I had you, Jesse, and my mother. In fact, if I hadn't been attacked, I never would have met you and never would have become a profiler. How can I be angry when the greatest loss of my life led to the greatest gain in my life?"

Alex smiled, marveling at Julian's logic and his endless positive outlook. "You are truly remarkable, Julian."

Julian leaned in closely and put his forehead against hers. "I know." He grinned.

"Are you the people that brought Molly McClelland in tonight?" a man in blue scrubs asked as he approached them.

Alex popped up quickly. "Yes. Is she okay? Can we see her? What's wrong with her?"

"Whoa. One question at a time. She's resting but wants to see someone named Julian. Are you Julian?"

Julian stood and nodded. "How is she?"

"She's a tough little one, that's for sure."

Julian shook his head. "You don't know the half of it."

The man chuckled. "Anyway, her MRI was normal. Her blood pressure is highly elevated though, so we'd like to keep her for observation. It's rare for a child so young to experience such high blood pressure. Has she had a lot of stress in her life recently?"

Alex nodded. "She's lost her entire family in the last twenty-four hours, doc."

"Oh my God. Poor girl. No wonder. That would explain it, but I still want to keep her here for a while, just to be sure."

"Can we stay with her?"

"Of course."

"We appreciate all you've done," Alex breathed. "Can we see her?"

The doctor shifted on his feet. "Well, actually she asked only for Julian. How about we let him go in first, and then he can talk to Molly about whether you can come in as well?"

"Sure, sure, whatever she wants," Alex answered, but Julian could hear the hurt in her voice.

"I'll be back to get you soon, Alex. Doc, may I place my hand on your shoulder for guidance?"

"Absolutely." Julian reached out and put his left hand on the doctor's right shoulder as Alex's phone rang. Grateful for the distraction, she turned away from the two men as they walked away. "Alex Hayes."

"Alex, it's Vinny. How are you?"

"Vinny! Long time no talk. I'm good, fine … well, I'm okay. How are you?"

"Got a new lady in my life since I last spoke with you, and she's great."

"Ah, good to hear, my friend. Can't wait to meet her. What's her name?"

"Annabelle Andrews."

Alex paused. "Why do I know that name?"

"She's a Boston ADA and is smart as a whip."

"Ah yes, now I remember. She prosecuted a guy I brought in for killing his wife after he had beaten her senseless for fourteen years. The guy got off on a technicality and returned home to his three sons. I'm sure he's beating them as well and raising them to follow in his footsteps. She blew that case and blamed it on us. She said we didn't give her a lot to work with. I guess his confession wasn't enough. But seriously, Vin, I'm glad you're happy."

Vinny paused. "Gee, Alex. You gotta stop holding in your feelings. Otherwise, you're going to get an ulcer."

"Sorry, Vinny. I'm sure she's a nice person, and I'm glad she makes you happy. Maybe when I meet her in a social situation, my feelings will change."

"Yeah, well, the reason I'm calling is because I spoke with the Winchester police chief, and he told me that you'd contacted him about a little girl named Molly—"

"McClelland. Yes, I did. Why? What does the FBI have to do with Molly McClelland?"

"Nothing yet."

"What do you mean, yet?"

"How is it that a Boston cop ended up getting involved with little Molly?"

"Julian and I were going away for the weekend and came across a car accident that she had caused."

"Molly caused a car crash?"

"Yeah. It's a long story, but she's with us now in the hospital."

"The hospital?"

"Yes. Everyone's okay, but the doctor wants her to stay here for observation. It's something about her blood pressure being high. Anyway, Vinny, why are you asking me about Buttons?"

"Who's Buttons?"

Alex was exasperated. "It's Molly's nickname. Why are you asking me about her?"

"Because her father was a confidential informant for us and now he's dead."

The hairs on Alex's arms stood at attention, and she deliberated on her next words. "Exactly why was Buttons' father a CI for you?"

"You don't know who Jimmy McClelland was? He was the Torchia family money man, and I'm not sure he killed himself. I think he might have been murdered, and one of my guys might have been in on it."

CHAPTER 37

His last conversation with the Ogre played on a loop through Sid's memory.

"Nothing's going to happen to them."

"Well then, that's up to you now, isn't it?"

The man had made it crystal clear that the well-being of Sid's family correlated directly with finding and delivering pertinent information Jimmy might have collected.

Sid cruised by Jimmy's house to see which forensic personnel were still there and then drove around the block twice while he talked himself into and out of breaking the law. On the third pass, he parked his unmarked car along the curb and cut the engine. Knowing what he must do to save his family did not jibe with his moral compass, and his stomach ulcer burned like a ball of fire in his belly.

Popping two TUMS into his mouth, he noted that one police cruiser and one crime scene tech van sat in the spacious driveway. Crime scene tape surrounded the entire house and yard. As he exited his car, a woman pushing a stroller approached him.

"Terrible what happened here, huh?" the woman asked, unable to remove her eyes from the yellow tape.

"Yes, ma'am."

The woman looked eagerly at Sid. "Are you a police officer?"

Sid evaluated the mother and determined that she enjoyed being first with new information in the neighborhood. He envisioned her surrounded by her bunco club and on her third glass of wine. Each member would be leaning in to glean the most recent grisly information regarding the McClelland family tragedy. Sid determined to give her nothing. "No, ma'am, I'm not."

She looked offended. "I'm not an idiot. Clearly you're some type of government official. You're dressed for it and have a Ford Crown Victoria. I mean, *come on.*"

Sid wanted to laugh openly at this woman's craving for validation. Instead, he changed the subject. "That's a beautiful baby there, ma'am. Enjoy this short time you have before he grows up. You know, they say that we're only borrowing our children. They never really belong to us. It's true. Trust me."

The woman glanced at her sleeping son and then at Sid. She cut her eyes at him and then laughed. "Now I see that you're not a cop after all. Are you a family friend of the McClellands?"

Sid smiled. "You might say that. I worked with Jimmy from time to time."

The woman pouted and was clearly disappointed with Sid's answer. "Oh, I see. Well, I have to finish walking Teddy and then get to yoga, so have a nice day."

Sid watched as the thirty-something mother walked away, her yoga pants swinging back and forth as she sipped her Starbucks. He shook his head as she glanced at him once more and removed her cell phone from its holder on the stroller, eager to update her friends. *When did strollers get cell phone holders?* Sid wondered as he crossed the front lawn.

"Hello, sir. Good to see you again."

"Officer Sinnex, good to see you as well."

"Boy, the FBI has a strong interest in this suicide, if I may say so, sir."

Sid clapped the young man on the back. "And how did you piss off your commanding officer to land door duty two days in a row?"

Officer Sinnex shook his head. "Nothing gets by you, sir. I screwed up some paperwork on a robbery. The chief wants to make sure I don't do that again."

"By giving you mind-numbing door duty?"

"Exactly."

"Is it working?"

"Yes, sir. No more paperwork mistakes for me, sir."

Sid smiled and squeezed the young man's shoulder. "No more paperwork mistakes, Sinnex, but you'll make other ones. Count on it." Sid made his way past the cop.

"Yes, sir, I'm sure I will. Sir?" Sid turned around slowly with his eyebrows raised. "Why is the FBI so interested in this case? It seems like a cut and dry suicide to me."

"Does it?" The man nodded. "Well, Sinnex, all I can say is that sometimes things aren't always what they seem to be."

Sid entered the house, closed the door behind him, and made a quick visual sweep of the downstairs. He determined that the techs were all upstairs in the master bedroom. He climbed the stairs, popped his head in the room, and proffered his badge. "Hi guys. Sid Nickerson, FBI. Just here following up on a loose end. Carry on." The techs paused just long enough to acknowledge Sid's words and then continued their argument regarding which contestant should win the current season of *The Voice*.

Sid ducked into the one room he had not searched the day before. Despite the seriousness of his situation, Sid couldn't help but smile as he glanced at the letters M-O-L-L-Y that hung above the pink chenille-blanketed canopy bed. A photo hung on each side of the name. The picture next to the "M" showed Molly with her big brother. Joey was at least four inches taller than his younger sister, yet her left arm was slung awkwardly over his shoulder and a wide smile graced her face. The picture next to the "Y" was a family portrait, and Molly wore the same open smile. *Not a care in the world*, Sid thought as he examined the photos.

A burst of laughter emanating from the master bedroom sobered Sid and recalled him to his task. He quickly but efficiently rifled through the drawers. Finding nothing of note, he turned his attention to the closet and reviewed its contents. Dresses, shoes, and toys were hung and stacked neatly in the small space.

Sid started to close the sliding doors when a rectangular cutout in the ceiling of the closet caught his eye. Grabbing Molly's desk chair, he positioned it directly under the opening, stepped on it, and gently lifted the wood covering the hole. He turned the piece of wood sideways so that he could pull it out through the opening and placed it on the floor next to the chair. He wasn't tall enough to actually see into the opening without a ladder but instead, felt around the inside of the opening with his right hand. As he turned his body on the chair, his hand traced the inside edges of the opening. He had come almost full circle when his hand touched something hard. Using his fingers, he coaxed the object to the edge of the opening and then let it fall down into his left hand.

Glancing at the bedroom door, he realized the laughter and speech of the techs had altered. Cocking his head, it sounded as if they had packed up and were heading his way. They had either finished their work or were wondering what he was doing. Sid dropped the object into his jacket pocket and quickly replaced the wood piece to cover the ceiling's opening. He had just replaced the desk chair when the lead tech rounded the doorjamb.

"We're all set. Gonna head out. Hey, you okay? You're sweating."

Sid wiped his forehead. "Yeah, yeah. I'm good."

The tech squinted at Sid. "Didn't I see you here yesterday?"

"Yeah, you did. I'm working this case. I think I have what I need now, so I'm all set."

CHAPTER 38

"What do you mean, one of your guys might have been in on it, Vinny?" Alex whispered into the phone.

"I'm not sure, Alex, but one of my longtime agents is acting weird. He's lying to me."

"No offense, Vin, but isn't lying your business? You tell me all the time that your agents withhold information in the interest of keeping it on a need-to-know basis."

"That's true, Alex, but this time it feels different."

"It *feels* different?" Alex repeated.

"Yeah, it does. My agent flipped Jimmy McClelland six months ago. Jimmy was given immunity in exchange for delivering as much information as it took for the state to build a winnable case against the Torchia family. We were so close, and then Jimmy turns up dead, and his family dies in a car crash on the same day. It's highly unlikely, don't you think?"

Alex shrugged. "Could be a coincidence, Vin."

Vinny exhaled heavily. "Maybe, but my gut says otherwise."

"Why do you think your agent might be lying to you?"

"I don't think, Alex, I *know*. He walked into my office yesterday all banged up. He told me that he had sustained the injuries while crashing into another car. He told the ER staff that he'd hit a bridge."

"Vinny, the man had just been in some type of car wreck. Maybe he was confused. Why don't you ask him about the discrepancy?"

"I will. But it's not just that. He's acting strangely. I don't know. Maybe you're right. I'll talk to him. So is Molly okay?"

Alex glanced in the direction of where Julian and the doctor had walked. "I think so. She's an incredible kid, Vin. You should see her."

"Is this the same Alex Hayes who has heretofore expressed a severe distaste for children and all things children-related?"

"Ha ha. Yes, I like this kid. She's tough, stoic, and girly—all at the same time."

"Sounds like someone else I know." The smile in Vinny's voice was unmistakable.

"Uh-huh. Anyway, the doctor wants to keep her overnight for observation because her blood pressure is really high."

"Is Julian with you?"

"He's with Molly in her room. I'll join them after we're done."

"What will happen to the girl? Where will she go?"

"Julian has a social worker friend who's researching whether Buttons has family she can live with."

"That's good. Why do you call her Buttons, by the way?"

Alex laughed. "It's the funniest thing, Vinny. You know how some kids carry around a blanket or a teddy bear?"

"Yeah."

"Molly carries a jar of buttons that her father gave her. It means the world to her."

"Buttons." Vinny stated the word rather than asking a question.

"I know it's weird, but yes, it's a jar of buttons. When we met her she wasn't speaking, so Julian nicknamed her Buttons, and it kind of stuck, I guess. She likes it anyway. It matches her tiara." Alex smiled.

"Her tiara? You know what? Never mind. As long as she's safe and happy, I don't care what she carries, wears, or is called."

Alex's smile abruptly dropped. "Do you think she's in danger, Vinny?"

Vinny shook his head. "Honestly, I'm not sure, Alex. I'm about to call the ME who's completing the autopsy on Jimmy's body. I'm hoping he can give me a better idea of the cause of death. If this wasn't a suicide, perhaps the Torchia family dispatched Jimmy and his family as well. If they were targeting the entire McClelland family and discovered that Molly was still alive, they might come after her."

"Over my dead body, literally," Alex growled as her hand found its way to the grip of her pistol.

"Alex, I gotta go. Someone else is calling me. Talk to you soon." Vinny pressed the call swap icon on his phone and said, "Vinny Marcozzi."

"Hi. It's me. Just calling to see how your day is going," Annabelle said.

"Hey, you. It's going better now that I'm talking to you."

"What do you mean it's going better? What's going on?"

Vinny sighed heavily. "Jimmy McClelland's kid is in the hospital."

Annabelle was quiet for a moment. "Which one?"

"The little girl, Molly."

"No, I meant which hospital?"

Vinny paused. Perhaps his brain was working overtime, or perhaps he felt paranoid because Sid was already trying to play him for a fool. Either way, he noted that this was the second time Annabelle had asked about Jimmy's family.

"Why do you ask?"

"Jesus, Vin. I was just wondering."

"Why didn't you ask about Jimmy's son?"

"I was getting to him, Vin, but I thought I'd ask about the girl first. God, what's up with you?"

Vinny shook his head. "I'm sorry, I'm sorry. There's a lot going on right now."

"Why don't you tell me about it? Lighten your load."

"It's just that I'm wondering if one of my guys is working both sides."

"What do you mean?"

"You know I can't say too much, Annabelle, but I'm pretty sure that one of my agents had something to do with Jimmy's death."

"Vin, we talked about this. It was a suicide, remember? Have you talked to the ME? I'm sure he'll verify that for you."

"I'm going to call him now."

"You'll feel better after you talk to him. Once you're confident Jimmy took his own life, you can address whatever the issue is with Sid and move on."

"Yeah, I guess you're right. Annabelle?"

"What?"

"I didn't tell you that Sid was the agent I was worried about."

Annabelle laughed. "Vinny, seriously? At my apartment you told me that Sid was running Jimmy. It wasn't a giant leap to assume that Sid was the agent you were worried about, right?"

Vinny smiled, feeling relieved. He *had* mentioned Sid's name last evening. "You're right. Sorry. I'm just a little jumpy. Will I see you later?"

"Of course. My place. Eight o'clock. Be there or else."

"I think I might take my chances with 'or else'."

Vinny whispered, "You're a wicked woman, Annabelle Andrews."

Annabelle laughed throatily.

"Oh, you have no idea, my dear. See you at eight."

CHAPTER 39

The doctor led Julian to Molly's bedside and deposited a chair behind Julian's knees, saying, "I'll give you some time together," before disappearing.

Julian eased himself into the chair and whispered, "You awake, Buttons?"

"Yes," she whispered back. "Julian?"

"Yes?"

"Why are we whispering?"

Julian continued quietly. "Because I thought you might be sleeping."

"But I'm not!" Buttons said loudly, sitting up in bed.

"Sh, Buttons. There are other patients that might want us to keep our voices quiet."

"Sorry," she said. "Oh!"

Julian reached forward. "What is it?"

"The room is all swirly, Julian."

"Listen to me. Lie back on your pillow right now, okay?"

She lay back on her pillow and breathed deeply. "The room isn't squiggly anymore, Julian."

Julian smiled. "Glad to hear it. It's important that you don't get up by yourself, Buttons. Your blood pressure is high, so—"

"I don't know what you're saying, Julian."

Julian thought for a moment. "You go to kindergarten, right?"

"I'll be going into first grade when school starts again," she corrected him.

"Right. Sorry. Anyhow, when you're coming in from recess, do the kids stand in a line to come in, or does everyone run toward the door and try to jam their way through it?"

"Well," Buttons said, dramatically elongated the L, "we used to run to the door where Miss Mary was waiting, but then she'd yell at us, and we'd get in a line. But one boy always used to—"

"Okay, okay. Listen. When you used to run toward the door, weren't there so many kids trying to get through the door, no one or only a few kids could get through?"

"Yup."

"That's what's happening to the blood in your body. Just like too many kids pushing to get through the door, a lot of blood is trying to get through your veins fast, which can make the room feel like it's—"

"Swirly?" she finished for him.

"Yes, swirly."

"That makes sense. You explain things really good, Julian. Oh no!"

"What's wrong?"

"My button jar, where is it?" The girl's breathing came faster, and Julian could feel her beginning to shake.

"It's okay, Buttons. It's okay. It's at home. I promise it's safe."

"It needs to stay with me. I have to have it with me." She tumbled out of bed and landed with a thud on Julian's shoes. He reached down to grab her, but she eluded him by twisting out of his grasp.

"Buttons!" Julian commanded, and the girl stopped abruptly. She hadn't known he could speak to her in such a tone. "You must stay here with me."

She approached Julian but remained far enough away that he couldn't touch her. "Julian, I'm sorry, but I need my jar." Her voice sounded exhausted yet defiant, and Julian's heart melted.

"I promise your jar is safe."

"I can't disappoint my daddy, Julian."

"I know, Buttons, and you won't. Please come back to your bed." The little girl took two steps toward Julian and then bolted out of the room.

"Buttons, get back here!" Julian stood up and felt his way to the door.

Buttons rounded the corner, plowed straight into someone's legs, and was knocked backward.

"Well, hello there. Where do you think you're going, Ms. McClelland?"

CHAPTER 40

Dr. Hamilton Lippincott placed his used apron and surgical mask in the dirty laundry bin. His plastic, protective glasses were splattered with bodily fluids, and he tossed them in a biohazard bucket labeled "to be sterilized." He scrubbed his hands and forearms in the large, surgical sink and then dried them on paper towels from the dispenser. Returning to his office, he awoke his computer from sleep mode and plopped down in his desk chair to dictate notes on his latest autopsy.

"Dr. Hamilton Lippincott performed a forensic autopsy on James McClelland today, July 13th, 20—"

His mobile phone buzzed, and he pressed the space bar on his computer to halt the recording while he answered, "Dr. Lippincott here."

"Hi, Dr. Lippincott. My name is Vinny Marcozzi, and I'm with the FBI. I was referred to you by Daniel Schmidt of the Winchester Police Department. I understand that you're performing the autopsy on James McClelland?"

"That is correct. In fact, I just completed his case and was just starting my notes on it when you called."

"Good timing, I guess. Look, doc, I'm just going to cut to the chase because I have a lot of irons in the fire right now, okay? Was James McClelland murdered, or was it truly a suicide?"

Dr. Lippincott smiled. "I don't think it's that simple, Mr. Marcozzi. Mr. McClelland definitely died due to hanging as opposed to an event that might have occurred prior to his hanging, if that's what you're asking."

"You're saying that he died because he was hanging from the rope and not from a blow to the head before he was strung up?"

"That is correct."

"What did you find under his fingernails?"

"A very tiny amount of dirt but no hairs or fibers indicating a struggle, if that's where you were going with your line of questioning."

Vinny slumped in his chair. "Can you tell me the time of death?"

Dr. Lippincott paused. "This is not an exact science, Mr. Marcozzi, but I would say that Mr. McClelland had been dead for about an hour or two when he was discovered."

"And you're basing that assertion on …?"

"His gastric contents, of course. I found a masticated but undigested bagel in his stomach, indicating that he'd eaten maybe an hour or two before he died."

"How long have you been performing autopsies, Dr. Lippincott?"

Hamilton sat straighter in his chair. "Forty-one years."

"And in all of those years, how many suicides eat breakfast on the morning they plan to end it all?"

"About half."

Vinny was shocked. "Really?"

"Sure. Did you know, Mr. Marcozzi, that more than one hundred Americans commit suicide every day? It's the tenth leading cause of death overall and the fourth among twenty-five to forty-four year olds, which is the category into which Mr. McClelland falls."

Relief washed over Vinny like a cool shower. Maybe Marcie was right. Maybe Sid hadn't lied on purpose about being in a car accident. Maybe his injuries had left him confused and shaken, and he had simply misspoken. Vinny's shoulders relaxed as he blew out a mouthful of air.

Dr. Lippincott continued. "Now, let me ask you a question. Do you know why Mr. McClelland would want to take his own life?"

"No, I don't. The fact is that one of my agents knows him and not me. I'm simply following up on a lead from my agent and helping him out."

"I see."

"So, you're confident that this is a suicide then?"

"I never said that, did I?"

"You said that he died by hanging and that nothing was found under his nails indicating a struggle."

"Correct."

"So, either he died from hanging himself or allowed someone to place a noose around his neck and pull him up?"

"That about sums it up."

Vinny shook his head, "Doc, you been doing your thing for forty-one years, and I've been doing mine for about twenty. I can tell you that no man will walk to the gallows voluntarily without having second thoughts or perhaps fighting for his life."

Dr. Lippincott thought back to the stool that had been kicked far away from the body. He wondered if Mr. McClelland had kicked it further away by mistake or if in fact, he might have been trying to reach it to regain solid footing.

"Mr. Marcozzi, contrary to popular belief, death by hanging is not often instantaneous. It actually happens in stages. Mr. McClelland's death was caused by a combination of asphyxia and venous congestion. That is to say, the rope around his neck compressed the larynx and trachea. This forced the root of his tongue against his pharynx and folded the epiglottis over the entrance of the larynx, which blocked his airway. At the same time, Mr. McClelland's jugular vein was blocked by the rope's compression, which caused cerebral circulation to stop."

"So you're saying …"

Dr. Lippincott sighed. "That he strangled and suffocated."

"Ah, okay. Thank you."

"Aren't you going to ask me about the rope he used?"

"Um, sure. Tell me about the rope he used."

"It was thick—about three-quarters of an inch in diameter—which is why it didn't sink more into the skin of his neck. A hybrid clinch and Palomar knot was used in the rope, which indicates to me that whoever secured the knot might have been a fisherman."

"What? Why do you say that?"

"Clinches and Palomar knots are well known to fisherman. They are strong, reliable knots that are used to fasten hooks to fishing lines. Using both together indicates that the person absolutely did not want the knot to untie. Using the thicker rope indicates that whoever killed Mr. McClelland—even if his death was self-inflicted—did not want the rope to break as it bore the weight of his body."

"Interesting."

"Yes, it is. And what's even more interesting is what I found in Mr. McClelland's hair."

"Tell me."

"Tiny splinters of wood that match the rafter from which his body was hung."

Vinny creased his brow in thought. "That makes sense. After all, he was hanging from the rafter, so some wood might have fallen as his body swung back and forth."

"Perhaps. But if that were the case, I believe that we would see wood splinters on the floor under his body, right? Can you picture it, Agent Marcozzi? As Mr. McClelland's body swings, the rope rubs from side to side against the wood, causing small pieces to break off and fall to the floor."

"I take it you didn't find much wood on the floor?"

"Some, but much more in his hair. It was as if the body were stationary as the pieces fell. Furthermore, I ascended a ladder and examined the rafter. You'd think that if Mr. McClelland slung a rope over the rafter, placed the noose around his neck, and kicked out the stool underneath him, the marks on the rafter where the rope rubbed against it would be horizontal as his body swung back and forth, but they weren't."

"I don't understand."

"What I'm saying is that the marks on the wood were vertical, up and down, as if a heavy object had been hoisted up using the rope like a pulley system."

"Were there *any* horizontal marks on the wood?"

"Minimal, indicating—"

"Indicating that there was little movement from side to side and little swinging of the body."

Dr. Lippincott smiled broadly. "You are a quick study, Agent Marcozzi."

"Which further indicates that Jimmy McClelland didn't fight as he was hanged. Wouldn't that assumption corroborate suicide then? I return to my question: What person in his right mind would willingly walk to the gallows?"

"I don't know. You tell me."

Vinny leaned back in his chair and closed his eyes. Annabelle popped into his mind, and it suddenly occurred to him that he would die for her. She was the one reason why he might put his life on the line—to save her.

Vinny's eyes popped open. "He gave his life to save his family. That's why he allowed himself to be strung up."

"My, my, Agent Marcozzi. I believe that you've hit the jackpot."

"Well, thank you for your time, doctor. You've been a great help."

"You're most welcome. Can you please do me a favor? Can you tell your associate about my findings? I was supposed to alert him upon completion of the autopsy."

"My associate?"

"Yes, the gentleman I met at the McClelland house. Let me see. I have his business card here somewhere." Vinny heard him rummaging through papers. "Here it is. A Mr. Sidney Nickerson. Do you know him? I assumed you did because he's with the FBI."

"I know him."

"Wonderful. He told me to report my findings to no one but him. I hope he doesn't mind that you and I chatted. Can you please pass along my conclusions then? It would save me a telephone call."

Vinny set his mouth. "Oh, I'll tell him. You can count on it."

CHAPTER 41

Buttons hoisted herself off the floor where she had fallen after slamming into Alex's legs in her attempt to retrieve her button jar. She brushed off her gown and glared at Alex. She had one hand on her hip and one pointing to her squinted eyes, her brows lowered ominously. "Do you know what these are, Alex?"

"No."

"These are angry eyes. These are very angry eyes because I'm very mad right now. I need to go home. I mean, I need to go to Julian's to get my button jar!"

Alex knelt down and reached out to the little girl, who didn't move a muscle in response. Alex let her hands drop to her knees as she said, "I'd love to let you do that, Buttons, but the doctor said that you need to stay here tonight."

The girl's bravado cracked a bit, and suddenly, Alex could see nothing but the five-year-old that she was. Buttons collapsed to the ground, defeated. Her large brown eyes stared dully at Alex and seemed devoid of emotion.

"Oh, Buttons," Alex sighed as she scooped her up and returned to her room where Julian waited quietly listening to the exchange. Alex gingerly placed the girl in her bed, pulled the covers up to her chin, and then pulled up a chair on the other side of the bed. As Julian patted Buttons' arm, Alex stroked her hair and began humming a tune her mother had sung to her as a child. Buttons' breathing steadied and then slowed until it was deep and even. Alex stopped humming.

"Is she asleep?" Julian whispered.

Alex cleared her throat and blew her nose. "Yes."

"Are you crying, Alex?"

"No," she lied.

Julian smiled. "Alex, you're not alone in your sorrow. There's no shame in grieving for those you love."

"Don't be dramatic, Julian. I'm not grieving."

"Yes, you are. You're grieving for the child you have gotten to know and care for in a very short time. You know that her life has been altered forever, and you feel powerless to do anything about it. That makes you sad ... and it's okay to feel that way."

Alex examined the little girl's features. "She's beautiful, Julian. Her eyes are a rich brown, and when she looks at you, it's as if she sees inside you. She has these great orange ringlets ..." Alex trailed off as she twirled some hair around her pointer finger. "Women pay a lot of money to get hair like this."

Julian tilted his head. "And if she's anything like you, she'll want to dye her hair a different color and straighten it."

Alex smiled as she traced Buttons' profile with her finger. "You're probably right."

"What song were you humming, Alex?"

"It's called 'Go Tell Aunt Rhody.'"

"How does it go?"

Alex sang quietly.

"Go tell Aunt Rhody,
Go tell Aunt Rhody,
Go tell Aunt Rhody
The old gray goose is dead.
The one she's been saving,
The one she's been saving,
The one she's been saving
To make a feather bed."

"My goodness. That's absolutely awful, Alex."

"I never thought about it, but yeah, you're right. It is awful. Did Buttons think she was going to run to your house to get her button jar?"

Julian sighed deeply. "I don't think she'd thought that far ahead. She panicked when she realized that her jar was at my house. She just flew out of the room. It's a good thing that you happened to find her because she might have made it outside if you hadn't."

Alex smiled. "She found me, actually."

The same physician who had approached them in the waiting room poked his head in the room and said, "How's everybody doing?"

Alex glanced at Buttons, whose eyes were darting back and forth under her lids. They reminded Alex of a hummingbird that flits from flower to flower desperately trying to satiate its never-ending need for sustenance. Much like a hummingbird, Buttons looked tiny and frail in the large hospital bed.

"She's doing okay, I guess, but why don't you tell us, doc? What's going on with her blood pressure?"

The doctor walked in and folded his arms. "I'm not sure yet. I'll have the nurse come in and retake her blood pressure to see if it has fallen while she's been sleeping. I may want to get some more blood work on her too, just to rule out any anomalies."

"Oh my God! What's going on? What happened to Buttons?" Jesse rushed in the room, completely out of breath.

"Hush, Jess. She's sleeping. How did you know where we were?" Julian asked.

Alex responded. "I called him to let him know. I thought he could get a head start on rescheduling tomorrow's patients if necessary."

"Good thinking." Julian updated Jesse on the girl's nightmare and escape attempt.

"Poor little thing," Jesse said, taking a seat.

"Well, one thing's for sure," the doctor said. "For an orphan, this kid sure does have a lot of people in her life. I'll send the nurse in shortly."

The doctor exited the room, and Alex said, "I'm going to get some coffee. Anyone else?"

"Coffee sounds good, Alex. Thanks. Hey, Jess, would you mind swinging by my house and getting the jar of buttons? When she wakes up, I want the jar to be the first thing she sees. I think it will go a long way in calming her down."

"Sure thing. I'll be back as soon as I can with the jar of buttons and the tiara."

Jesse was almost at the door when a nurse entered. He waited as she took Buttons' blood pressure. She murmured, "Huh," as she worked.

"Huh what? What does that mean?" Jesse asked urgently.

"It means that even at rest her blood pressure is still very high."

Jesse huffed. "And what does *that* mean?"

"It means that Buttons' world is still all swirly," Julian whispered as he leaned over Buttons and gave her a kiss on the cheek.

CHAPTER 42

Vinny felt very much out of sorts. The conversation with Dr. Lippincott did nothing to assuage his fears that Sid was lying. The fact that Vinny could not determine with certainty whether Sid was lying or not also bothered him.

In all of his years at the bureau, he was incredibly proud to say that his agents had remained loyal to their country, the agency, and to him, in that order. Of course, he expected nothing less from his agents than he demanded of himself. Vinny knew that protocol required that if he questioned an agent's motives and actions, he must place that agent under surveillance. But Sid was his friend, and Vinny wanted to give him another chance to clarify what had happened to cause such awful injuries.

Vinny crossed to his office window that overlooked the bull pen, where about thirty agents toiled in their cubicles, chasing down leads and connecting global dots, which allowed American citizens to sleep soundly at night. His eyes fell on Sid, who sat rigidly and stared blankly at his dark computer screen.

"Sid, you got a minute?" Vinny leaned out and spoke over the other agents' voices.

Sid started at the sound of Vinny's voice and awakened from his reverie. "Yeah, sure, Vin."

With effort, Sid lifted himself from his desk chair and walked slowly to Vinny's office, where Vinny sat patiently waiting behind his desk. "Why don't you close the door, Sid."

Sid's eyes locked on Vinny as he swung the door shut. "What's up, Vin?"

"How are you feeling?"

"Oh, fair to middling, I'd say," Sid replied with an attempt at light humor.

Vinny remained stoic and unsmiling. "You don't look good, Sid."

"Don't I?"

"You're sweating again."

"Yeah, well, it's kind of hot in here."

"I spoke with the ME that did Jimmy's autopsy."

Sid sat straighter in his chair. "Oh?"

"Uh-huh. He's not convinced it was a suicide."

Sid's eyes glazed over as he shifted uncomfortably in the chair. "Why?"

"I don't know. Something about wood fragments found in Jimmy's hair. Why don't you tell me everything Jimmy communicated to you before he died—right now."

"I put it all in a memo that I wrote last night. I need to go through it once more before I give it to you, just to make sure I didn't forget anything."

"What color was the car you hit?"

"What?"

"The car, Sid. It's not a hard question. What color was the car you plowed into that caused such severe injuries?"

"Oh, uh—"

"What color, Sid?"

"It was uh—"

"Or was it a bridge?"

Sid started shaking his head. "I don't understand."

Vinny stood, came around the front of his desk, and then leaned against it. "Did you hit a blue car or did you drive into a bridge piling, Sid? Or was it something else altogether?"

With effort, Sid stood as he stuttered and then retched on the floor next to the chair. The smell of vomit filled the small room as Vinny jerked himself out of the way. Quickly regaining his footing, he continued. "How about the name of Jimmy's mistress, Sid? What was her name?"

"Listen, Vinny. I gotta go. I don't feel well." Sid staggered backward to the door.

"No, Sid. What was her name?" Vinny raised his voice.

"It was, uh, it was Jimmy's cleaning lady, Kellie Moser. I need to leave, Vinny. Sorry, but I have to get home."

Sid threw open the door of Vinny's office to find the entire bull pen of agents staring at him. The walls closed in as his eyes traveled quickly around the room. He wiped his mouth on his sleeve and then gathered his keys and briefcase, avoiding all of the accusatory questions in his colleagues' eyes.

Vinny returned to his office, emotionally drained. "God dammit," he mumbled under his breath as he accessed the internet. He googled Kellie Moser, and her Facebook profile appeared. In it she promoted her cleaning company, Dirty Secrets. Several photos of Kellie and her family graced the page as well. They looked like a happy American family—Kellie, her husband, and a young boy, who presumably was their son.

Marcie entered Vinny's office cautiously. "Vin, you okay? What the hell was all that about with Sid? God, it smells in here ..." Her voice trailed off as she saw the pool of vomit.

Vinny glanced up from his computer and saw Marcie's worried look. "I'm fine, Marcie. Thanks. Listen—could you do me a favor and get someone to clean up Sid's mess?"

As Marcie left, a wry smile crept to Vinny's lips as he considered the irony of the cleaning company's name, Dirty Secrets. Vinny's entire career was composed of dirty secrets, but until now, none of them had crossed into his personal space. Vinny leaned back in his chair and realized he had recently come to two very important conclusions: Sid, who had been Jimmy's handler since he had flipped six months ago, was definitely lying to him, and Jimmy's death had not been a suicide but a murder.

CHAPTER 43

Sid sat in his rental car hyperventilating. He grabbed a paper bag on the passenger seat and breathed into it, forcing some carbon dioxide into his over-oxygenated body. A full minute later after having regained control over his breathing, his mind was still racing. Retrieving his phone, he stabbed out a text message that read,

Meet me at Dobson Park in ten minutes

Then he raced out of the parking lot. He commanded Siri to call his wife on speakerphone, and as the call connected, he thought back to the births of his two children. Annie had come into the world easily and without incident, but Joshua's birth had been much more dramatic.

Joshua had suffered from microcephaly, and his doctors had thought that his corpus callosum (the area of the brain that connects its two hemispheres) might not have been fully developed. Sid and his wife had been told that Joshua might end up with epilepsy or worse. But his development had progressed relatively normally. After a period of three years, he had been formally released from the neurologist's care. The last thing Sid remembered saying to the man was, "Thanks for everything, doc, but honestly, I hope we never see you again."

Kathleen interrupted Sid's thoughts. "Sid, is that you?"

"Hey, honey. Yeah, it's me. I'm just calling to say hi."

"That's sweet. How was your day? I'm sitting here at brunch with—"

"Kath, remember when Josh was born, and we thought that he was really sick, but it turns out that he wasn't? Remember how worried we were? That could've broken some relationships, but it made ours even stronger, don't you think?"

A long pause ensued followed by Kathleen excusing herself from the table to speak privately.

"Okay, Sid, enough. What's going on? You've told me to not ask questions, but this is ridiculous. You know I love reminiscing, but there's obviously something else going on."

"I can't. … I just …"

Kathleen pursed her lips. "Are you in trouble, Sid?"

"I'm not sure."

"Oh my God! Are *we* in trouble—the kids and me? Should I take the kids and go to my parents? Oh my God, Sid! Tell me!"

"You can't take the kids and go anywhere, Kath. They'll know. They're watching us."

"Who is watching us?"

Sid pulled into a parking space at the park and stared dully at the Ogre, who was seated on a bench. His legs were crossed, and he was smiling as he threw crumbs to the pigeons.

"Sid, answer me! Who are you in trouble with? Who's watching us?"

Sid's face crinkled as he leaned his forehead against the steering wheel. His cracked ribs ached as he struggled not to cry. "I can't tell you, Kath. It'll just make it worse. You and I never had this conversation. Whatever you do, act normal. I want you to know that I'm sorry and that whatever happens, you need to understand that everything I'm doing is for you and the kids, okay?"

Kathleen sniffled through the phone before whispering, "Okay."

"Do you remember how years ago when I first started at the bureau, you and I made a plan just in case?"

Kathleen nodded. "Yes, and I told you that you were being dramatic."

"Do you remember where the extra money is and where we said we would meet?"

"Yes."

"I hear there's a tornado in the Midwest. Have you heard that as well?"

"Oh no, Sid," Kathleen moaned.

"Did you hear about the tornado?" Sid whispered urgently as the Ogre waved at him, indicating that he should come over to the bench.

"Yes, I've heard," she whispered so quietly that Sid had to strain to hear her.

"Good. But, Kath, you *must* act normal until then. Understand?" She didn't answer. "Kath?"

"Yeah, I understand, okay."

"I love you so much, you know?"

"I know, Sid. We love you too."

Sid ended the call, wiped his eyes, and exited the car holding his briefcase. He thought back to his recent encounter in Vinny's office. His boss obviously suspected that Sid was lying. It was only a matter of time before he put all of the pieces together, and Sid was arrested for treason. Sid hadn't called Kathleen with the intent of planning their getaway, but the idea had formed as they had been speaking. Now he saw a way out of this mess, his family alive and intact. Walking toward the bench, Sid discovered a renewed strength and even managed a small smile as he approached the Ogre.

"Hello, my friend," the Ogre smiled. "You look almost happy to see me. I told you we'd get along."

"I have something for you," Sid said as he sat down and opened his briefcase. Removing the small book he had found in the ceiling of Molly's room, he presented it to the Ogre, who turned it over and laughed.

"What is this, Sid? It looks like a girl's diary."

"It probably is."

The Ogre looked confused. "What's in it?"

"I don't know. As you can see, I left the lock intact so that you could be assured that I didn't alter it in any way."

The Ogre patted Sid on the back. "Ever the conscientious FBI agent, aren't you? Nice work. Shall we open it together? Do you have the key?"

Sid looked at the man as if he had lost his mind. "No, I don't have the fucking key!"

"Well then, how are we going to open it?"

Sid laughed in disbelief while shaking his head. "Look at me! If you can do *this* to me," Sid pointed to his bruised face and broken ribs, "I think you can manage to break open a girl's fucking diary."

"Whoa, whoa, buddy. Easy with the language. There's no need to be rude."

Sid rolled his eyes. "Give me the diary, and I'll open it." Sid grabbed the book and forced the lock open with a pen.

"Where did you find it?"

"It was hidden in the ceiling of Molly McClelland's room. I didn't find anything in Jimmy's house related to the business, but this was hidden, so I thought it might be pertinent."

"Pertinent? What does that mean?"

"Important to your … investigation."

"Pertinent. I like that word. I'm going to use it in the future."

"Anyway, here." Sid handed the unlocked book to the Ogre and watched as he opened it. Although Sid had no particular expectations of the book's contents, he was surprised to find personal entries accompanied by pages of notations in Jimmy's handwriting. He didn't know what they meant.

"What is all of this?" the Ogre asked, flipping quickly through the book.

Sid leaned in to see better. "I have no idea. Maybe some entries about his dry-cleaning stores? I'm assuming that because it's divided into different colors."

"What do you mean?"

"Each of Jimmy's seven stores had a dominant color theme. You know, one was red, one was blue, etc. These entries might be related to each store. But why?"

The Ogre glanced sideways at Sid while closing the book. "Maybe this has nothing to do with my boss. Listen, Sid, if you're yanking my chain and brought me this ridiculous book in an effort to get off the hook—"

"No, no, no. I'm telling you. This book was hidden, and it was the only thing—the *only* thing—I found that might be related to the Torchia family and their business dealings. Why would Jimmy have hidden it if it weren't important?"

The Ogre squinted at Sid while making an evaluation. "Okay, Sid. I believe you. But you gotta figure out what all of this writing means."

Sid shook his head and raised his eyebrows. "No way. That wasn't part of our deal. My job was to bring you the information, and I did that." Sid tapped the diary for emphasis. "I'm done. I'm outta here." Sid snapped his briefcase shut, stood, and began to walk away.

The Ogre didn't move. "Sid?"

Sid stopped, turned around, and was exasperated. "What?"

"Your safe word is *tornado,* and I hear that Argentina is lovely this time of year. I thought the fact that I know both of those items might be *pertinent* to you as you make your decision as to whether or not you will continue to help me."

CHAPTER 44

Vinny's car sputtered to a stop in the hospital parking lot. After popping a stick of gum in his mouth, Vinny exited the vehicle and made his way through the automatic doors into the lobby where an elderly lady sat primly at the front desk. As he approached, she tilted her head and welcomed him with a warm smile. "Good morning, sir. Welcome to Winchester Hospital. My name is Rose. How may I help you?"

"Good morning, Rose. I'm looking for Kellie Moser's room."

"Are you a friend or a family member?" she inquired politely.

Vinny leaned forward and proffered his badge while speaking quietly. "Well, neither actually. I'm with the FBI."

The octogenarian's eyebrows rose dramatically as her eyes focused on Vinny's shield. "Really?"

Vinny gave her his best toothy smile. "Really. Can you please tell me where I might find Ms. Moser?"

Rose nodded somberly, as if her duty was a burden. Employing the hunt-and-peck technique, she typed Kellie's name into her computer while Vinny waited patiently. "Ms. Moser is in room 507. Elevators are to your left." Rose smiled and added, "I hope you get the bad guy, whoever he is."

"Thanks, Rose. I hope so too." *As soon as I can figure out who the bad guy is*, Vinny thought as he entered the elevator.

Vinny made his way to the fifth floor and walked slowly down the intensive care unit's hallway, noting how subdued the area felt. He passed a doctor and nurse discussing a patient. As they used the words *terminal* and *imminent* in their verbiage, he was reminded of how sick someone needed to be in order to come to the hospital at all, much less in the ICU. He braced himself for what he might see upon opening Kellie Moser's door.

He inhaled deeply as he gently rapped on the door. Vinny was surprised to hear a strong voice say, "Come in!" He pushed the door open and found three faces staring at him.

"Are you another doctor?" Kellie asked.

"No, Ms. Moser. My name is Vinny Marcozzi, and I'm with the FBI. May I speak with you a moment?"

"Um, sure. Come in."

Vinny entered the dimly lit room and stood at the foot of her bed. Turning to the man seated at Kellie's bedside, he asked, "Are you Mr. Moser?"

The man looked as if he hadn't slept. "Yeah. I'm Frank Moser, and this is our son, Connor. Connor, say hi to Mr. Marcozzi."

Connor was seated on a couch near the window, rocking back and forth while staring at the floor. Suddenly, he jumped up, ran over to stand directly in front of Vinny, said, "Hell-hell-hello, Mr. Marcozzi. Nice to meet you," and then darted back to the couch to resume his prior posture.

"Nice to meet you too, Connor."

Frank Moser walked over to his son. "Good job being polite, Connor. What's this about, Mr. Marcozzi. Why are you here?"

Vinny turned his attention to Kellie, who was sitting up in bed. Upon closer inspection, however, Vinny realized that she wasn't actually sitting up. She was propped up in her bed and held in place by straps and strategically placed pillows. Her head was supported by a metal brace. A sporadic whirring sound erupted as the bed automatically adjusted to ensure Kellie's comfort.

"I'm following up on the death of Mr. James McClelland. Is it okay if I ask you some questions, Ms. Moser?"

Kellie glanced quickly at her husband, who nodded his silent agreement. "C'mon, Connor. Let's go to the cafeteria and get Mom some of that chocolate pudding she loves."

"I love that pudding, Dad!" Connor announced too loudly.

"I know, buddy. You can have some too. Say goodbye to Mr. Marcozzi."

Connor rushed toward Vinny again, stopping within a half an inch of hitting him. To Vinny's credit, he didn't flinch. "Goodbye, Mr. Marcozzi. Be nice to my mom. She's real sick."

Vinny smiled. "I promise I'll be nice, Connor. Enjoy your pudding."

As the boy and his father left the room, silence descended. Vinny cleared his throat. "May I sit down?" he asked as he pointed to the bedside chair.

"Of course."

"Ms. Moser—"

"Please call me Kellie."

Vinny nodded. "Kellie, can you tell me your version of what happened the day you found Mr. McClelland?"

Kellie recounted the story and finished by shrugging her shoulders. "I can shrug my shoulders now. I couldn't do that yesterday."

"What do the doctors say about your prognosis? Will you regain movement?"

"They're hopeful. Although I have two cervical fractures, this halo brace I'm wearing immobilizes my neck so that the breaks can heal. I'm told that as the fractures heal, I'll most likely be able to move the areas below my shoulders again. Meanwhile, I look like the bride of Frankenstein with the brace drilled into my skull for support."

Vinny smiled, marveling at her ability to crack a joke under the circumstances. "You're resilient. I'll give you that."

Kellie's eyes darted to the door. "I have a good teacher, Mr. Marcozzi. My son is autistic, if you hadn't noticed. Every day is a challenge for him. If he can do it, so can I. We'll get through it together as a family. I will walk again. You can count on it."

Vinny believed her. "That's some kid."

"Yes, he is, and so is his dad. When Connor was diagnosed at two, Frank and I decided that Frank would be my son's primary caregiver so I could build my cleaning business. Frank's amazing with Connor."

Vinny paused, not wanting to pose the question he had come to ask. Kellie stared at him. "What is it, Mr. Marcozzi? Why are you really here?"

"Kellie, I'm not sure how to ask this, so I'm just going to come out with it. Were you and Mr. McClelland having an affair?"

Kellie simply stared at him. "Why are you asking me that?"

"Mr. McClelland left a note indicating that he took his life because of the guilt of cheating on his wife."

"What does that have to do with me?"

"You've been implicated in that affair."

"By whom?" she demanded.

"I can't tell you that, ma'am."

Kellie looked disgusted. "Oh, so you're back to calling me ma'am now? Official FBI business, I suppose. Well, let me tell you something. Jimmy McClelland loved his family as much as I love mine, and neither of us would ever do anything to breach that trust and love. Not to mention that I don't have time to do anything but work. My God, I haven't been out with my husband in months. Between work and taking care of Connor, we're both too physically and emotionally exhausted to do anything but fall into bed at the end of the day. You've got to be freakin' kidding me! An affair?"

"Okay, so it wasn't you. Could Mr. McClelland have been having an affair with someone else?"

"Listen—family and loyalty were paramount to Jimmy. There's absolutely no way that he would have cheated on Isabella and the kids. Hey, where are they anyway?"

Vinny examined his shoes.

"Oh no," Kellie started as her eyes welled up with tears.

"Mrs. McClelland and her son were killed in a car accident."

"What about little Molly?"

"She's okay. She's with friends of mine."

"Thank God," Kellie said, her face relaxing somewhat. "That kid is special. There's just something about her. She's going to do something really important someday. Mark my words."

CHAPTER 45

Julian sat silently while he listened to the footsteps of passersby outside Buttons' room. Then he focused on the little girl's steady breathing and synched his breath pattern with hers. It was the first time since yesterday that he had taken a moment to just breathe. He felt his shoulders relax and his mind calm. Reaching his hand out to the bed, Julian traced Buttons' arm with his fingers, eventually finding her hand. He placed his palm against hers and was struck with how small her hand was. Her skin was as smooth as velvet, and Julian imagined it to be an alabaster color.

"You're going to be alright, Buttons," Julian quietly assured her. "You're stronger than you know. You have lots of people who care about you, including me."

The door opened, and Alex whispered, "It's me," as she handed Julian a cup of coffee. "How's she doing?"

"You were gone only a few minutes, Alex."

"I know, but … you know."

"You're really worried about her, aren't you? I've never seen you like this."

Alex sighed heavily. "I just can't imagine what she's going through, that's all."

"I think it's more than that, Alex. What's going on?"

"I spoke with Vinny, and he told me something that could change the whole trajectory of this case."

Julian shook his head in confusion. "Case? What case, Alex?"

Alex leaned closer to Julian and whispered, "Do you know who Jimmy McClelland was?"

"Yes. He was Molly's father."

"Yes, but do you know what else he was? Who he worked for?"

"Yeah. He owned some dry-cleaning stores, and—"

Alex grabbed Julian's arm to silence him and led him to a corner of the room. "He was the chief accountant for the Torchia family. He became an FBI confidential informant in the last six months."

Julian raised his eyebrows in disbelief. "*The* Torchia family?"

Alex sighed. "There's really only one Torchia family in Boston to which I might be referring, Stryker."

"So, what does Vinny have to do with ..." Julian's voice faltered as the full weight of revelation settled on his shoulders. "Oh my God. Vinny thinks that the mob discovered Jimmy had flipped and that they murdered him."

"And he thinks that one of his guys might be involved," Alex added.

Julian's mind raced. "And Molly's mother and brother?"

Alex shrugged. "Hard to know what caused the car accident that killed them. It does seem coincidental that they died the same day as Jimmy though, doesn't it?"

"And Mrs. McClelland had no ID on her, which made it difficult for the authorities to identify her and Joey. That's something the mob would do, isn't it? Make sure there was no ID?"

"Absolutely," Alex said sadly as her eyes wandered over Buttons' tiny frame.

Julian gripped Alex's arm tightly. "Alex, does Vinny think that they'll come after Buttons?"

"He doesn't know, but I think to be safe, we should continue to keep her with us."

"I'd be sick if anything happened to her."

"Me too," Alex agreed.

The little girl stirred, yawned broadly, and stretched. When she realized where she was, her eyes commenced a wild, terrified spree around the room and finally settled on Alex and Julian, who stood huddled in the corner. Alex rushed to her side, put one hand on the girl's chest, and clutched Buttons' hand with the other. "It's okay, Buttons. Julian and I are here."

"I dreamed you were gone just like my mommy and daddy," she whimpered as her lips quivered.

"No, Buttons. Alex and I are here just like we said we'd be." Julian approached the bed and smiled. The girl's breathing slowed, and she leaned her head back on the pillow.

"What is that beeping sound?" she asked.

Alex glanced at the machine, which was connected to its patient via rubber-coated leads that were attached to Molly's chest. "This machine keeps track of your heart rate and blood pressure, Buttons. If you get too stressed, it gets stressed too and makes more noise."

Molly crinkled her brow and stared at the machine. "I don't like those beeps."

"Then stay relaxed, and the machine will too, okay?" Julian smiled.

Buttons shrugged. "Okay."

The door creaked as it opened slightly. Jesse, wearing the tiara, poked his head inside. "I thought I heard a little princess speaking."

"Jesse!" Buttons called out, reaching toward him with outstretched fingers wiggling with excitement. "That's my tiara, silly!"

Jesse glanced upward toward his crown. "Are you sure this is yours? Because I have one just like it at home."

Buttons dipped her head and squinted at him. "I'm sure."

"Well then, let's place it where it belongs." Jesse made a show of removing the tiara and placed it gingerly on her head. "Ah, you are correct. That is definitely yours. It fits you much better than me. I brought you another surprise."

As Jesse presented the button jar, Buttons' hands flew to her mouth, and she started crying. "Thank you, Jesse. My daddy is happy now."

"You're most welcome, my beautiful princess."

The door opened, and an orderly entered with a wheelchair. "Am I to understand that a princess abides in my palace?" he asked good-naturedly.

Buttons smiled and giggled. "Yes."

The orderly bowed and said, "Your presence has been requested in the hematology lab, my princess. Your carriage awaits." The man spread his arms wide, indicating the wheelchair.

Julian asked, "Why is she going to the hematology lab? Why can't they draw her blood here?"

"Because the doctor might require another brain scan and wants to do everything all at once so that it's less stressful for her royal highness, if that's okay?" The man looked questioningly at Buttons, who giggled once more.

Julian touched Alex's arm. "Why don't you go with her, Alex?"

"Good idea. Let's go, Buttons."

"Can I bring my jar?"

"How about I take care of your button jar until you get back?" suggested Jesse. "It'll be right here waiting for you."

"What about my tiara?"

The orderly smiled. "You may bring it, but you'll have to take it off for one of the tests, okay?"

Buttons smiled. "That's a deal."

The orderly came over and removed the leads from Buttons' chest, laying them gently on the bed. Buttons climbed into her carriage, wiggled to find a comfortable spot in the large chair, and announced, "Onward!" The procession exited the room, leaving Jesse and Julian alone.

"How're you doing?" Julian asked Jesse.

"God, Julian, she breaks my heart. What's going to happen to her?"

"I'm not sure, Jess. I guess that depends on what Stacey finds in terms of Buttons' relatives."

"Stacey called the office earlier but didn't leave a message. Why don't you call her back now?"

Julian commanded Siri to dial Stacey's number, and it went straight to voicemail. "Hey, Stace, it's Julian. I'm hoping you called my office earlier to give me some good news about finding Molly's relatives. Please get back to me when you can. Thanks for all of your help."

As Julian ended the call, a nurse popped her head into the room. "I thought my monitor was broken when it showed that Molly's leads had been removed. Why are Molly's leads on the bed?"

Jesse smiled. "Because she's getting her blood work done."

The nurse shook her head. "She already had her blood work done."

"Yes, but earlier the doctor said that she might need more. Plus, she's getting another brain scan," Julian said.

The nurse entered the room and examined her iPad. "There's no record of another MRI being ordered. Which doctor ordered it?"

"How should we know?" Jesse asked. "Shouldn't *you* know that?"

"Yes, I should. And I'm telling you that no other testing has been ordered for Molly. Where did she go?"

"I don't know," Julian said as he rose from his chair, "but one of your orderlies took her in a wheelchair."

"We don't have any orderlies."

Julian felt his way to the door, threw it open, and yelled, "Alex!"

Alex came running breathlessly down the hall. "What? What is it, Stryker? What's wrong?"

"Where's Molly?" he asked frantically.

"She went with the orderly through those doors—the ones that say, 'Magnetic Imaging Do Not Enter,' so I had to stay behind. Why?"

"Because this nurse says that the hospital doesn't have orderlies and that no new orders were processed for Buttons."

Without responding, Alex drew her gun and sprinted down the hallway ignoring the screams and cries of people who were unfortunate enough to be in her way. Kicking open the doors, she staggered to her knees in front of an empty wheelchair that had a diamond-studded tiara swinging from its handle.

CHAPTER 46

Molly's limbs were heavy and difficult to move. Glancing down at her torso, she realized why. She was stuck in quicksand up to her chest and was struggling against the suction. She was trying to disentangle her arms, a centimeter at a time, out of the muck. Once her arms were free, she frantically searched for something she could grab onto to pull herself out. A man she didn't know extended a pole out to her. Molly tentatively reached out as the man smiled and encouraged her to take hold of the pole. With eyes unblinking, Molly extricated herself from the quicksand and stared at the man.

"Hello, Molly. I'm going to get you out of here. You're safe with me. Don't worry. I'm taking care of you to help a friend."

Molly tilted her head. "Are you helping my daddy? Is he your friend?"

The man looked sad. "He was my friend. But I'm taking you out of here because I'm helping another friend."

Molly examined her surroundings and saw only blackness. Confused, she looked back to see the man, but he had disappeared and had been replaced by her father, who was seated in front of her.

"Daddy! I'm so glad you're here." The little girl threw her arms around her father's neck and breathed in his scent. "I have so much to tell you, Daddy."

Her father fixed her in his warm gaze and smiled calmly. "I know all about it, little one. You've been very brave and very strong."

Molly looked down. "I don't have the button jar, Daddy. A man took me before I could go back to my room and get it. Why did he take me, Daddy? Is he your friend?"

"He is not my friend, Molly, and bad things are coming. It's good you don't have the jar."

"Why?"

"Because they want it."

"But why?"

"When I was young like you, I was picked on by other children and had to learn to stand up for myself. My father left when I was young, so I had to do everything on my own. I promised myself that if I ever had children, they would be taken care of. But I'm gone now, and you're going to have to stand up for yourself like I did. Can you do that?"

"I don't know, Daddy."

"You can, Molly. You're stronger than you know. Now I want you to wake up and be strong. They're going to ask you questions that you can't answer, but as long as you don't have the button jar, you're going to be okay."

Molly didn't understand. "What do you mean? Why do they want the jar, Daddy?"

Molly's father vanished as she gasped for air and sat up quickly. "Where am I?" she whispered as she stared out the back window of a car. She turned around and met the eyes of the car's driver in the rearview mirror. They were the eyes of the same man who had helped her out of the quicksand in her dream.

"Well, hello, Ms. McClelland. Welcome back. How was your nap?"

Her father's words echoed in her head, "Bad things are coming. Be strong. Stand up for yourself." Molly lifted her chin in defiance.

The man smiled and shook his head. "I guess I should have expected nothing less from Jimmy McClelland's daughter. I knew your father well, Molly. May I call you Molly?" The man's eyebrows rose in a questioning gesture. Receiving no response, he continued. "Your father and I worked together, Molly. I'm sorry that he died, by the way."

Molly's eyebrows came together as her face reddened in anger. Like a volcano simmers and then slowly rumbles to life, Molly's fury bubbled to the surface. "You know nothing about my father!"

"That's not true, actually. I knew a lot about your father. We worked closely together on several projects, you see. I would even say that he was my friend."

Molly looked down at her hospital gown and wondered why it was shaking. Holding her hand in front of her face, she noted that it was shaking too. Suddenly she realized that her entire body was shaking. Closing her eyes, Molly heard her father's voice from the dream, "He is not my friend. Be strong."

Breathing deeply, Molly opened her eyes, stared out the window, and counted the trees as they drove.

"Molly, who were those people with you in the hospital?"

Molly thought about Julian, Alex, and Jesse. Did they even know she was gone? Were they going to look for her? Julian had promised that he would always be there to help her no matter what. Deciding that Julian would find her, she shrugged and said, "Friends."

She returned her gaze to the rearview mirror and locked eyes with the driver. "They're going to come looking for me, you know."

The man smiled. "There will be no need for that, Molly. I'm going to have you back in the hospital before you know it. This is just a quick trip."

Molly searched the man's eyes as they darted back and forth between the road and her. "I think you're lying, and lying is wrong." Molly hugged her knees to her chest. "They're going to come looking for me, and they're going to find me, and you're going to be in big trouble."

"You think so?" The man shook his head again. "You're something else, Molly McClelland. Your father was right about you. You're a pistol."

Molly didn't know why her father would say that she was a gun but decided against asking. "Do you have clothes for me?"

"Yes, I do. You can change when we arrive at our destination."

Molly looked out the window again. "Where are we going?"

"To a place with toys and fun stuff to do while we wait."

"Wait for what?"

For a second time, the man's eyes danced between the road and Molly. "For information, Molly. You and I are going to read a book together and try to figure out a puzzle."

Molly made a face. Joey loved puzzles. He would sit for hours at a time constructing puzzles and building Legos while Molly would draw or help her mother. Sometimes, she would simply sit with her father in his study while he did "business work." He would set up a writing area for Molly, and she would observe and imitate him. It always made her father smile when she would tap her pen on a pad of paper like he did or chew on the end of a pencil while thinking. She smiled at the memory.

"Doesn't that sound like fun?"

Molly shook her head. "I don't like puzzles."

"Oh, this one is special, Molly. Your father created it for you and me to play and figure out."

Molly scrunched up her face. "My daddy made this puzzle?"

"He sure did, Molly. And I think you hold the key to figuring everything out."

Molly raised her eyebrows. She didn't remember her father ever talking to her about a puzzle. She certainly didn't think that she could help this man.

"Anyway, I'd like you to help me, Molly. The sooner we figure out the puzzle, the sooner you can go back to your friends. I promise."

Molly didn't believe this man. She was so tired. Tears welled up in her eyes and spilled out onto her red cheeks. She frantically wiped them away as quickly as they came because she had to be strong for her father.

The car stopped at a red light, and the man turned around, smiled, and gave her a tissue. Molly snatched the tissue and then remembering her manners, mumbled, "Thank you," as the car moved forward once more.

CHAPTER 47

Julian rushed down the hall as fast as he could tap his cane. "Alex! Alex! What's going on? Where are you?"

"Julian! This way! Down here!" Jesse yelled.

Julian walked faster toward Jesse's voice as Alex spoke urgently but quietly to a nearby nurse. "Listen—a child was just abducted. I don't know what your protocol is for a situation like this, but whatever it is, put it into effect now. Now!" she ordered.

The nurse nodded and picked up the nearest phone. "Code pink. I repeat, code pink!"

Less than four seconds later a voice erupted over the loudspeakers across the entire hospital. "Code pink in effect. Code pink in effect immediately." Before the disembodied voice had completed its transmission, the hallway was abuzz with activity. Nurses, physicians, and non-medical personnel filed through the hallways to predetermined posts. Within minutes, all doors in the building were guarded by sentries whose job was to deny access, in or out.

Alex pulled out her phone and dialed 911. "Alex Hayes, Boston PD. Amber alert from Boston Children's Hospital. Five-year-old female by the name of Molly Elizabeth McClelland. Ginger hair, brown eyes, approximately forty pounds and three-and-a-half-feet tall. All access to the building has been denied, but we need uniforms over here right now!"

A hospital security guard appeared. "Sam Stafford. How can I help?"

Alex placed her hand on the man's shoulder. "Sam, you have two jobs. The first is to make sure, without an iota of a doubt, that every single door is covered. The guy that took Molly may still be here, hiding her somewhere until the hubbub dies down and it's safe to bring her out. Secondly, how many people do you have on your security staff?"

"Fifteen."

"Okay. Your second job is to dispatch your people and have them examine all the nooks and crannies in this place. We want to determine whether or not Molly is still here. Got it?"

"Yes, ma'am." As Sam Stafford turned on his heels, he was already executing Alex's orders over his radio.

Alex took a breath and turned to find Julian standing quietly against a wall. His cane drooped from his right hand. "You okay, Stryker?"

Julian slowly shook his head as he sank to the ground. "No, Alex. I am not okay. I let her down again. I promised I would take care of her, and I let her down again. Oh my God, what have I done?" he trailed off and covered his face with his hands.

Alex knelt in front of him. "Listen—we're going to find her, Stryker. I told Vinny that I wouldn't let anything happen to her, and I won't."

Julian lifted his head and laughed mirthlessly. "What are you talking about, Alex? We *have* let something happen to her. She was kidnapped by the mob, no less!"

"We don't know that, Julian."

Julian vehemently nodded his head. "Yes, Alex, we do know that. And we know what they did to her dad and maybe to the rest of her family too. Do me a favor and call Vinny. We need more than the Boston PD on this."

Keeping one hand on Julian, Alex accessed the favorites screen on her phone and pressed Vinny's name. He answered on the third ring.

"Vinny Marcozzi."

"Vinny, it's Alex."

"Hey, Alex. Twice in one—"

"No time, Vin. You remember I told you about Molly being in the hospital?"

"Yeah, How's she—"

"She's gone. She was taken."

"What? By whom?"

"I think it was the Torchia family, Vin. We could use your help on this."

"How did they know where to find her?"

"Good question. I don't know."

"I'll be there in fifteen minutes."

As Alex ended the call, she heard sirens approaching the hospital. "Vinny will be here soon," she said, patting Julian's arm. "How about you and Jesse go back to Molly's room and wait for me there? I'm going to meet the uniforms downstairs and update them. Then I'll wait for Vinny and bring him back up here."

Julian nodded and stood. "I'm sick about what happened, Alex, but I'm glad you're here to oversee everything."

"I shouldn't have let her go with that man."

Julian shook his head. "No. Don't say that. There's absolutely no way you could have known that he wasn't legit. Taking her down the restricted hallway where he knew you couldn't follow was brilliant. From there, it was easy for him to carry her away. She weighs next to nothing."

"Why did he leave her tiara?" Alex and Julian turned toward Jesse's voice. He sat in the wheelchair twirling the sparkling crown. "Is it because she might no longer need it?" he whispered, choking back a sob. "This kid has been through so, so much. Why can't they just leave her alone?"

Julian made his way to Jesse and knelt next to the chair. "Jesse, I know you care about Buttons. We all do. Alex is going to find her, and when she does, you can be the first person to scoop her up and smother her with love."

Alex knelt on Jesse's other side and whispered. "And while you're hugging Buttons, I'm going to find the man that took her and make him pay. You can count on that."

Jesse turned to face Alex. "Do you remember how lost I was when I first came to work for Julian?"

"I do," Alex said, smiling.

"Me too. I know that's what Buttons is feeling right now. She is completely lost. We are her only family. Do you understand, Alex? Just like you and Julian are my only family. We have to protect her. We have to find her because that's what families do. They protect and love each other, no matter what. Through the good times and bad. Do you understand?" Jesse was crying openly now, the tiara twirling quickly through his fingers.

Alex reached out a hand to still his movement. "I do understand, Jesse, and I promise you—do you hear me? I *promise* you that I will not stop until I find her, okay?"

Jesse's wild eyes examined Alex's and found determination and calm.

He inhaled a staggered breath and wiped his eyes. "Julian and I will wait in Buttons' room until you need us."

As Alex helped Jesse out of the chair and hugged him hard, Julian's cell phone rang. Julian spoke quietly, sighed, and then disengaged from the call.

"Who was that?" Alex asked.

"It was Stacey."

"What did she say?" Jesse urged. "Did she find Buttons' extended family?"

Julian shook his head. "There's no one. You're right, Jess. We truly are Buttons' only family now."

CHAPTER 48

Sweating profusely, Sid sat on the top level of the long-term parking garage at Boston Logan International Airport. The air in his car had reached a stifling one hundred degrees, but he refused to crack a window as he pondered his next move. The Ogre had made it very clear that his escape plan was compromised, and Sid knew he could no longer place his family in harm's way. *He* had chosen to join the FBI. His family had not. It wasn't fair to them that his sins be absolved with their blood.

"How did they know what our escape plan was?" Sid wondered aloud. As he spoke, the answer materialized immediately. "The house is bugged. Our phones are tapped. Jesus." The full realization of his predicament came crashing down as sweat dripped off of his nose onto his wrinkled suit.

Sid picked up his phone and then paused. They could probably hear him speaking on his cell phone or in his car as well. Was the Ogre listening to him right now? Looking around, he exited the car and continued to scan the area to ensure he wasn't being watched. No one wanted to park on the top level during the summer months when temperatures could easily exceed 120 degrees inside the car. Satisfied that he was alone, he popped the trunk and removed a prepaid phone he'd purchased several months earlier. He dialed Kathleen's number and was relieved to hear her voice after two rings.

"Hello?" she ventured even though she did not recognize the caller's number.

"It's me, hon."

"Oh, Sid. Where are you? I'm about to get the kids from school, and then we'll make our way to the airport—"

"Change of plans, Kath."

"What? Why?"

Sid stared out over the airport, appreciating the beauty of planes taking off and landing. Those steel birds, so heavy and awkward on the ground, seemed to have such freedom in the air.

"I can't do this anymore, Kath. I've done some things."

Kathleen held her breath while she waited for her husband of seventeen years to give her something to hold onto. Something she could use to move forward and out of this hellish quagmire that had enveloped them. "Sid, I know you can't tell me exactly what's going on but at least tell me if you're safe."

Sid didn't answer.

"Oh my God. Okay. What do you want me to do?"

"I want you to take the kids and drive south, maybe to Florida. Buy a prepaid cell phone along the way and use it to contact me once you've arrived. Stay in a hotel and pay with cash."

"So we can't be tracked?"

"Yes."

"What about the minivan?"

"It's probably bugged, so you're going to have to ask Ginny Eckersly if you can borrow hers. Tell her yours is in the shop, and you need to make a quick trip to the grocery store or something. We'll figure out a way to reimburse her later."

"When do you want us to leave?"

"It's critical that nothing looks out of the ordinary. Leave your car in our garage so no one can see it. Pick up the kids in Ginny's car, okay? Tell the school they have an appointment or something. Don't even pack a bag, Kath. You can buy what you need when you get there. Not even a toothbrush. And remember, pay only in cash. In fact, leave all of your credit cards at home, understand?"

Kathleen's voice caught as she managed a whispered, "Yes."

"Kath? I love you and the kids more than anything in the world."

Although she was trying to be stoic, tears breached her lids. "I know, Sid. We love you too. When will we see you?"

"I'm not sure, hon. But I want you to know that whatever happens and whatever you hear about me, I did it for the right reasons."

"Sid, you're really scaring me. It's sounding as if you think you may not see us again. Tell me, is it really that bad?"

Sid heard his other cell phone ringing inside the car. Turning toward the sound, he caught his reflection in the car window and was astonished to see an exhausted, haunted face staring back at him through bloodshot eyes. "Yeah, Kath. It's that bad."

***

The Ogre smiled at Molly in the rearview mirror. Her eyes were listless and flitted from the mirror to the window and back again. "This will all be over before you know it," the Ogre said. "I need to make a call, sweetheart, so please be quiet while I'm on the phone, okay?"

Molly nodded and picked at a tear in her hospital gown. She absent-mindedly wondered when the fabric had ripped.

"Hey, Sid. It's me. Just a quick call to let you know that I have a surprise for you that's guaranteed to make you smile. I told you before that I like you, so I wanted to help you out and make your job a little easier. We can't bring Mohammad to the mountain, so I'm bringing the mountain to you." The Ogre laughed. "I never understood what that meant, but I think it kinda fits in this circumstance. Anyway, meet me at the Conley Terminal in Southie in half an hour, and you'll see your surprise. I think we'll be able to wrap this thing up so all of us can get on with our lives, including that beautiful family of yours. See you soon."

"Do you have a surprise for me?" Molly asked.

"What?"

"You have a surprise for the person on the phone, but do you have a surprise for me?"

The Ogre stopped at a red light and turned around in his seat. "You betcha, brown eyes. I've got a big surprise for you." He winked and turned back around, feeling proud of how well things were going. He was sure Sid would be pleased when he realized the lengths to which the Ogre had gone to help him. After all, that's what friends were for.

CHAPTER 49

Vinny swore under his breath as traffic crawled along Storrow Drive. After his phone call with Alex, Vinny had told Marcie he would be gone for a while and had instructed her to put all of his calls into his voicemail. Having worked with Vinny for several years, Marcie had recognized Vinny's stress level and had accepted his orders without question.

Vinny tapped the steering wheel with his left thumb while his right hand danced on his thigh. As he was contemplating how he might circumvent traffic and wind through Back Bay toward the hospital, his cell phone chirped loudly and made Vinny jump. He scooped it up from the passenger's seat and swiped the screen to answer it. "Vinny Marcozzi."

"Hiya, handsome. How goes your day?" Annabelle's perky tone was at once endearing and irritating.

"From the sound of your voice, it seems as if your day's going much better than mine."

"I'm having a great day, actually, but I'm sorry you're not. What's going on?"

"Well, let's see, where to begin? My day started with Sid lying outright to my face, followed by a visit to Winchester Hospital to see Kellie Moser, who's most likely going to be paralyzed and informed me that she was not having an affair with Jimmy McClelland. After that, I found out that Jimmy's daughter, the only surviving member of his family, has been kidnapped from Boston Children's Hospital, where I'm currently in route to now, except that I'm stuck on Storrow Drive in so much fucking traffic, my car hasn't moved in five minutes!"

Annabelle remained silent as Vinny closed his eyes and inhaled deeply, held the breath, and then released it slowly. "Feel better?"

A smile crept to Vinny's lips. "A little, thanks. But seriously, Annabelle, this has been one of the shittiest days in a string of shitty days."

Annabelle's voice dropped seductively. "What can I do to make it better?"

Vinny's interest was piqued, along with his man parts. "What did you have in mind?"

"How about I just show you tonight?"

"Sounds amazing. Why is your day so good anyway?"

"I just finished deposing someone, and it went better than expected. Chris said that I might be looking at a promotion if things keep going this well."

"Wow! High praise from the DA, Annabelle."

"Did you know that Chris isn't running in 2020?"

"No, I didn't know that."

"That's not public knowledge yet, so please don't say anything."

Vinny fully digested the implications of what Annabelle was going out of her way *not* to say. "Wait a minute, are you thinking about running for the office of Suffolk County District Attorney?"

Annabelle hummed on the other end of the line.

"Does Chris think you can win?"

Annabelle lowered her voice almost to a whisper. "With his endorsement, yes."

"And he's planning on endorsing you?"

"Uh-huh. Can you believe it?"

Vinny smiled as traffic started to move again. "Of course I can believe it. You're incredibly talented. I've been telling you that since I met you. But are you sure you want to get into politics?"

Annabelle laughed. "Vinny, what makes you think I haven't been playing politics since I took the ADA job several years ago? This has been a dream of mine since I was a little girl. One step at a time, I've built a resume and a group of loyal supporters and donors who are willing to help me make my dream a reality, for the betterment of Suffolk County, Massachusetts, and the United States."

"Wow! You sound like you're already on the stump, but why am I not surprised? And what's after the DA position?"

"What do you mean?"

"C'mon, Annabelle. You're not going to stop there, are you?"

Annabelle laughed. "Like I said, Vin, one step at a time. But really, who knows? Maybe the White House isn't out of reach. You gotta start somewhere, right? And maybe, just maybe, if you play your cards right, you might end up as director of the FBI."

"Oh yeah?" Vinny laughed.

"I said 'maybe,' if you're nice to me."

"I'll show you how nice I'm going to be later tonight."

"That's a good start."

CHAPTER 50

Jesse sat on the bed in Buttons' hospital room and hugged her pillow to his chest. Leaning his chin on the pillow, he smiled. "Julian, I can still smell her on the pillow."

"We'll get her back, Jesse."

"How can you be so sure?"

"Because Alex won't stop until she finds her, and Vinny's on his way here as well."

Jesse nodded and stood, replacing the pillow as he spoke. "Who was the guy that took her? The orderly. How did he even get in here?"

"Was he wearing a badge, Jess? What did he look like?"

Jesse closed his eyes and tried to remember. "Average height, dark hair, fiftyish. He was wearing a badge attached with a clip to the bottom of his shirt, but I couldn't see his name."

"It was probably stolen anyway."

"Maybe he actually does work for the hospital."

"Maybe. But it's more likely that Buttons was taken by the same people that killed her father, and maybe the rest of her family as well."

"What do you mean?"

Julian hesitated a second too long.

"Oh my God, Julian. What are you *not* telling me?"

"Don't freak out, Jess, but Alex told me that Buttons' father was the head accountant for the Torchia family."

As Jesse leaned toward Julian, his eyes were like saucers. "Are you fucking kidding me right now?" Jesse's voice rose as he raked his fingers through his hair. "The mob?"

"Sh, Jesse! Stop it! I told you not to freak out! That's not going to help anyone."

Jesse paced the room. "Let me get this straight. Molly McClelland's dad worked for the mob, and the day after her entire family was demolished, she was kidnapped? Jesus, you can't make this stuff up, Julian."

"It's just a theory, Jess. It could be something completely unrelated."

Jesse violently shook his head. "No, no. I think you're probably right. Is that why Vinny's coming? Because the mob's involved?"

Julian nodded with his arms crossed over his chest.

"If it was the mob, how did they know she was here?"

"I don't know. Vinny asked the same question," Alex said as she entered the room out of breath. "Okay. All exits are manned by local law enforcement. Sam Stafford, the head of hospital security, has dispatched all of his officers to various areas of the building to search. Maybe the guy who took her is hiding somewhere until it's safe to bring her out."

"Do you think that's the case?"

Alex placed her hand on Julian's shoulder. "Honestly, no. I think he took her and ran, but we have to be thorough."

"What about airports, train stations, and bus depots?" Jesse asked.

"An amber alert has been disseminated to the entire New England region, so any places like that have been notified."

"How can we help, Alex?"

"I have a sketch artist coming here to draw a picture of the guy who took her so we can post it as soon as possible. Jesse, can you focus on that?"

"Sure. Absolutely."

"Julian, is there anything you remember about the man who took Buttons?"

"He was wearing funny shoes."

Alex cocked her head. "What do you mean?"

"At the time, it didn't really strike me as odd, but looking back, I should have realized something was a little off. Health-care workers tend to wear clogs, which have a distinctive heavy clop, clop sound to them. Or they wear sneakers, which squeak, or Crocs, which are almost silent.

"But this guy's shoes clicked on the floor tile like ..." Julian turned to Jesse. "Like those expensive Italian leather shoes you like to wear, Jess. I remember hearing the clicking on the floor and thought it was interesting that a health-care worker—someone who's on his feet all day—would wear shoes like that. But it was one of those passing thoughts you have, you know? In and out of your head in an instant."

Alex patted Julian's arm. "That's good, Stryker. That's good. Anything else?"

"His voice was gravelly, and he had a distinct Revere accent."

"Revere, Massachusetts has its own accent?"

"Of course, Alex. All of the Boston towns have slight but distinct differences in their residents' speech patterns."

"Okay. Good to know. I'll add the shoe and accent information to the amber alert."

"Speaking of expensive Italian shoes, here comes Vinny." Julian smiled. "I can hear his loafers clicking down the hallway."

Vinny knocked and entered. "Hey guys. Sorry it took so long. Traffic was awful."

Alex hugged Vinny and pinched his cheek. "Look at you. You look great. Tired but great."

Vinny made the rounds with hugs to everyone. "So, what's the story here?"

Alex updated Vinny on the last thirty-six hours, finishing with Julian's observations of the kidnapper.

"If Molly's abductor is with the Italian mob, then the Revere accent would make sense. There's a huge Italian population in that town," Vinny noted.

"You had mentioned on the phone that one of your guys might somehow be involved with Jimmy McClelland's death," Alex said.

Vinny stuffed his hands into his pockets. "Yeah. A guy named Sid Nickerson. He was Jimmy's handler for the last six months, and recently he's been acting really squirrelly. I wanted to talk to you first and understand the situation here, but my next stop is Sid's house. If he is involved in Jimmy's death, he might know more about the rest of the McClelland family, including where Molly might have been taken."

Vinny turned his attention to Jesse, who was twirling something in his hand that was catching sunlight from the window and creating prisms across the walls. "What's that, Jess?"

Jesse looked down at the tiara in his hand. "Oh, this is Buttons' tiara.

She left it when she was taken …" Jesse trailed off as the words caught in his throat.

Julian rose and crossed to where Jesse sat on the bed. Rubbing his friend's back, he said, "Between the tiara and her jar of buttons, that's all that little girl had left in the world that meant anything to her."

Vinny picked up the jar and tilted it toward the light. "What's with the buttons anyway?"

Alex smiled sadly. "Her father had given her the buttons from his dry-cleaning stores. They meant so much to her because they reminded her of her father. She even told us that she had a dream in which her father told her how important they were."

Vinny nodded, gently replacing the jar on the nightstand. "Kids are funny, aren't they?"

"Alex, where's that key that you found at my house?"

"What key?" Jesse asked.

"The button jar spilled on the floor in the living room while Buttons was watching TV with Oscar, and Alex found a key that looked like it belonged to a diary or something."

Alex thought for a moment. "I think it's still on the dining room table at your house, Stryker."

"Do you think the key could help us?" Vinny asked.

"I don't know. Buttons didn't seem to know what it went to, but it was in her button jar, so it must hold some significance. If not to her, then to her father."

Sam Stafford appeared in the doorway and glanced at each person in the room. "Detective? May I have a word?"

"Of course." Alex made introductions and told Sam to speak freely.

"We found a male nurse passed out in a storage room, propped up against the door. He'd been hit from behind, and his ID badge had been taken. His name is Zach Casciano, and he claims to know nothing about the kidnapping. I'll let you talk to him, but he seems to be telling the truth. He was in the wrong place at the wrong time, that's all."

"Or maybe he's part of the Torchia family and told them she was here," Alex grumbled.

"He was hit from behind, Alex. I doubt he's involved."

"Jesse, I've seen people allow themselves to be shot in order for a scene to look convincing. Trust me. He's probably in on the kidnapping."

Jesse stood. "Did you find any evidence that Molly might still be in the building?"

The large man shook his head, "No, sir. Nothing yet, but all exits continue to be blocked. If she's here, we'll find her."

"And if she's not?" Jesse asked, turning to Alex with pleading eyes.

Alex set her mouth in a grim, tight line. "Then I'll find her."

CHAPTER 51

Molly was jolted awake by a brain-numbing, screeching sound. She squinted at the sunlight bouncing off of the windows, covered her ears with her hands, and spoke over the noise. "What is that awful sound?"

"Sorry, hon. It's just the metal gates opening. They need some WD-40 or something, but no one's around anymore to take care of that sort of thing. Cutbacks."

Molly yawned and looked out the window. There was a large sign that was secured to the fence which surrounded the property. It had large letters on it, and she recognized the name. "Hey, that's my friend's name."

The driver turned around. "Wow, kid, you can read? Aren't you young to be reading?"

Molly rolled her eyes. "I can't read books, but I know what my friend's name looks like. Those letters are the same as her name: C-o-n-l-e-y."

"You mean her last name, right?"

Molly shook her head. "No, her first name."

The driver turned back around and steered through the open gate, mumbling about how kids had strange first names these days.

Molly leaned toward the window to follow the neck of an incredibly large crane to its head. The machine reminded her of a giraffe she had seen in the Boston Zoo when she had last visited with her mom and Joey. She and her brother had been chosen to feed the giraffe. As they had climbed twenty-eight steps (she had counted), she became fearful that the giraffe might harm her. The keeper had been very kind and patient and had coached her to extend her hand. Molly had been awestruck as the animal's black, impossibly long tongue had wrapped around her small arm before finding its way down to the lettuce in her hand. She had giggled as saliva dripped down and tickled her arm.

Turning her attention back to the crane, she watched, mesmerized, as the mouth gently placed a metal box atop a pile of other metal boxes. The boxes reminded Molly of her brother's Legos, which he snapped together to form larger units. "What is this place?"

The man looked in the rearview mirror and smiled. "You like it?"

"Uh-huh. It's cool."

"It's a shipping yard. Stuff comes in from all over the world."

"Why?"

The man shrugged. "People need things, Molly. Sometimes from other countries. Lots of things come through here. Cars, refrigerators, washing machines, and toys."

Molly smiled. "What kinds of toys? Legos?"

"Absolutely."

Molly nodded. That made sense to her.

"Here we are."

Molly's inquisitive, adventurous mood morphed into cautiousness as the car slowed. "Where are you taking me?"

"Just inside this building." The man put the car in park and shut off the engine. After unfastening his seat belt, he turned to find Molly shrinking against the back seat with her knees drawn up against her body and hands covering her head in a protective posture.

"Hey, hey, sweetheart, listen." Molly drew her hands down just enough to see the man looking at her with concern in his eyes. "I'm not going to hurt you. I promise. I could never do that. I told you before. You're here to play a game with me, and then I'm going to take you back to the hospital—back to your friends. Okay?"

Molly wanted to trust this man, but her father's words danced through her mind like a song on repeat. Her eyes betrayed her equivocation, and the man sighed. "Molly, you're a smart girl, so I think you understand that this is going to happen, one way or another. So let's decide together that we're going to have fun, okay?"

Molly's eyes bored into the man's. "Are you having fun right now?"

The man's shoulders fell as he glanced about his surroundings. After a time, he sighed heavily once more. "No, Molly, I am definitely not having fun right now. But let's go inside, get you some clothes and something to eat, and then we can play our game."

CHAPTER 52

Vinny stared absent-mindedly at the car ahead of him at the stop light. Ironically, it was a blue Toyota, and Vinny was reminded of Sid's dishonesty. Although Sid had not been in a car accident, he *had been* seriously wounded. Vinny wondered if Sid had been compromised in some way and vowed to get answers when he spoke with him again.

The light changed, and Vinny crept forward slowly, trying to get onto Route 1 from Storrow Drive. He was on his way to visit Sid at his home in Melrose. It was bad enough that Sid had lied to Vinny, but now a little girl's life was in jeopardy, and Vinny was convinced that Sid had some information pertaining to her disappearance. Even if he didn't, perhaps he could provide some guidance with regard to how Vinny should proceed in the search.

Vinny's phone buzzed, and he touched the answer button. "Vinny Marcozzi."

"Vinny, Chris Smith, it's been forever. How are you?"

It took Vinny a moment to realize to whom he was speaking. "I'm well, Mr. District Attorney, very well. You?"

"I'm great actually. I have a real go-getter working for me and making me look good."

Vinny chuckled. "Yeah, she makes everybody look good."

Now it was Chris's turn to laugh. "She talks about you a lot. Did you know that?"

Vinny was shocked. "Annabelle talks about me in the office?"

"Well, not to everyone, but she talks about you with me. You two seem to have a good thing going. Don't screw it up, Marcozzi."

"Is that why you're calling me, Chris? To tell me to take care of Annabelle?"

He paused. "Well, yes. That and to find out what you have on the McClelland case."

Vinny balked. "You gotta be kidding me, Chris. I've come to you at least a half dozen times asking for help on federal cases, only to have you tell me to go fuck myself. Now you want federal help to bring down the biggest fish in your career? No way."

"Whoa, whoa, my friend. Why so hostile? I just thought I'd ask, that's all. We can do it on our own, but it might be easier if we had some help. I was thinking maybe you had some information we didn't."

"You didn't get enough from Jimmy working with you guys in exchange for full immunity? I would've thought that he'd have given you enough information to burn down the Torchia house."

"Well, like I said, we have a lot, but we can always use more. I thought that perhaps you and Annabelle had discussed working together in a more professional capacity, but I guess not."

"Is that what she said?"

"Not in so many words, but she indicated that you might be open to an arrangement."

Vinny thought back to his pillow talk with Annabelle and tried to discern if he had inadvertently offered the idea or missed an invitation. "Does she know you're calling me?"

"No."

"How is it that you allowed your ADA to authorize full immunity without your consent, by the way? Who's running your office, you or Annabelle?"

The comment drew a long whistle from Chris, followed by a deep breath. When he spoke again, his volume was so low that Vinny found himself leaning toward his speaker to hear. "I never burn bridges. I never speak before having thought it through. And I never, *never* turn my back on an opportunity."

Vinny whispered back. "What the hell opportunity are you talking about?"

"Annabelle."

Vinny squinted in confusion. "You have an opportunity with Annabelle? I'm confused. Are you calling because you're interested in dating her, Chris? If so, you—" Chris blew out air on the phone. "No,

I'm talking about—you really don't know, do you?" Chris chuckled. "You work for the fucking FBI, and you didn't research the love of your life? Are you kidding me?"

Vinny set his jaw in a tight line as beads of perspiration broke out on his forehead.

"Do you know who Annabelle's great uncle is, Vinny? Paolo Torchia, that's who. I guess she never mentioned it. I let her get away with offering full immunity to Jimmy because I knew that with her intimate knowledge of the family, she would close the deal."

Vinny was astounded. How had he missed it? Thinking back, they had discussed their immediate families, but they hadn't gone past that. They had been too busy screwing each other. Maybe while Annabelle was screwing Vinny, she was *screwing* him. How much had he told her about his cases? Was there any possibility she was working both sides?

Vinny gave his concerns voice, and Chris laughed outright. "No way, man. She's a straight arrow. If she was working you for information, it was simply to further her own case and her own career." As if reading Vinny's mind, Chris added, "And she really, genuinely talks about you a lot, Vin. She really likes you."

Vinny's head was spinning. "So why did you call me again?"

"Just to see if you'd like to get together to discuss what each of our offices has on the Torchias. Maybe we can help each other."

Vinny didn't know what to think or how to feel. "Uh, let me think about it and get back to you, okay?"

"Sure, yeah, Vinny. Sounds good. Don't be a stranger. Bye."

Still analyzing the call, Vinny watched the blue Toyota in front of him veer off an exit on the right. He realized too late that he should have turned there as well. "Dammit!" He continued to the next exit and turned right, using back roads to wind his way to Sid's house.

At the intersection across from the entrance to Sid's neighborhood, he thought he recognized Sid's wife driving a minivan directly across from him. He waved at her, and as she raised her hand to wave back, recognition crossed her countenance, and she quickly lowered her hand and stared straight ahead. When the light changed, she sped by Vinny without looking at him. *That was weird*, Vinny thought, as he continued to Sid's house.

Vinny had visited the Nickerson household only twice during Sid's tenure with the bureau. The first time was for a family picnic, and the second time was for a brunch after a colleague's funeral. He recognized it immediately, however, because the yard had Sid's fingerprints all over it- a neatly trimmed hedge, color-coordinated flower bunches, and grass that was cut just so. Vinny smiled at the pride he knew Sid felt at keeping his house and his family organized and safe.

Then his smile died as he remembered why he was there. He was relieved that Kathleen wasn't home so he and Sid could get to the bottom of Sid's dishonesty.

Vinny exited the car and approached the sunshine yellow front door. Knocking loudly, he glanced through the windows on either side of the door as he called Sid's name several times.

"They're not home."

Vinny turned to find an overweight woman wearing gardening gloves and sporting a hose. Using her wrist to push long bangs out of her eyes, she added, "You just missed Kathleen. She borrowed my car 'cause hers is in the shop."

"Thank you, Miss ..."

"Eckersly. *Mrs.* Eckersly, actually. Who are you?"

"A friend of Sid's. Is he home, by the way?"

Mrs. Eckersly examined Vinny carefully. "No, like I said, they're not home. Sid's at work like he usually is during the day. What did you say your name was?"

Vinny smiled broadly. "I didn't, Mrs. Eckersly, but the name's Vinny. I think I'll look for Sid at work. Thanks for your help though."

As Vinny walked back to his car, he glanced in the garage window. Sid's car was there. It was completely undamaged, and the minivan was beside it. "You're sure Sid isn't home, Mrs. Eckersly?" Vinny called out to the neighbor who had recommended watering her flowers.

"Yes, I saw him leave this morning."

"And you said that Kathleen borrowed your car because hers is in the shop?"

Mrs. Eckersly widened her eyes and nodded her head slowly, as if she was speaking to an idiot. "That's what I said."

"What kind of car does Kathleen drive?"

The neighbor abruptly stopped watering and faced Vinny. "A black Chrysler Town and Country minivan. Why are you asking all of these questions?"

Vinny examined the minivan in the garage. It was a black Chrysler Town and Country minivan.

"Just wondering. Thanks, Mrs. Eckersly. Have a great day."

CHAPTER 53

The man opened Molly's car door and extended his hand toward her. Ignoring the gesture, Molly scooted out of the car and crossed her arms snugly across her chest. Stealing an upward glance at the man, she found him gazing at a large metal building with a worried look settling into his features.

"What's wrong?"

He turned to her and knelt down. "Okay, Molly. You need to be polite and answer any questions that are asked of you. If you don't know the answer, don't lie or make something up. Just say you don't know, okay?"

"You're scaring me," she replied as she pressed herself against the car.

"No, no, it's nothing like that, honey. Just ... just—"

"Be myself."

The man's face broke into a lopsided grin. "Yeah, do that. Be yourself. Okay, let's go. Follow me and stay close." The man offered his hand once more. Molly considered it and then squinted up at the man's face, whose grin remained fixed. Twisting her mouth, she slipped her hand into his. It felt rough and huge. It was nothing like her daddy's hands, which fit hers perfectly and were really soft.

Gravel crunched under her feet, and at one point. she stopped to remove a pebble from between her toes. "We'll get you some shoes inside," the man stated as he helped her brush off her feet. "How about I carry you the rest of the way?" Before she could protest, the man swept her into his arms, and despite herself, a giggle escaped.

"Oh, you like that?" As he walked he threw Molly up into the air and caught her, letting his arms drop precariously low to the ground in the process. Each time he laughed with her as her hands rose and fell in rhythm with her body.

They approached the large metal doors, and the man suddenly stopped and placed Molly on the ground next to him. Molly's laugh died in her throat as she saw an even larger man glaring at them from the open door. "Took you long enough," he growled. Pointing at Molly, he said, "So *this* is what all the fuss is about?"

Molly shrank back and clutched the man's hand. Her father's words of warning were all but forgotten. The man holding her hand might not have been her father's friend, but right now, he was being nice to her.

"Stop it! You're scaring her." To Molly he said, "It's okay, Molly. Ignore him. He's just a dumb jerk." Molly wanted to remind the man not to call people names, but her mouth wouldn't form any words.

"Get in here. He's waiting for you."

The dramatic change from bright sunlight to relative darkness made Molly blink as she entered the cavernous space. She walked quickly in an effort to keep pace with the man, whose mood had changed once more. His hand was squeezing hers as they rounded a corner and climbed a set of metal stairs. At the top of the stairs, they took a sharp right and traversed a walkway that Molly could see through. She examined all of the people working below who were watching her closely.

"Almost there, honey."

Molly looked up at the man to say something and tripped. As she fell, one of her legs draped over the side of the metal walkway, and the man grabbed her hospital gown to retrieve her. The man gasped and covered his face with one hand while gripping her gown with the other.

"Oh my god, Molly. Don't do that!"

Molly looked down as a tear trickled down her cheek. "I didn't mean to. It's just that you're walking fast, and my feet hurt." Although her daddy had told her not to complain, she was tired and scared and didn't know whom to trust.

The man wiped the tear away. "I'm not mad, Molly. I was just scared, that's all. I'm sorry I spoke loudly. You're the bravest girl I know. Hang in there."

Molly sniffled and then stood once more with her head held high. Ahead of them, a door opened, and from it emerged a woman with a lot of hair and too much lipstick. "Hiya, hon. Come here and let's get you dressed."

Molly grabbed the man's hand and shook her head. The man pulled his hand free from hers and said, "It's okay, Molly. This is my friend, Sheri. She'll take good care of you. Go with her and get some clothes on, okay?"

Molly hesitated. Not seeing a way out of it, she walked toward the woman's outstretched arms. "You probably don't remember me, but we've met before. In fact, we had so much fun together you were calling me Aunt Sheri. Do you remember?"

Molly looked skeptical, and the woman laughed. "Of course not. You were too young. Your daddy and I were friends. We worked together."

Molly perked up. "At the dry-cleaning stores?"

"Yeah, yeah. There and here," the woman gestured to the large space. "Lots of places." Molly's eyes followed Sheri's hands as they swept across the open space.

"Where am I?"

"Oh, this is just a warehouse where we keep stuff until we move it somewhere else."

Molly looked at the workers moving wooden boxes using little trucks that had flat metal arms sticking out of their fronts. "What kind of stuff?"

Sheri patted Molly's head. "Jimmy was right. You are a curious one, aren't you? Come with me."

Molly followed Sheri into a bathroom that looked old and smelled bad. She pinched her nose to block the odor.

"I know. It's awful, right? You'd think they'd do better for the one woman that works for them, but they don't. I've complained and complained, and nothing changes. Here are some clothes for you."

Molly accepted the clothes and entered the stall to change. The shirt was too small and looked babyish, but she knew better than to complain. The pants fit in the waist but were two inches too long. She pulled them away from the floor as she exited the stall to find Sheri filing her nails.

"Oh, Jesus, hon, look at those pants. You're a tiny one, ain't ya?" Sheri knelt down and rolled up the pant legs so Molly could walk.

"Do you have shoes for me? The man said you'd have shoes."

Sheri pulled out a pair of lime green crocs from the bag that was on her shoulder. Although they were way too big, Molly was grateful she wouldn't have to feel either gravel or cold metal under her feet anymore. "Thank you."

Sheri shook her head as she took in Molly's appearance. Removing a brush from her oversized bag, she drew it gently through Molly's hair and then tied it up with an elastic. "You sure are cute. I'll give you that. Let's go."

Molly didn't move. "Where are we going now?"

"To meet the big guy, hon."

"And play games?"

"What?"

"The man said that we'd play some games."

Sheri's shoulders slumped, and she looked sad. "Sure, hon, to play some games. C'mon."

Molly didn't know why she was there or what was going to happen, but she knew one thing for sure. This woman was lying, and lying was bad.

CHAPTER 54

After exhausting all possible hiding places in and around the hospital, Alex instructed Sam Stafford and the rest of the hospital security team to call it quits on the search for Molly. Alex had personally questioned Zach Casciano, the nurse whose badge had been taken. Although she was fairly certain he was involved in some way and wanted to arrest him on suspicion of involvement in a kidnapping, she'd been unable to find any hard evidence or extract any information from him that would be useful in finding Molly.

The local BOLO was still in effect, as was the national Amber Alert, and Alex was certain that the man who had taken Molly was nowhere near the hospital campus. Alex thanked the security force for their time, effort, and professionalism and requested that they not discuss the missing child with friends or family in an effort to maintain some control over the case. Director of Security Stafford asked Alex to keep him updated on the search for Molly, as he felt responsible for her disappearance. Alex smiled, shook his hand, thanked him once more, and promised to keep him in the loop.

Sam Stafford and his colleagues exited, leaving Alex, Jesse, and Julian alone in Molly's hospital room.

"What do we do now?" Jesse asked.

Alex turned to Jesse, who sat on Molly's bed hugging a pillow. "I think you two should go to Julian's house and get the key I found the other day. It's the only lead we have. That key and the damn button jar. There's got to be something important in that jar."

Jesse nodded. "Okay. At least we'll be doing something."

"Where are you going, Alex?"

Alex turned to Julian. "I need to complete the paperwork related to Molly's abduction. You know it's not official until there's paperwork to back it up."

"As if Molly weren't really taken?"

"Exactly. She has not officially been taken until the paperwork says so."

Julian spread his arms wide, and Alex went in for a hug. "After you finish your paperwork, come to my house, okay?"

"I'll be there as soon as I can."

Julian held her longer than necessary.

"Oh, I know that look. I'll get the car, Alex. Bring him down when you're done." Jesse grabbed the button jar and left the room.

"Your hair smells good. You feel different."

Alex smiled into his shirt. "What do you mean?"

Julian made a face as she drew back and looked up at him. "I don't know how exactly, but you feel different."

"Bad different? Fat different? I think I've gained some weight."

"No, no. Just … different. It's probably your body reacting to extreme stress, Alex. Nothing to worry about."

Alex chuckled mirthlessly. "Sure, Stryker. Nothing to worry about. We only have an orphan who was entrusted to our care and has been abducted by the mob. No stress there."

"Sh, Alex, breathe. You'll work better, smarter, and faster if you breathe." They breathed together for several moments. "We're going to find Buttons. I feel it. I know it."

Alex looked at the man who knew her better than anyone else on the planet. She placed both hands on either side of his face and kissed him. "I love you, Stryker. Thanks."

"For what?"

Alex shrugged in his embrace. "For everything. For being there whenever I need you. For understanding me. For being … you. It's just who you are."

Julian nodded. "I am pretty special, aren't I?"

Alex pushed him away and playfully hit his chest. "And … there goes our beautiful moment. I'll bring you downstairs."

Alex walked Julian to the car where Jesse was waiting. "I'll be over as soon as I can. Call me if you find anything related to the button jar or key."

Jesse nodded as he placed the button jar in Julian's lap. "Got it. See you soon."

As they pulled away from the curb, Jesse chewed the inside of his cheek. "I'm really worried about Buttons, Julian."

"I am too, Jess, but the reality is that the man who took her probably needs her."

"What do you mean?"

"Chances are we're not dealing with a run-of-the-mill wacko who took her for his own enjoyment. If the guy works for the mob, he took her because he needs her."

"For what?"

"I don't know. As a negotiating tool perhaps."

Jesse cringed. "What does *that* mean?"

"I'm just guessing, Jess, but maybe whoever has her is going to use her life as leverage in a negotiation. Or, maybe ..."

Jesse waited impatiently. "Or what, Julian?"

"Or maybe she has knowledge she doesn't know she has. Maybe the mob knows that she knows something that she doesn't know that she knows. You know?"

Jesse rolled his eyes. "Julian, she's five years old. What information could she possibly have?"

Julian smiled. "She's no normal five-year-old, Jesse. You'd agree with that, right?"

"Yeah, for sure."

"She was very close to her father, so perhaps he shared some information with her without her even knowing. I'm convinced that button jar holds the key. Pun intended."

"If what you say is true, then as long as she doesn't tell them what they need to know, she's safe, right?"

"In theory, yes."

"On the flip side of that argument, if she gives them the information they need without knowing it, then she may make herself vulnerable because she'll no longer be necessary."

Julian nodded. "Or she may know nothing, and they may bargain with her life, as I first suggested."

"Either way, it's bad."

"Either way, it's really bad."

CHAPTER 55

Vinny's jaw was working overtime as he chomped on the three pieces of gum he had stuffed in his mouth after leaving Sid's house. Kathleen Nickerson's minivan sat parked in the garage, and she had lied to her neighbor in order to borrow her car. That meant only one thing to Vinny. She was running. And Sid was either going to run with her or follow her later. Vinny knew that Sid had kids and that he and Kathleen would never leave without their children. If Kathleen was running, she had to get her kids first.

Vinny pressed "Marcie work" on his cell phone, and she answered on the second ring.

"Hey, Vin, what's up?"

"What are Sid's kids' names?"

"Annie and Joshua."

"Where do they go to school?"

"I don't know. Want me to look it up?"

"Yes please. Hurry, Marcie." Vinny tapped the steering wheel as he listened to Marcie's fingers flying across her keyboard.

"Catholic Memorial on Baker Street."

"Thanks." Vinny disconnected the call as he pulled a U-turn in the middle of the road. His only chance of getting to Sid was to catch up with Kathleen.

As he drove, he commanded Siri to dial Sid's number. Sid's voice came on the line asking the caller to leave a name and number. After the beep, Vinny tried to sound normal as he said, "Hey, Sid. It's Vin. Just checking in to see how you're doing. I hope you're at home resting. We miss you and want you back in the thick of it soon. Call me when you get this."

As he disconnected the call, he tried to imagine what might make a man like Sid Nickerson turn against everything he had ever known and believed in. Money? Vinny didn't think so, unless Sid was hiding some serious gambling debt or—Vinny laughed out loud at this—another family somewhere in Connecticut. If someone was to ask Vinny who the least likely person was to break the code of ethics, he would have named Sid. No, it had to be something bigger than himself. Vinny would have thought Sid's family was in trouble, but he had seen Kathleen with his own eyes. Maybe the kids were in some sort of trouble?

Vinny's thoughts drifted to Annabelle. He reviewed his last conversation with her boss, Chris Smith. Chris had assured Vinny that Annabelle spoke often of him, but Vinny was still uneasy. He had fallen hard and fast for her. Was it possible he'd missed some warning signs? Chris had assured him that she wasn't using him to further her career, but now Vinny wasn't so sure. Why hadn't she mentioned her connection to the Torchia family, especially when she knew that Vinny's team had been investigating and building a case against them? Shit, she shouldn't even be involved. She should have recused herself early on. Vinny shook his head, wondering if she'd broken any laws in her quest for greatness.

His attention shifted when he saw the car Kathleen had been driving parked in front of Catholic Memorial School. He pulled in behind the minivan and waited. Within minutes, Kathleen exited the building with her two children in tow. They each wore a look of worry as Kathleen spoke fast and gesticulated with her hands. Vinny got out of his car and leaned against the passenger door with his arms crossed. "Hey, Kathleen."

Kathleen Nickerson stopped short and instinctively reached out both hands to touch her children, who stood on each side of her wearing confused expressions. She didn't respond but started pulling on the kids' clothes in an effort to steer them toward the minivan.

The boy stared at Vinny and then at the car Kathleen was driving. "Who's car is this, Mom?"

Vinny smiled. "Where are you going, Kathleen?"

"Um, to the doctor's office. The kids have their physicals today."

"We do?"

"Yes, hon. Now get in the car."

"Isn't this Mrs. Eckersly's car? Why do you have her car?"

"Mine's in the shop. Get in please, Josh."

Vinny shook his head. "Your car is in your garage, Kathleen."

Kathleen's eyes narrowed, and she closed the distance between them in three strides. "If you have something to say to me, say it. Otherwise, leave me and my family alone! Get in the car, kids."

As she walked quickly to the minivan, Vinny said, "I can help you, Kathleen. The bureau protects its own."

Kathleen, who had opened the driver's door, stared hard at Vinny. A humorless smile formed on her face. Slowly, she shook her head. "I don't think so. If I have to choose between my husband and the bureau, I'm going to choose my husband every time." She hoisted herself into the driver's seat.

Vinny came to stand next to the driver's door. "I need to find Sid, Kathleen. It's a matter of life and death."

Kathleen paused with her hand poised on the armrest, ready to close the car door.

"Who's life?"

Vinny leaned in and whispered, "I know you're a smart person, and I know that Sid is a really good person. But something's going on that's making Sid act different. He's not making good decisions, and I'm worried about him. Also, there's a little girl's life at stake."

Kathleen glared at him and then turned her gaze downward as she thought. Vinny interpreted that as a good sign and continued. "This little girl's name is Molly, and she's five years old. She's been kidnapped, and I think Sid is involved somehow."

Kathleen's eyes flared. She glanced at her children, who were engrossed in their phones, and then got out of the car, slamming the door. "You listen here," she hissed. "My husband is a good man. He would never, *never* do *anything* to harm a child!" She was shaking now, and angry tears were forming in her eyes. The finger she had been pointing at Vinny fell limply to her side as she dropped her arm. "But you're right. Something is going on, and he hasn't told me what it is."

Vinny softened his tone. "What has he told you, Kathleen? Do you know where he is?"

Kathleen's shoulders slumped, and she shook her head. "No. I think he hasn't told me on purpose. He always says the less I know about his work, the better."

Vinny nodded. That's how he would do it if he ever had a wife. Ignorance equals safety. Hell, he had shared information with Annabelle, and look where it had gotten him.

"What's the little girl's name again?"

"Molly."

Kathleen smiled through her tears. "That's a cute name."

"Think, Kathleen. What did Sid tell you?"

She shuddered and sighed. "He told me to take the neighbor's car and to drive south, to use only cash, and to bring nothing but the kids with me. He said he would meet us when he could."

"That's it?"

"That's it, but he's been acting really strange recently. He's been asking me if he's a good man. Things like that. I'm really scared because I've never seen him like this." As she swiped at her tears, new ones formed and took their place.

Her son knocked on the window and said, "Hurry up, Mom, or we'll be late to the doctor."

Kathleen shook her head. "What am I going to tell the kids?"

Vinny blew out air. "I'm not a dad, Kathleen, but I think they're old enough to hear the truth or some of it at least."

"And what exactly is the truth?"

"That their father has been working a case that requires his complete attention. For their safety, the bureau has asked them to leave town for a while."

A wan smile formed on Kathleen's face. "You clearly don't have kids. That explanation would invite more questions."

Vinny shrugged. "You're probably right. But if you don't want to come with me, and Sid told you to get out of town, he must have had a good reason. If I see Sid, I'll tell him that you and the kids are safe and are following his instructions."

Kathleen took both of Vinny's hands in her own. "You've always been good to Sid. I thank you for that. If he's done something that violated the law or bureau policy, you know as well as I do that he had a damned good reason to do it. Remember that."

"Please let me know if he gets in touch with you, Kathleen." Vinny extended his business card, to which she held up her hand. "I know the number, and we both know that I won't be calling."

Kathleen nodded once and got in the car. As they pulled away, Sid's daughter turned around and stared at Vinny. *She understands on some level that she's not returning home,* Vinny thought as he watched the minivan speed away.

CHAPTER 56

Molly followed Sheri out of the bathroom and down a long, dirty hallway. She could hear men yelling at each other below her where the funny machines were. She heard one man call someone a dumbass. Molly didn't know what that meant, but she noticed that the other man stopped talking, and the argument seemed to be over. She rolled the word *dumbass* around in her mouth and decided that she liked it.

"Here we are, sweetheart." Sheri knelt down in front of Molly and smoothed her hair. "You are a looker. I'll say that for you. Now be good, speak only when spoken to, and don't be fresh." Sheri stood up quickly and adjusted her skirt before opening the door.

"Well, here she is. She's as fresh as a daisy of sorts," Sheri announced with a sweep of her hand toward Molly.

Five men turned at once to examine Molly. She stared at each of them in turn until her gaze finally settled on an impossibly large man whose bandaged arm stuck out from his side and was propped up like the wing of a broken bird. Molly bit her lip to stop from smiling. He looked ridiculous.

"You have something to say, young lady?" the man bellowed.

Molly twisted her mouth in an effort to not laugh, but the urge overwhelmed her ability to stifle it. She barked out a laugh as she pointed to his arm. "What happened to your wing?"

The room drew a collective breath and held it. The man rose carefully from his chair and made his way slowly over to the little girl. As he towered over her, she realized she'd been rude—or fresh as Sheri had put it—and dropped her gaze to her lime green shoes.

"What is your name?"

Molly twisted her right foot around on the carpet while her hands writhed. She mumbled a response.

"I cannot hear you."

Molly quietly repeated her name.

"Are you not Jimmy McClelland's daughter?"

At hearing her father's name, Molly's head bolted upright. "Yes."

"Then what is your name?" the man repeated, raising himself to his full height.

Molly lifted her chin in defiance, knowing that her father would want her to be brave and strong. She spoke loudly and clearly. "My name is Molly Elizabeth McClelland."

A smile crept over the man's face as he squinted at her with his head tilted. "Yes, that's better." A collective sigh filled the room as the man turned on his heel and returned to the leather chair behind his desk. Molly glanced at Sheri, who smiled weakly at her and then gave her a thumbs-up.

The man leaned back in his chair while examining Molly. "Do you know who I am, Molly?"

She shook her head no.

"I cannot hear you."

All of a sudden Molly realized that this large man with the broken arm couldn't see very well. That's why he had gotten up and crossed over to her. She looked at Sheri, who seemed confused as to what she was planning, and then crossed behind the desk to the man. She gently took the man's hand in her own and made the "no" sign on his palm just as Julian had taught her.

"What are you doing?"

"It's okay that you can't see very well. I have a good friend who can't see at all, and he uses this sign to say 'no.'" She made the sign again on his palm to ensure that he understood. "And this is how you say 'yes.'" She rubbed her knuckles against his palm.

The man cleared his throat as the people in the room exchanged nervous glances.

"I see. Well my name is Mr. Torchia, and I wanted you to come here so that you could help me figure something out."

Ignoring his last remark, Molly traced her fingers along his cast. "What happened to your arm?"

"That's none of your business, Molly."

"Did you fall?"

The man sighed. "Yes, I did, but—"

"Is it because you couldn't see? Maybe you need new glasses."

Nervous twitters rippled through the room as people shifted back and forth. The man's face turned red, and he was breathing deeply.

"My friend Julian, the one who can't see at all, wears glasses too, but those are sunglasses. I think he wears them to hide his eyes. His eyes aren't normal because one of his patients made it so he can't see anymore. I miss him." Molly's voice trailed off as she remembered being taken from the hospital. "He's going to come looking for me."

"Who is this person you're talking about? Does Julian have a last name?"

Molly considered the question. "I don't know. He must have a last name. Sometimes Alex calls him Stryker." The man gave an imperceptible nod to the Ogre, who slid out of the room like a serpent.

"Well then, if this Julian Stryker is going to come looking for you, perhaps we should start talking about why you're here."

With his one good hand, the man opened a drawer in his desk and withdrew a small book. "Come closer, Molly, so we can look at this book together."

Molly ducked under the man's broken arm and leaned over the desk to examine the book. "I've seen this book before."

"Good, good, Molly. Where have you seen it?"

"At my daddy's store and at home."

"I see. Do you remember which store it was? Was it the red one, the blue one, the yellow one, or the—"

"That's easy. All of them."

"Okay. You say that you saw this book at home too?"

"Yes."

"Where at home? In your daddy's office?"

Molly tapped her head and willed herself to remember. "Sometimes, yes, but he would always carry it away from his office when we were done with work."

The man smiled. "Did you enjoy working with your father in his office, Molly?"

"Yes, I did. I miss him. He died, you know."

"I know that, and I was so sorry that we had to … that he's gone."

"Yeah." Molly looked at the carpet and felt sad and tired at the same time. "Can I go back to the hospital now?"

"Not yet. Tell me, do you know what these letters and numbers mean?"

Molly leaned in to examine the writing more closely. She noticed many letters from the alphabet that were followed by numbers, but none of them spelled a word that she knew. Suddenly, she saw a word she recognized. "Hey, that's my name! But I can't read the rest of it. What does it say?" The man motioned Sheri over, and she read it aloud.

June 22, 2018

> Molly continues to amaze me. Not only is she bright and kind, but she's incredibly intuitive. Today she saw a turtle in the middle of the road and asked me to stop the car. I watched as she examined the turtle, looked around to see why the turtle had been crossing the road, and figured out that the turtle had been searching for water (It's been so dry recently). She then had me lift the snapping turtle (I have the bite marks to prove it), carry it safely across the road, and place it next to a stream where it promptly slid in and began drinking. How many five year olds have that kind of empathy and intuition? Incredible.

While Sheri read, a huge grin spread across Molly's face as she recalled "The Great Turtle Salvation," as her father had come to refer to the event. The bite marks had scarred her father's hand, but he had told her that she should not worry about it and that he would do it all over again in exactly the same way.

Molly took the book from the man, flipped through it, and recognized her and her brother's names sprinkled throughout many entries her father had made. In addition to the entries, her father had made many scribbles that contained only letters and numbers as well. She suddenly remembered that although her father hadn't told her exactly what the notations meant, he had told her that they were extremely important. He had said that they were as important as the buttons in her jar.

"Molly, answer me. Do you know what these letters and numbers mean?"

"No."

"But you know something, don't you? I can tell. Molly, I know that these letters and numbers are a code, but I don't know how to figure out what the code says. There must be a key to this code."

Molly brightened. "Yes, there is a key! It locks the book. I remember daddy had it." She was pleased that she could help them without telling them something her daddy had told her to keep secret.

The man chuckled. "No, Molly, not that kind of key. A code is a secret way of hiding information in plain sight. Each of these letters and numbers must stand for something else. So I need to know any other places I might find information that can help me break this code."

Molly became uncomfortable. "Why do you need to break the code?"

The man's tone changed as he leaned forward and exhaled heavily on her. His breath smelled bad, and she tried to draw away from him. "I don't have any more time to waste, so here's the truth, Molly. Your father stole information from me, and I need it back."

Molly shook her head vehemently. "My daddy would never, ever steal. Stealing is wrong."

"Yes, you're right. Stealing is wrong. That's why I need this information back, Molly. I asked your daddy about the information, and he didn't help me. Now he's no longer here to help me, but you are. That's why I asked to see you. Tell me. Did your father give you anything that might have the information I need? Did he give you or your brother presents and tell you to hide them or keep them safe?"

Molly shook her head. "Nope. The only thing he gave me was my buttons."

The room became very quiet. "Buttons, you say?"

"Uh-huh. Daddy gave me beautiful buttons from his stores. I keep them in a jar."

"I see. And where is this jar of buttons now?"

"At the hospital."

The Ogre entered the room, crossed to the desk, and whispered to the man, who nodded and turned his attention back to Molly. "Tell me more about your friends Dr. Julian Stryker and Alex Hayes, Molly."

"What do you want to know?"

"Well, let's see. That jar of buttons you mentioned. Since you're no longer at the hospital, would they have taken the jar with them, or would they have left it in your hospital room?"

Molly thought hard. Julian and Jesse knew how important her jar was, so she decided that they'd take care of it for her until she returned. "I think they would take it with them because it's important."

"Why is it so important?"

She shrugged. "I don't know, but it is. That's what Daddy said."

"And where do you think your friends would have taken your important jar after they left the hospital?"

"I don't know. Maybe to Julian's house?"

The don glanced at the Ogre again with an unspoken directive in his eyes. "Thank you, Molly. You've been so very helpful."

CHAPTER 57

The car ride from the hospital to Julian's house was eerily quiet. Julian sat listening to the sounds of a busy city, as Jesse drove slowly and with great care. The tension caused by Buttons' kidnapping sat quietly and ominously between them.

"What are you thinking, Julian?"

Julian faced the passenger window, as if he were watching the passersby. He took a moment before answering. "About how incredibly resilient children are."

"You mean Molly?"

"Yes. I was also thinking about how ironic it is that Alex and I found her as opposed to someone else. Who knows? Maybe if it had been someone else, she would still be safe."

Jesse thought for a moment. "Or, perhaps you were meant to find her because she'll need your special expertise when this is all said and done and she's back home."

"Yeah, maybe."

"Julian, we can play this what if game all day long, but it serves no purpose except to make us feel shitty. Do me a favor and activate that analytical brain in that big old head of yours. Work your magic."

Julian turned toward Jesse and smiled weakly. "Thanks, Jess, but no amount of analysis is going to tell us where Molly is. If she truly was taken by the mob, she could be anywhere, including in a trunk or on a plane taking her to be trafficked or worse."

"But they took her for a particular purpose, right? I m-m-mean … you said earlier that they probably took her because she knows something." Jesse was stammering as he imagined the worst. "They wouldn't, like, sell her, right?"

Julian reached out his left hand and touched Jesse's shoulder. "I'm sorry, Jess. My imagination is getting the better of me. I shouldn't have said that. No, you're right. If her family was murdered by the mob, they took her for a specific reason."

"To kill her?"

Julian returned his sightless gaze to the window once more. "I don't think so. If they wanted her dead, they would have done it in the hospital. I'm convinced one of Torchia's guys took her." Julian shook his head as he thought out loud. "It would have been easy to kill her in that hallway once he took her from the room, but he didn't. He took her somewhere for safekeeping."

"You don't know that, Julian. Maybe he took her so that he could kill her and dump her body without anyone ever finding it. If he had killed her in the hospital, there might have been witnesses and screaming."

Julian shook his head. "No. The Torchia family is professional. If they had wanted her dead, they would have been as efficient with her death as they were with her father's. They wouldn't want to complicate the situation by taking her somewhere and then killing her. Too risky. I think she's still alive."

"Okay, assuming that's true, why would they take her? For a ransom?"

Julian turned to face Jesse. "And who exactly would they call to give their ransom demand? Her entire family is dead."

"Well then, why else would they take her if not for ransom money or to kill her? You said she might have some information, but it just doesn't make sense."

Julian inhaled deeply and thought about Molly, the smart, empathetic, sweet, tenacious girl who loved her family and her father most of all. Jimmy was an intelligent, organized, disciplined, thorough businessman who loved his daughter very much—enough to give her presents like the beautiful buttons that she coveted and protected with her life.

Julian shook the jar and listened as buttons rattled. "We're almost home, right?"

"Yeah. How do you do that? How do you know?"

"I can feel the turns and hear the noises that are particular to my street, but that doesn't matter, Jess. It's this jar. We've got to get inside and see what is so damn special about these buttons."

"What? Why? The only reason Molly was so vehement about holding onto that jar is because it was the one remaining link to her dead father."

Julian was shaking his head. "No, it's more than that. Molly said that her father would give her buttons every once in a while and that she needed to keep them in the jar and guard them with her life. He told her that they were her freedom, remember?"

"Yeah, so?"

"So why would some buttons represent freedom?"

"Um ..."

"What pops into your head when I say the word *freedom*? What represents freedom to you?"

"Let's see ... money to be able to do what I want, time in which to do it, and the knowledge to do it, whatever *it* is."

"Yes, that's right. Money, time, and knowledge. Maybe the buttons are linked to a lot of money."

"Then why didn't the mob just steal the button jar?"

"Because they must not know about it—unless Molly tells them."

"So, they took Molly because she knows how to get to the money."

"Or she simply has information. Maybe there is no money."

"But you just said—"

"That was one theory, Jess. Maybe the buttons aren't about money. Maybe they're related to something else. Either way, if Molly tells her captors what they want to know ..." The unfinished thought hung in the air like a lead balloon.

Julian shook his head. "The most ironic thing is that I don't think Molly knows she has valuable knowledge. She might tell them what they want to know without even realizing she's divulging important information."

"We're here."

Julian exited the car and climbed the porch stairs to a cacophony of howling emanating from the house. The door had barely opened when Oscar came bounding forward and put his paws up on Julian's chest.

"Get down!" Julian bellowed.

"Hey, don't get mad at poor old Oscar. He's just glad to see you."

"You're right." Julian opened his arms, which was his unspoken permission for Oscar to officially greet him. Because the large dog was still unsure, he whined. "C'mon, boy. I'm sorry. Jesse's right. Come here and give me some love." The dog paused only a split second before resuming his welcome. "Okay, that's enough. Down, Oscar."

Now appeased, the gentle giant loped into the kitchen for some water. Julian and Jesse followed, fed him some kibble, and sat down in the dining room. Molly's button jar sat on the table between them.

Julian unscrewed the top and reached into the jar, extracting a few buttons. "Describe these to me please."

Jesse took a button from Julian and examined it under the light. "Light blue, rhinestones of the same color, about a half an inch in diameter."

"And this one?"

"Army green, kind of plain looking."

One by one, they dissected the jar until the entire tabletop was covered in buttons of various shapes, sizes, colors, and textures.

"There's got to be something here," Julian said, running his hands through his hair. "Let's group them by color and see if anything pops up."

"You mean Roy G. Biv?"

Julian smiled. "The rainbow colors spell out 'Roy G. Biv.' That's right. Yes please, Roy G. Biv the heck out of those buttons and see if anything strikes you."

Jesse did as instructed. "There are about the same number of each color and about an equal amount of fancy to non-fancy buttons. Nothing stands out to me."

"Damn it," Julian muttered as he picked up a button and rubbed it between his forefinger and thumb. "What about that key that Alex found when the jar spilled?"

"It's right here." Jesse picked it up and examined it. "I don't know, Julian. I don't think there's anything special about it. It looks like it might belong to a diary or something, but who knows? Maybe it just happens to be in the jar. Maybe it means nothing."

"But why would it be in the jar if it weren't important or linked somehow to these buttons? By that logic, the key is as important as the buttons. Remember, Molly didn't know where the key came from, so that means that her father must have placed the key in the jar. He was so specific about each button he put in. I can't imagine he would have slipped the key in there by accident."

Julian focused on the button he had been holding. One

side—presumably the side that would face out on a shirt—was bumpy. The other side was smooth, except for a miniscule area that felt slightly uneven, as if it had been scratched.

"Jesse, there's something on the back of this button. There's a tiny scratch or something."

Jesse took the button and tilted it toward the light. "I'm not sure. There might be something there, Julian, but God, it's so tiny. I think it's just a scratch."

"How would scratches get on the underside of a button like that?"

"I don't know. From being in the jar with other buttons?"

"Maybe, but let's be sure. Can you please go up to my closet and get my microscope? It's on the top right shelf."

"Why does a blind man have a microscope in his closet?" Jesse asked as he rose from his seat.

"It's from my grad school days. Go get it. Hurry."

Jesse bounded up the stairs while Julian opened the back door for Oscar, who was pawing to go out. Jesse returned, placed the instrument on the table, and removed the leather cover. "Wow. This is really nice, Julian."

"Thanks. Take a look at the back of this button and tell me if you see anything."

Julian waited impatiently, shifting back and forth. After several tries and five excruciating minutes, Jesse eventually found the right distance, lighting, and magnification to examine the button's detail.

"Well, what do you see?"

"A35."

"What?"

"I said that I see A35 on the back of this button. It's carved into the plastic. It's so incredibly tiny, but clear under magnification."

"I knew it!" Julian breathed. "Check all of the others, Jess, and let's keep track of which colors have which numbers and letters carved into them."

Jesse looked hopelessly at the array of buttons spread across the table. "Do you know how many buttons we're talking about, Julian?"

"Do you have a better idea as to how we can help Molly?"

Jesse cringed and grabbed another button.

CHAPTER 58

Adrenaline surged through Sid's body, causing his heart to beat wildly. His pupils were dilated, and everything seemed brighter and louder than usual. Sweat dripped down his back as he cut across Boston toward Southie. Although he felt almost giddy contemplating the Ogre's comment about having a surprise for him, Sid didn't really care what it was, as his priority- the safety of his family- had been removed from the equation. Confident that Kathleen would heed his warnings and start driving South with the kids, Sid's only job now was to stall the Ogre long enough so that Kathleen could put a lot of miles between herself and danger.

Sid hoped that he would be able to meet Kath and the kids in the near future, but he certainly wasn't counting on it. Once the Ogre discovered that he no longer had Sid's family with which to bargain, Sid presumed that he'd be killed. He was too far into the shit to be able to walk away anyway. It would take some sort of miracle for his life to be spared, and Sid was not a religious man. Even so, he found himself asking God to look after his family once he was gone. Between God and the letter in his personnel file, which each FBI agent writes and leaves for his family in case something unthinkable happens, Sid figured Kath could finish raising the kids. After all, Sid had stashed away quite a bit over the years, and his letter to Kath outlined when and how to access the cash.

Sid wiped a tear from his eye and shifted his focus to his boss and good friend Vinny. He hated that he had been lying to Vinny, but believed he had made the correct choice in order to protect his family. If the situation were reversed, he believed that Vinny would have made the same decision. Besides, Sid felt that on some level Vinny knew he was lying. When he had read suspicion in Vinny's eyes at their last meeting, Sid had known that he had to fully commit one way or the other- continue to lie in order to save his family or put the agency first and sacrifice his family. All he needed now was a little time—just enough for Kath to escape with the kids.

Sid drove slowly along the large metal fence that surrounded Conley Terminal. Cranes, forklifts, and flatbed trucks zigzagged the tarmac on their way to load and unload cargo ships. Men in hard hats whistled, motioned, and yelled to unhearing freight-elevator operators, who gestured wildly in return.

Sid stopped his car in front of a gate that had a number pad and a speaker. Not having been given any directions, he simply pressed the "CALL" button on the pad and waited. Static popped through the speaker, followed by a gruff voice. "Yeah?"

"Um, I'm here to see ..." Sid realized he'd never learned the Ogre's real name. "I'm here to see, uh ..."

With a tremendous squeak and groan the monstrous gate started moving. Sid drove quickly through the gaping hole, afraid that the unseen operator might change his mind and slam the gate shut. Ahead of him there were three identical warehouses, mammoth steel structures that each spanned the length of a football field.

The center warehouse's sliding door opened a crack to reveal someone motioning to Sid and guiding him toward the structure. Sid obeyed and drove slowly toward the building as he evaluated his surroundings. The machine noise accosted his ears as people scrambled chaotically. Sid decided that no one would notice one more person walking into a warehouse or a body being removed.

He shifted the car into park and powered down the driver's window as the Ogre walked quickly toward him. "Hey, buddy, good to see you."

"I wish I could say the same."

The Ogre ignored the comment. "Wait till you see what I have in there for you," the large man gestured toward the warehouse. "Boy are you gonna be happy. Follow me. Oh, but make sure you leave your phone and your gun in the car. We wouldn't want any accidents to occur." The Ogre donned a genuine smile and winked.

Sid creased his eyebrows while removing his gun and placing it in the glove box. Removing his phone from his jacket pocket, he noticed a pop-up on the home screen that indicated that he had a message. "I'll be right in. I need to listen to this message."

"Is it from Kathleen?" the Ogre asked, as if he were a longtime friend of the family.

"Yeah, I think so. Do you mind?"

"No, no, not at all. Come in when you're done. We're all friends here, aren't we?" His gaze lingered on Sid as a silent threat was implied. *Fuck you*, Sid thought as he replied, "Sure thing."

Sid unlocked his phone and pressed the voicemail button.

"Hey, Sid. It's Vin. Just checking in to see how you're doing. I hope you're at home resting. We miss you and want you back in the thick of it soon. Call me when you get this."

Sid stared at his phone while contemplating Vinny's tone. *He definitely knows something isn't right, but he's not completely sure what it is*, Sid thought. *That's good.*

Sid tapped the "Call Back" icon on the screen, leaned his head back, breathed deeply, and thought, *Time ... I need more time.*

"Vinny Marcozzi."

"Hey, Vin. It's Sid."

"Oh, hey, Sid, how're you doing, man? Feeling any better?"

"Not really. I just got your message though and thought I'd call back. Listen—I won't be in for a couple days. I just feel like I need to take some time off, you know? Get my head back in order."

"Okay. But you'll be back in by next Monday then?"

"Yeah, Monday for sure. Hey, Vinny?"

"Yeah?"

"Thanks for everything."

"What do you mean?"

"I mean, well, for standing by me ... and caring. You're a good boss and an even better friend."

"You think so?"

"Yeah, I do."

"Sid?"

"Yeah?"

"Kath and the kids are safe." The comment was thrown carelessly and was meant to catch him off guard. Sid held his breath while his mind flew through possibilities. When he spoke again, the pitch of his voice had risen. "Of course they're safe. Why wouldn't they be?"

"I just wanted you to know. I saw Kathleen earlier at the kids' school. Apparently they have a doctor's appointment today. Kids sure do keep you busy, don't they?"

All of a sudden, Sid realized that Vinny wasn't trying to trick him or even corner him. He was trying to inform Sid of his family's safety without alerting anyone who might be listening to the fact that his family was following his directions and was safely on the run. Gratitude and relief made Sid dizzy. "Yeah, they sure do keep us busy."

"Listen, Sid, I know you've had a rough time of it recently with your car crash and all. If you need anything—I mean *anything*—please let me know. You and I have been a strong team for a long time, and I'd hate to see your career suffer because of some error in judgment like falling asleep at the wheel. You hear me?"

Vinny knows that I lied about not only the car crash but the reason for it. What else does he know? Sid thought but then said, "I absolutely understand, Vinny."

"You know I have an obligation to help you as my employee, right?"

"Sure."

"I mean, even if you felt like you didn't need my help, I would always go out on a limb for you. You might need help and not even know it. You ever been in a situation like that, Sid? Where you needed help but didn't realize it?"

"Um ..."

"Where are you now, Sid?"

The door to the warehouse opened suddenly, and the Ogre stood staring at Sid, tapping his watch. Sid's time was up. "I need to go, Vin. Again, thanks."

"Where's Molly, Sid?"

Sid shook his head. "I have no idea."

"Are you sure? Because she was kidnapped from her hospital room."

"What?" The Ogre lifted his arms with his hands outstretched. It was a clear indication of his growing impatience with Sid. "I don't know, Vinny. Really, I don't. I'll see you on Monday. I need to go now."

Vinny dropped all pretenses with his next comment. "We gotta find her, Sid. Otherwise she might get hurt like her family did. If you know where she is, you need to do the right thing—the moral thing. Tell me where she is!"

"I'm telling you that I don't know where she is. I swear!" As Sid held up his pointer finger toward the Ogre, indicating he needed a little more time, he noticed the man gesture to his left. A little girl wearing lime green shoes appeared, and fixed her gaze on Sid while chewing on her thumbnail. Sid's face blanched as he stared at the Ogre, who was clearly pleased with himself as he stroked Molly McClelland's ginger curls.

CHAPTER 59

Vinny pressed on, determined. "Sid, I believe that you don't know where Molly is. I also believe that you've gotten yourself into—"

"Oh my God," whispered Sid.

"Sid, let me help you. I can—" The call cut off abruptly. "Sid? Sid! Damn it!" Vinny commanded Siri to call Marcie, who answered immediately.

"What's up, Vin?"

"Put a trace on Sid's phone. I need to know where he is. Now, Marcie, please. I should've done this a while ago."

"You got it. Anything else?"

"Yeah. If Sid or anyone from his family calls in, patch it through to my mobile immediately."

"Of course."

"I'm going to check in with Alex Hayes and see if she's learned anything new in the disappearance of Molly McClelland. If you hear anything, Marcie, please let me know."

"Absolutely. Vinny?"

"What?"

"You okay?"

Vinny's shoulders slumped. "To be honest, I don't know."

"And Sid?"

"I have no idea what to think about Sid at this point, Marcie. Do me a favor and pull all files for his active cases. I'm going to have go through them one by one to see if they've been compromised. Jesus, what a fucking mess!"

"I'll get on it right now. We'll get through this."

Vinny shook his head. "I know, but Sid ... of all people ... I just—"

"I know, Vin, I know. Call me if you need anything else."

"Thanks, Marcie." Vinny disconnected and dialed Alex.

"Alex Hayes."

"Hey, Alex, it's Vinny."

"Hey, Vin, any luck on your end?"

"I wish I could say yes, but I can't. I spoke with the agent that I suspected was lying. The good news is that I now know he's lying. The bad news is that he can't lead us to Molly."

"But you think he knows something?"

"Yes, but he hung up before I could get it out of him."

"Where is he? I'll get it out of him."

"I have my office tracing his phone. As soon as I hear anything, I'll let you know. Where are you?"

"I'm just finishing paperwork regarding Molly's abduction, and then I'm heading over to Julian's house. Jesse and Julian are there waiting for me. Can you meet me there?"

"Sure. I can get there in about twenty minutes."

"See you then."

Vinny took a right onto the road that wound around the arboretum. He loved that about Boston. In the middle of a major city, there sat pristine, colonial homes that surrounded a lush pond and trees. It was an oasis in a desert, so to speak. Vinny gave himself a moment to simply enjoy his surroundings. Powering the windows down, he inhaled the fresh scent of recently cut grass and remembered that there was an entire world out there where people lived normal, non-chaotic lives—the kind of life he had begun to imagine he might have with Annabelle.

He didn't know how he felt about her not divulging her connection to a major crime family. Between her nondisclosure and Sid's recent lies, Vinny felt wounded, vulnerable, and angry. The more he thought about it, the more he realized that he felt angry.

The words of his deceased mother floated through his mind. "Vincenzo, whenever possible, do not speak to someone with whom you're angry while you still hold the *palla di fuoco* in your stomach. Wait until it dulls, and only then, you speak." The ball of fire in Vinny's stomach was burning brightly. He knew he should heed his mother's warning but couldn't. He commanded Siri to call Annabelle's cell phone.

"Annabelle Andrews."

"Hey, it's me."

"Ooh. I was just thinking about you."

"Stop, Annabelle, please. I'm going to ask you something, and I want you to answer it honestly, okay?"

"Jeez, Vin. So serious. Okay."

"Why didn't you tell me that you're related to Paolo Torchia when you knew I was running agents on him for almost a year? I mean, Jesus, Annabelle. I've probably told you things that could cause my ass to be hauled in front of the senate for a hearing."

"You haven't told me anything I didn't already know or couldn't have easily discovered with a little digging, Vinny."

Vinny shook his head. "Answer the question. Why didn't you tell me?"

Silence buzzed across the line. "It wasn't relevant."

Vinny spit out a laugh. "Wasn't *relevant*? Are you kidding me? Of course it was relevant!"

"No, it wasn't. Think, Vinny. You and I were running two separate investigations on the Torchia family—"

"You mean your uncle," Vinny interjected, unable to restrain himself.

Annabelle paused. "Yes, my *great* uncle and his associates. We were working on parallel planes. Eventually the two paths would have run together, either when you arrested him or when we indicted him. You see, we're actually working on the same side."

"Except you had knowledge that I didn't have, Annabelle, which puts me at a disadvantage."

"How? How does not knowing that I'm related to Paolo Torchia put you at a disadvantage?"

"Because whether you know it or not, you might have inadvertently learned something that aided your case."

"And why would that be so wrong?"

Vinny waved his hand as if swatting away a fly. "It's about morality, integrity, and honor, Annabelle."

"Oh my God, Vinny. It's about rounding up some thugs and making sure they go to prison. Or do you have a different agenda?"

"No, that's my agenda, but the process is just as important as the outcome. If the process is flawed, the outcome is tenuous. Do you know that your boss called me today asking if we could get together to discuss the case?"

"He said he might do that."

"And even then, did it not occur to you to call me and give me a heads-up about your uncle?"

"Great uncle."

"Stop splitting hairs, Annabelle."

"No, it didn't because I thought we were working toward the same goal."

"At the end of the day, it's about trust, Annabelle. Even if we were working toward the same goal, I had a right to know about your familial relationship. The conflict of interest is glaring."

"Chris didn't think so, and neither do I. I suppose we're going to have to agree to disagree."

She sounded smug and trite, and Vinny was having a difficult time reconciling the woman he had known thus far and the person who was now speaking to him so condescendingly.

"I think the idea of becoming the DA has gone to your head."

"I could not disagree more. I think perhaps you're scared of seeing a powerful woman rise in the ranks."

Vinny physically drew back in the car. "What did you just say to me?"

"You heard me. Be careful, Vinny. You're old-school Italian beliefs are showing. You may want to tuck those back in."

"God, Annabelle, what's happening here? I don't even know you."

"Maybe you don't, Vinny. It's been fun, but I have work to do. Talk to you later."

"Annabelle?" Vinny's phone beeped two times, indicating that the call had ended. Stunned, Vinny stared straight ahead while he wondered what had just happened. The *palla di fuoco* was searing him. He realized his mother had been correct. He shouldn't have called her when he was angry, but would the outcome have been any different? He glanced at a family playing Frisbee on the bank of the pond and realized his chance at normalcy with Annabelle had quickly disintegrated.

CHAPTER 60

Sid fixed his eyes on Molly as he slowly exited the car.

"Did you leave the items in the car like I asked?" The Ogre was using a singsong voice, presumably so that he would not scare the little girl.

"Yes."

"And the SIM card has been removed from your phone? We wouldn't want anyone to know you're here, would we?"

Sid attempted to smile at Molly, who simply stared, wide-eyed.

"The SIM card is in the glove box, along with the other items. Hi, Molly. Do you remember me?" Sid asked.

Molly tilted her head in thought. "Yes. You're the man that used to work with my daddy."

"That's right," the Ogre responded. "And the three of us are going to put our heads together to figure out what the letters and numbers in the book mean, aren't we, Sid?"

Sid ignored him and knelt down in front of Molly. "Are you hurt, sweetheart?"

Molly scrunched up her face. "No. Why?"

Sid placed a hand on her bony shoulder. "It's nothing. Just making sure. Because if anything were to happen to you, I might get angry at my friend here."

Molly looked up towards the Ogre, whose smile faltered slightly. "I don't think you're in any position to make threats, Sid."

"What were you thinking, bringing her here?" Sid hissed as his frustration and anger boiled over.

"Hey, she's the only one who can help us find the information we need—*you* need, Sid—to ensure everyone's safety." The Ogre raised his eyebrows to ensure that Sid understood his implication.

213

Sid swallowed hard, forcing himself to remain calm so he could buy more time for his family's escape.

The Ogre sounded hurt as he said, "Besides, I thought this would be a nice surprise for you, Sid. I was trying to help. The sooner we can put this unpleasant business behind us, the sooner we can get little Molly back to her friends and you back to your family."

Sid glanced quickly at Molly and whispered, "I'm not sure you have any intention of returning either of us."

"Well now, that's just mean, Sid. You know I could never hurt you or Molly."

Sid huffed as he shook his head. "Yeah, right."

"Let's go inside and look at the book, okay?"

The Ogre took Molly's hand as Sid fell in step behind them. The warehouse was buzzing with activity as they traversed the main floor and climbed a set of rickety metal stairs.

"What's going on here anyway?" Sid said as he indicated the bustling activity with a sweep of his hand.

The Ogre barely glanced behind him. "Getting ready for a shipment."

"Of what?"

The Ogre stopped on the top stair and turned fully toward Sid. "You can take the man out of the FBI, but you can't take the FBI out of the man, can you? Do you really want to know?"

Sid evaluated the wooden pallets being relocated and boxes being nailed shut. Under normal circumstances, he would have eagerly accepted the Ogre's offer, but these circumstances were in no way normal. Sid thought better of his request. "No. I don't want to know."

The Ogre raised his eyebrows. "I didn't think so. C'mon."

They walked across a dilapidated metal catwalk that groaned under their weight. "You may want to invest in some infrastructure."

"And you may want to stow that sarcasm of yours when we enter the office. Not everyone in our establishment is as forgiving or kind as I am."

Sid pursed his lips but heeded the Ogre's advice. The three of them entered an office that could only be described as extravagantly tacky. Rich, blood-red drapes adorned the windows that overlooked the warehouse. The velvet couch was sheeted in plastic to protect it from dirt. The Persian carpet was of good quality, albeit somewhat threadbare. An obese man whose casted arm poked out from his side sat behind a huge oak desk.

An involuntary, "Wow!" escaped Sid's lips.

The Ogre turned to him sharply. "Not a word," he whispered.

Three other people stood in various locations around the room, including a badly dressed woman with bright red lips and the man who had helped to damage Sid's body and pride several days ago—the Muscle. Sid glanced at the man, who nodded slightly as if to say hello.

"You must be Mr. Nickerson. Welcome to my humble abode. I can see that you're impressed." The large man behind the desk leaned back in his chair, relishing the moment.

"Oh yes, very impressed," Sid noted sarcastically. The Ogre shot him a look, and Sid immediately regretted his comment. His goal was to buy time, not to annoy Molly's kidnappers and his blackmailers any further. "It's really very nice."

The large man smiled. "There you go. That's the cooperation we're looking for. Mr. Nickerson, I assume that you know my name."

"His name is Mr. Torchia," Molly interjected while crossing over to Sid and taking his hand. She leaned into him and whispered, "And he can't see very well." Sid squeezed Molly's hand while looking at Paolo Torchia to measure his response.

The mafia boss simply chuckled. "She's precocious, isn't she?" The room's occupants twittered in unison. They were all sycophants. "You know, Mr. Nickerson, I'm usually not interested in children, but there's something about this girl that fascinates me. She's much like her father was—"

"Before you killed him and his wife and son?"

The woman with red lips drew a quick breath, and Sid froze. He hadn't meant to say it aloud, but somehow the venomous words had taken on a life of their own and had escaped.

Molly's hand dropped from his. When he looked at Molly, she was staring openmouthed at Paolo Torchia with a look of pure astonishment. Her eyes were huge and searched the large man's face. "You killed my daddy? Why? Why would you do that?"

"Molly, I didn't kill your daddy."

Everyone watched in fascination as she crossed to him and looked into his rheumy eyes. After a moment, she backed away. Placing her hands over her ears as if to block out sounds only she could hear, Molly shook her head and sank to the ground. "I remember now. I remember all of it: my daddy hanging, my mommy driving too fast, my brother yelling at my mommy." Suddenly she was dry-eyed and factual as she turned to Sid. "He died, you know. My brother, Joey."

Sid's heart melted. "I know, Molly. I'm so sorry."

"Enough!" Paolo Torchia bellowed, stunning everyone into silence. He turned to Molly. "Yes, Molly. I killed your daddy because he was a no-good, lying sack of shit who stole from me. But hear me when I say that I did *not* kill your mother or your brother. I don't know why they were driving so fast, and I'm truly sorry that they died. Now if you want to leave here and go back to your friends, you and Mr. Nickerson need to focus on helping us figure out this code. Understand?"

Molly looked hard at each person in the room and then nodded very slowly. Sid marveled at her stoicism until he realized that she was in shock and had entered survival mode. Her glassy eyes traveled across his face, causing him to kneel once more and speak to her. "Molly, we're going to get out of this. I promise you."

As if registering him for the first time, she said, "My daddy didn't steal anything from Mr. Torchia because stealing is wrong."

Taking both of her small hands into his own, he said, "I know, Molly. Your father was a good man, and he loved you and your brother so much."

"Yes," Molly whispered. "So much."

CHAPTER 61

"You're not helping at all, you know," Jesse sighed as he looked up from the microscope and watched Julian pace across the living room for the umpteenth time.

"I'm sorry, Jess. I can't do anything, and it's killing me. If I could see, I'd help you, but I can't." As if sensing his master's frustration, Oscar whined and pawed at Julian's leg, prompting an unconscious ear rub from Julian.

"You could take notes. You know, write down the names and numbers I find on the buttons. That would make this process go much faster."

Julian's shoulders sagged. "Think, Jesse. If I took notes in braille, how would that help? I'd be the only one who could read it."

Jesse tilted his head back and forth, acquiescing. "True."

"How many buttons have you reviewed?"

Jesse took stock of the tabletop, which was covered in a rainbow of multi-shaped, tiny objects. They had been arranged first by color and then by shape. After multiplying quickly, he answered, "I'd say that I've looked at two hundred buttons so far, with about another two hundred to go."

"And how many of them have markings?"

"About twenty-eight so far."

"What are the markings?"

Jesse leaned back in his chair and rubbed his tired eyes. "All just letters and numbers."

Julian sat down on the floor next to Oscar, who thumped his tail happily before rolling onto his back.

"That dog will do anything for a belly rub, won't he?"

"Yeah, he will, won't cha buddy?" Julian said as he scratched Oscar's stomach.

"I'm going to take a break and get something to eat, Julian. Want anything?"

Julian shook his head. "I'm too worried."

Jesse entered the kitchen, made two ham and cheese sandwiches, and returned, setting one down on the floor next to Julian. "Eat. That's an order."

Oscar flipped upright and sat at attention as Julian prepared to eat. "Thanks. Hey, how many of each color of button has writing on it?"

Julian ate his sandwich as Jesse counted. "Three red buttons have A35, T17, and C12, respectively. Two yellow buttons have M12 and S7. Four green buttons have A14, T5, S5, and T4. One blue button has—"

"Okay, okay. So, we know that Jimmy owned seven stores, each of which was painted a different color of the rainbow, right?"

"Yes."

"What if the colors of the buttons that have writing on them are associated with the same color of store?"

"You're saying that the red buttons have something to do with the red store, et cetera?"

Julian nodded, swallowing the last of his sandwich. "Exactly, and what if the numbers correspond to something inside the store?"

Jesse twisted his mouth in thought. "Like what?"

Julian shook his head. "Clothes maybe? What else is inside a dry-cleaning store but clothes?"

"Julian, Jimmy couldn't just take buttons from clothes in his store. Don't you think the customers would notice?"

"I wouldn't notice if someone had taken the extra button that comes with my shirts. You know, in case a button falls off, many manufacturers include an extra one on the inside of a garment. The only time I'd notice it is if I needed it. If it was missing, it wouldn't make me suspicious. I would just assume that it had fallen off."

"Okay. That would make sense for the regular buttons like on the shirts that you and I wear. But there are fancy buttons here that have rhinestones on them. Do those clothes come with extra buttons too? I don't think so. Too expensive for the manufacturer, I would think."

Julian's excitement waned. "So you're saying that some of the buttons with letters and numbers on them have rhinestones?"

"Yeah. Sorry."

"Damn it! I thought we were on to something."

Jesse thought for a moment. "What are the chances of us getting into Jimmy's stores?"

"So we can look for the clothes that are missing these buttons?" Julian asked, pointing toward the table.

"Yes."

"To what end?"

"As you pointed out a while ago, we don't have any other way to help Molly. This is our only lead and our only remaining connection to her. We have to try."

The front door opened. Alex entered and drank in the scene: Julian sitting on the floor next to Oscar, and Jesse leaning over a microscope on a table covered in buttons. "What's going on here?" At the sound of her voice, Oscar leapt to his feet, jumped over Julian, and howled while rubbing his head against Alex's leg. "Hi, Oscar. I love you too."

"Did you find any information on Molly?" Julian asked, standing up quickly.

"Absolutely nothing. What are you doing, Jess?"

"I have to keep examining these buttons, Alex. Julian, you explain."

Julian updated Alex on their discoveries and assumptions, ending with, "All of this is to say that we need to get into Jimmy's stores to see if we can find any information that might lead us to Molly."

"They're all closed pending the investigation."

"I know, but we figured that you could get us in."

"Sure, but I don't see how this is going to help us figure out where Molly is."

"We're thinking that maybe the letters and numbers on these buttons are a cypher. Given the fact that Jimmy told Molly to guard the jar with her life and that the buttons were her freedom, the cypher must contain information that protects Molly somehow."

"It certainly didn't protect Jimmy or the rest of his family."

"True, but it might be Jimmy's insurance policy against the mob, even after his death. Everyone says how cautious, meticulous, and detailed Jimmy was. If that's true, he would have had a backup plan in case something happened to compromise his position in the mob or his life."

"Okay. I guess that makes sense. But why would he safeguard such important information by giving it to a little girl?"

"Two reasons: No one would suspect that he would trust his young daughter with that kind of information, and he thought she was safe because she didn't know that she had the information. If I'm right, it's brilliant on his part."

"Brilliant until his adorable daughter got kidnapped, that is," Jesse grumbled.

"Yeah, up until that point," Alex echoed.

"Jesse, gather the buttons that have writing on them—"

"Julian, I still have a bunch more to go."

"I know, but we have enough to investigate several stores to see if we're on the right track. The information in the stores might lead us to Molly's whereabouts."

"I'll get my car." Alex opened the front door to find Vinny standing on the front porch, his hand poised to knock. "Hey Vin. Any news about Molly?"

"Not yet, but I'm working on it. What's happening here?"

Alex glanced behind her at Julian and Jesse as they leaned over the table gathering the buttons. Vinny's gaze followed.

"Are those buttons?" Vinny asked. "Why are they playing with buttons?"

"Too long to explain. Get in my car, and I'll explain on the way over."

"Where are we going?"

Alex sighed. "Just get in the car. C'mon, guys. Vinny's coming with us."

CHAPTER 62

Sid Nickerson sat at a small table with the Ogre. Taking in the surroundings and current company, Sid couldn't help but marvel at how far and how fast he had fallen. *How had this even happened?* he wondered. Perhaps he should have stood his ground when the Ogre first approached him. If he had not been broken during the beating or if he had told Vinny the truth when he had been asked, things might be different.

He hadn't done either of those things. He had bent his morals and had lied. Here he was with the potential destruction of an innocent little girl on his hands in addition to the destruction of his family and his career.

"Don't blame yourself," the Ogre said as he read Sid's face. "It's not your fault. Anyone would have done the same thing and made the same decisions to protect his family. You're a good father and husband."

Defeated and utterly exhausted, Sid met the Ogre's concerned eyes. He looked at the plastic-covered couch where Molly had retreated after learning the truth about her father's death. She lay still and stared at the ceiling with unblinking eyes. She hadn't spoken since the discovery, and Sid was terrified she had gone into some type of living coma. Leaning forward, he whispered, "Tell me the truth. You owe me that at least. Molly and I aren't getting out of here alive, are we?"

"Sid, how many times do I got to tell you? I'm a man of my word. You hold up your end of the bargain, and I'll hold up mine. You help us figure out this writing thing, and we'll let you go." Sid glanced in the direction of the Muscle, who stood immediately outside the open door and then asked, "But what if we can't?"

The Ogre shrugged. "Well then, I'm honestly not sure what Mr. Torchia will decide as to your living or dying." Sid's heart beat wildly as adrenaline pumped hotly through his body. "You can't tell me that you'd kill an innocent little girl. C'mon ... really?"

The Ogre looked at Sid for a long time as sadness descended over his visage like a veil. Sid's eyes morphed from disbelief, to anger, to pleading, in a matter of moments. He looked away as a tear ran down his face.

"Oh, come on now. Let's figure out these letters and numbers and be done with it," the Ogre said. Handing Sid a tissue, he gently pushed the book in front of Sid. "You knew Jimmy well. What could he mean with all of this writing?"

Sid wiped his eyes and blew his nose. Running a hand through his hair, he examined Jimmy's handwriting. Small, neat, precise strokes for each letter and number. He thought, *just like Jimmy—small, neat, and precise.* Flipping through the pages, he read some of Jimmy's entries. Most were about his children, especially Molly, to whom he was clearly devoted.

Sid wondered if Jimmy would have allowed his daughter to follow in his gangster footsteps. He thought not, as her father would have wanted a better, safer life for her. He would have wanted to keep her away from people like the Ogre. *Hell, people like me,* Sid thought, grunting.

"Anything?" the Ogre asked.

"Not yet. Give me a minute."

Sid turned the page and read through a list written in red ink:

2, A, 27
4, C, 14
7, F, 2
3, D, 28

Underneath the list was a personal entry for that day. Even though Sid knew reading Jimmy's words about his children would make him feel worse, he couldn't help himself.

> I gave Molly the most beautiful button today. It was red with rhinestones, and she loved it! I told her how incredibly important these buttons are and how she needs to guard them with her life. She placed it, ever so gently, atop her others in the jar, which is becoming close to full.

What to do when the jar is full? Perhaps then, our future will be secure. On the other hand, perhaps it will never be as complete as … Wishful thinking … In the meantime, Molly continues to impress me with her intelligence and sensitivity. It brings me such joy to watch her examine each treasure I give her. They're only buttons, but to her, they're the world.

"Huh."

"What is it, Sid? You got something?"

"I don't know. Maybe." Sid quickly thumbed through the rest of the book. "Have you noticed that Jimmy used different ink throughout the entries?"

"So?"

"So maybe the ink color corresponds to the color of the store."

"Go on."

"Maybe these letters and numbers match something in his stores." Sid turned to another page. "See? This entry is in green ink. There are letters, numbers, and a personal entry as well." He turned yet another page. "But this entry is only personal. There are no letters and numbers, and he used black ink. In fact," Sid continued flipping the pages, scanning each one, "Jimmy included letters and numbers only when using colored ink. There are absolutely no letters and numbers when he used black ink."

The Ogre's eyes were boring into Sid's. He was trying to understand and failing miserably.

"Don't you get it? Leave it to Jimmy to play both sides."

The Ogre shook his head. "What do you mean?"

Sid laughed out loud. "It was brilliant. Jimmy was gathering information from his work for the Torchia family as an insurance policy in case anything happened to him. At the same time, he was also playing me because the entire time that I was running him as my CI, he was feeding me tidbits of information to keep me interested but not fully informed. Wow."

Sid ran his hands over his face as he continued to process. "He was playing both of us. I would bet money that he was planning on running with his family in the near future and using this cypher to protect himself from being whacked by you guys and from going to prison by me. Brilliant, simply brilliant."

"Obviously not that brilliant. He's dead."

Sid turned to the Ogre. "That's where you're wrong. It was brilliant because Jimmy gathered information that Paolo Torchia is willing to kill for, which means that it implicates the don personally, as opposed to some of his lieutenants. If I'm right, and the FBI gets to this information before we do, then it will destroy the entire Torchia dynasty." A slow smile spread across Sid's face as he watched the Ogre process what he had said.

Once he'd caught up, the Ogre glared at Sid. "Why are you smiling, Sid? If someone figures out the puzzle before we do, you and the girl will die. Not so funny now, huh?"

Sid glanced at Molly, who hadn't moved. He gestured toward the Ogre, drawing him closer. "You know what, asshole? I don't give a shit about me anymore. But you're right. I don't want her to die, so I'm going to continue to help you. Get your thug out of the doorway, and let's go to one of Jimmy's stores to see if we can find the next piece of the puzzle."

The Ogre tilted his head toward Sid. "I'm going to allow you that one, Sid, because I know you're stressed. But understand this, my friend. The girl comes with us, and if you don't make the progress I think you should be making or if you try to trick me in some way, she dies."

Sid pulled back with a smirk on his face. "Now, then, how could I ever possibly hope to outwit a mastermind like you?"

"That's just mean, Sid. Why do you have to be so mean?"

CHAPTER 63

Alex drove her Mustang recklessly, her frustration and anger channeled into her right foot as it pressed hard on the accelerator.

"Jesus, Alex. Slow down, or none of us will live to see Molly found."

"Shut up, Vinny."

Julian reached out and placed his hand on Alex's forearm. "We're going to find her."

"What if we don't?"

"We will."

Her voice cracked. "I hope you're right, Stryker. You know I'm not a religious person, but I've basically promised everything to God if he lets us find her."

"Alex, I know you're taking this burden completely on yourself, but please let Jesse, Vinny, and I shoulder some of it with you. The burden won't be as heavy if we share it."

"You weren't there, Julian. I literally gave her over to her kidnapper—literally. I was pushing her wheelchair, and then I handed it over to him." Alex choked back a sob.

"Alex, how could you possibly have known that he was going to take her?"

"I should have known."

"Because he was wearing a T-shirt that said 'kidnapper' or because your extrasensory perception should have alerted you?"

"Don't be ridiculous."

"You're the one being ridiculous. *You could not have known.* So stop beating yourself up and focus on what you can control."

Alex rolled her eyes. "That's the thing. We have absolutely no control in this situation."

"I disagree. You can control your reaction to what's happening. You can choose to channel your energy into a positive outcome for Molly. That's absolutely a choice."

Wiping the mascara from under her eyes, she said, "I guess that's true."

"You're feeling this case more than others because it's personal. Completely understandable, but you're a strong person. Don't let this overwhelm you or get in the way of finding her."

"Okay. I'll try."

"Now, having said all of that, if you feel the need to hug me at any point, I'm just letting you know that I'm very open to that."

Alex smirked wryly. "Thanks. I'll take that under advisement."

"I bet you will."

"Stop it, you two. This is definitely not the time," Jesse said while leaning forward from the back seat.

"Yeah, seriously," Vinny added, "How do you two keep it so fresh?"

"What? The relationship?"

"Yeah."

Julian found Alex's hand and brought it to his lips. "Because neither of us takes the other for granted. In fact, can I tell them?"

"Tell us what?" Jesse asked excitedly.

Alex sighed dramatically. "Well, now I think you have to. They're not going to let it go until you do."

"Alex and I have made the rather large decision to take our relationship to the next level."

"Oh my God! You're getting married?" Jesse asked and then put his hands over his mouth.

"No, no, no." Alex said irritably. "We're moving in together."

"Oh. Well … that's good too, I guess."

"Sorry to disappoint you, Jess, but we're pretty excited about it."

"No, no, that's great. It's just that you basically live together now."

"It's different, Jess. Even though Alex and I spend a lot of time together, there's a real psychological effect when people live together."

Alex pulled a face. "What do you mean?"

"There's actually substantial evidence that associates cohabitation with negative relationship outcomes."

Alex shoulders slumped. "Then why are we doing it?"

"Because we love each other. Remember, research is generalized and based on hundreds or even thousands of subjects. The real outcome depends on the couple and their reasons for moving in together."

"Wow, Dr. Stryker. Thanks for the analysis. I thought you were a romantic."

"I am, but I'm also a realist. Studies suggest that people who cohabitate because they want to spend more time together do better than people who do it out of financial convenience. Also, people who are planning to get married at some point after they live together do better than couples who aren't sure about marriage."

"I see. And where do we fall?"

Julian grinned and waggled his eyebrows. "My dear, you'll have to just wait and see."

"Fantastic. Can't wait," Alex responded as she rolled her eyes at Jesse in the rearview mirror.

Vinny, who'd been quiet throughout the exchange, stared gloomily out the window. "What's with you, Vin?" Alex asked.

Vinny waved his hand in the air. "Oh, it's nothing. Annabelle and I broke up."

"What? Why?"

"Get this. Turns out she's related to Paolo Torchia."

"What?" Alex almost shrieked. "And she didn't find the time to tell you this because …?"

"I know. I agree, Alex. She should have said something. I challenged her about it, and she told me that her relationship with the Torchias isn't relevant."

Alex snorted. "Yeah, right. Of course it is! She should have told you."

"I know."

Julian turned slightly in his seat. "How are you doing? I know you care for her quite a bit."

Vinny shrugged. "Okay, I guess. I'm going to miss her, but this is kind of a deal breaker for me. I'm still not completely convinced she doesn't have some skin in Torchia's game, if I'm being honest."

"You think she's crooked? Seriously?" Alex asked, craning to look at Vinny in the back seat.

"Seriously. She says she's not, but … looks like we're here."

Alex parked the car directly in front of the dry-cleaning store. The lights were off, and a sign on the door read "Closed Until Further Notice Due To Unforeseen Circumstances."

"Unforeseen circumstances. That's an understatement," Jesse muttered under his breath.

"A Winchester cop is supposed to meet us here. Oh, here she is."

A Winchester police car parked next to Alex's car. A female officer emerged and jogged over. "Sorry to keep you waiting. I'm Officer Thelma Grace. Let me get this open for you." She removed a ring of keys from her jacket and used the red one to unlock the door.

Alex made introductions. "Wow. He was organized, wasn't he? Red key for the red store. Let me guess. The blue key is for the blue store, et cetera?"

"Correct. These keys were found in the desk of Mr. McClelland's study after his death. If I may ask, why are you working this case, Detective Hayes?" Thelma asked.

"Call me Alex, please. We have a, um, a personal interest in the last remaining member of the McClelland family, who's still alive. She was kidnapped, and we're hoping something in the store might help us in our search."

"Oh, my goodness. Let me know if I can help. I'll be out here while you do whatever it is you need to do."

"Thanks, Officer Grace."

"Thelma."

Alex smiled. "Thelma."

Vinny's cell phone chirped. Looking at the screen, he said, "You guys go in. I'll follow shortly." As the rest of the group entered the store, Vinny turned away from Officer Grace and answered. "Hey Marcie. You got good news for me?"

"I do, but it's not what you think."

"Okay. Shoot."

"Sid must have removed his SIM card, or his phone is dead because I haven't been able to track him for the last hour or so."

"That's not good news."

"No, it's not, but prior to an hour ago, his phone was at Conley Terminal in Southie."

"Conley? Why would he be there?"

"I don't know."

"Wait a minute. I asked you to track him less than an hour ago, Marcie. You said his phone wasn't trackable during that period of time. So how do you know where his phone was prior to that?"

There was silence.

"Were you tracking his phone before I asked you to?"

"Maybe."

"Why would you do that?"

"Because I saw the writing on the wall, Vinny, and I knew you'd eventually ask me to. We've worked together a long time, and I knew that tracking his phone would be your next step."

Vinny rubbed his eyes. "That's against the rules, Marcie."

"I know. That's why I said I had good news but that it wasn't what you'd think."

"Okay. Well, thanks for breaking the rules. If you hadn't, I wouldn't know where I had to go to ream Sid out. Seriously, thanks."

"So you're not mad?"

"Why would I be mad? You and I never had this conversation. As far as I remember, I asked you—wait, when did you start tracking his phone?"

"This morning."

"Right. As far as I remember, I asked you this morning to track his phone."

The relief in Marcie's voice was palpable. "Thanks, Vin."

"Thank *you*, Marcie."

Vinny rang off and opened the door to the cleaners. "Guess what? I know where my agent is, and I'm going to bring him here so he can help us."

"Do you think he knows where Molly is?" Jesse asked as he hurried forward.

"He says he doesn't, but he must know something."

"Well then, I'm going with you," Alex said, striding toward the door. Throwing her car keys to Jesse, she added, "You two stay here and work through your ideas about the notations on the buttons. Vinny and I will be back when we can. Take my car if you need it. Thelma, would mind driving Vinny and me to where, Vin?"

"Southie. Conley Terminal."

"Sure. Happy to help. Climb into my cruiser."

As they left, Alex turned to Jesse and said, "Be careful with my car, Jess. And don't let Julian drive."

Jesse smiled. "That never gets old!"

CHAPTER 64

After updating Mr. Torchia on Sid's discoveries in the diary, the Ogre asked permission to take Sid and Molly to one of the dry-cleaning stores to determine if Sid's theories were accurate.

"What about the button jar that the girl mentioned?" Torchia asked. At the mention of her beloved jar, Molly rose from the couch. "Didn't she say that her father had given her buttons that she kept in a jar? They might be related to the cypher in the diary, no?"

Sid's insides turned over. The idea of the button jar containing critical information had already occurred to Sid, but he was hoping to draw out the hunt, much as Jimmy had drawn out feeding him information. "I don't think the jar would have—"

"No one is speaking to you, Mr. Nickerson!" Torchia barked. "Keep your mouth shut!" Turning to the Ogre, he continued. "Go to Dr. Stryker's home. Get the jar, and then go to one of Jimmy's stores. Here's Dr. Stryker's address." He handed the Ogre a slip of paper before returning his attention to Sid. "Mr. Nickerson, this entire situation is becoming tiresome. You've got very little time to figure out what dirt Jimmy had on me and my organization."

Turning to Molly, he closed one eye and gave a wry little grin. "Perhaps Ms. McClelland should stay here with me as insurance." Molly rushed to Sid and shrank against his pant leg, trying to make herself small. She had determined that the big man with the broken arm wasn't very nice. The woman, Sheri, had been okay, but the man with the broken arm scared her.

"I don't think that will be necessary, boss. Besides, she might be useful in the store. She might know more than she thinks. When we get there, she might be able to help us."

The large man considered the Ogre's words as he reached into his cast with a long stick to scratch an itch. "Very well. Take her too."

As the trio turned to leave, Paolo Torchia cleared his throat loudly. "Oh, and Elliott?"

The Ogre turned to face the mob boss. "Yeah?"

"If you don't find the information I need, don't bother coming back."

The Ogre took several seconds to fully digest the implications of his boss's words before responding, "Yes, sir."

As they crossed the rickety metal catwalk, Sid couldn't help himself. Grabbing the Ogre's arm, he laughed. "Elliott? That's your name? Elliott?"

"Shut up, Sid. Your name ain't so great either."

"It's better than Elliott. That's, like, a cat's name or something."

"Just get moving, will ya?"

Exiting the building, Sid saw that a car was waiting for them, idling amidst the boatyard mayhem. The Muscle sat in the driver's seat, and Sid realized that his and Molly's time clock was ticking loudly. There was only one reason for the Muscle to go with them, and it wasn't to further the thought process.

Sid and Molly slid into the back seat while the Ogre sat next to the Muscle in the front. The Ogre turned around and lifted his gun. "My ass is on the line now too, so no funny business, Sid. For her sake." All heads turned to Molly, whose eyes were locked on the weapon. She had never seen a gun before.

"For God's sake, Elliott, put that thing away. You're scaring her!" Sid ordered, glancing at Molly again.

"Okay, but you get my point, right?"

"Yes, yes. Of course." Sid took Molly's limp hand and gave it a squeeze before she pulled it away and crossed her arms.

They rode in a silence that was broken only by the British GPS voice alerting them of a turn. "In five hundred feet, turn right, and the destination will be on your left," she purred.

As they pulled onto Julian's block, the Ogre said, "Okay, here's the deal. Leonard will knock on the door to see if anyone's there."

Sid's eyes became big. "Leonard? His name is Leonard?" he said while pointing to the huge, muscled driver. Sid gave him a dry look and continued. "If someone's there, Leonard will deal with it."

"What does that mean?" Sid asked, horrified.

"Don't worry, Sid. He'll be gentle but efficient. Anyway, that's only if someone's home. Hopefully no one's home, and we go in, grab the jar of buttons, and get out of there quickly."

Sid dropped his head and wondered once more about his predicament. Not seeing a way out, he agreed, noting that Molly seemed indifferent as the Muscle approached the door, knocked, and then rang the bell. He could hear what sounded like a large dog barking wildly.

After perusing the area to ensure no one had seen them, the Muscle turned to the car and motioned for everyone else to join him. Sid had to push Molly out of the car and carry her up onto the porch.

"Isn't this where your friend lives?" the Ogre asked. Molly nodded listlessly. Sid glanced at the Ogre with a worried look on his face. "I'm not sure she's okay."

The Ogre pursed his lips and raised his eyebrows. "Then let's get this over with as soon as possible, Sid." Sid looked at Molly again and nodded.

The Ogre leaned toward the little girl. "Honey, do you know the dog on the other side of this door?" Molly nodded. "Is he big?" Molly nodded again. "Is he nice?"

Molly looked at the wood door, as if she could see through it to the dog. "Oscar is very nice," she whispered.

The Ogre nodded to the Muscle, who removed a device from inside his coat. Within ten seconds, the front door was open, and Oscar came bounding through the doorway to greet them. Upon recognizing Molly, he broke into a howl and rubbed his head against her until she fell on the porch laughing. Sid smiled as he watched the scene unfold. Glancing at the Ogre and the Muscle, he saw that they were smiling too. Sid shook his head, trying to reconcile the two sides of the Ogre. His monster outside could shoot someone in the head while his marshmallow inside would be distraught about what he had done. It just didn't make sense.

"All right, all right. Let's get inside," the Ogre announced, businesslike once more.

Molly stood shakily and patted her hip so Oscar would follow. The motley crew entered the house where Sid immediately saw the buttons spread out on the dining room table.

Pointing, he said, "Look on the table."

Molly's face lit up as she followed the line of his outstretched finger. Jumping up, she dashed to the table and started scooping up her buttons and returning them to the jar.

"Whoa, whoa, Molly. Let me look at those for a moment." Sid crossed and took note of the microscope. Bending down, he closed one eye and peeked through the lens. A green button sat underneath it. It lay facedown so that he was examining the back of the button. Noting nothing unusual, he opened his other eye and adjusted the distance and focus using the metal wheels on either side of the instrument. Suddenly the image popped into focus, and Sid could clearly see "C12" engraved in tiny script. He looked up from the microscope and smiled at the Ogre. "Bingo. Another piece of the puzzle."

Once the Ogre understood the import of Sid's discovery, his mind leapt forward. "So Molly's friend, this Julian Stryker guy, already knows about this."

Sid nodded. "I would presume so, seeing as we're in his house."

"So what do you think he's gonna do next?"

Sid thought. "I'm not sure, but an obvious place to start would be one of the dry-cleaning stores."

"So we gotta get to the dry-cleaning store before he does."

Sid nodded as he thought. "Jimmy has seven stores. Odds are we're not going to end up at the same store looking for the same information." Sid glanced at the green button on the glass slide. "I'm guessing that Julian went to the green store once he realized what he was looking at."

The Ogre nodded his assent. "So we want to go to a different store. But which one?"

Sid reviewed the array of buttons, which had been divided by rainbow color. "Roy G. Biv."

"Excuse me?" the Ogre asked. His face was a mask of confusion.

Sid repeated, "Roy G. Biv."

"Who the hell is that?"

"The rainbow. That's how you remember it. You never learned that in school?"

The Ogre's blank look spoke volumes.

"Did you even go to school?"

The Ogre dropped his head in frustration. "Again, Sid, so mean. Yes, I went to school, but I never learned that."

Sid nodded. "Okay. R is for red, O is for orange, Y is for yellow—"

"Ahhh," the Ogre said as realization dawned. "That's cool!"

"Assuming Stryker went to the green store, how about we go to the red store, seeing as that's the first color in the rainbow?"

The Ogre nodded his approval. "Very logical, Sid. Good job."

"May I please have my buttons now?" Molly's soft voice broke through.

All three men turned in unison toward the little girl who had lost so much. The Muscle stepped forward, grabbed the jar, and started sweeping the buttons into it. In his high tenor voice he said, "Of course you can, sweetheart. Here you go."

Molly mumbled, "Thank you," as she gripped the jar to her tiny frame. It was the only solid item that still remained in her broken world.

CHAPTER 65

Julian smelled the odor of plastic sheeting as he followed Jesse into the dry-cleaning store. After three steps, Jesse stopped abruptly. "Okay, Julian. The store is about twenty feet wide with two counters in front. It's separated by a two-foot opening in the middle that has a metal bar above it, which is used for hanging clothes on for pickup. You with me?"

"Yup. Keep going."

"Behind the left counter is a doorway to the back of the store. You want to go back there?"

"Of course. Lead the way."

Jesse bent his left elbow, and Julian took his arm with his right hand while tapping his walking cane with his left. Normally Julian would have wanted to investigate the space on his own, but given their short time frame and the demanding circumstances, he acquiesced to being guided.

They had taken two steps forward when Julian hit his head on the metal bar separating the counters. "Ow!"

"Sorry. I sometimes forget how tall you are. I'll do better."

They entered the back area of the store where two distinct scents competed for attention: dirty clothes and steam.

"What's that smell? Yuck."

Julian smiled. "Have you never been in a dry-cleaning store before?"

Jesse pinched his nose. "Not in the heart of one, no. Have you?"

Julian smiled. "When I was in high school, I worked at a dry-cleaning store on weekends. It's tough, smelly work. Really hot in the summer despite the air-conditioning." He held up his right forearm, exposing the underside. "See that scar? It's from the huge flat irons we used."

"I've never noticed that before. Must have been painful."

"Absolutely. Now, describe the space please."

Jesse examined the area, deciding how best to start. "Same width, twenty feet, and I'd say about fifteen feet long. One of those irons that you burned yourself on is to your left—about two feet away—and there are several machines that have little holes in them with a bar above."

"Those are the industrial steamers."

"There are two steamers ahead about six feet to your right. There are many bins on wheels that hold clothes, and there are about thirty blue drawstring bags."

"Those are clothes that have been tagged already and are awaiting processing."

Jesse turned to Julian. "You are a veritable fountain of useless information."

"You have no idea. Go on."

"Anyhow, all around us is what looks to be a monorail for clothes. It's a conveyor belt, I think. It starts on the left of where we entered and rises to a height of about twelve feet as it winds around to the back of the store. It descends as it comes around to the right side of this space. It looks like all of the clean clothes that are waiting to be picked up are on it."

Julian nodded. "What about sweaters?"

"What?"

"There should be an area that holds folded items like sweaters."

Jesse led Julian past the iron and there on the left, was shelving that contained sweaters, shirts, comforters, and UGG boots. "You were right. There are shelves back here on the left."

"Anything else?"

Jesse led Julian to the right and craned his neck. "No. That's the entire store."

"You brought the red buttons and your written list of the engravings, right?"

"Yes."

"Great. Okay, let's be methodical about this. What's the first letter/ number combination on your written list?"

Jesse consulted the paper. "A35."

"Do you remember which of the three red buttons A35 is?"

"No, and the engraving is too small to see without the microscope."

Julian shook his head. "I guess it doesn't matter because if we find the clothes the button comes from, it'll be clear. The item will be missing a button, right?"

"Right."

"Okay. How are the clothes on the conveyor belt organized? By ticket number? Is there an A35?"

Jesse returned to the front of the conveyor belt and grabbed a paper tag. "It seems that each clothing item has a ticket on it. There's a name—the customer's, I'm assuming—and an eight-digit order number on the tag but nothing like A35."

"That would have been too easy, I suppose. If Jimmy went to all of this trouble to hide something that would protect his family, he would have been more clever about it." Julian chewed his lip in thought. "Maybe the A has something to do with color. Jimmy clearly liked to categorize by color, so maybe A is a color. What are some colors that begin with A?"

"Alabaster, almond, amaranth."

Julian tilted his head. "What's amaranth?"

"It's a beautiful rosy red color. It's a weed but has a gorgeous flower. It's often called pigweed, which I think is unfair because—"

Julian help up his hand. "Sorry I asked. Anyhow, the colors you mentioned are too obscure. I don't think he would have used those."

"Well if you were trying to hide something, wouldn't obscure be a useful trait?"

"Yes, but Jimmy was also very practical. He would have picked a more obvious color."

"Maybe the letter doesn't refer to a color. Maybe it refers to a customer name."

"Good thought. How did you say the clean clothes were organized on the belt?"

"By customer name and an eight-digit number."

"Check and see if all of the *A*'s are grouped together."

Jesse pressed the green button that activated the conveyor belt. The gears groaned to life, and the clothes started moving. "*H, I, J.*" Jesse stopped speaking as the clothes continued their circular journey. "Here we are. The *A*'s." As Jesse searched, the plastic rustled and reminded Julian of opening Christmas gifts as a child. "The *A*'s are all together."

"And what about the numbers? Are they in sequential order within the *A* section?"

Jesse sifted through ten hangers. "It would seem so."

"So A35 must be in that group somewhere if our theory is correct. Check the entire *A* section and see if any clothes have buttons matching the three red buttons you brought."

Jesse groaned. "The *A* section has at least fifty hangers, Julian."

"Do it. We're running out of time."

Julian tapped his way around the back area of the store as he listened to Jesse rummage through clothes. After several minutes, Jesse announced, "Nothing. No match. Besides, I told you that each tag has an eight-digit code. The engraving only says A35. I think we're barking up the wrong tree."

"Is there anywhere we can sit for a minute?"

Jesse looked around. "Not back here, but we could go to the front and sit on the counters. You okay?"

"Yeah. I just need to think."

Returning to the front, each man hoisted himself up on a counter. Julian dipped his head and placed himself in Jimmy McClelland's mind. He spoke softly and slowly. "What we're looking for has to be here. Maybe not in *this* store but in one of his stores. He wouldn't be stupid enough to simply rent a post office box or a locker at the bus terminal. He was smarter than that and cunning. He would keep his insurance against the mob close to him where he could monitor its safety. He would hide it in plain sight. It has to be in one of his stores. Maybe we should try a different store." Julian paused for a moment and then said, "Did you hear me, Jess?"

"What? No. You were mumbling, and I was reading the signage here. Do you know that people lose the right to their clothes if they don't pick them up within thirty days of dropping them off? That doesn't seem right."

"That's a typical policy for most dry-cleaning stores. Otherwise, you run out of space. Maybe we should try another store. What do you think?"

"What do they do? Give the clothes away to charity? Sell them?"

Julian shook his head. "When I worked in dry-cleaning, although we posted a sign saying clothes were forfeited after thirty days, in reality, we just kept them at the back of the store for another thirty days while we tried to contact the owners. Hey, can we get back on topic please? Should we go to the green store and check out their clothes?"

"Yeah, sure. It'll give me chance to drive Alex's zippy car." He jumped off the counter and walked toward the front door. "Should we lock the door from the inside as we're leaving? That cop didn't tell us how to lock up, so …" He turned around and Julian was gone. "Julian?"

"Back here! Come quick!" Julian called.

"What is it?"

"You're brilliant, that's what."

"I know, but can you be more specific?"

"Remember I said that despite the posted policy, we actually kept the clothes for another month?"

"Yeah."

"Well, that got me thinking that sometimes there are clothes that are never claimed. People die or forget and move away."

"Really?" Jesse was skeptical.

"Yes, really. Happens more than you'd think. You know my gray Irish knit sweater that you hate?"

"You mean the one that smells and has holes in it? Yes."

"That's from the dry-cleaning store where I worked. It was unclaimed, so the owner gave it to me as a gift when I went to college."

"Some gift," Jesse sniffed.

Julian ignored the comment. "Anyway, let's find the unclaimed clothes and check their buttons against our three red ones. Go to the *Z* section and then look past it. I bet the unclaimed clothes are there."

Jesse pressed the green button once more, and the conveyor lurched forward. Singing an incredibly slow version of the alphabet song as each letter passed, he finally arrived at *Z*. "Good news. There aren't many *Z*'s. Let's see … Ah. You were right, Julian. The alphabetic listing starts all over again back here, but they still have eight-digit codes."

"How many *A*'s are there?"

"I'd say about eight."

"See if any of them have the number 35 on them anywhere, maybe at the beginning of the eight-digit code or at the end."

Jesse sorted through the unclaimed items and found one whose last two numbers were 35.

"Please tell me that it's missing a button."

Jesse withdrew the suit and removed the plastic. Based on Jesse's sigh, Julian knew the answer before Jesse spoke. "All of the buttons are on the suit jacket, Julian."

"Dammit! Do any of the three red buttons you brought from the jar match the ones on the suit?"

Jesse removed the three red buttons from his pocket and compared them. "Yes! One of them does."

Julian stood up straighter. "There's got to be something here then. Check the pockets of the jacket to see if anything's in there."

Jesse methodically lifted the flap over each of the four pockets and then reached in to scour their insides. "Nothing in any of the pockets."

"What about the pants?"

"It's a woman's suit, and it has a skirt."

"Whatever. Check it."

Jesse lifted the suit jacket and examined the skirt. A line of buttons that matched the ones on the jacket was sewn across the waistline, and one was missing. "The skirt is missing a button, Julian. I'm checking the pockets." Jesse checked both pockets and came up empty.

"It doesn't make sense," Julian said, shaking his head. "What were the codes on the back of the other two red buttons again?"

Jesse referred to his written list. "T17 and C12."

"Go to the *C* section and find the item that has the number 12 as the last two numbers in its eight-digit code."

Jesse did as instructed and discovered a missing button on the shirt but nothing in the pockets.

"Check T17."

A minute later Jesse said, "It looks like a blanket. No, actually it's a gorgeous red duvet cover."

"Any buttons missing?"

Jesse ran his fingers along the line of buttons that were used to close the cover around the duvet. "Yup. The last button on the corner is missing. But there are no pockets to check."

"Jess, a duvet cover *is* a giant pocket. Remove it from the hanger, and let's spread it out."

Jesse pulled it off the hanger and gave Julian two sides while he held the other two. Together they walked backward away from each other, spread the cover out completely, and laid it on the floor. There was a small bump in the middle of the duvet. Jesse reached into the cover, scrunching it up as he went, and pulled out a thumb drive. Handing it to Julian, he said, "What does this feel like to you?"

Realizing what it was, Julian grinned. "It feels like we're one step closer to finding Molly. That's what it feels like."

CHAPTER 66

Officer Thelma Grace drove faster than usual. She was excited to be peripherally involved in a case that commanded not only the Boston Police Department's attention, but also the FBI's. "My last involvement with this case was the day I found Mr. McClelland and Ms. Moser at his house. I heard that they were having an affair and that's why he hung himself." She glanced to her right where Vinny sat staring out the passenger window.

"Not true. I saw Kellie Moser in the hospital. She said there was no affair, and I believe her. McClelland's death was a mob hit. He was murdered."

"What?"

Alex picked up the thread from there and updated Thelma on the rest of the case to date. When she was done, Thelma shook her head and sighed. "I can't believe all of that was happening in Winchester right under our noses. And my father was worried that I'd be bored working in the Winchester PD. Holy cow. So, you think that McClelland was hiding something in his stores to protect himself against the mob?"

Vinny nodded.

"Like what?"

"Information most likely. Stuff that could put Paolo Torchia away for a long time."

"And you think that your friends will find it?"

"Julian has an uncanny ability to get inside other people's heads to determine what they've done or might do. If anyone can figure this puzzle out, it's Julian," Alex said confidently.

Thelma turned to Vinny. "You said that you saw Ms. Moser in the hospital. How is she?"

Vinny continued to stare outside. "She's regained some movement, and the doctors are hopeful that she won't be paralyzed."

"That's good to hear."

Thelma thought for a moment. "The only McClelland left alive is little Molly?"

"Yes."

"We have to find her."

Alex, who was in the back seat of the cruiser, locked eyes with Thelma in the rearview mirror. "Yes, we do. That's why we're going to Conley Terminal. It's the last place Vinny's agent's phone was tracked to. Vinny thinks the owner of the phone can lead us to her. Can you go a little faster please?"

Thelma increased her speed. "So you're that agent's boss?" Vinny nodded. "And where is he now? Did something happen to him?"

Vinny turned to face the young officer. "I'm hoping that he's still at Conley and that he's okay. We've worked together since I started at the bureau. All of this is completely out of character for him. At first, I thought maybe the mob was threatening his family, but I know they're safe, so now I don't know what's going on or why." Vinny resumed his window vigil. "All I know is that I have to talk to him."

The police cruiser approached the entry gate and slowed. A burly man, who was sporting a goatee, eyed the car and its occupants.

"Help you?"

Thelma tried to sound official. "Please open the gate. Police business."

"What kind of business?"

Thelma pulled out her badge and stared him dead in the eye. "Police business. Open the gate—now."

The man backed away, pulled out his phone, and dialed. After a quick conversation, the gate slid open, and the car was waved through.

"I wonder what that was about," Thelma said as she watched the man in her side mirror.

"Doesn't matter. Drive," Vinny ordered.

"Where should I go? There are three warehouses."

Vinny swiveled his head around and looked for any sign of Sid. Not finding any, Vinny said, "Just drive straight ahead to the middle warehouse."

Thelma did as she was told and stopped the car in front of a large steel entrance at the front of the building. "Now what?"

Before Vinny could answer, the sliding doors parted and an obese man wearing a cast emerged. "What the hell happened to his arm?" Vinny asked.

"Must have broken it," Alex mumbled. "Oh my God, Vin. That's Paolo Torchia."

Vinny sneered. "Broken arm, huh. Couldn't have happened to a nicer guy. Stay in the car, Thelma, but let your precinct know where we are. Alex, come with me."

They exited the car as Paolo Torchia removed a cigar from his pocket, bit off the end, and spat it on the pavement. "Classy," Alex whispered.

As they approached, Alex could feel his eyes crawling over her body. With the unlit cigar perched in one side of his mouth, he asked, "Can you do a crippled man a favor and light my cigar?" Vinny stepped forward. "Not you," he stated while still examining Alex. "Her."

His mouth curled into a grotesque smile, and as she approached, he whispered, "*Mio dio.* You are breathtaking, my dear." Alex met his eyes as she took the lighter from his hand and drew a flame. She leaned in close as the flame met the cigar. "No, no, my dear," he said, pulling away from her. "You must never let the flame actually touch the foot of the cigar. You remain still while I rotate the cigar around the flame, like this." He bent his head at a forty-five-degree angle and turned the cigar in his fingers while drawing on it. Once he was satisfied that it was burning evenly, he removed it from his mouth and blew on it gently to ensure that it remained lit. All the while, he watched Alex watching him. "If only *you* were this cigar, *mio amore.* The process is quite seductive, is it not?"

Alex raised her eyebrows. "It is not. Tell me, Mr. Torchia, have you seen Sid Nickerson anywhere around here recently?"

He regarded her for just an instant before throwing his head back in laughter. "My, but you are a firecracker! As a matter of fact, I have no idea of whom you speak. I've been working in my office all afternoon. Would you like to come in and see?" With his one good arm, he gestured toward the open door behind him. He was clearly enjoying himself.

"Why did you murder Jimmy McClelland?" Alex asked.

Paolo Torchia's arm dropped as his smile evaporated. After a long, languid draw on his cigar, he said, "I'm sorry. Who?"

Vinny stepped forward quickly. "Listen, asshole, we know that you killed Jimmy, and we know that Sid was here earlier. We also believe that your people kidnapped Molly McClelland from the hospital. If you know where either Sid or Molly are, you better tell us right fucking *now!*"

Paolo regarded Vinny as one might consider a mosquito before helping it meet its maker. Stepping toward Vinny, he smiled and said, "Or what, Mr. Marcozzi? You need to understand that I am used to dealing with ... your kind and do not intimidate easily. If you had any proof of these so-called crimes, you'd be arresting me." Placing the cigar in his mouth, he proffered his one good hand toward Vinny. "Would you like to cuff me?"

A guttural sound escaped Vinny's throat. "I'd like nothing more."

Paolo turned to Alex suddenly and dropped his eyes. "Would *you* like to cuff me?" Alex contorted her face in disgust.

He drew on his cigar again and smiled broadly. "Well, what a lovely chat it's been. Ms. Hayes, you are welcome here anytime in an unofficial capacity of course." He shifted his eyes toward Vinny as his smile fell. "You, Mr. FBI man, are not. Good day." With that, he turned on his heel and reentered the building. The large steel doors closed behind him as if by magic.

"Why do I feel like we were just part of a stage show?" Vinny muttered.

"Why do I feel like I need a shower?" Alex responded, her face a mask of revulsion. "Yuck!"

They returned to Thelma, whose window had been open to hear the exchange. "Wow! So that's Paolo Torchia. He seems a little ..."

"Crazy?" Vinny asked.

"Gross?" Alex offered.

"Yes on both counts. Listen—why don't we take a look around while we're here."

"We don't have any authority. No warrant."

"I thought the FBI didn't need a warrant or probable cause."

"Technically, you're correct. The FBI can initiate an investigation without a warrant, but the Torchia family is a state and federal problem. Alex and I want to ensure that every move we make is on solid legal footing. A lot of what we're doing is based on gut feeling, Thelma. We don't want you to get in trouble because of our potential mistakes."

"Are you kidding me? This is awesome!" They both looked at her simultaneously. "Well, I didn't mean awesome. I meant—"

"We know what you meant, Thelma," said Vinny tiredly. "I remember when I felt like that about my job."

"Hey, how did he know your names, by the way?"

Alex lifted her head. "What?"

"He called you both by your names. How did he know your names?"

Alex looked at Vinny, who returned her stare and said, "The only way he would know my face and name is if he'd been talking to Sid."

"And the only way he'd know me is if he'd been talking to Molly."

Thelma looked from Alex to Vinny. "Well, I don't know about you guys, but in my world, that information is probably enough to get a warrant."

CHAPTER 67

"How are we going to see what's on that thumb drive?" Julian asked.

"There's a computer on each counter out front. Let me see if they have USB ports." Jesse rushed to the front of the store and turned one of the computers around. "There's a port on the back of this one. Give me the drive."

Julian handed Jesse the drive, and he inserted it. Almost immediately, Julian heard two soft dings, which indicated that the drive was active. "What do you see?"

"Too many files are on this drive. It's completely full. I don't know where to begin."

"Just open one of them, and let's see what we're dealing with."

Julian heard Jesse double-clicking the mouse and then the computer's innards working to retrieve the file. After what felt like an interminable length of time, Jesse said, "Ah-ha!"

"What is it?"

"It's an Excel file with many, many sheets and tons of rows and columns in each sheet. Wow, this thing is huge."

"Jesse, it's been a while since I've looked at a computer, and I don't think I ever used Excel in grad school. Can you please describe what you are seeing?"

"Yeah, sorry, Julian. Excel is an application used to create spreadsheets in order to manage financial information—or anything really. Each Excel file can have many spreadsheets. Each spreadsheet can contain many cells. The first spreadsheet's tab starts with *A*, but you can rename it to whatever you like. The next tab is *B*, which is followed by *C*, et cetera. And when those twenty-six sheets are full, the tabs start all over again with *AA*, *BB*, et cetera. Understand?"

"Yes."

"This particular file that I opened has—wait." Julian listened while Jesse counted out loud. "It has eighteen sheets, each of which has exactly …" The mouse clicked as Jesse scrolled. "It has ninety-three rows and thirty columns. Holy moly, that's a ton of data."

Julian did some quick math in his head. "So if I'm understanding you correctly, each spreadsheet would contain 2,790 cells of data, and the entire file would contain … let's see, 50,220 cells of information."

Jesse swiveled his head and regarded Julian suspiciously. "Why, exactly, am I doing the bills and the financial work at your practice if you can do that kind of math in your head?"

Julian grinned broadly and patted Jesse's back. "Because we need each other. We're a team. You're the yin to my yang, the peanut butter to my jelly, the—"

Jesse was shaking his head as he interrupted. "Anywayyyy, each tab in this file is labeled with a date. The dates are spread about three weeks apart, it seems. The first tab is January 1, 2018. The next tab is January 20, 2018 and so on. The last tab is December 12, 2018."

Julian stood up straight and rubbed his back. "This is just one file on one thumb drive, and it has this much data. Didn't you say that this thumb drive has many files on it?"

"Yes."

"We have to assume that there are other drives or information of some sort that correspond with the other buttons' engravings. How many buttons had engravings on them?"

"I didn't finish examining them, remember? But there are seven colors in the rainbow, and each color had at least two or three buttons. Out of three red buttons, we found only one drive in this store, but we can't assume Jimmy did it that way in his other stores. So I'd say that there are between seven and twenty drives in his stores waiting to be found."

"Those other drives probably have the same amount of information too." Julian rubbed his face.

"Let's say we find all of them. How do we know what's important? How do we know what information corresponds to Torchia's empire and what are simply numbers that Jimmy threw in to hide the real data?"

Both of them were silent as they thought through the enormity of the situation. Jesse was quiet for so long that Julian wondered if he was still at the computer. "Jesse?"

"What do you think Molly is doing right now?" he asked softly.

"I don't know, Jess. But we're going to find her. We found Jimmy's hidden information, and we'll find her as well."

"But do you think she's scared?"

Julian didn't want to lie and knew how much Jesse had grown to care for her in the short time he had known her. "I hope not."

"I think she's scared, Julian. I think that she believes we abandoned her."

"But we haven't, and we won't. Let's focus on the problem right in front of us, which might help lead us to her. I was just thinking about your question. You asked how we'll know which numbers are important in all of this data."

"Do you have an answer?"

"No, I don't."

Jesse threw up his hands in frustration.

"But how did he know?"

"Who?"

"Jimmy. How did he keep track of which numbers were important? He was smart and organized, but no one could keep track of fifty thousand numbers in his head. Besides, he created these spreadsheets to safeguard his family while he was alive and after he was gone, although I'm sure he was hoping it wouldn't come to that. While he was alive, he must have had a way to keep track of the important information. If the mob figured out that he was collecting info on them and killed him, he was probably relying on someone being able to decipher his codes and to continue to protect his family."

"What about Vinny's agent, Sid? Maybe Jimmy thought that if something happened to him, Sid would figure out the code and bring the Torchias to justice, thereby protecting his family."

"Exactly. Maybe it was Sid. My point is that Jimmy must have had a way to keep track of information related to the Torchia business versus dummy numbers." Suddenly, a thought illuminated his mind so clearly that Julian was shocked he hadn't seen it sooner. "Oh, my goodness."

"What?"

"The key."

"What key?"

"Remember the key that was in the button jar? Maybe the reason it was kept in the jar was because it guarded the second part of the puzzle—the part that would indicate which numbers were important. The key looked like it might open a diary or a small book."

"So where is the key now?"

"Still back at my house with the jar."

"And where's the book that it opens?"

"I don't know. I think we're still missing that piece of the puzzle."

"You mean this?" a gravelly voice asked from the doorway. Jesse looked up to see a man in a bright Hawaiian shirt holding a small book in his hand.

"Who are you?" Jesse asked.

"Doesn't matter."

"His name is Elliott," another man interjected as he stepped from behind the first man. The Ogre gave Sid a withering stare.

"And you are ...?" Jesse asked the newcomer.

"That *really* doesn't matter," Sid said. The Ogre cleared his throat. "His name is Sid Nickerson. He's with the FBI."

"Ah, Sid." Julian smiled. "We've been looking for you. Well, Vinny's been looking for you."

Sid looked around quickly. "Is Vinny here?"

"No, no, but I'm sure he'll be here soon. Anyone else we need to know about?"

The Muscle stood outside with his back to the store and ensured that the encounter remained private. "My friend Leonard is outside, but you don't need to worry about him," the Ogre said. "He's only here in case we need backup."

Julian raised both of his hands in a supplicating gesture. "There'll be no need for that, I assure you."

"I couldn't help but overhear your discussion about this diary," the Ogre said, paging through it. Then he saw the thumb drive sticking out of the computer. "Anything interesting on that drive?"

Jesse eyed the screen. "Not really. Just some statistics about this dry-cleaning store. Very boring actually."

"Hmm, I see. Then you won't mind if I take it? You see, in order to understand what's written in this book, I think I need that thumb drive. Until now, I was missing some *pertinent* information." He turned to Sid. "See what I did there? I used the word *pertinent* correctly, didn't I?"

Sid ignored the comment and looked pleadingly at Jesse. "Please just give the drive to Elliott, and we can be on our way."

Jesse whispered to Julian without moving his lips. "What do we do now?" Although they only had the red buttons with them, Julian knew that the other buttons were safe and sound on the table at his house. So if they had to surrender the thumb drive, they could use the other buttons' engravings to find the remaining drives and to turn them over to the police. Perhaps they could use this thumb drive as a negotiating tool to find Molly and still use the other buttons to gather enough evidence to shut down the Torchias.

Julian drew a long slow breath through rounded lips and started the negotiation. "We could do that, Sid, but then you'd have all the cards."

The Ogre laughed. "What's so funny?" Jesse asked.

"You guys. You guys are what's funny. I don't think you get it. We already hold all of the cards, or all of the cards that matter to you, that is."

"What do you mean?" asked Julian.

"How's this for a card?" the Ogre asked as he reached behind him. Molly, who had been hiding behind Sid, was dragged out and held in place by the Ogre's large hands. The buttons rattled in the jar she was holding as she struggled against the Ogre's grip.

Jesse's hand flew to his mouth as his breath caught in his throat. After a moment, Molly stopped resisting. In a tiny, halting voice she said, "Hi, Julian. Why didn't you find me? You said you'd come ... but you didn't."

CHAPTER 68

Vinny was on the phone with Marcie, updating her on recent events. He also asked her to obtain a federal warrant to search Paolo Torchia's warehouse at Conley Terminal on the grounds of suspicion of kidnapping and endangering a minor.

"Do you think the little girl is inside?" Marcie asked.

"I have no idea, but if the warrant gets us inside the building, that's all I need. I have to find Sid and Molly. If Paolo and his goons go down in the process, so much the better."

"I'm on it, Vin."

"How long will it take?"

"I'm going to call Judge Connelly's office. His chief of staff owes me a favor. Let me see if I can expedite this for you. I'll be in touch."

"Thanks for working your magic, Marcie."

"Don't thank me yet."

As Vinny disconnected, Thelma said, "You know, technically Paolo Torchia invited you guys into the warehouse, remember? You shouldn't need a warrant."

Alex shook her head. "He invited me in but not Vinny, and we want everything by the book so that when this goes to trial, there will be absolutely no wiggle room for him to get off on a technicality."

"Makes sense," Thelma nodded.

Alex noted that Vinny's mouth was twisting in thought. "What? You think I should go in?"

"Thelma's right. He did invite you in, and Molly could be in there."

"Vinny, I'll go, but if something goes wrong—"

"I'll be your backup," Vinny interjected.

"No, you dumbass. I'm not worried about my safety. I'm worried about protocol, like you said earlier. How many times have these mobsters used a get-out-of-jail-free card because of some deal that was made behind closed doors related to a technicality. If I go in there and Torchia's high-priced lawyer weaves an argument that I wasn't invited in, our case will go down the tubes. It will be finished. Do you want to risk failure after all of the time, effort, and taxpayer money the FBI has put into Torchia's case? Think before you answer, Vinny. I'll do whatever you think is right."

Vinny hesitated less than a second. "Go. Molly might be in there. If she is, they might move her before we can get the warrant, and then she's gone forever, literally. I couldn't live with that. Could you?"

Alex looked at the building. "Absolutely not. I'm going."

Alex removed her gun from its holster and unlocked the safety. She replaced the gun, closed her eyes, placed her hand on her belly, and breathed deeply. Exhaling, she said, "Here we go. Get in there as soon as the warrant gets here."

"I will. Good luck."

Alex pulled hard on the sliding steel door. After two tries, it separated from its twin. Success was slow, but finally, a gap emerged through which she slid sideways. Giving one last wave to Vinny and Thelma, she entered the cavernous space, leaving the door ajar behind her. As her eyes adjusted to the building's dim light, she was able to discern small forklifts moving various sizes of wooden crates from one end of the building to the other. She noted that all of the men were yelling, which made it difficult to discern who was in charge. Keeping close to the wall, she forged ahead, unsure of where she was going but displaying confidence in her stride and demeanor. She had stopped at an elevator and was pressing the button when a voice called out, "Hey, you, stop! What are you doing?"

Standing up straighter, Alex turned slowly with her palms facing outward. "Hi!" she yelled over the noise. "I'm here to see Mr. Torchia."

The man glanced at her gun holster and then smirked. "Who?"

Alex smiled in response. "Paolo Torchia. I know he's here because I was recently speaking to him outside. Where might I find him?"

"I'm sorry, lady, but—"

Alex stepped closer so she wouldn't have to yell. "He invited me in."

The look of doubt on the man's face struck Alex as comical. He was obviously not a key player in the organization, and she could see that he was calculating the options. If she was telling the truth and had been invited and he didn't allow it, he would get in trouble. If she hadn't been invited and he brought her to Mr. Torchia, he'd be in trouble. No one wanted to be in trouble with Paolo Torchia.

Taking a step backward from her, he yelled, "How do I know you're telling the truth?"

Just to torture him, she replied, "You don't."

He glared at her and then shook his head. "Get the fuck outta here."

He lurched forward and grabbed her wrist, which she had hoped he would do. Twisting her wrist out of his grasp, she encircled his throat with her left arm while simultaneously grabbing his right arm and twisting it up behind his back. He grunted and stood on his toes in an effort to alleviate the awkward, painful position his arm was in.

Alex leaned close to his ear. "Have you seen a little girl about five years old around here?"

His grunted response was incoherent, so Alex applied more pressure to his arm. "Aaahhh," he breathed.

"You must not have heard the question. Have you seen a little girl recently?"

"Yeah, yeah. She was here before. Please, please stop. I'll take you to Mr. Torchia."

"Do you promise to be nice?"

"Yeah, yeah."

Alex released his arm, and he backed away quickly, trying to put as much distance between himself and her as possible. Rubbing his right shoulder, he mumbled, "Crazy bitch."

"What was that?" Alex asked as she closed the distance between them in one stride.

He held up his hands in front of him. "Nothing! Sorry. Follow me."

The man kept glancing behind him as he led Alex through the warehouse. She wasn't sure if he was nervous she would jump him or if he wanted to ensure she wouldn't run off somewhere. Either way, it made her smile. Vinny had been right. This *was* a good idea.

They ascended a metal staircase ending in a catwalk that swayed as they crossed. Finally, the man stopped abruptly in front of a large metal door. He knocked three times as he kept looking at Alex nervously while they waited. The door opened about two inches, and the man leaned forward to speak to the person inside. After a brief conversation, the door was closed but was reopened thirty seconds later. Paolo Torchia was standing there smiling with his broken arm outstretched like an awkward scarecrow. The man who had led Alex stumbled backward, fell into her, and then scrambled to right himself as Paolo Torchia waved him away. To Alex's astonishment, the man bowed before taking his leave from the godfather.

"Wow," she said. "It's kind of like you're a king."

Paolo raised one eyebrow while spreading his good arm wide in a welcoming gesture. "I am a king, of sorts, and let me tell you ..." He leaned forward conspiratorially. "It is very good to be king, my dear."

"So I hear."

"Now, to what do I owe this very, very pleasant surprise?"

Now it was Alex's turn to smile. "You did invite me in, didn't you?"

He stared at her for a moment with a smile frozen on his face. "Did I?" he answered with a finger to his lips as he feigned confusion. "A man of my advanced years, you know, sometimes we forget things or speak out of turn."

Alex nodded. "Oh, you definitely invited me in, Paolo. May I call you Paolo? But it doesn't really matter, because my friend outside, the FBI agent you didn't invite in, is in the process of obtaining a warrant to search the warehouse. I just thought I'd come visit and take a look around myself. You know, since you invited me."

Their eyes locked in a silent war of wills as a full minute crept by. Without warning, he bowed theatrically and said, "But of course. Do come in and make yourself at home. Look around as much as you want. We always want to be of assistance to our men and women in blue."

Alex crossed the threshold and was greeted by wide-eyed stares from several of the room's occupants. A ruby-lipped woman with big hair sat draped across a plastic-covered couch while a young man, whose pants were too tight, gawked at her from a corner. A small well-dressed, mustached man was leaning over the desk reading. He looked up briefly as she had entered but quickly returned to his task.

"Is this where Jimmy McClelland worked?" At the sound of Jimmy's name, the small man behind the desk straightened quickly and glanced nervously at Paolo.

"I'm sorry. Did I hit a nerve?" Alex asked innocently. "Are you his replacement? You kind of look like an accountant."

The man's eyes widened as they flitted between Alex and Paolo, who laughed. "You're very good at your job, Ms. Hayes. Yes, this is Jimmy's replacement."

"I see," Alex said, staring the little man straight in the eye. "If I were you, I'd get out while I could because once you're in, you're in for life. Isn't that right, Paolo?" Not waiting for an answer, she continued. "Has anyone in this room seen a little girl who is five years old, cute as a fricking button, and has ginger hair?" She looked from person to person, but no one met her eye. "That's what I thought. She was here. Is she still here somewhere?"

Alex started for the door, but Paolo placed his good hand on her arm. "Don't bother, my dear. She's no longer with us."

CHAPTER 69

Julian couldn't speak. "I ... I ..."

"It's okay, Julian. Everybody leaves me. It's okay. Don't be sad."

"Molly ..." Julian knelt down and spoke quietly. "Molly, we never, ever stopped looking for you. We're here because we thought it might bring us closer to finding you. Jesse, Alex, and I have been searching, and we weren't giving up until we found you. And now you're here."

Molly took a step toward Julian but was stopped by the Ogre. "Oh, no, missy. You're staying with me. We're all going to get in my car and go see Mr. Torchia."

Molly looked up at the Ogre. "You mean the big fat blind man with the broken wing?"

The Ogre, who was caught off guard, guffawed. "Yeah. That's him. He'll know what to do."

"How did you get your button jar, Molly?" Jesse asked softly.

Molly looked guilty. "These men took me to Julian's house to get my jar. Sorry we went in without you, Julian, but Oscar is okay. He licked me a lot and made me laugh."

Julian smiled. "Thank you for telling me that Oscar's okay. Are you okay?"

She simply stared in response with large unblinking eyes.

"Molly?" Julian tried again.

"Let's go," the Ogre interrupted.

The Ogre led the way. He opened the rear door of the Yukon XL to ensure that Julian and Jesse sat in the very back seat with Molly sandwiched between them. The Muscle sat in the second row and faced the back so he could keep an eye on them as the Ogre drove with Sid in the passenger seat.

Jesse wanted to hug Molly but didn't want to risk angering their captors. Instead, he gently placed his hand over hers and whispered, "Your tiara is waiting for you at Julian's house."

Molly withdrew her hand and shook her head as she stared straight ahead. "I don't want it anymore."

"Why?"

"Because I'm not a princess, Jesse. I'm just a girl with no … a girl with no …" A sob burst forth so strongly that it caused her little body to double over. She sat with her chest on her thighs and was wracked by grief that had not yet been expressed. The stresses of the last few days came roaring over the lip of the waterfall, and the flow that followed was unstoppable. She cried for the family she would never see again, for the promises that new friends had broken, and for the life that would be forever altered.

Jesse reached over her and squeezed Julian's shoulder, silently asking what he should do.

"Let her cry," Julian responded aloud. "Molly, you have every right to feel the way you do. You cry as long as you want. When you're done, Jesse and I will still be here to talk to you when you're ready."

The Ogre met Jesse's eyes in the rearview mirror. "Hey, buddy. Tell your blind friend that he shouldn't make promises he may not be able to keep." Jesse glared at the Ogre and then glanced at the Muscle, who shifted uncomfortably in his seat. He was clearly moved by Molly's tears.

The little girl's sobbing slowly subsided to briefs bouts of quick inhalations followed by quiet moaning. Eventually she stopped altogether, asked for a tissue, and collapsed against Jesse. Ignoring the Ogre's warning looks, Jesse placed his arm around her and pulled her close. "Feeling better?"

She nodded, reached for Julian's hand and pulled it into her lap. "I remembered, Julian."

"Remembered what?"

"What happened the day my family died."

Jesse stiffened as Julian pressed on. "Do you want to talk about it?"

Taking his hand in her own, she signed "yes" on his palm.

"Okay. Take your time and talk when you're ready."

She looked at Jesse for reassurance. He nodded and smiled. Taking a deep breath, she began. "Mommy, Joey, and I were at the grocery store getting food for dinner when Mommy talked to Daddy on the phone and then started crying when she hung up. She told us to get in the car right away, and we left our cart right in the middle of the store. We ran to the car, and Mommy put her phone and her purse in a trash can. She took the—what's the thing called on the back of cars?"

"The bumper?"

"No. It's a rectangle made of metal."

"The license plate?"

"Yeah. That's it. She took a license plate out of the box in the front seat and put it on the back of the car. Then she took the other license plate and threw it in the trashcan. Joey was yelling, 'Where are we going?' and she said that we were driving and that Daddy would meet us later. Then I asked her where we were going, and she told me to stop talking.

"I started crying because she was being so mean. I told her that I had to get my button jar, and she said a bad word. But then she told me that I was right and that we had to get it, so we went home, and I got it. That's when I saw my ..." Molly stopped talking as her eyes took in the scene unfolding in her memory. "I saw my daddy swinging. I was so scared, but I got my jar and ran back to the car. Mommy asked if I was okay, and I nodded, but I wasn't. I couldn't talk. I couldn't talk," she repeated, trailing off.

Jesse's lips were tight as he watched Molly relive that horrific day in her memory. He knew from working with Julian that he shouldn't interrupt her or bring in any emotion of his own. He stifled the sob that was crawling up his throat and stamped down his anger at the people in the car who had caused this innocent little girl so much chaos and pain. He stroked Molly's hair while staring out the window.

"Mommy was driving so fast, and Joey and I were scared. Joey was in the front seat, and he's not supposed to be there. He's too little. I wanted to be in the front seat too, but Mommy told me to shut up." Molly started to cry again. "She was being so mean." Molly covered her face in her hands as she breathed rapidly. "It wasn't fair that Joey was in the front seat, and I wasn't. I wanted to be there too, so I kept asking. I shouldn't have asked. I shouldn't have asked ..."

Jesse shook his head and wiped his tears on his sleeve. He glanced at Julian for guidance. Julian sat stoically listening with his head tilted toward Molly and his fingers still entwined with hers. Jesse knew that Julian was evaluating and determining the correct time to ask a question or interject a thought.

Molly took a deep shuddering breath and then exhaled raggedly. "It's my fault. It's all my fault."

"What's all your fault, Molly?" Julian asked.

Molly worked her fingers among Julian's, trying to displace her discomfort. "They died because of me. Mommy turned around to yell at me because I wouldn't stop asking to sit in the front seat. While she was looking at me, an animal—what are those animals that have black masks?"

"A raccoon?"

Molly nodded. "A raccoon ran in front of Mommy's car. She tried not to hit it. She turned the driving wheel like this." Molly imitated a severe clockwise rotation. "We crashed into the tree. Do you remember the tree, Julian?"

"I do," he said quietly.

"It was a beautiful tree, wasn't it?"

Julian smiled sadly, "Yes, Molly. It sure was." Everyone was quiet for a moment. The only sound was the Muscle sniffling and blowing his nose. Jesse realized that Sid, too, was crying. The Ogre appeared solemn as he gazed at Molly in the mirror.

Sid suddenly turned around. "None of this is your fault, Molly. None of it. I'm so sorry that this happened. I'm going to do everything that I can to make this right for you."

Jesse stared. "Really? And how are you going to do that?"

"I'm—well, I *was* with the FBI."

"Yes, I know. But you seem to be part of the problem and not the solution," Jesse retorted.

Julian held up his hand to silence Jesse. "Sid, Vinny told us that you're a good agent. You can still do the right thing here and let Molly go. You have the button jar, and you have the book. Jesse and I can help you figure out the cypher. Let her go."

Sid twisted around fully so that he could face Julian and Jesse. "I—"

The Ogre threw out his right hand, which landed squarely in the middle of Sid's chest. "What Sid was going to say is that he'd love to let the little girl go, but he can't because it's not up to him. At this point, all decisions must go through Mr. Torchia, who you will find is a kind and fair man."

Julian felt the car slow and heard gravel crunch under the tires. "And where is Mr. Torchia exactly?" Julian inquired.

"Just inside these gates."

"Are we at Conley Terminal?" Julian asked.

"Yeah." The Ogre stared at Julian in the rearview. "How'd you know where we are, blind man?"

Jesse looked quickly at Julian and understood that Julian had surmised they were heading to Conley because that's where Sid's phone had been last detected. He also knew that Alex and Vinny were either somewhere in the area or had already come and gone. He prayed it was the latter and answered before Julian could respond. "I read the sign and he heard me."

The Ogre squinted his eyes, trying to determine Jesse's veracity. The ear-shattering squeak of the opening gate broke his concentration, and he winced. "We really gotta do something about that." He drove to the left toward the first of the three warehouses and wound his way around the back of the structures. He parked directly behind the second building.

"Have you met Mr. Torchia, Molly?" Julian whispered.

"Yes. He's big and has a broken wing. It's not really a wing. It's an arm, but he looks like a big bird. And he's blind like you, Julian."

Julian was taken aback. "Really? He can't see?"

"Uh-uh. Can't see good at all. He's a blind, broken, big bird."

CHAPTER 70

Vinny checked his watch for the fourth time in as many minutes. Alex had been inside warehouse number two for twenty minutes, and he was beginning to get worried. Without taking his eyes off of the large doors that still gaped open where Alex had entered, he commanded Siri to dial Marcie.

"Marcie, what's going on? Where's that warrant?"

"I told you not to thank me too soon, Vin. Judge Connelly is on vacation, so I had to go with Judge Abati, who's not as forgiving as Connelly when it comes to probable cause. I'm still working on it."

"Dammit! Okay. Let me know as soon as you know."

"I will. Sorry, Vin."

"Not your fault, Marcie. Bye."

Vinny continued to stare at the door, willing Alex to walk through it. *Five minutes*, he thought. *Five minutes, and then I'm going in. Warrant be damned.*

***

A chasm opened in Alex's stomach as she digested Paolo's words. Fearing the worst and not trusting her emotions, she looked at the ground and spoke evenly and clearly. "What do you mean when you said, 'She's no longer with us.' What exactly does that mean?"

Paolo Torchia gestured with his good hand. "Do you see her here? No? Well, she's no longer here. That's exactly what I mean."

"Where is she then?"

The large man shrugged, the movement made challenging by his arm brace. "How should I know, Ms. Hayes?"

"But she's still alive?"

Paolo looked shocked. "I should think so."

"Who took her?"

"Ah, now *that* I can answer for you. An FBI agent named Sid took her."

"Nickerson." It was a statement and not a question.

"Yes, I believe that's his surname."

"And you don't know where they went?"

"Alas, I'm afraid I do not."

"Bullshit."

Paolo wrinkled his nose. "I find vulgarity so distasteful in young, beautiful women."

Alex stepped forward until they were almost nose to nose. The man sporting the tight pants turned quickly and pulled a gun, but Paolo Torchia extended his hand toward him in a gesture that indicated he should stand down.

Alex leaned forward and whispered in his ear. "Fuck you, Paolo. I know you killed Jimmy McClelland because he was gathering evidence on you and talking to the FBI. I'm pretty sure you're blackmailing Jimmy's handler, Sid, to help you find the evidence that was hiding. But here's something you don't know. My friends are close to figuring out exactly where that evidence is. When they do, we're going to bring your heinous reign to an earth-shattering end."

Paolo Torchia smiled as he withdrew from Alex. His eyes flared and then sparkled as he spoke. "And here's something *you* don't know, Ms. Hayes. Sid and one of my associates have paid a visit to the home of a man named Dr. Julian Stryker to obtain a jar of buttons."

Alex's shoulders tensed at the mention of Julian's name, and the subtle movement did not go unnoticed. "I don't see well, my dear, but even I can see that this Julian Stryker is important to you. Good to know. Once we obtain the buttons, we believe that we'll possess the necessary knowledge to discern where the information is hidden. Then this unpleasantness will be over, and we can all go back to our normal lives."

"Except for Molly, whose family no longer exists because of you."

"I had absolutely nothing to do with her mother's and brother's deaths, I assure you."

"But you're admitting to murdering Jimmy and staging it to resemble a suicide?"

Paolo smiled condescendingly. "I admit to absolutely nothing, my dear. All I'm saying is that her mother's and brother's death had nothing to do with me or this unfortunate situation. Now, I believe that I have answered all of your questions. I would suggest that you seek Mr. Nickerson if you wish to find little Molly. You never know, her time might be running out, so you'd best hurry."

Alex held his gaze for a moment longer and then looked each of the room's occupants before turning toward the door. "My friend and I will be back soon with a warrant. Count on it." As she reached the door, she turned. Speaking directly to the new accountant, she said, "Think on what I said about getting out. It would seem that Paolo's accountants don't have an especially long life expectancy."

Alex exited the room and retraced her steps to the large metal doors. As she passed the man who had shown her to Paolo's office, he pointed to her and whispered to another worker, whereupon they both started laughing. Alex slid through the opening to find Vinny walking toward the door. "Please tell me you have the warrant."

"Oh my God! There you are. I don't have a warrant, but I was coming in anyway. You took so long!"

"Vinny Marcozzi, were you worried about me?"

"No, no. I just, you were just—alright, yeah, I was worried."

Alex smiled. "You needn't have worried. I dealt with things just fine in there. Even managed to have a little fun."

"What did you find out?"

"Molly's still alive. Sid and some other guy took her to Julian's house to get the button jar."

"Recently?"

"Near as I can figure, it was about the time we were at the dry-cleaning store."

"Good thing Julian wasn't home."

"I thought of that too."

"So you and Julian were right. Those buttons are important. Are you sure Sid went too? Cause that would mean that he's now a party to Molly's kidnapping." Vinny dropped his head in his hands. "Jesus, Sid's way more involved with the Torchias than I was hoping."

Alex raised her eyebrows. "I'm sure, Vinny. Paolo said that Molly went with Sid and someone else. Why don't you have the warrant, by the way?"

"One judge is on vacation, so Marcie's working another angle."

"I'm going to call Julian and see how they're doing at the dry-cleaning store. They must have found something by now."

CHAPTER 71

"Okay, everybody out. Let's go talk to Mr. Torchia," the Ogre ordered. Jesse exited the car and held Molly's hand as she slid off the seat. They watched Julian emerge, shake out his cane, and tap his way toward the group.

Molly slid her small hand into his as he approached. "Because we all need help sometimes," she said quietly.

"Thank you, Molly," Julian answered, giving her hand a small squeeze. The Ogre opened his jacket and showed Jesse the gun that was stored inside. Giving him a knowing look, he asked, "Understand?"

Jesse glared at him. "You won't be needing that."

The Ogre looked almost guilty as he looked at Molly. "I really hope not, my friend. But I want to make sure that you understand."

Jesse glanced at Molly and nodded. "I understand."

"Here are the ground rules. We're taking you up to meet Mr. Torchia. You'll speak only when spoken to, and you'll address him as 'sir' or 'Mr. Torchia.' Got it? Also, give me your phones, you two."

Jesse and Julian handed their phones to the Ogre, and the ragtag group started walking in single file. Molly followed the Ogre closely, repeatedly looking at Julian to ensure that he would not fall. As they approached the stairs, Molly said, "These stairs are woozy, Julian. Be careful."

As soon as he felt the insecurity of the metal stairs, he was grateful that Molly had warned him. Tucking his cane under his arm, he held tightly to Molly's hand while keeping the other on the handrail. "Anything else I need to know about?" he asked Molly.

"Yeah. There's a funny, skinny floor coming up."

Julian turned to Jesse for clarification. "Old, metal catwalk. One wrong foot, and you'll be over the edge. She's right. Be careful."

"Noted. Thanks." Julian reinstated his walking stick and uneventfully tapped his way across the catwalk.

The Ogre knocked on Paolo's door, and they were ushered into his office. "You must be Mr. Julian Stryker," Paolo gushed. "Welcome. Please sit down."

Julian tapped his way over to the couch and was surprised to hear plastic squeak under him as he sat.

"It's actually *Dr.* Julian Stryker," Jesse said with more confidence than he felt.

Paolo turned toward him. "And you are?"

"Dr. Stryker's assistant, Jesse James. What do you want from us?"

Paolo laughed. "Jesse James, you say? How original. What do I *want*, Mr. James? I want the information you have."

Jesse turned to Julian for guidance. "Julian?"

Julian patted the seat next to him, and Molly came and snuggled with him. "Mr. Torchia, I'm sure you're a reasonable man. All we want is to get out of here safely with Molly."

"We're on the same page then, Dr. Stryker. How is it that you came into Elliott's company?"

The Ogre answered. "We went to his house, got the button jar, and noticed that these two had been using a microscope to look at some buttons. When Sid looked, he saw that some of the buttons had engravings on them: letters and numbers. So we went to one of Jimmy's stores to see if we could find anything related to the letters and numbers and found these two looking at some information on the computer."

Paolo turned to Julian. "Care to take the story from there, Dr. Stryker?"

"Everything Elliott said is true. Jesse found the engravings, and we reasoned that Jimmy must have hidden information in his stores. It was just bad luck that we ended up at the same store. But we were missing another piece of the puzzle, which Elliott graciously pointed out upon entering the dry-cleaning store."

"The diary?" Paolo asked.

Julian nodded. "Using the codes on the back of the buttons, Jesse and I found a thumb drive that contains thousands of cells of data. We don't know which information applies to your business or even how to figure that out."

"That's what this must be for," the Ogre said as he opened the diary.

"Well done!" Paolo bellowed. "Now you need to figure out how the diary and the thumb drives intersect."

Julian nodded. "That is the obvious last step, except that we have no motivation to do that for you."

Paolo's jocularity vanished. "Of course you do. If you figure this out, you can all go free."

Sid burst out laughing. "Go free or get dead? No offense, Paolo, but we weren't born yesterday."

Paolo's nod was almost imperceptible. The man in the tight pants, who'd been standing in the corner of the room, lifted his gun and walked toward Sid. Taking aim at his head, he looked to Mr. Torchia for guidance. "Do you want to rephrase your comment, Mr. Nickerson?"

Before Sid could respond, tight pants lowered the gun and shot Sid in the left knee. Molly screamed as Sid collapsed to the ground howling and clawing at his leg.

Paolo walked over to where Sid lay on the floor, writhing in pain. "Next time, please mind your manners, Mr. Nickerson." He turned to Julian. "I trust you're sufficiently motivated now?"

Julian, who had had no advance warning of the gunshot, sat rigidly on the couch with a mute and trembling Molly in his lap.

***

Alex's head whipped toward the open door of warehouse number two. "Did you hear that?"

Vinny turned toward her as he disconnected a call with Marcie. "Still no warrant. Did you talk to Julian?"

"No. The call went straight to voicemail. Vinny, did you *hear* that?" Alex repeated urgently.

"Did I hear what?"

Alex strained to discern specific noise within the cacophony of the warehouse chaos. "I thought I heard a gunshot."

"Are you sure?"

She hesitated. "No."

"Then we wait for a warrant."

***

Julian was incredibly angry, not for himself but for Molly. Allowing himself to feel anger was rarely useful in his practice, so it took him a few moments to realize exactly what he was feeling. Once he allowed himself the luxury of the emotion, however, he embraced it. Gently disentangling himself from Molly and laying her against Jesse, who had come to sit on her other side, Julian rose from the couch.

"What's the matter with you? There is a little girl right behind me that has recently lost her entire world, and you have the audacity to shoot a gun in her presence? Who the hell do you think you are?" Julian walked forward. He was unsure of where he was going but didn't care. "And you, Sid," Julian gestured into the air, unsure of Sid's actual position in the room, "you deserved that shot. Vinny trusted you, and you sold him out for what? For *what*?" Julian yelled.

Sid's breath came in short, ragged bursts. "My family, dammit! But I'm done. I swear it. I'm done. Fuck you, Torchia!" Sid screamed. "Kill me! I won't help you anymore." Sid sobbed as he lay on the floor. He was broken but secure in the fact that his family was safe.

An uncertain quiet quickly descended on the room. The only sound was the ticking of a grandfather clock and the drone of never-ending machinery downstairs.

"Are you both finished?" Paolo asked patiently. "Can we get started on the diary?"

"I told you that I'm done, asshole," Sid gasped between groans of pain.

Paolo approached Sid and extended his hand palm up. Tight pants laid the gun in his hand. "I don't do this kind of thing myself very often, Mr. Nickerson, but I'm embarrassed to say that you have my dander up." He shot at Sid's other knee but missed. Sid inhaled quickly as Paolo shot again. This time, the bullet found its mark.

As Sid screamed in pain, Paolo chuckled. "I really need to get my eyes checked, I suppose." He regarded Sid, who had soiled his pants. "Mr. Nickerson, you asked me to kill you. I will, eventually. But it will take an extremely long time. Or …" Paolo turned toward the couch, smiling. "I can rethink how to achieve my goals. I should have started here. How silly of me. Molly, come here."

"No," Julian said, striking at the air with his cane. "No. Take me."

Jesse gripped Molly against his chest, shaking his head. "No, no. Please. Please don't take her. Take me. Take Julian. Kill Sid. Please don't take her. Please."

"Molly, come here or I will kill Julian." Paolo lifted the gun and placed it against Julian's head as the Ogre lifted his weapon and pointed it at Jesse.

Jesse whimpered as Julian spoke calmly. "Molly, listen to me. Do not go with this man. He will not hurt me. Do not go with him. You hear me? Molly?"

Molly had already wriggled out of Jesse's arms and was standing next to Paolo. "That's a smart girl," he cooed as she was ushered out of the room by Sheri.

CHAPTER 72

"I definitely heard that one, Alex. That was a gunshot. We don't need a warrant. Let's go." Alex drew her gun and followed Vinny closely. As they approached the door, they encountered some workers running out of the building. The man who earlier had led Alex to Paolo's office stopped in front of Alex, momentarily stunned to see her once more. Eyeing her gun, he glanced at Vinny, who said, "If I were you I'd keep running, asshole."

Vinny poked his head through the gap and surveyed the area, ensuring there was no immediate threat on the other side. Satisfied, he entered and gestured for the remaining workers to gather around him while Alex stood nearby with her gun drawn and pointed at the ground. As machinery slowed and ground to a halt, the sudden silence was unnerving. Vinny quickly gestured again, indicating that the machines should remain turned on while the men spoke with him. Confused and wary, they restarted the machines and then approached him.

"Look at my eyes, people. This is a onetime offer only. Capisce? If you leave now, this won't come back to bite you in the ass. If you choose to stay, then we'll assume that you work for Paolo Torchia, and we'll arrest you. Does everyone understand me?" Most people nodded, but several simply stared. Vinny tried again. "Do you understand?"

"They don't speak English," a worker offered, referring to some of his colleagues.

"What language do they speak?"

"Spanish."

Vinny quickly repeated his offer in Spanish and was met with more nodding heads. "Okay, not a word about this to anyone. Got it? *Silencio.*"

There was murmured agreement all around as they exchanged glances of assurance. "What are you waiting for. Vamanos!" The men scampered out of the warehouse. Many of them gawked at Alex as they ran.

"Why did you let them all go? Those guys obviously work for Torchia. They're accessories, if not worse."

"They're small potatoes, Alex. We want the big fish. It's safer this way too. Less people to potentially turn on us as we hunt. Come on. Follow me."

"You don't know where Torchia's office is, and I do, so why don't *you* follow *me*?" Alex smiled smugly.

Vinny fell into step behind Alex, who led him across the warehouse, up some stairs, across a catwalk, and to a large metal door. She mouthed, *Ready?* and then held up her fingers as she counted down: three, two, one. Turning the knob, she threw the door open to find the room empty. Two large, fresh pools of blood stained the carpet.

"Jesus," Alex breathed. "God, Vinny, what if that's Molly's blood?" Alex's heart started to race and sweat broke out on her forehead. Her breath came quickly as she started to hyperventilate. She bent over to regain her breath.

Vinny rubbed her back and said, "You okay?"

Alex shook her head. She had seen more death, gore, and mayhem than many of her colleagues, but for the first time in her career, she was not okay. Plopping onto the couch, she placed her head between her knees. "I'm either going to throw up or pass out."

"Jeez. You stay here while I clear the rest of the building, okay? Stay here."

Alex nodded, not trusting herself to speak.

As Vinny left the room he saw a trail of smeared blood they hadn't noticed on their way in. It was as if someone had been dragged through the hallway. Following the trail down a short hallway that ended at a restroom, he placed his back against the wall, pushed the door open with his foot, and came around quickly while aiming his gun ahead of him.

Sid sat slumped against the bathroom wall. His two destroyed knees were splayed out in front of him. "Oh my God, Sid!" Vinny rushed forward and squatted beside his friend. "What the hell happened?"

Sid roused himself and tried to smile. "Vinny. It's all my fault. I'm so sorry. So sorry. I tried to be a good man. I did. Kath and the kids ..." he trailed off and was unable to finish his thought.

"They're okay, Sid. I promise. They're okay. I'm going to get you some help—"

"Stand up, Mr. Marcozzi." Vinny felt the cold steel of a muzzle press against the back of his head. He glanced at Sid, who closed his eyes and whispered, "I'm sorry, Vinny."

"You set me up." Vinny shook his head as he placed his gun on the floor and stood with his hands raised.

He turned to face the Ogre, who sighed. "It wasn't supposed to be this complicated."

Vinny sneered. "It never is."

The Ogre led Vinny back down the hallway past the office and into a small conference room where they found Jesse hunched over a laptop while Julian paced. "How did you guys get here?" Vinny asked in disbelief.

Julian's head turned toward Vinny's voice. "Vinny?"

"Yeah, it's me."

"Mr. Marcozzi, thank you for joining us. I trust that Ms. Hayes is comfortable in my office? It was clever of you to keep the machines running while you let my men go, but the sudden, momentary silence when they turned off the machines struck me as odd, so we looked out my window and saw you speaking to them. Kind of you to give us just enough time to get Mr. Nickerson to the bathroom."

"Hello, Paolo. I'm assuming that you or one of your men shot Sid. You realize you can't kill all of us and get away with it, right?"

"I only want what is mine. Dr. Stryker and his assistant have figured out Jimmy's code, haven't you?"

Julian nodded. "The buttons lead to thumb drives that contain financial transactions. The diary, it turns out, identifies which of those many transactions are real and which are fake. Jimmy did an amazing job gathering and coding."

Julian tilted his head toward Paolo as he crossed his arms and hardened his tone. "It must be infuriating to know that one of your employees outsmarted you. He was systematically gathering information that will destroy everything you and your family have built over generations."

"I think you forget who is in control here. You don't know what you're talking about, Dr. Stryker."

"I know exactly what I'm talking about, Paolo. You're pathologically narcissistic, so you insist that your employees kowtow to you and treat you like a king. You crave complete control, and when you don't have it, you blow like Old Faithful, and everyone scampers. Everyone is terrified of becoming the object of your wrath. You enjoy other people's fear. It makes you feel powerful. But in reality, you're a pathetic, big broken bird, just like Molly said. That's exactly what you are: *pathetic*. Like I said, Jimmy did a fantastic job of tricking you out of information. Hell, maybe he was even skimming money on the side. His one mistake was including Molly."

Paolo stepped toward Julian, his face a mask of white rage. "You will pay for your words, Dr. Stryker, more than you can possibly imagine." Leaning even closer he hissed, "Or should I say that Molly will pay for your words."

Julian clenched his fists as Vinny asked, "Where is Molly, asshole?"

Paolo smiled. "She is all tucked away. An incredible child, really."

"You have your information. Now let Molly go."

The large man shrugged. "She's already gone."

They all turned to him at once. "What do you mean?" Julian demanded. "Gone where?"

Paolo chuckled. "Come here to the window, all of you. Oh, except you, Dr. Stryker, since you cannot see, poor thing." They joined him at the window, which overlooked the shipyard and harbor. "See that tanker with all of the shipping containers on it?"

"Yes."

"She's in one of those, all tucked away."

"You bastard!" Jesse jumped at Paolo and hurled punches, some of which found their mark on Paolo's torso. The Ogre coldcocked him, and Jesse's body collapsed in a heap at Julian's feet, causing him to stumble backward and fall against the wall. Vinny backed away with his hands raised as tight pants aimed a gun at Vinny's chest.

"Enough!" Paolo roared.

Julian breathed heavily. "Mr. Torchia, you've done many, many bad things in your career, but to my understanding, you have never harmed a child. Don't make Molly the first. Please call that tanker back."

"I cannot do that, Dr. Stryker. And I hope you realize that all of you have brought this on yourselves. Sid started everything in motion when he took Jimmy under his wing. Sid is responsible for Molly's fate. This is all his fault."

"And I'm going to make it right. As much as I can, at least." Having hauled himself from the bathroom using only his arms, Sid lay in the doorway, his breathing ragged. Braced on his elbows, he held the gun tightly in both hands. It looked like a yoga pose gone wrong. "I've made a lot of bad decisions recently, Vinny, but this one I'm sure about."

"Sid no!" Vinny yelled. In a split second, a bullet crossed the small space and found its target in tight pants' chest, the impact thrusting him backward onto the conference room table. Before anyone could react, a second bullet pierced the Ogre's head, which erupted like a ripe watermelon and sprayed brain matter on Julian.

Sid lay panting. "Paolo, I'm not going to shoot you unless I have to. I'd prefer you to rot in prison." The effort had exhausted Sid as he stole a glance at Vinny. "Smart move, Vin, laying your gun on the bathroom floor where I could reach it."

Vinny nodded. Hoping that the agent still retained some of his former self, Vinny had taken a calculated risk leaving his gun within Sid's reach. The gamble had paid off. Paolo stood with his broken arm extended, shocked into submission.

Suddenly, a scream erupted from down the hall. Without hesitation, Julian leapt up and rushed from the room with his cane in his hand. "Alex!" He felt his way down the hall with Vinny on his heels. Opening the door to Paolo's office, he said, "Alex? Alex? Are you okay?"

"Oh my God," Vinny said.

"What is it? Is Alex okay?"

"I'm okay, Julian." Her voice sounded strained and contained an unspoken warning. Julian turned to Vinny, silently asking for clarification.

"Molly," Vinny said, "put the gun down, sweetheart. Put the gun down."

Julian involuntarily gasped and lowered himself to his knees so he was at eye level with Molly. "What's going on, Vinny?" Julian asked calmly.

"Molly is waving a gun back and forth between Alex and another lady who, I'm assuming, works for Paolo."

"How did this happen, Alex?"

"Does it really matter, Julian?" Alex asked through gritted teeth.

"No, no. You're right. Molly, can you please put the gun on the ground?" The terrified girl continued to wildly alternate her aim between the two women.

Alex tried. "Molly, honey, can you talk to Julian? Do you hear him speaking to you?" Keeping her eyes on Molly, she said, "Julian, I don't think she's hearing us. It's the same look I saw when we first met her and when she had that night terror."

"What do her eyes look like?"

"Wild!" Sheri whispered as her voice broke. "All of this time, and I'm gonna be taken out by a kid. Unfuckingbelieveable."

"Unfuckingbelieveable," Molly echoed and pointed the gun directly at Sheri. "Swearing is bad."

Sheri's hands flew to protect her face as she mumbled, "Sorry! Sorry!"

"I'm glad you're talking, Molly. Do you hear me?" Julian spoke soothingly.

"I hear my daddy." She smiled and kept the gun still for a moment.

"What is your daddy saying, Molly?" Julian asked as he sat down on the floor and inched closer to her.

"He's smiling and saying that I've done a good job."

"Do you see him in the room with us?"

"No. I can't see him, but I hear him, and I feel him."

"I agree with your father, Molly. You've done a wonderful job. But it's time to stop now because you're safe."

She turned to him with a questioning expression while she kept the gun trained in the direction of Alex and Sheri. "I don't know what that means, Julian."

"It means that no one will hurt you anymore."

The little girl's eyes glazed over as she listened to a voice only she could hear. "I don't like that story, Daddy."

"What's your daddy saying, Molly?" Julian asked as he moved toward her.

"He's telling me a story about a princess who was taken away from her family. Mean people made her play dumb games and wear stupid clothes that were too big for her. Mean men killed her daddy and stole her button jar!" The gun lurched violently as she sobbed. "I don't want to do that, Daddy. I can't do that!"

"What does your father want you to do, Molly?"

"He wants the mean people to go away." She raised the gun and pointed it at Sheri, who cowered against the desk trying to make herself as inconspicuous as possible.

"Julian, do something … please," Alex whispered. "I'm not sure she's going to last much longer."

"Molly Elizabeth McClelland, look at me. Are you looking at me? Put the gun down and take my hands. Please. You're safe now." His tone was kind but adamant as he stretched out both hands in her direction.

Molly's eyebrows came together in confusion as she considered Julian's words. She shook her head slowly at first, but then it gained momentum as she stared through Julian. "No! No! You said you'd come, but you didn't, Julian. You didn't *come*!" She screamed the last word as her tears choked her. "No one came. I was all by myself. *I'm all by myself*!" The gun jerked recklessly as it mirrored her emotions and sent all sighted people scrambling for cover.

"*Molly!*" As Julian crawled toward her, Sheri lurched for the door, pulling Alex in front of her as a shield. The movement made Molly lose her footing and she fell forward, causing the gun to explode, sending sound crashing around the small office. Sheri bounded out the door as Alex clutched her abdomen and fell backward onto the couch.

"Julian!" she managed before fainting.

CHAPTER 73

The surgeon approached the waiting area where Julian and Vinny sat silently. The surgery had lasted a long time, and all small talk had been spent hours earlier. Vinny tapped Julian's knee as the physician came closer. "The doctor's coming."

"What does his face look like?" Julian asked anxiously.

"Tired."

"That's not good." They both stood. "Hello, Doctor."

"Hi Dr. Stryker, Mr. Marcozzi. I have good news and bad news." Julian reached over, and Vinny took his hand.

"Good news first please." Julian took a deep breath and held it.

"Ms. Hayes is going to recover nicely, although it might take some time. The bullet entered her abdomen and traveled upward. It just missed her spleen. Another quarter of an inch and she might not have made it."

Julian exhaled. "Thank God. What's the bad news?"

The surgeon hesitated. "There's never an easy way to say this, so I'll just say it. She lost the baby. I'm so sorry. She's awake and in recovery if you want to see her."

Time slowed and sound vanished as a rushing sound filled Julian's ears. He remembered hugging her the other day and noting that her body felt different. A baby. "Boy or girl?" Julian whispered as Vinny squeezed his hand.

"She was only about six weeks along, so I can't answer that question. Again, I'm so sorry." He shook their hands and walked away, his heels clicking on the tile floor.

Julian stood still for what seemed like an eternity. After a time, he realized that Vinny was speaking. "Julian, did you hear me? Do you want to visit Alex?"

"What? Oh, yes, please." Julian allowed himself to be led to Alex's bedside.

"I'll go get some coffee and come back in a while," Vinny whispered, patting Julian on the back. Julian nodded, found Alex's hand, kissed it gently, and placed his forehead against it. Tears came freely as he contemplated the loss of the baby. His child. *Their* child.

"Why are you crying?" Alex whispered. "I'm going to be okay. I promise." She attempted a weak smile.

"I know. Thank God," Julian said and kissed her hand again. "It's just that …"

"Did I lose her?"

Julian nodded. They were silent in their shared grief. "Why didn't you tell me?"

Alex closed her eyes. "Because I actually wasn't sure. I missed my period, but I hadn't taken a pregnancy test yet. I wanted us to do it together." She began to cry.

Julian rose, traced her face with his fingers, and then placed his forehead against hers. "We're going to be okay, Alex. It's going to be okay."

CHAPTER 74

Jesse sat across from Molly, who was devouring her third Nutella and jelly sandwich. "You're going to explode," Jesse commented, laughing. The rhinestones on her tiara caught the light and sent a prism of colors flying across the wall of Julian's kitchen as Oscar lay panting at her feet. Molly reached down and patted the dog, who returned the favor by licking jelly off her hand.

Molly giggled and asked, "How come you don't call me your royal highness or Buttons anymore, Jesse?"

Jesse regarded her carefully. "Because you didn't want me to. Do you remember that?" It had been four weeks since the warehouse fiasco and Molly had been slowly reconstructing her memory. Her brain had chosen various events to review each day. Using drawing and games, Julian had been working with Molly to rebuild trust and to regain a sense of safety. He had commented to Jesse that she was making great progress but still had a long way to go. Moments like this one, which seemed so innocent, had a funny way of turning quickly if not handled appropriately.

Molly looked at Jesse and rolled her eyes. "I never said that I didn't want you to call me Buttons, Jesse. Don't be silly. I told you that I wasn't a real princess. And that's true. I'm not. But," she reached over and pinched Jesse's side playfully, "I know that I'm very special!" She stood quickly, bent down to Oscar's head, and planted a sticky kiss. "Come on, Oscar. Let's play!" She ran into Julian as he was entering the kitchen.

"Whoa there, camper!" Julian laughed.

As the little girl collapsed on the floor in the family room with the dog who was twice her size, Jesse asked, "Are you sure it's a good idea to be fostering her?"

Julian smiled. "I told you, Jess, she needs some consistency right now.

I've consulted with other child psychologists, and we all agree that the best thing for Molly is a safe, solid place for her to heal. When she's stronger, we'll consider next steps in terms of adoption."

"She's so happy here. Would you ever consider adopting her, especially given the fact that Alex lost the baby?"

"Whom Alex insists was a girl, by the way," Julian commented.

Jesse smiled sadly. "Yeah."

"To answer your question, I don't know if we'll consider adopting Molly or not. The first priority is getting both Alex and Molly back on their feet. After that, who knows?"

"Yeah, who knows?" Jesse echoed.

Julian tilted his head as a smile blossomed. "Jess, are *you* thinking about adopting Molly?"

Jesse shrugged. "Well of course, I've thought about it, Julian. How could I *not* think about it? I mean, that perfect little girl has gone through so much. But I'm not sure it's a good idea."

"Why not?"

Jesse made a face at Julian. "Seriously, Julian? I'm a single gay man working as a secretary for a child psychologist who deals with troubled youth and works as a criminal profiler on the side. In the last several years, I've been kidnapped, shot at, and generally put in harm's way. I'm not sure Child and Family Services would view me as an ideal candidate to be Molly's parent."

Julian shook his head. "First of all, you're not a secretary."

Jesse laughed. "That's what you took from everything I just said?"

"And second of all, it's because of all of those things that you'd be the perfect parent for Molly. You know exactly what she's been through and possess the physical and emotional resources to continue her healing. After all, you have access to an exceptional child psychologist."

"I do, huh? Exceptional you say?"

"Seriously, Jess, I think you adopting Molly is an excellent idea, and I will offer my opinion in family court when it's time."

"I'll continue to think about it. Thanks, Julian."

"Always my pleasure, friend."

They listened to Oscar grunt in pleasure as Molly scratched his belly. Her laughter floated into the kitchen, and a sense of normalcy was reviving.

"What's going on with the Torchia trial?"

"Vinny said it's being fast-tracked given the evidence that we found and decoded. I'm sure Paolo won't see the light of day for a very long time—maybe forever given his age."

Jesse sighed. "But you know there will be someone to replace him soon, if not already."

"I know."

A knock sounded at the front door, followed by Vinny yelling at Oscar, who was greeting him with long howls. "Shut up, dammit!"

"Swearing is bad, Vinny," Molly admonished.

"Sorry, Molly. You're right," Vinny said, tousling her hair. He entered the kitchen and plopped into a chair. "How goes it, gentlemen?" he asked.

"You're chipper."

"Sure am. Annabelle and I are back on again after working out our differences."

"You mean now that Torchia's going to jail," Jesse commented wryly.

"That too. If I play my cards right, I might become Mr. Annabelle Andrews."

"Nothing wrong with a strong, assertive woman, as long as she's on the up-and-up. Speaking of the up-and-up, what's going on with Sid?" Julian asked.

A cloud crossed his countenance as Vinny picked lint off of his jacket. "He's still in the hospital. He'll probably end up with two new knees. After the surgery and rehab, he'll go to jail."

"Are you okay with that?" Julian pressed.

Vinny shrugged. "Sid was being blackmailed, but he made idiotic choices along the way. He could have come to me at any point, and we could have figured things out together. Do I want to see him go to jail? No. Is it warranted though? Hell, yeah. Obviously his career is over, and his pension is gone, but I'll try to help him get back on his feet once he's out. And I'll be sure to check in on Kathleen and the kids while he's in."

"You're a good man, Vin." Julian paused and then said, "I wonder what we would have done if we had been in Sid's position." No one spoke as each person pondered how quickly life could take an unexpected turn.

"Hey, how's Kellie Moser?" Jesse asked.

Vinny smiled. "There's good news on that front. I just stopped by yesterday to see her. She's home now and in physical therapy five days a week. She's going to walk again, but it's going to take some time."

The stairs creaked, and Julian jumped to his feet, rushing out of the kitchen. He entered a moment later with Alex holding his arm and rolling her eyes. "Hi guys."

"Hey, how are you feeling?" Vinny asked.

"Almost back to normal, although you'd never know it with nervous Nellie here." She hooked her thumb toward Julian, who brought her in for a bear hug.

"Me too!" Jesse said as he wiggled his way between them.

Vinny looked on in disdain with his arms crossed and a scowl on his face. "Get in here, Vin," Julian ordered.

"No, I'm okay."

Julian turned to Vinny and extended his arm. "Get in here, buddy. You've earned a group hug."

Vinny shook his head and rolled his eyes. "Really, I'm good."

Molly entered the kitchen, grinning from ear to ear. Eyeing Vinny, she said, "Why aren't you in the hug? Don't you love them?"

They all turned to Vinny, daring him to challenge this resilient child. Seeing no alternative, Vinny reluctantly stood and wrapped his arms around all three of them. "Of course I love them."

Molly stood with her hands on her little hips, evaluating the best entry point. Raising an eyebrow, she said, "There better be room for me," before wriggling into the middle of the fray. They stood in a huddle for a moment enjoying the simplicity of contentment.

When they separated, Molly smiled at each of them as tears rolled slowly down her face. Alex knelt and wiped away her tears. "Why are you crying, Buttons?"

Without speaking she grasped Alex's hand and joined it with Julian's. Then she placed her hand on top of theirs. She glanced at Jesse and Vinny, who followed the unspoken direction by joining their hands with the group. Molly looked at each person in turn while grinning through her tears. "Look. We're a family."